"I KNOW NOTHING
OF THE ART OF LOVE . . ."

Her kiss was inexpert, amateur, and she knew it. She cupped his neck in her palms. The powerful muscles were as rigid as steel. Gareth remained unmoved by her softness, as unrelenting as a statue in her embrace.

She leaned forward and drew her small tongue gently along the seam of his lips, feeling them part beneath the coaxing motion. His smoky lashes veiled his eyes as he returned her kiss, his mouth spreading hers, his tongue sweeping out to possess hers.

Gareth tilted her face, studying her features in the gentle glow of the firelight. He punctuated each word with the brush of his lips down the purest curve of her cheekbone. "What do I offer you but a slow ride to hell?"

His lips came to rest against the thundering pulse in her throat. Bewitched by the lingering heat of his mouth, Rowena's head fell back in languorous surrender . . .

SHADOWS AND LACE

**A timeless novel of dark passion
by the author of LADY OF CONQUEST,
TERESA MEDEIROS**

"A VIVID IMAGINATION!"—*Madisonville
Messenger*

Berkley Books by Teresa Medeiros

LADY OF CONQUEST
SHADOWS AND LACE

SHADOWS AND LACE

TERESA MEDEIROS

BERKLEY BOOKS, NEW YORK

SHADOWS AND LACE

A Berkley Book / published by arrangement with
the author

PRINTING HISTORY
Berkley edition / September 1990

ISBN: 0-425-12262-X

A BERKLEY BOOK® TM 757,375
Berkley Books are published by The Berkley Publishing Group,
200 Madison Avenue, New York, New York 10016.
The name "Berkley" and the "B" logo
are trademarks belonging to Berkley Publishing Corporation.

PRINTED IN THE UNITED STATES OF AMERICA

10 9 8 7 6 5 4 3 2 1

DEDICATION

*To Kim-Poo, who writes her own happy endings,
and to Michael, my hero*

PROLOGUE

1279 England

The boy slipped into the bower without a sound. His steps faltered as the ethereal scent of rosemary raked like tender claws down his spine. He closed his eyes briefly, letting the scent envelop him as it had the night before when his stepmother had curtsied to him in the dance. Her raven curls had brushed his cheek, unmanning him with their softness as she taught him each step of the carol with the sweetest of patience. He opened his eyes; dark lashes fringed their bleak depths.

He should not have come here. Writing music could be learned at his father's desk. Courtesy, in the great hall. What knightly skill might he learn in his stepmother's chamber? His father would be home from battle within the fortnight. He only wanted to see her—to offer his thanks for her kindness and attention in his father's absence.

A clash of lances followed by a roar of laughter spilled through the open window. The courtyard below where the squires played at tilting seemed a world away. Before him, sunlight bathed the empty chamber. Disappointment and relief gripped him. He slipped forward with a grace beyond his fourteen years. The shoulders of his tall form had already begun to broaden.

Damask curtains the same deep, rich blue of her eyes were drawn back from the rumpled bed. He ducked under the carved canopy, his hand shaking as he touched the hollowed cave in the feather pillow where her head had rested.

A tiny sound came from the alcove behind him. He rapped his head on the canopy and swung around, wide-eyed with guilt. His smooth brow furrowed with annoyance.

He had forgotten the babe. His stepsister stood in the oaken cradle, the tangled remnants of her swaddling hanging from her tiny paws like a shroud. Sunlight kissed the halo of golden curls poking out of her silken coif. Her lower lip trembled. Her round, blue eyes welled with tears, but she did not cry. Her forbearance seemed to be such that she would have stood there forever, waiting for someone to come by and pick her up. He supposed he should see to her before she tumbled out of the cradle and cracked her silly head.

As he approached the cradle, she held out her chubby, little arms and smiled through her tears. What if her napkins were wet? He looked around as if to make sure no one was looking before gingerly lifting her. She was solid, as heavy as a baby piglet in his arms. 'Twas impossible to imagine his stepmother's lithe, dark grace giving birth to such a clumsy creature. He held her awkwardly over one arm as if she might bite him. What should he do with her now?

She knew what to do with him. With a soft coo, she laid her head against his breast. Her fist curled around a strand of his dark hair. She tugged as if to remind him of her presence.

Without warning, tears stung his eyes. He had not cried for as long as he could remember, not even when his mother died. He buried his face in the child's sweet-smelling curls as the knot in his throat choked him. She was so fresh and untainted, so free of the guilty stain of his feelings for her mother. He felt twisted and ugly to hold such innocence in his arms.

The door swung open. His stepmother swept in, her eyes darkening unaccountably for a moment at the sight of the golden head next to the dark one.

She snatched the child from his arms. "Is the silly babe troubling you? Forgive me. I don't know how she manages to wiggle out of her swaddling."

He watched, his arms empty, as she stuffed the plump limbs back into the binding linen. The child's lips trembled, but she did not cry. Her eyes were not on her mother. They were on him. "Is she not old enough to toddle about?" he said faintly.

"Toddle into mischief! What do lads know of babes? The swaddling will help her limbs grow straight and strong." She gave him a flash of a vivacious dimple. "And contribute to the sweet demeanor that every man prizes in a wife." She took his hand, her soft, ivory-colored fingers playing over his knuckles. "Come. Forget the bratling. You've much to learn before your father returns. I've yet to see you make a proper kneel."

She drew him away from the cradle. "Now, pretend I am your queen."

He was not pretending as he cleared his throat awkwardly and dropped to one knee. He reached for her outstretched hand. Her middle finger bore the rubies and emeralds of his father's betrothal ring. His head dropped. He could not touch her. His hands clenched into fists at his sides. He hardly dared breathe as she touched him, her fingernails gently tracing the shapes of his ears beneath his thick, dark hair.

"My man," she crooned. "My sweet, young man. I've so much to teach you."

He closed his eyes as she drew his face into the rosemary-scented velvet of her bosom. But as he buried his face in her softness, 'twas not darkness he saw but the reproach in young, round, blue eyes the color of the spring sky.

PART I

Take thou this rose, O rose
Since love's own flower it is
And by that rose
Thy lover captive is

—*Anonymous*

CHAPTER 1

1298 England

The hare's nostrils quivered an inch from hers. If anyone had been as near to Rowena as the hare was at that moment, they would have sworn her lightly freckled nose also quivered. She lay in the sweet-smelling grass of the moor, her chin nuzzled in the crook of her arm. Her cap slipped over her blue eyes, and the slight movement startled the hare into flight. Rowena swore softly and climbed to her knees, adjusting the cap with a jerk. With stinging fingers she plucked thistles from her overtunic. She had lain motionless in the tall grass for hours to gain the trust of the hare that went bouncing cheerfully toward the rosy pocket of the western sky.

She shook her fist at the animal, then laughed ruefully. Sheathing the long knife that hung forgotten in her hand, she trudged toward Revelwood where eight hungry boys were doomed to be hungrier.

As the only girl in a family of seven brothers, one cousin, and a father given to long disappearances, it had taken Rowena both time and ingenuity to convince the family she was indifferent to the cobwebs festooning the grim remnants of Revelwood. She had learned at a tender age that her only escape from a life of perpetual drudgery lay in becoming a terrible cook and a clever huntress. She tackled both tasks

with enthusiasm, leaving her brothers to till the stony ground
and freeing herself to roam the wild moor.

Rowena spread her arms, emphasizing their emptiness as
she leaped from stone to stone across a sparkling stream.
Little Freddie would even now be preparing the spit for the
game she did not bear. Her youngest brother had rescued
the doomed family from a life of raw cabbage when his first
tottering steps had led him to the dusty kettle on the hearth
where he promptly fell in. His hollow cries had echoed
through the castle until Rowena's oldest brother, Big Freddie, fished him out.

Dead drunk on the occasion that marked the birth of his
youngest son and the death of Rowena's mother, Althea,
Papa had promptly christened the red, squalling infant
Frederick, just as he had christened his firstborn Frederick.
In the years to come, Papa would fondly brag that he had
named the babe Roderick in honor of his oldest son—the
first fruit of his loins whom he cherished beyond all measure. With a gentle poke, Rowena would whisper in his ear
that the name was Frederick. Papa would shrug and smile
and turn up his goblet again.

The dry grass crackled beneath Rowena's heels. The late
summer twilight descended around her in a lavender haze—
a gentle reproof for the long hours she had spent running
through the meadows, whistling at the larks and tracking a
wide-eyed doe at the edge of the forest. To come home
empty-handed would be to admit the folly of her day and
succumb to a supper of boiled turnips for the third time in
a week.

Setting her jaw in determination, she unsheathed the knife
and turned to the forest. The sour, cracked note of a badly
blown trumpet shattered the quiet like a golden fanfare.

Papa! Papa was home. Rowena sprinted toward the decrepit castle she called home and the charming braggart she
called Papa.

Eight months had passed since he had left without a word
to pursue his fortune. In the past those same pursuits had

brought him home with a leather pouch of golden coins which he had scattered among his children like a jolly harbinger of happier times. Rowena had laughingly scrambled for the coins, knowing all the while that the gold would be regathered in time for Papa's next expedition. She dreaded the times he returned with nothing but a massive headache and a kick for the cur that skulked around the hearth. He never dared raise a hand to any of his children; even Rowena outmeasured him by two inches.

However hapless his journey, he never returned without some scrap of a present for his only daughter. The tattings of lace and velvet bows had been tucked away, forgotten, to be replaced by soft-beaten leather and a curved dagger. Rowena expressed her needs with a candor not inherited from her father.

With a hint of the ingenuity they did share, she thought with glee that Papa's return would draw attention from her empty hands, especially if he packed the carcass of a deer on his aged gelding as he was wont to do when his wagers had been successful.

The weatherbeaten stones of Revelwood came into view as she topped the hill. She paused to grasp her side and rub away the stitch that stole her breath away. Her mother's ancestral home crouched on the edge of the moor, the battered walls no longer a defense against the wind that roared through the widening cracks in the mortar. But in the rapidly dying light of the summer sun, the ancient castle gleamed in a poignant reflection of its former glory.

Rowena's joy overflowed in a whoop as she skipped down the hill. The sound died. Her throat went dry. Papa's slope-backed gelding was tethered to a post, an empty pouch draped over its heaving flanks. She ran her hand over the horse's withers, then wiped the slimy film of sweat on her braies with a grimace. The horse gave a gurgling snort, its head buried in a wooden bucket. Shaking off a shiver of foreboding, Rowena bounded up the splintered planks that served as a bridge over the dank moat.

Arrow slits set deep in the masonry held the twilight at
bay. Rowena blinked away blindness as her eyes adjusted to
the gloom of the cavernous hall. A fire dwarfed by the im-
mense hearth strove to add cheer to the vaulted room but
succeeded in casting more shadows than light. The corners
of her mouth tilted upward. The slight form of Little Freddie stirred the contents of an iron kettle. The pungent odor
of turnips floated to her nose.

She leaped out of the doorway, the clatter of large feet
on the planks a warning. Her brothers burst into the hall
bearing an array of hoes and rakes.

''Where is Papa?'' bellowed Big Freddie.

He led five men who could have been smaller, paler twins
of himself with their lank hair and hunched shoulders. He
tossed his scythe to the flagstones. The others exchanged
doubtful glances, then dumped their tools with equal care-
lessness.

Rowena's cousin Irwin stepped out from the stairs. His
plump face held an oddly glum look; he twirled a rusty
trumpet between his fingers.

''Your father is abovestairs,'' he announced. ''He wanted
you gathered. Said there wasn't much time.''

Even as he spoke, a deafening crash sounded from the
upper reaches of the castle followed by a bellow and a flurry
of imaginative curses. They all stared upward as if an explanation for Irwin's cryptic speech would float down with
the dust motes loosened from the beams.

Big Freddie knuckled his eyes. ''Is Papa in foul spirits,
Irwin?''

Irwin scratched his head with the trumpet. ''I don't believe he is in spirits at all. I believe he is sober.''

Rowena's brothers nodded to each other, accepting the
news with puzzled solemnity.

Rowena snorted. ''Nonsense. Have you ever seen him
sober, Irwin?''

Her cousin turned to her, unable to stop blind adoration

from conquering his calflike eyes. "Nay. But I've never seen him like this before, either."

Rowena tweaked Irwin's nose with fond contempt. "If you say he is sober, then I say you've been dipping into the ale with your own greedy paw."

Irwin choked out a meager chuckle. The others laughed aloud at the thought of their pasty-faced cousin swilling a goblet of brew.

"Papa is probably just hungry," Rowena pronounced with conviction.

The look Little Freddie gave her was so devoid of reproach that she ducked her head in shame, regretting her thoughtless fling with the summer day. The mention of food sent all their stomachs rumbling. The black bread crusts dipped in lard they had broken their fast with that morn were a fond but distant memory. Rowena started for the wall that housed the old bow and arrow. Little Freddie's words stopped her.

"Apples, Ro. We can spare a few. I can cook them on the coals the way Papa fancies them."

With a grateful smile she took the sack he held out. Little Freddie seemed to have inherited intelligence equal to all that was divided so sparingly between her older brothers. Pulling her cap over her ears, she ducked into the deepening night.

The door had hardly closed behind her when Papa came stumbling down the stairs.

My God, thought Little Freddie. Irwin was right. Papa never stumbles when he's drunk.

Gone was the strutting gait, the bleary, sated gaze. In their place were feet that took each step as if mired in molten lead and eyes that shone with the weight of unshed tears. Sir Lindsey Fordyce, Baron of Revelwood, stood at the foot of the stairs and surveyed his sullen sons as if seeing them for the first time.

"Sweet Christ. I didn't know there was such a godawful

lot of you." He rubbed his eyes as if to make some of them
disappear.

"There are nine of us, Uncle Lindsey, counting Rowena," said Irwin, ever eager to please.

He peered around the hall again. "Where is Ro? I do not
see her."

Little Freddie stepped away from the hearth. "Gone to
fetch apples, Papa."

" 'Tis just as well." Papa dragged his right leg as he
crossed the hall, his faint limp painfully pronounced. He
sat heavily in an ancient chair. The wood creaked beneath
his weight. "Water, Freddie," he croaked.

Papa leaned back and closed his eyes, missing the struggle that ensued as Big Freddie and Little Freddie tugged at
the stoneware flagon, sloshing tepid water over their bare
feet. With a choked mutter, Big Freddie jerked the flagon
out of his brother's hands and poured the water into a rusty
goblet. He allowed Little Freddie the honor of presenting it
to their father with a flourish.

Papa's hands shook as he took the goblet. He drained it
as if it contained something far more tasty than dirty water
and an errant gnat.

"Gather around, sons. I have glad tidings," he announced.

Spreading his arms wide as if to embrace them to his
bosom, he grinned. His sons took a hesitant step forward,
and Irwin took a step backward.

"Join us, Irwin. I would not choose to cheat you of a
chance for adventure simply because you had the misfortune
to spring from another man's loins."

Irwin blushed and sidled closer. "Adventure, Uncle
Lindsey?"

The boys exchanged blank glances, unable to comprehend the idea of any existence or experience beyond their
own. Surely farming turnips in rocky fields that were never
meant to be farmed was adventure enough.

Papa leaned forward with a conspirator's wink. "You see,

my boys, I truly found my elusive fortune in the course of this expedition. I was on my way home to share the prosperity with my precious offspring.'' He clucked sadly. ''But my purse was weighted down by so many gold coins that the old gelding could hardly bear it.''

Little Freddie crossed his arms, his eyes narrowing.

''So I stopped for a night's rest at the castle of a friend.''

Irwin wondered what it was like to have a friend. He had never met anyone he was not related to.

''And they had a jolly game of hazard going at the castle, did they not, Papa?'' Little Freddie interrupted.

Papa rumpled his son's silver-blond hair. ''Roddy, you never cease to amaze me.''

''It's Freddie.'' Ducking away, Freddie returned to the hearth, busying himself once again with the kettle.

''So,'' Papa continued briskly, ''seeking to rid myself of some of this cumbersome load—for the dear gelding's sake, of course—I entered into a game of hazard with an old acquaintance of mine, the son of an earl whose fief I held long ago. The lad once bore me a great fondness and is now grown into a great and noble knight.''

Something about the way Papa spoke the last two words sent a chill down Little Freddie's spine. He straightened, the turnips forgotten.

''First I wagered what I had. Then I wagered what I didn't have. Mayhaps I had imbibed a tad too much ale.'' He held his thumb and finger apart in illustration.

Little Freddie's arms spread as wide as they could go, adjusting the inaccurate measure. Irwin smothered a giggle behind his plump hand. Little Freddie pretended to stretch as his father's gaze fell upon him.

Papa shrugged. ''So I lost my fortune. When my old friend discovered my penniless straits, I fear he lost his temper. With the unfortunate memory of a winner, he recalled my boasts of the eight strapping lads who tended my castle while I sought my fortune. So the gist of the matter is that one of you lucky lads is going to serve an earl for the period of one year.'' He beamed at them, his bright pig-eyes awaiting their congratulations.

Only silence greeted him.

"You wagered one of your children?'' Little Freddie pushed through the forest of shoulders to face his father.

Sir Lindsey Fordyce's smile faded. He rubbed his head, peeling back the hair to reveal the bald spot he usually struggled to hide.

"Not precisely. The choice was not mine to make.'' He surveyed them glumly, dropping all pretense of happiness. "He said he would journey to Revelwood to choose one of my lads for service, or he would journey to Revelwood bearing my head on a pikestaff.''

"Oh, Uncle,'' breathed Irwin, paling to an unpleasant shade of green.

" 'Tis your good fortune he was not your enemy. Does this virtuous knight have a name?'' Little Freddie's eyes narrowed to slits.

Fordyce mopped his brow with his sleeve, the heat from the small fire suddenly oppressive. He froze as the thunder of hooves echoed in the courtyard. Silence followed. Then the door flew open with a mighty crash that nearly shook it from its hinges.

Rowena came bursting in like a ray of sunshine cutting through the stale layer of smoke that hung over the hall. The wild, sweet scent of the moor clung to her hair, her skin, the handwoven tunic she wore. Her cheeks were touched with the flushed rose of exertion; her eyes were alight with exuberance.

She ran straight to her father, her words tumbling out faster than the apples dumped from the sack she clutched upside down.

"Oh, Papa, I am ever so happy you've come home! Where did you have the stallion hidden? He is the most beautiful animal I ever saw. Did you truly find your elusive fortune this journey?''

Falling to her knees beside his chair, she pulled a crumpled bunch of heather from her pocket and dumped it in his lap without giving him time to reply.

"I brought your favorite flowers and Little Freddie has promised to cook apples on the coals. They will be hot and sweet and juicy, just as you like them. 'Twill be a hundred times better than any nasty old roasted hare. Oh, Papa, you're home! We thought you were never coming back."

She threw her arms around his waist. The uninhibited gesture knocked the cap from her head to unleash a cascade of wheaten curls.

Fordyce's arms did not move to encircle her. He sat stiff in her embrace. She lifted her face, aware of a silence broken only by the thump of a log shifting on the fire. Her father did not meet her eyes, and for one disturbing moment, she thought she saw his lower lip tremble.

She followed his gaze. Her brothers stood lined up before the hearth in the most ordered manner she had ever seen them. Irwin beamed from the middle of the row.

Bathed in the light of the flickering fire, the stranger stepped out of the shadows. Rowena raised her eyes. From where she knelt, it was as if she was peering up from the bottom of a deep well to meet the eyes of the man who towered over her. His level gaze sent a bolt of raw fear through her, riveting her to the floor as if she stared into the face of death itself. A long moment passed before she could pull her eyes away.

"Papa?" she breathed, patting his cool, trembling hand.

He stroked her hair, his eyes distant. "Rowena, I believe 'twould be fitting for you to step outside till we have concluded our dealings."

"You made no mention of a daughter, Fordyce." The stranger's gaze traveled between father and child.

Papa's arm curved around Rowena's shoulders like a shield. The stranger's mocking laughter echoed through the hall. Only Rowena heard Papa's muttered curse as he realized what he had done.

"Your interest is in my sons," Papa hissed, a tiny vein in his temple beginning to throb.

"But *your* interest is not. That much is apparent."

The man advanced and Rowena rose, knowing instinctively that she did not want to be on her knees at this stranger's feet. She stood without flinching to face the wrought links of the silver chain mail that crossed the man's chest. From broad shoulders to booted feet, his garments were as black as the eyes that regarded her with frank scrutiny. She returned his perusal with arms crossed in front of her.

A closer look revealed his eyes were not black, but a deep, velvety brown. Their opacity rendered them inscrutable, but alive with intelligence. Heavy, arched brows added a mocking humor that gave Rowena the impression she was being laughed at, although his expression did not waver. His sable hair was neatly cut, but an errant waviness warned of easy rebellion. His well-formed features were saved from prettiness by an edge of rugged masculinity enhanced by his sheer size. The thought flitted through Rowena's mind that he might be handsome if his face was not set in such ruthless lines.

He reached down and lifted a strand of her hair as if hypnotized at its brightness. The velvety tendril curled around his fingers at the caress.

Rowena's hand slipped underneath her tunic, but before she could bring the knife up to strike, her wrist was twisted in a fearful grip that sent the blade clattering to the stones. She bit her lip to keep from crying out. The man loosed her.

"She has more fire than the rest of you combined." The stranger strode back to the hearth. "I'll take her."

The hall exploded in enraged protest. Papa sank back in the chair, his hand over his eyes.

"You cannot have my sister!" Little Freddie's childish tenor cut through his brothers' cries.

The man leaned against the hearth with a smirk. "Take

heart, lad. 'Tis not forever. She is only to serve me for a year.''

Rowena looked at Papa. His lips moved with no sound. Her brothers spewed forth dire and violent threats, although they remained in place as if rooted to the stone. She wondered if they had all taken leave of their senses. The stranger's sparkling eyes offered no comfort. They watched her as if delighting in the chaos he had provoked. The tiny lines around them crinkled as he gave her a wink made all the more threatening by its implied intimacy. A primitive thrill of fear shot through her, freezing her questions before they could leave her lips.

Papa's whine carried just far enough to reach the man's ears. ''We said sons, did we not?''

The man's booming voice silenced them all. ''Nay, Fordyce. We said children. I was to have the use of one of your children for a year.''

Rowena's knees went as slack as her jaw. Only the sheer effort of her will kept her standing.

''You cannot take a man's only daughter,'' said Papa, unable to keep the pleading note from his voice. ''Show me some mercy, won't you?''

The knight snorted. ''Mercy? What have you ever known of mercy, Fordyce? I've come to teach you of justice.''

Papa mustered his courage and banged with force on the arm of the chair. ''I will not allow it.''

The stranger's hand went to the hilt of the massive sword sheathed at his waist. Beneath the rich linen of his surcoat, the muscles in his arms rippled with the slight gesture. ''You choose to fight?'' he asked softly.

Lindsey Fordyce hesitated the merest moment. ''Rowena, you must accompany this nice man.''

Rowena blinked stupidly, thrown off guard by her father's abrupt surrender.

Little Freddie charged forward, an iron pot wielded over his head like a bludgeon. The knight turned with sword drawn. Rowena lunged for his arm, but Papa sailed past both of them and knocked the boy to the ground with a brutal uppercut. Freddie glared at his father, blood trickling from his mouth and nose.

"Don't be an idiot," Papa spat. "He will only kill you, and then he will kill me."

Still wielding his sword, the stranger faced the row of grumbling boys. "If anyone cares to challenge my right to their sister, I shall be more than happy to defend it."

The broad blade gleamed in the firelight. Big Freddie returned the man's stare for a long moment, his calloused paws clenched into fists. He turned away and rested his forehead against the warm stones of the hearth.

The stranger's eyes widened as Irwin's plump form stepped forward, trumpet still clutched in hand. Papa took one step toward Irwin, who then plopped his ample bottom on the hearth and studied the trumpet as if seeing it for the first time.

"A wager is a wager." Papa ran his thumbs along the worn gilt of his tattered surcoat. "As you well know, I am a baron and a knight myself—an honorable man."

He sighed as if the burden of his honor was too much for him to bear. The short laugh uttered by the knight was not a pleasant sound.

Papa gently took Rowena's face between his moist palms. "Go with him, Rowena." He swallowed with difficulty. "He will not harm you."

The stranger watched the exchange in cryptic silence, his arms crossed over his chest.

Rowena searched her father's face, blindly hoping for a burst of laughter to explain away the knight's intrusion as a cruel jest. The hope that flickered within her sputtered and died, smothered by the bleakness in the cornflower-blue eyes that were a pale, rheumy echo of her own.

"I shall go with him, Papa, if you say I should."

The man moved forward, unlooping the rope at his waist. Papa stepped back to keep a healthy sword's distance away from the imposing figure.

Rowena shoved her hands behind her back. "There is no need to bind me."

The man retrieved her hands. Rowena did not flinch as he bound her wrists in front of her none too gently.

Her soft tone belied her anger. "If Papa says I am to go with you, then I will go."

The dark head remained bowed as he tightened the knot with a stiff jerk. Coiling the free end of the rope around his wrist, he led her to the door without a word. She slowed to scoop up her cap. Feeling the sudden tautness in the rope, the man tugged. Rowena dug her heels into the flagstones, resisting his pull. Their eyes met in a silent battle of wills. Without warning, he yanked the rope, causing Rowena to stumble. She straightened, her eyes shining with angry tears for an instant. Then their blue depths cleared and she purposefully followed him through the door, cap clutched in bound hands.

The boys shuffled after them like the undead in a grim processional. Papa meandered behind. Little Freddie was gripped between two of his brothers; a fierce scowl darkened his fair brow.

Night had fallen. A full moon cast its beams through the scant trees, suffusing the muted landscape with the eerie glow of a bogus daylight. Big Freddie gave a low, admiring whistle as a white stallion seemed to rise from the thin shroud of mist that cloaked the ground. The fog entwined itself around the graceful fetlocks. The creature pranced nervously at the sound of approaching footsteps.

Rowena's eyes were drawn to the golden bridle crowning the massive animal. Jewels of every hue encrusted its length. Why would a man of such wealth come all the way to Revelwood to steal a poor man's child? The knight's forbidding shoulders invited no questions as he mounted the horse and slipped Rowena's tether over the leather pommel. The horse's iron-shod hooves twitched. How close could she follow without being pounded to a pulp?

Irwin stepped in front of the horse as if accustomed to

placing his bulk in the path of a steed mounted by a fully armed nobleman. The knight leaned back in the saddle with a sigh.

"Kind sir?" Irwin's voice was a mere squeak, so he cleared his throat and tried again. "Kind sir, I hasten to remind you that you are stealing away our only ray of light in a life of darkness. You pluck the single bloom in our garden of grim desolation. I speak for all of us."

Irwin's cousins looked at one another and scratched their heads. Rowena wished faintly that the knight would run him through and end her embarrassment.

"You make an eloquent plea, lad," the knight replied, surprising them all. "Mayhaps you should plead with her father to make his wagers with more care in the future."

From behind Big Freddie, Papa dared to shoot the man a look of pure hatred.

"You will not relent?" asked Irwin.

"I will not."

"Then I pray the burden of chivalry rests heavily on your shoulders. I pray you will honor my sweet cousin with the same consideration you would grant to the rest of the fair and weaker sex."

Rowena itched to box his ears, remembering the uncountable times she had wrestled him to the ground and pinched him until he squealed for mercy.

The stranger again uttered that short, unpleasant laugh. "Do not fear, lad. I will grant her the same consideration that I would grant to any wench as comely as she. Now stand aside or be trampled."

Irwin tripped to the left as the knight kicked the stallion into a trot. Rowena broke into a lope to avoid being jerked off her feet. She dared break her concentration only long enough for one last hungry look at her family. She heard the soft thud of fist pummeling flesh and a familiar cry as Little Freddie tackled Irwin in blind rage and frustration.

Then they were gone. She focused all of her attention on the rocky turf beneath her feet as her world narrowed to the task of putting one foot in front of the other without falling nose first into the drumming hooves.

CHAPTER 2

The ground blurred beneath Rowena's pounding feet, slipping out from under her with alarming frequency. The tangled grasses of the moor were left behind as they entered a forest. A thick net of branches diffused the brilliant moonbeams into a treacherous web of shadow and light. A dead branch she did not see slammed into her knees even as she stumbled over a rock that was only a reflection in the slick leaves. Surely her whole life had been spent following the flowing tail of this monster steed and the forbidding back of its demon rider. The aching rhythm of her heels faltered, and she stayed on her feet only by entwining her fingers around the strand of rope that bound her wrists. Her cap was now crushed, but she refused to drop it. Tiny droplets of blood welled from her knuckles.

"Pardon me," she gasped.

The broad shoulders did not turn.

"Excuse me . . . sir?"

Nothing. Rowena could think of only one way to get his attention. She sat down, throwing her legs around the rope to keep from being pulled to her stomach. She had counted on the nests of pine needles to cushion her. She had not counted on the knight continuing for several feet until her bottom was dragged into a shallow stream with a defeated splash.

He halted and pivoted the prancing mount to face her. Rowena was not sure who she hated more—the smug stal-

on or the knight who raised one inquisitive eyebrow at her.
he collapsed against the bank and closed her eyes. The
ope relaxed as he dismounted. She sighed at the sheer lux-
ry of stretching her bound wrists over her head and slowly
pened her eyes. The man knelt a few feet away, filling a
eather canteen from the stream. His dark eyes never left
er.

Water filled her braies. The annoying sensation fanned
er flames of indignation. "Would you drown me like an
nwanted kitten, milord, or is there that much compassion
n you?"

"Why did you not ask me to halt?"

"Would you have listened?" Rowena fought to steady her
reathing.

"Aye."

Rowena rolled her eyes and turned her face away to hide
er obvious skepticism.

"How did your little rooster of a father manage to raise
uch a spiritless brood?" he demanded, rising to his feet
nd tucking the canteen into his belt.

"We are not spiritless," she protested. "You've no right
o call us that."

He crossed the stream with one stride and squatted in
ront of her. "Your father is a knight. Has he no skill with
a sword?"

Rowena's eyes sparkled with pride. "Papa had to lay
down his arms through no fault of his own. He was lamed
n a fierce battle with the Welsh devils."

Gareth snorted. "Devils, indeed. What of the six grown
men besides your papa? They let me dance out of there with
you as if it was naught. You do not call that spiritless?"

"You could have slain every one of them, could you
not?"

He shrugged. "Perhaps."

"Then they were not without courage. They were intel-
igent."

The knight's face dissolved into hearty laughter, dispel-

ling its menace and softening its lines to boyishness for a
elusive instant.

"I fear the only quality more lacking than courage wa
intelligence. Who was the plump boy? I feared he was goin
to trumpet me to death."

" 'Twas Irwin. And he is not a boy. He is as old as I.'

"I suppose that makes him a man?"

Rowena searched her mind for some weapon to wipe th
smirk from his haughty lips but knew the moment she spok
that she had chosen poorly.

"Irwin is my betrothed."

She sniffed with injured pride as the man burst into nev
peals of laughter.

She spoke quickly. "He is my cousin. Papa took him i
as my betrothed when he was but a lad. Knowing he coul
provide no dowry, Papa sought to make me an early matcl
and save me embarrassment."

"I sense you are still embarrassed."

Rowena sighed, missing the absurdity of sitting in
stream and discussing matters of the heart with this ster
stranger.

"Do you love this Irwin?"

"I feel a sort of affection for him. He has always bee
around."

"Like a faithful hound?" he offered.

Nodding briskly, she admitted, "I'd sooner love a toad.'

"I found his display of affection rather touching. Did
not melt your heart?"

She shook her head. "You don't know Irwin. He ha
probably been waiting his whole life for a chance to wa:
poetic before a peer of the realm."

A smile touched the man's lips. He tilted her face witl
one finger, studying its softened planes in the moonlight
Round blue eyes, suddenly wary, blinked back at him.

"I'd have fought to the death to keep my betrothed fron
falling into the hands of a man like me," he murmured

His finger traveled upward to trace the curve of her wide lower lip.

Rowena's heart slipped into a thunderous rhythm she did not recognize. She tried to smile, less than comforted by his words. He stared down at her, his dark eyes succumbing to the shadows of the forest. The last traces of laughter vanished from his face. Rowena shifted, painfully aware of her vulnerability as she lay half in and half out of the stream with her hands bound and this enigmatic stranger crouching over her. The wet braies clung to her thighs; her skin glistened with the water's mist.

He pried the crumpled cap from her hands. Placing it on her head, he tucked each strand of flaxen hair beneath with great care.

"If you must go about sprawling in streams like a wanton nymph, pray do wear your cap to discourage would-be assailants." He hauled her to her feet.

He unbound her wrists. Water dripped steadily from the seat of her braies. He mounted the horse without a word.

She smiled hopefully. "I daresay Papa has learned his lesson by now. I believe I can find my way home from here."

"Will you mount with me or shall I bind you again?" The knight stared down at her, his dark eyes hooded.

She approached the massive steed, dwarfed by the man who sat with such ease upon its back.

She swallowed. "You wish for me to ride with you?"

She was suddenly astride the horse as he lifted her with one powerful arm and placed her on the saddle in front of him. Her wet braies tangled beneath her but she barely had time to focus on that discomfort before he kicked the horse into a canter. She realized how much time her pride had cost them since leaving Revelwood.

The horse flew down the path, the thunder of its hooves muffled by the luxuriant carpet of pine needles. Rowena leaned forward to place a safe distance between her back and the broad chest of her captor, only to find herself jerked against him by a muscular arm wrapped around her waist.

"Be still. You'll spook the horse," he commanded.

Rowena surrendered to his iron grip as the horse careened off the path and darted among the trees as if following some esoteric equine map. The knight's chest became a haven that protected her from being crushed as tree trunks lurched into their path with frightening regularity.

When she realized the arm locked beneath her breasts would not allow her to sail off the horse, she settled back, lulled by the novel sense of security the warm chest afforded. She slipped into sleep with uncommon ease.

Rowena awoke in time to keep from falling to her knees as the knight lowered her unceremoniously to the ground. She yawned and rubbed her eyes. Halos of torchlight shone through the trees. The sounds of clumsily plucked lutestrings and voices blended in drunken laughter floated into the night. She blinked up at the forbidding knight.

"Trot behind me like a good squire," he commanded. "Keep your hair up. Perhaps 'tis late enough and they are drunk enough to believe you a lad."

"This is not your home?"

"Nay. But 'twill do to pass the night."

He urged the horse into a walk. Rowena fell into an awkward swagger behind him, at a loss as to how the squire of such a man would appear.

The knight spoke without turning. "You will be left to your own devices when I retire. If you have any thoughts of escape, think again. If you run, I shall return to your home and slay your entire family. When I find you, as I most certainly will, you will wish you had been among the ones slain."

Rowena forced her feet to keep moving. His words sent the skin at the nape of her neck crawling. She pictured Little Freddie, lifeless, a gaping sword wound where his heart should be. Anger flared in her eyes only to be

quenched by common sense as the man turned in the saddle
and fixed his dark eyes on her. She nodded, eyes wide and
without guile.

The merriment within the castle courtyard came spilling
out with the light as couples stumbled down a drawbridge
that spanned a twenty-foot moat. One of the men faltered
in front of the knight's horse.

"Welcome all. The feast is just beginning," he announced, his words slurred. His eyes rolled back in his
head. He fell straight into the dirt, arms spread wide in
greeting.

The woman on his arm flounced back into the castle as
the other couples dissipated like giggling phantoms in the
night.

The knight guided the horse around the prostrate form
without so much as a flick of an eyebrow. Rowena followed,
cutting a wide swath around the fallen man.

Gareth dismounted, handing his reins to a pockmarked
lad who materialized out of the shadows. Before they could
take three steps, the same woman reappeared on the arm of
another stumbling man. Rowena dodged them as they passed
within inches of her. The woman's brittle laughter rent the
air. Rowena gaped as the man's hamlike hands caught the
woman's hips and bore her backward. Her grimy toes curled
into an embrace at the small of his back. With a grunt and
a grind of his hips, he pinioned her to the wall.

Rowena had forgotten the knight until she felt his firm
grasp on her forearm as he tugged her away from the lurid
scene. She was so intent on peering over her shoulder at the
mingled pain and ecstasy on the woman's florid face that
she did not see the man that leaped in front of them until
she slammed into his hauberk with a force that set her ears
to ringing.

"Who goes there? Gareth, my man, could that really be
you?" came the urgent voice.

"Nay," she replied without thought. " 'Tis Ro—"

The knight clapped his hand over her mouth.

"Aye, Blaine. 'Tis Gareth. I do believe you've knocked my squire insensible. Clumsy lad, Ro is. I shall have to beat that out of him." The knight loosed his grip on her mouth and boxed her ears with gentle force.

This was followed by a hearty slap on the back from the slender gentleman. He peered drunkenly into her face, and a smile quirked the corners of his thin lips. Rowena gasped, unable to remember a time when she had been knocked about with such relish.

"Who would be foolish enough to trust their young whelp into your blackhearted hands?" Although he addressed her captor, Blaine's gaze traveled from her face to her felt-clad feet with insinuating slowness.

"Need I remind you how many times these blackhearted hands have unseated you in a tourney?" Gareth replied.

Blaine ignored him and circled Rowena. "Small, is he not?"

"You were small yourself once, Blaine." Gareth slapped a muscled arm around Blaine's shoulders and guided his stumbling steps away from Rowena and toward the drawbridge. "Have you forgotten the time I pitched you out the window with one hand when we were but lads?"

"How could I? I landed in a bramble bush and spent the rest of the night soaking my finer parts in a barrel." Blaine shielded his eyes from the torchlight and hooked one arm around Gareth's neck. "Yet still I welcome you to Arden-donne. What a fool I am! I should feed you to the man-eating fish in my moat."

Gareth rolled his eyes. "After the camels ran away, I thought you'd give up on exotic animals."

"When the Prince of Wales took to bragging about his pet lion, I had to find some way to best him." Blaine shook his head sadly. "I lose two or three guests every feast day. One splash and they are no more. Nothing left but bones to be fished out when the sun rises. Ah, well."

Gareth jerked him back as he swayed toward the side of the drawbridge. Rowena hugged herself and edged closer to

the center of the bridge, refusing to raise her eyes for fear
of finding bleached bones floating in the bubbling water.

She followed the men through the bailey and into the
vaulted hall, her eyes locked on Gareth's back as he steered
Sir Blaine away. She read a thousand warnings in the glance
he threw over his shoulder as they disappeared into the milling crowd.

She halted, feeling oddly at a loss by her captor's deser-
tion. Thrusting her hands deep in her sleeves, she whistled,
pretending to be unaffected by the strangers reeling about
her in various states of drunkenness and dishabille. As her
gaze traveled the room, it lit on a sight that made her mouth
water. The rest of the hall faded to invisibility.

She shouldered her way through the galloping dancers
and halted as close as she dared.

A man in a red velvet mantle grinned and nudged her.
"Make haste, lad. 'Tis been picked to bare bones, but you
might yet find a few choice morsels."

Rowena started to laugh and cry at the same time. The
man sidled away, believing her daft or drunk or both. On a
table that stretched twenty feet along the wall lay the remnants of Ardendonne's feast. Revelwood would not see this
much food in a year.

Rowena's stomach rumbled a warning. She placed her
feet farther apart to keep from swaying. A half-eaten boar's
head stared her down with glassy eyes from the center of
the table. With a hasty glance around her, she plucked the
apple from its mouth and shoved it up her sleeve. Her trembling hand dipped into a silver bowl and came out with a
mound as golden as the sun that floated over the moor on a
spring day. She dared to lick it. Sweetly seasoned apples
coated her tongue. She closed her eyes in rapture.

With the hunger of a lifetime unleashed, Rowena darted
up and down the table, dipping a hand into each bowl and
snatching at each platter, pausing long enough to stare at
what could have only been the remains of a whole cow
sprawled at the end of the table. A mean-eyed yellow hound

stood on the table with his hind legs in the gravy. Rowena
wrestled a turkey leg from him and washed it down with a
half-full tankard of ale found abandoned in the honeyed
plums.

With a huge sigh, she plopped down on the stale-smelling
floor rushes, lulled by her sated belly. The hall spun around
her. The silken veils of the dancing women swirled in violent splashes of purple and peach against the bright red and
blue of the men's surcoats. She reached a hand to her mois-
tened, fair brow. What sort of peculiar people would waste
a roaring fire on a summer night?

"See how he charms," came the hissed whisper above
her.

Rowena's gaze followed the stained satin skirts of the
woman beside the table, to a round face wreathed in a ma-
levolent smile.

"I daresay Alise will lift her skirts before morning is
nigh," murmured the tall, bony woman beside the other.
"Sir Gareth garners few refusals."

Rowena's eyes widened as she followed their gazes to her
captor. The unadorned black of his garments was unrelenting against the backdrop of bobbing reds and greens. He
stood with one foot propped on a stool, his dark head inclined toward a laughing woman. The woman's hand slipped
farther up his thigh with each of her whispered words. A
tight smile curved his lips in a mocking travesty of the smile
he had given Rowena at the stream. His hand lightly caressed the woman's slender neck even as his gaze pulled
away and traveled the hall. Rowena leaned deeper into the
shadows under the table, not wanting to be found by those
dark eyes.

"Charmed the king himself into knighting him, he did,
at the tender age of seventeen."

"Oh, go on! If you'd have stepped between a Welsh sword
and old Longshanks on a battlefield running with England's
blood, I daresay he would have knighted you, too." The
plump woman plucked something off the table and tossed it

in her mouth with a satisfied smack. "Dare I pop a fly in Alise's pudding?"

"If you refrain, the dark lord will pop more than a fly in her pudding tonight," the thin woman replied.

"Alise can handle de Crecy. She has outlived two husbands, has she not?"

"I'll wager she wouldn't outlive that one." Both women cackled.

"See how Mortimer watches with jealous eyes. I believe he fancies Gareth himself. Let us determine if he is drunk enough to be stupid."

"Or stupid enough to be murdered." The thin woman giggled. She stumbled away from the table, treading on her friend's embroidered train until the woman snatched it up and threw it over her arm, slapping several dancers more insensible than they were.

The women descended on a pasty-faced minstrel. His long, delicate fingers continued to pluck his lute. The women flanked him, leaning forward to capture both ears with sly, sidelong glances at Gareth and his lady. At a quick shake of his head, the plump woman leaned closer, smothering him with her ample bosom. He shrugged and nodded. The women backed away, whispering behind their hands. Rowena tugged a strand of her hair from her cap and tucked in into her mouth.

The jolly tune halted abruptly, to the groans of the dancers. A man near Rowena continued in the dance, slinging invisible partners to and fro with a regal air. The minstrel pulled a flask from his vest and took a long swig. Most of the wine missed his mouth and dribbled down his chin.

A stumbling knight cried out, "Play now, Mortimer. Quench your infernal thirst later."

"Play and I shall send my squire to your chambers after the revelry to quench it for you," called Sir Blaine.

At the hoots and catcalls of the crowd, Mortimer wiggled his fingers at Sir Blaine in an effeminate salute of thanks. Blaine made the sign of a cross as if to ward him away. The

crowd rocked with laughter. Rowena smiled without understanding. Sir Gareth still leaned over the canary-garbed
woman on the stool, oblivious to the musical entertainment
or lack of it. As Rowena watched, his hand slid beneath the
woman's wimple. His lips brushed her swanlike throat. How
could such a pale, delicate neck support a brocade wimple,
much less a head?

Rowena's fingers brushed her own throat. She was comforted by its sturdy familiarity. No matter how much her
head was spinning at the moment, she knew it would not
fall off.

Mortimer's fingers gently teased the lutestrings. The
crowd fell silent as he drew bittersweet chords out of the
stained instrument with a skill they had forgotten he possessed.

"You see, my dear lords and ladies, I have a new tune,
a new song," he said softly.

Tears started in Rowena's eyes at the haunting melody.
Longing for home, she wiped them away with the same
strand of hair she had been chewing on. The crowd crept
nearer to Mortimer, starved even in their drunken stupor for
fresh words and melodies. His lank hair fell across his face.
They leaned forward to hear his muted words.

" 'Tis a tune I first heard a fortnight ago at a castle across
the channel in Touraine."

Sir Gareth straightened with a frown. A chill of appre-
hension shot through Rowena as his brow darkened. But he
was not seeking her; he was staring at the minstrel.

Mortimer began to sing, his voice deep and pleasant.

> The fair Elayne
> Unfairly slain
> Her faithless hand
> Stilled by a name.

With a nervous murmur and clearing of throats, the crowd
took a step backward.

The fair Elayne
Hath fled the pain—
With fearful flight
From one dark knight.

The fair Elayne—

Rowena was humming brokenly along when Mortimer's words choked to a halt. The lute crashed to the stones with a discordant thump. The minstrel lay on the floor with Gareth's boot on his throat and the chiseled tip of a sword at his breast. The crowd cleared a healthy circle around the two of them. Rowena saw the two women who had accosted the minstrel duck out the door. She came to her feet, tucking her hair into her cap.

Gareth's eyes glittered like black diamonds. His broad chest rose and fell in uneven rhythm. "If you care to sing another day, canary, tell me who wrote that song," he growled. Mortimer's pale hands fluttered upward in a mute plea. Gareth lifted his shiny boot half an inch, as his sword pressed deeper into the man's tunic. "Speak now or forever hold your tongue."

Mortimer coughed weakly. "I told you. I learned it in Touraine. At a castle."

"What castle? And from whom?"

"I cannot remember."

"You lie." Gareth's boot came down on his throat again.

The crowd parted to let Sir Blaine through. The master of the castle cast a careless arm around Gareth's shoulder. Gareth whirled around, and for a breathless moment, Rowena thought he would draw his sword on his friend.

"Come now, my brother-in-arms. Skillful minstrels are hard to find. I will be hard-pressed to find another if you skewer this one. Pardon his insolence this once. Perhaps 'twas an honest mistake." Blaine's smile was a shade too bright.

Gareth stared down at his friend, his face as drawn and

expressionless as a mask. He looked back at the minstrel. Mortimer grimaced hopefully. Gareth sheathed his sword with a snarl of contempt, but kept his boot on Mortimer's throat.

He leaned forward, his whisper audible throughout the hall. "If those words ever leave your throat again, they will be your last."

The crowd fell back as Gareth crossed the hall in long strides. Rowena started after him, uncertain if she should follow. She stopped when he reached the doe-eyed woman on the stool. Without a word he caught the woman's hand in his. She rose and followed him up the stairs, casting a look back at the crowd that was both demure and triumphant. Gareth stopped on the landing. His eyes searched the hall and found Rowena standing in the middle of the floor, feet poised for movement if he should beckon.

He nodded, and she had no way of knowing if it was a nod of approval or warning. Then he disappeared with the lady into the shadows at the top of the stairs.

A giggling squire emerged from the crowd and pulled Mortimer to his feet, brushing him off with a suggestive leer. The crowd cut a wide swath around the splintered lute. Without the music, the dance and the revelry died. Those who could walk paired off and stumbled up the stairs or out into the night. Those who could not wrapped their cloaks around them and stretched out on the tables and floor. A short blond boy beside Rowena cleared off the table with a single swipe and rolled onto it with a gurgling snore. She watched him sleep for a moment, wondering with longing what Little Freddie might be doing at that moment. Her stomach ached. She sighed and curled up in the corner, bunching a grimy handful of rushes into a pillow.

A vision of the man and woman she had seen outside the castle drifted through her weary mind. The thought of the lady Alise's delicate face screwed up into such an expression of pleasure and pain made her smile. She found it hard to imagine Gareth's strong form caught in such a graceless act as skewering a woman like a trapped bug against a wall. Even the hogs at Revelwood, when they still had hogs, had possessed more finesse in their mating. Her smile faded. When the yellow cur sank down beside her and lapped at her nose, she threw an arm over him and drawing him to her chest, went to sleep.

As Gareth climbed the steps, the weight of Alise's hand in his felt cold and insubstantial. The melody of Mortimer's song echoed in the back of his skull, taunting him with its eerie refrain. Curiosity shone in Alise's hazel eyes. Perhaps she could hear it, too. He snatched his hand out of the web of her fine-boned fingers without explanation. There was no time for her gentle reproof. The door of a chamber lay before them.

A baby-faced squire and blushing maidservant pushed past them with knowing glances as they entered. Their giggles floated back as they fled down the stairs. Gareth slammed the door and jerked the tousled counterpane off the mattress. At the violence of the gesture, a tingle of fright shuddered down Alise's spine, deepening the sparkle of anticipation in her eyes. Gareth felt sickened.

She glided toward him, twirling like a leaf in the wind when he caught her arm and drew her into his embrace. Her lips spread hungrily, drawing him into a lake of fire. Even as his body responded in all the right ways, his mind wondered how many women bedded him out of curiosity, seeking the razor-edge thrill of danger, and hoping what others said about him was true.

Alise backed away, her eyes darkening pools of invitation. Her fingers caught like claws in the edge of his leather gauntlets. She peeled them from his forearms like a second layer of skin.

A chord of memory chimed within him. He remembered the nightmares that had beset him after he had buried Elayne. He dreamed her moldering corpse would come dragging up the hall. Her skeletal claws would paw his

bolted door until he would awaken, screaming and drenched
in the scent of his own fear.

He pulled Alise to him, burying his face in her smooth
throat to vanquish the memory. His broad fingers splayed
over the ridges of her ribs through the heavy brocade.

His eyes opened of their own volition as he remembered
without warning the warmth of something more solid against
him—the girl sleeping in his arms on the journey to the
castle. Her body, vulnerable and warm, nestled against him.
Her head had fallen to the side, and her gentle breath had
passed through his chain mail like a spring wind. She was
so young, and he suddenly felt very old trapped in the sharp
embrace of a woman he hardly knew. He could see the girl
standing in the center of the hall, her golden mass of hair
caught in the shapeless confines of her cap, looking more
self-possessed than any of those who stumbled around her.
Only her eyes had lacked certainty. They had locked on him
as if his will could determine the very direction of her
thoughts. The vision made him uneasy. Would she flee, or
would she heed his warnings? Stumbling across her father
had been a stroke of fate. He had searched for her too long
to lose her now.

Alise moaned against his lips, bringing him back to the
teasing ache of her fingertips gliding over his hip and downward with practiced skill. With a groan, he dragged the
wimple from her head. Her hair came spilling out in a pale
cloud around their faces.

Rowena awoke with a firm hand clamped over her mouth.
She struggled for consciousness through a groggy haze and
reached for her knife. Her hand came up empty. A rough
hand plunged inside her overtunic.

"If you are a lad, sweet squire, then I am a vestal virgin," came a hoarse whisper against her ear.

The fire had died to embers. Her attacker's face was in
shadow. His wandering hand slid downward outside the
coarse braies and clamped between her legs. Panic sliced

through the last vestiges of sleep, and Rowena struck out in earnest. The man's cry of triumph was cut short as her fist connected smartly with his smooth chin.

He caught her wrist and wrenched it. "Damn you, wench. You may fight like a lad, but I swear I'll make you glad you're not one before this night is done."

A heated breath of ale filled her nostrils. Wet, greedy lips closed on hers. Rowena drove her knee toward his groin but found only air as a shadow fell over them and the man's weight vanished. She sat up, struggling to catch her breath. Her cap fell off, her golden hair tumbling over her face. She tossed it back from her eyes to find her host, Sir Blaine, slammed against the wall with Gareth's misericord pressed to his throat.

Blaine shrugged as well as he could in his awkward position. "What did you expect, my friend? Did you think me so drunk as to believe her a lad? That mouth may have been fashioned by heaven to service a knight, but not as a squire."

Rowena touched her lips. They felt hot and swollen.

Gareth's gauntlets were gone. The muscles of his forearm knotted beneath dark curling hairs. "The lady is not to be troubled." The small dagger in his hand did not waver.

Blaine's eyes narrowed. "If you cannot offer this . . . lady any more protection than leaving her unattended in my hall, how can you dare reproach me for offering her my protection?"

"You were offering her more than your protection. If you find my care lacking, old friend, mayhaps you would care to challenge me to a joust."

Blaine looked away from Gareth's steady gaze. A muscle in his cheek twitched.

Gareth's smile held no humor. "I thought not." He loosed Blaine and sheathed the dagger. "Now be a good drunken boy and find your bed. I fear I had to disappoint Alise. Perhaps she will consent to soothe your wounded pride."

Blaine forced a rueful smile and rubbed his chin. "I suggest you armor yourself ere you take this chit abovestairs. She tosses a nasty punch."

"I know. I saw."

Gareth pulled Rowena to her feet. She had no choice but to follow him. She glanced back to find Blaine staring after them, his smile gone and his eyes smoldering with an emotion deeper than annoyance.

CHAPTER 3

The climb up the stairs was far too brief, and Rowena found herself in the middle of a modest bedchamber, twisting her cap in her hands, as a heavy door slammed behind her. Would this night never end? She tried not to tremble as Gareth's knuckles trailed gently over her cheek.

"Did he hurt you?"

She shook her head, exhaustion making her honest. "Have you brought me here to paw me yourself?"

He turned away with a disparaging laugh. "God forbid. I've no taste for dirty little moor urchins."

Rowena opened her mouth to protest that she had been swimming in her clothes only that afternoon, then snapped it shut. If the sweet, pure dirt of the moor would protect her from the attentions of honorable knights like Sir Gareth and his friends, she would give up bathing altogether.

Gareth turned his back to her and drew his tunic over his head. A web of pale scars crisscrossed his broad shoulders. Rowena wondered which scar should have belonged to the king.

" 'Tis no wonder," she murmured. "You've challenged everyone but me to a tournament this eve."

Gareth turned on her, his eyes bright. Dark, curling hair furred his chest. His lips quirked upward in what might have seemed amusement in a less guarded man. Rowena realized she had spoken her thoughts aloud. She sank down on the woven rug beside the bed and nervously began to braid her hair.

The feather mattress shifted as he lay his solid weight on it. His dark head appeared over the edge of the bed. "No one accepted my challenge, did they?"

"Are you that good?"

He threw his weight back on the bed. She took his grunt as one of assent. She abandoned the braids, longing for Little Freddie's competent hands. She was tying her hair in knots. She lay back and hugged her overtunic around her, missing the musty warmth of the hound in the hall. Encompassed by the weight of the day, her tired eyes fluttered shut. She sensed a shadow fall over her.

Gareth loomed above, and Rowena's breath caught in her throat. She waited for his strong hand to cover her mouth, his smooth lips to clamp down on hers in demand. Instead, a coverlet fell on her chest. His misericord thumped to a halt on top of it.

"If anyone else attempts you tonight—including me—gut him."

Her unblinking blue eyes met his dark gaze. The bed creaked again. She waited in silence for the sound of steady breathing that would tell her he slept. It did not come. She curled up on her side, her hand clenched around the hilt of the tiny dagger.

Rowena awoke to a sun-warmed and empty chamber. She uncurled her stiff back and stood, rubbing her eyes. The goose-down coverlet slid around her ankles. The rumpled tick on the deserted bed was its only sign of recent occupancy. She glanced around guiltily, then threw herself on the feather mattress with a sigh. The bed frames at Revelwood had been sold long ago, leaving only moldy heaps of straw in the hall for all to share. She rolled over, burrowing her face in the luxuriant softness. Her body fit neatly into the larger imprint of the man who had slept there. She breathed in a scent of leather, deeper and more evocative than the smell of old feathers. She flopped to her back and bounced up and down with a giggle. The timber frame creaked a shrill complaint. Rowena was still gleefully bouncing when the door flew open.

Gareth stood in the doorway with a pair of dripping chausses draped over one arm. Rowena froze, though the bed kept reverberating for an excruciating minute. Gareth's face revealed nothing, and for the first time in her life, Rowena wondered what she looked like. The hand she raised to her hair found it half braided and half matted around her face.

She grinned weakly. "Good morn, sir. I was awaiting your pleasure."

He lifted an eyebrow and Rowena bit her tongue. He shut the door.

"As your squire, I meant, kind sir." She casually sidled off the bed. "I was awaiting your pleasure as your squire this morn to learn how I might best serve you." Rowena winced and pondered taking a vow of silence. She started for the coverlet, but his tall form blocked her path.

"My dagger, please." He held out a broad palm.

"I was just going to fetch it."

" 'Tis what I feared."

When he stepped back a few inches, her hip was forced to brush against his thighs as she bent and scavenged through the blanket folds for the dagger. After a moment, she slapped the hilt into his palm with a step back. He tucked the jeweled weapon into his boot and bent to gather his scant belongings.

"You will find a tub in the chamber at the end of the corridor. The water remains from yestereve, but you're welcome to it if you desire."

Rowena shook her head with maddening complacency. "Nay, sir. There is no need. I bathed only last month."

Gareth's head jerked up. She struggled not to squirm under his frank scrutiny. Had it been only yesterday she had plunged beneath the chill, tumbling water of a stream and lain in the warmth of the noonday sun until her clothes dried crisp and hot against her skin? This tyrant would not learn of it.

He mumbled something unintelligible and laced up his leather gauntlets with swift, sure motions, then held out his arms expectantly. Rowena took another step backward, which brought the back of her legs in uncomfortable proximity to the bed frame.

Gareth cleared his throat. Leather thongs dangled from the burnished gloves. "Would you mind?" he asked, the very picture of pained patience.

Rowena crept nearer. A proper squire would help him dress, would he not? And that is what she was meant to be, was it not? Her tongue slipped out of the corner of her mouth at the effort of working the slick thongs into a proper knot. Twice she included her thumb in the tidy parcel.

On the third try, after she had tangled not only her little finger but a large strand of her hair in the endeavor, he snatched his hand back with a growl. "Unless I care to nip your fingers off, I'd best find another to assist me."

Rowena shoved her hands behind her back, lacing her fingers together in a protective knot.

He slipped the woven chain mail over his head. "Tarry here. I will seek out Blaine and thank him for his hospitality ere we take our leave."

Rowena remembered a heavy hand clamped between her legs and thought of myriad ways she would like to thank Blaine for his hospitality—most of them involving the blunt end of a cudgel. She hid her thoughts behind the hand that tucked her tangled hair back into her cap. Gareth left her sitting dutifully on the edge of the bed, hands folded.

A tiny spark in the pit of her stomach ignited a burning hole. After her sating last night, Rowena recognized the sting as hunger. She had lived with the ache so long it had taken on a certain normalcy.

She crossed her legs, uncrossed them, and rose to pace the chamber. She drank a bit of water, sloshed the remains out the window, and sat down again. The pit in her gut swelled, threatening to suck her in and swallow her completely.

She opened the door and peered both ways before creeping out. The hour must be earlier than she thought. Bodies still littered the stairs in various positions of sleep and stupor. She picked her way down the stairs and across the great hall. A man reached for her ankle. She nimbly skirted his fingers, eliciting a strangled murmur before he curled back into his cloak.

The table loomed before her, no less beautiful in the harsh light of morning than in the romantic hue of torchlight.

Rowena whirled around when Gareth came plunging down the steps moments later. He caught hold of the wall to steady himself. She knew from his expression that he had been to the empty chamber. As she imagined his confusion a sparkle of satisfied malice touched her eyes, but it was gone before he could cross the sea of bodies. Rowena took advantage of his concentration on that task by running her palms beneath the table, then rubbing her cheeks, leaving powdery smudges of dirt wherever she touched.

Gareth opened his mouth to speak, then closed it. His eyes traveled over her from head to foot, narrowing in suspicion as if wondering if the faeries had come in the night and left this pudgy, dirty changeling in place of his lithe captive.

Rowena smiled brightly. "I grew weary of waiting, milord. I trust I did not anger you."

"Of course not."

Rowena knew from his clenched jaw that he was lying. Her smile grew broader. She wished she had gained the time to black out one of her pearly teeth with soot.

"I would prefer in the future that you follow my commands," he said. "Unless you would prefer to fall into the hands of another Sir Blaine."

His barb stung. Rowena hid it behind flowery words that mocked his precise French without meaning to. "Where is our fair host? Has he no words of farewell at our leavetaking?''

Something like a grin touched Gareth's lips. "I fear Sir Blaine finds himself indisposed this morn. He bids us a safe journey with special good wishes for my new squire. He has even instructed his stableman to gift you with a horse for our journey to Caerleon.''

Rowena took the hand he proffered to guide her across the hall, wondering what fits of joy and jealousy it would give Mortimer to see Sir Gareth holding hands with his squire. She had always thought her blunt fingers heavy and ungraceful. They were dwarfed in the cup of Gareth's palm. She heard a snuffling noise at her leg and looked down to find the yellow hound. She scratched him absently on the head, considering it a fitting farewell for a faithful friend.

Horse was a kind word for the swayback nag Sir Blaine had provided her. The inverted hump between withers and rump was deep enough to hold three Rowenas. If the early morning silence had not been broken by a halfhearted stamp of one hoof at their approach, Rowena would have thought him dead. She heard a snort behind her far more lively than any she could expect from the horse. When she turned, Gareth's face was curiously stern.

"Blaine's judgment of women has always exceeded his judgment of horseflesh,'' he said.

A more experienced woman might have read a compliment in Gareth's words, but they sailed over Rowena's head. A warm muzzle poked at her hand. The yellow hound was still following her. He had been joined by a grizzled mutt and an oversized mastiff who stood as high as her waist.

The mastiff jammed his nose into the sleeve of her tunic. "Begone, please,'' she hissed.

Gareth frowned at her. His stallion pranced nearby, unnerved by the yelps and whines of the milling dogs. Rowena swatted at the hound. The mastiff tugged at her sleeve. Three tiny dogs came yipping down the drawbridge, their jeweled collars flashing in the morning sun. They made a straight path for Rowena. She decided this might be an opportune moment to ignore Sir Blaine's diabolical sense of humor and throw herself on the nag's back. She lifted one leg. The mastiff caught the cuff of her braies between his powerful jaws. She gritted her teeth and pulled, caught in an all-out battle of strength with the slavering beast.

Rowena's waist slid nicely into the groove of the nag's back, leaving the foot not encompassed in the mastiff's jaws dangling helplessly. Gareth stroked his short beard, his stance one of complete relaxation.

"Pardon me," she grunted. "I would be ever so appreciative if you would help me mount. I seem to be having some difficulty."

He scattered the dogs with a masterful bellow. The yellow hound crept away with a reproachful look at Rowena. Gareth's arms circled her waist, but she felt him pause and heard him sniff.

The ground beneath her feet was a more welcome sensation than Gareth's hand on her elbow as he spun her around. "I am not given to rudeness, but I must insist you bathe. When the dogs start following your scent, 'tis a hearty indication . . ."

He trailed off. His nose quivered. His gaze slid downward, caught by the spectacle of half a roasted hen hanging out of her torn sleeve. He gingerly plucked it from her and cast it in the midst of the widening circle of dogs gathered in the courtyard. They attacked it with snarls of satisfaction.

Gareth glowered at her. Rowena lifted her arms in mute surrender. He delved beneath the overtunic, fishing out a handful of bread crusts, two pork loins, a wad of stewed raisins and prunes, three whole onions and the rotting apple she had stolen from the boar's mouth. When he had removed the pudginess she had acquired so abruptly, he held out his hand. Rowena slipped out of her overtunic and laid it in his hands. The tattered garment followed the food to the dogs.

She could not hide her crestfallen expression as she

watched her succulent treasures disappear into their yawning maws. How Little Freddie would have savored the cinnamon and honey flavoring the raisins! Rowena shivered in her thin shirte. This knight was more than cruel; he was a monster.

Gareth unlatched a woven basket from his bridle, and dropped it at Rowena's feet. He tilted her chin upward with one finger. Her eyes were dry, but her lips were set in a bitter line.

"Did you think I would starve you?"

Her silence was reply enough. A thin layer of dust coated his fingertip where he had touched her chin. He swept back the lid of the basket to reveal two loaves of steaming bread, a crock of creamy yellow butter and three swollen strings of fresh sausage. He heard the teasing growl of Rowena's stomach before she felt it.

She slammed the lid with her foot and sat down on top of the basket. She clutched his leg, her eyes as blue and earnest as the brightening sky.

"You won't give it to the dogs, will you? You mustn't. Say you won't."

Her reaction mystified Gareth. He squatted beside her, convinced if he dared toss the basket to the dogs, he would have to toss her, too. Her arms were smooth and fair, unmarred by the dirt streaking her cheeks.

He spoke slowly and patiently. "I packed the food for our morning repast. I thought it might be more pleasant to partake of it away from the stench of yestereve's merriment."

She stood as abruptly as she had sat down. She handed the basket to Gareth, marveling at its weight in her hand. "Of course. A grand idea. To break the fast of the night. Some days at Revelwood we do not break the fast until nightfall. We are simply too busy and the delay heightens our anticipation and whets our appetites." Rowena was chattering because she knew if her appetite was whetted any more, she might gobble up Gareth where he stood, basket and all.

He hefted the basket to its rope. "Are you hungry?"

She poked the dirt with her toe and shrugged. From beneath downcast lashes, she watched him open the basket and tear off a hunk of bread so fresh that flour dusted its surface. Hardly daring to breathe, she waited for him to eat the bread and throw her the crust. Her hands almost did not react when he tossed the entire hunk to her. She caught its warmth between her palms.

Gareth mounted the stallion without a word. Clutching the miracle of flour and yeast between her fingers, Rowena dragged herself astride the nag and followed him over an arched bridge into the pocket of cool air hanging over the misty lake.

As Gareth had promised, they picnicked in a sunny meadow at midmorning. He ate little, seemingly content to recline in the grass a few feet away and watch Rowena polish off both strings of sausage and a creamy hunk of cheese. Sir Blaine's keep of Ardendonne crowned a distant hill, giving Rowena a shining view of the grandeur she had only guessed at in the night. Sunlight spilled over the tiled roof of the donjon, casting shadows behind the rounded tower. Rowena sighed at its beauty and gently sucked the sausage grease from each of her fingers with dreamy satisfaction.

She glanced up to find Gareth staring at her lips with hypnotic intensity. His gaze flicked guiltily to her eyes. He sprang to his feet, barking a command that she mount.

They left the meadows for a tangled forest thick with the bracken of late summer. The pit in Rowena's stomach had been soothed to a warm glow. Lulled by her sated senses and the melancholy rhythm of the nag's laggard pace, she began to hum absently. The words of Mortimer's ballad rose from her throat in a sweet, off-key alto before she even realized she remembered them:

The fair Elayne,
Unfairly slain—

Gareth moved with such speed that the nag was still
walking when he snatched Rowena down by the scruff of
her sleeveless shirte. He drove her backwards until she felt
the rough bark of a tree slam into her shoulders. Without
wanting to, she remembered again the man pinning the
woman against the castle wall.

His nostrils flared. "Do not sing that song. Not now. Not
ever."

A darkness deeper than color loomed behind his eyes.
Even when he released her, all she could do was nod, rendered mute by the oddly tender brush of his gauntlet against
her cheek.

He stalked back to the stallion, never hearing her faint,
"As you wish, milord."

Her knees shook. Gareth threw himself on the stallion's
back and spurred the horse forward. Had he forgotten her?
She was already wondering if she dared return to Ardendonne to ask directions to Revelwood when Gareth spun the
mount around. The stallion pranced sideways, its satiny coat
rippling in shimmering contrast to the black-clad knight on
its back. Gareth and the stallion could have been one creature, so sharp and precise were their movements. They
stopped, poised and waiting. Only the velvety lift of the
wind through the stallion's mane assured Rowena they were
real and not the product of a starved imagination fed on the
paltry dreams of Revelwood.

She mounted the nag without a word, lacing her hands
in the wispy mane to hide their trembling.

By late afternoon the sun had disappeared behind a solid
bank of gray clouds. Day faded painlessly into dusk as they
slipped off the old Roman road and entered a forest of tall
and ancient trees. Rowena stared upward. Through the
creaking boughs, the wind whispered of rain. The trees were

so huge, her arms could not have circled a single tree trunk. When she began to see faces twisted in the gnarled bark, she fixed her eyes straight ahead and edged her mount closer to Gareth.

The span of his shoulders lost its menace and became as much a comfort as the rhythmic jingle of the bridle in his steady hands. A wolf howled in the distance, sending pin-pricks of fear down Rowena's spine. Gareth glanced back at her, his eyes shadowed by the forest.

He might have been a wolf himself with his shaggy hair and the gleam of his white teeth. Irwin had told them all of werebeasts from hell, half-men and half-wolves who lured innocent damsels into the forest to feast upon their tender flesh. Her cheerful whistle held a hollow ring. She slowed her mount, putting a more healthy distance between herself and Gareth.

With an earsplitting screech, a silvery bat came swooping out of the trees to crash into Gareth. The impact unseated him with a clang that echoed through the still forest. The nag responded with his first indication of life in the long day by rearing with a half-paw at the air, dumping Rowena on the damp ground. Her hair spilled out of her cap, rendering her blind. She could hear nothing but Gareth's muffled curses.

When she untangled her hair from her eyes, Gareth lay flat on his back. An armored figure straddled his shoulders. His steady stream of curses brought a blush to Rowena's cheeks. She leaped to her feet in a frenzy of indecision.

"Surrender!" bellowed the helmed creature, bouncing up and down on Gareth's chest.

Rowena hopped from one foot to the other, pondering what to do. Why did Gareth not simply throw his assailant off? Perhaps he had been injured in the fall, though he certainly had enough wits and breath left to curse.

Deciding a known evil was preferable to an unknown evil, Rowena scooped up a stick and whacked the helmed figure on the head.

The creature fell off Gareth with a groan. Gareth rolled to his side and pounded the ground with his fist. Rowena took a step backward when she realized he was laughing. Her brow furrowed. She could find nothing amusing in his being rescued by someone who by all rights should have hit him on the head.

The armored stranger sat up with a moan. Rowena lifted her stick, prepared to dispatch them both if Gareth's hysteria persisted. Still weak with laughter, he reached out a restraining arm.

The stranger reached for the helm. From under the tarnished silver came a straight dark fall of hair. The one dark eye that glared at Rowena from beneath the stray locks was unmistakably familiar. Rowena stared between Gareth and the stranger, wondering if she or they had lost their senses.

Gareth gasped for breath. "Allow me to introduce my sister Marlys."

Marlys rubbed her head, her glare no less pronounced at the introduction. "Your new whore packs a powerful wallop."

"And a well-deserved one, I might add." Gareth sat up, flexing his long legs. He tucked a twig between his teeth, addressing Rowena although he was looking at his sister. "Marlys delights in ambushing me upon my return to Caerleon. She believes it keeps me on my toes. How long have you been hanging in that tree, dear? Two days? Three? A week?"

Marlys climbed to her feet, her rusty knee mail clanking. "As if I would waste so much time on you, brother. You've been letting your women swell your opinion of yourself again."

Rowena was too lost in Marlys's uncorrected impression of her to notice when the girl came to stand in front of her. Marlys rested her hands on her hips. Rowena squinted, trying to determine if the face was as formidable as the hair. Instead of pushing back her dark mop, Marlys shook it forward so even more of it fell over her face. It was impossible for Rowena to determine her age.

When Marlys reached out a hand and captured a wheaten strand of Rowena's hair, Rowena had to resist the urge to jerk it back. The golden strand curled around a fingernail tipped with a crescent of dirt. Marlys stared at it for a moment, then drew it across the tip of Rowena's nose in a gentle caress. Rowena swallowed the urge to sneeze.

"Pretty," Marlys pronounced, her lip curling in a sneer.

Gareth rose to stand behind Rowena. "Hands off, little sister. She belongs to me. Not you." He did not touch Rowena. He did not have to.

"Where did you come by such a find?"

"I won her with a throw of the dice in a game of hazard."

Marlys lifted the one eyebrow visible beneath her hair. "Original. Tell me—does she always dress like a boy, or have you acquired some new tastes on your journey?"

"I don't have to answer that question. Especially not for you."

Marlys circled them both. "Does it talk, or only hit?"

Rowena was beginning to feel like a Christian caught between two lions. "I talk," she said, a shade too loud.

Marlys ignored her. "Does it have a name?"

A pride she'd long forgotten fell into the silence with Rowena's clipped words. "Its name is Lady Rowena Fordyce."

A current so deep and swift that Rowena might have imagined it passed between Marlys and Gareth. The tiny hairs at the nape of Rowena's neck stood erect.

Marlys snorted, granting her the courtesy of addressing her directly. "You look like no lady I've ever seen."

"She might say the same for you," Gareth added smoothly.

Marlys screwed up her face in a childish gesture of defiance. She stuffed two fingers in her mouth and whistled shrilly. A piebald mare trotted into view, as shaggy and heavy-footed as its mistress. Marlys settled herself on the horse's back with a tremendous clinking.

She tossed her head at the nag. "Did you win that, too, or was he a penalty forced on you for losing?"

Gareth mounted. "The jade was Blaine's twisted idea of a jest. We had to travel slowly to keep from killing the poor beast." His disparaging glance seemed to take in Rowena, as well.

"Pity you didn't." Marlys kicked her mare forward.

A kindred sympathy for the nag welled up in Rowena. She stroked the beast's nose before mounting to follow them into the deepening dark.

As they reached Caerleon, the rain began, pelting them like fists from the sky. Rowena had a dim impression of a sloping drawbridge, a shadowy courtyard, black and towering stone. Strong arms circled her waist. Gareth pulled her off the nag and bustled her through a yawning door.

She stood breathless and dripping inside a well of vast darkness. She gazed upward but could find no roof to mark an end to the barren blackness. Only when her breathing steadied with an odd catch in her throat did she realize the darkness was only darkness because of tiny pinpoints of light trailing down each wall. Tapers. Tapers in a hall that demanded torchlight for any vision at all. A chill touched her damp clothes as Gareth moved away.

A sharp clang and a hearty volley of curses marked Marlys's progress through the hall. "Dunnla!" she bellowed.

A splash of light wavered into the hall. At first Rowena thought the torch had walked out of the wall itself, but a harder glance showed her an old woman, bent double by a crooked back, entering the hall from a narrow corridor. The torch she carried nearly brushed the floor. That would have been disastrous, for in the wake of the light she cast, Rowena discovered the stones were covered not by floor rushes, but by opulent Oriental rugs, embroidered edge to edge in a never ending sea of luxury.

The woman bobbed out of the darkness with a toothless

smile and crooked a finger at Rowena. Rowena bent forward. The stale smell of boiled sage brushed her nostrils as the woman touched her lips to Rowena's ear.

"Welcome!" she roared.

Rowena leaped backward, striking her shin on some immovable object. Gareth had to bend double to kiss the old woman's papery cheek. She beamed up at him.

"Dunnla is mostly deaf," he explained. "She thinks we all are."

"Aren't we, though, after being screamed at since we were babes?"

Marlys's voice thundered back to them on the heels of an echo. There had to be a roof above them somewhere. Rowena was forced to stagger back as Dunnla swung around, nearly igniting Rowena's braies with a sweep of the torch.

Gareth caught the corner of Dunnla's shawl. He made a tiny leap himself to keep from being torched. Rowena started to giggle but stopped when Gareth pointed at her.

She cocked her head to the side, watching Gareth's hands dart through a dance of foreign motions. Dunnla bobbed up and down, sending shadows billowing over Gareth's face. From somewhere in the darkness, Rowena could hear the harsh sound of Marlys's breathing. With a final bob, Dunnla gave Gareth a shove. He cast Rowena an unreadable look before making his way through the invisible chaos of the hall without a single pause or bump.

Rowena was still staring after him when she felt a tug on the leg of her braies. Dunnla started toward the corridor with Rowena's leg in tow, oblivious to the fact that the rest of her was rooted to the floor.

"What does she want?" Rowena whispered. "What did he tell her?"

Marlys's voice boomed out of the darkness. "He told her to feed you well and bring you to his chambers."

Rowena felt herself drawn irresistibly toward the corridor. The worn homespun of her braies groaned a protest as Dunnla tugged harder. Marlys's voice came again with a deep ripple of laughter. "He also told her to ensure you had a bath."

Rowena lurched forward to keep from falling. The look she threw over her shoulder caught the gleam of white teeth bared in a hungry smile through a web of dark hair. Somewhere in her mind she heard once again the cry of the wolf in the forest.

CHAPTER 4

Even a tray of cold mutton so fresh the grease beaded on it like drops of nectar failed to cheer Rowena. The word Marlys had used for her set up echoes that grew louder each moment against Gareth's pointed lack of denial. The scene played itself over and over with a different outcome each time.

"Whore?" Gareth would answer in a booming bass. "Nonsense. I thought she might help us plant corn this spring" or "Silly girl! Does she look like my whore? I've won her to help Dunnla in the kitchen" or best of all, "Bite your tongue, sister. This fair child is a lady. How dare you insult her by branding her with false names?" These imagined replies were always followed by the dissipating of Marlys's bravado and a heartfelt apology with Gareth, preferably on bended knee, kissing her palm.

The image of her forceful captor on his knees at her feet brought her back to reality with a jolt. The word went spinning through her head in dizzying circles. She was still picking at the meat with her knife when Dunnla entered the kitchen, dragging a round wooden tub twice her size. Rowena watched glumly as heated water was poured into the splintery vessel. She prayed Gareth would not wander in for his supper. Dunnla stripped her and cheerfully tossed her clothes in the fire. A puff of black smoke and they were gone up the chimney like her life at Revelwood.

She sank into the steaming water up to her chin and her

hair floated to the surface in a tangled skein. The warm water loosened the lump in her throat. If Gareth had truly intended to use her for his pleasure this long year, why had he left her untouched last night? He had gone so far as to give her his dagger to protect herself. Had it been only her supposed dirtiness he feared? Now he wanted her clean. And in his chambers. Dunnla scrubbed her face with a melting ball of soap. The hot, greedy feel of Sir Blaine's lips on hers seared her memory. The word darted again in a vicious circle between her ears.

When Dunnla raised the bucket to rinse her hair and screeched, "More?," Rowena thought she said "whore" and burst into tears. The night blurred as Dunnla extracted her from the tub with a sympathetic cluck, dried her, and dropped a clean white bliaut over her head. The tunic was long and shapeless, with no waist to speak of. Its fine linen brushed like feathers against her skin.

Before she realized what was happening, she was standing barefoot outside a massive oak door banded with iron. Her damp hair fell in a heavy weight around her shoulders. Dunnla's sturdy figure waddled away around the corner. Rowena touched the door, then drew her hand back. She could run now, but where would she run to? The castle with its dark mazes held as many terrors as the encroaching forest.

A low voice shot out of the darkness, giving Rowena no less of a start than if Marlys had jumped on her fully armored out of the rafters. "Why do you hesitate? Are you afraid?"

She peered into the shadows. Marlys sat with her back against the wall, her knees drawn up in a casual sprawl.

An uncharacteristic streak of stubbornness prompted Rowena to reply, "Nay. I am not."

Marlys took a long swig out of a grubby wineskin, then drew the back of her hand across her mouth. "He gobbles up little country girls like you just to whet his appetite." Rowena smoothed the unfamiliar skirt, praying Marlys could

not see the trembling of her hands. Marlys corked the wineskin and laid it aside. "He has not touched you, has he?"

Rowena searched her memory. "He threw me up against
a tree because I sang a song that displeased him."

Marlys rose and swaggered toward her. Rowena found
herself pushed against the door before she could even gasp.
Marlys's hands dug into her shoulders. The hair that fell
over Marlys's brow brushed Rowena's nose. Bullying must
be a family trait.

"What was the song? Tell me the words," Marlys rasped.

With a shiver, Rowena repeated the words she could remember. The corner of Marlys's mouth tightened in a smile
that held no hint of humor.

She pushed her face closer to Rowena's. "Go to him.
Hide your fear well. He hasn't murdered any of his women—
not lately, anyway." She threw back her head in a burst of
wild laughter, reached past Rowena, and threw open the
door. Rowena was thrust backward into the chamber. The
door slammed in her face.

She stood with her forehead pressed to the hard wood,
afraid to move. Exhaling a deep breath, she turned. At first
glance, the chamber appeared empty. A cheerful fire crackled on the long hearth, easing the dampness of the rain
pounding against the shutters. Candles flickered in iron
sconces, dripping wax down the stone walls in melting cas-
cades. A bed frame sat against one wall, devoid of orna-
mentation but ostentatious in its fine mahogany canopy and
sheer size. Rowena tiptoed toward the bed.

Gareth lay on his back, one leg thrown outward in surrender to exhaustion. His dark lashes rested on his cheeks.
Rowena crept forward, biting her lower lip without realizing
it.

Sleep did nothing to diminish his size and strength. The
hand flung out beside his bearded cheek could have crushed
her as if she were no more than a gnat. His mouth was
closed as if even in sleep there were thoughts to guard and
secrets to keep. Dark hair furred the muscular expanse of

his chest, trailing into a single line that flowed toward his hips and the thin sheet draped there. His chest was unmarred by nicks or scars, though Rowena remembered the web of scars on his back. The men who had bested Sir Gareth of Caerleon had bested him from behind. He stirred. Rowena took an involuntary step backward, fearful the camlet sheet might fall away and reveal more of his slumbering form than she cared to see.

Her feet were cushioned in unearthly softness. Her gaze dropped to find herself standing on a pile of furs heaped beside the bed. Gareth must have kicked them away when the warmth of the fire reached the bed. He stirred again with a deep moan, then was still. Rowena looked at the bed, then back at the floor. Her thigh muscles ached from the long hours of clinging to the slippery nag. With a small sigh, she sank to her knees and curled up in the nest of furs.

Rowena had been asleep for a long time when Gareth rolled out of the bed. He sank his heavy frame into a carved chair in front of the hearth. He rested his chin in his hand and studied the girl slumbering at his feet. Hair that had grown limp from the dusty journey shimmered as thick and ripe as wheat around her face. The kiss of fire gave her skin a rosy flush. Her fist was curled against her parted lips like a child's.

Gareth stirred restlessly at the thought. Lindsey Fordyce's hair had once been as thick as this girl's, his eyes as blue. Only days after Gareth's father had brought home his vivacious new bride, Fordyce had followed, swearing his fealty and skimming like the golden-haired tail of the sultry-eyed comet who would sweep their lives clean, leaving desolation in her path. The years had not been kind to him. At Revelwood his hands had trembled as if palsied. Dissipation had spun its web into the bags of flesh beneath his eyes. 'Twas no wonder the man had eluded him all these years. Gareth had been searching for a powerful baron with a fortified stronghold in the north, not a strutting wastrel with a crumbling castle. Within Fordyce's pudgy frame, Gareth could not find even a hint of the dapper, jovial knight who had taught Gareth how to dice and bragged ceaselessly each time he journeyed to his castle in the north to tuck another babe in his wife's belly.

Of its own volition Gareth's gaze followed the smooth planes of Rowena's bliaut down to her flat stomach. What would she do if she awoke to find his lips pressed to hers? A faint smile curved his lips. Like Blaine, he would probably taste the bite of her fist against his jaw. That would not be a hindrance. It would not have been a hindrance for Blaine if he had not intervened. He could subdue her with one hand, leaving his other hand free to plunder the ill-gotten gain of his wager with Lindsey Fordyce, Baron of Revelwood.

He remained in the chair by the fire. There was nothing to do but wait to discover if he had baited his trap well enough to awaken some sleeping vestige of honor in Fordyce. Surely even the most indifferent of fathers would not sacrifice a rose like her into his vengeful hands. When the last flame died to a glowing ember, he still sat, watching Rowena sleep and wondering if he had made a terrible mistake.

CHAPTER 5

The familiar fingers of dawn coaxed Rowena from sleep. She snuggled deeper into the furs. Grinning hares bounced across the backs of her closed eyelids. She twitched, believing for a moment that she must strap on her knife and take to the moors to hunt. A shutter creaked. She opened her eyes. Hazy light filtered through the open window, a surrounding mist turning Gareth's dark hair to a halo of silver. Rowena sat up, clutching the furs to her chest, forgetting for a moment the modest garment she wore.

Gareth turned at the movement. To her relief, he wore loose fitting chausses, though his chest was still bare. "You may sleep longer if you like," he said. "You were not abed as early as I last night."

"You were resting well when I came to the chamber. I did not see fit to awaken you."

"How thoughtful." His even tone implied the opposite.

Rowena looked away to escape his mocking gaze. Tapestries ringed the walls, their rich burgundies and russets granting an illusion of coziness to the chamber. Directly above her head in a delicately painted mural, the bright, dark eyes of a serpent beguiled a naked and demure Eve.

A loud crunch made her jump. Gareth stood a hand's breadth from her, cradling a half-eaten apple in his palm.

"Fruit?" he asked cheerfully.

Never one to refuse food, Rowena took the apple and snapped a hearty bite out of it. As her eyes glided between

Gareth and the serpent, she handed the apple back. He smiled and took another hearty bite.

He held out his other hand to her. "Come."

Rowena paled. Had she escaped his attentions in the night only to earn them now? She touched her hair, praying that sleep had left her rumpled and dirty. If Gareth's sparkling eyes were any indication, she was not rumpled enough. She slipped her hand into his. Rowena held her breath as he brought it to his lips. He paused, studying the thin line of calluses marring her palm. His brow furrowed and Rowena thought she had somehow angered him. She knew he must be accustomed to the downy softness of a lady's hand. She would not need dirt or untidy hair to repulse him. She tried to draw back her hand, feeling unaccountably ashamed. He gently tucked it into the crook of his arm and led her to the window. She followed, intensely aware of the feelings that his touch had ignited, and the warmth now that seemed to overwhelm.

He leaned an elbow on the stone ledge. The apple core fell from his fingers to disappear into the mist below. "Welcome to Caerleon. The grandfather of my grandfather christened it after Uther Pendragon's Caerleon. He was a romantic soul. Quite touched in the head. He adored the Pendragon legend."

"Irwin told me stories of the Pendragon and his court. Your Caerleon must be as lovely as his."

The castle sprawled below was not fashioned of black obsidian as Rowena had fancied in the pouring rain, but of deep gray stone kissed with the wearing of rain and wind. Mist drenched the battlements. Outside the castle walls, the early morning sun slanted through the fog, burning it away in patches to reveal a forest so thick it glistened black instead of green. In the distance, cut off from its hill by a shimmering platter of mist, stood another castle with pennons flying a red and yellow welcome in the ethereal light.

"Ardendonne," Gareth said when he saw her lips part. "I expect to see Blaine's banner come flying over the hill at any moment. His curiosity is insatiable, especially when it involves a comely damsel who scorns his advances.''

His gaze strayed from her lips to her eyes. Rowena propped her hip on the ledge and began to braid her hair. The clean strands slipped through her fingers like corn silk.

"Allow me," Gareth said, plucking the coil from her hand. "I thought to provide you no maidservant."

Rowena hardly dared to breathe. His broad fingers intertwined the sections of hair with a deftness that implied an intimacy with womanly grooming she did not care to examine. Such lazy grace in a man of his size was jarring. Rowena stared at the top of his head. His hair was still tousled from sleep.

"Irwin said I was too lazy to tend to my own hair."

"But not too lazy to be up at dawn to hunt the game to stuff his plump face."

Rowena started to nod, then stopped, squirming under a pinprick of disloyalty. "Little Freddie helped me with my braids."

"Hmmm," he said noncommittally. "Would Little Freddie be the gray-eyed gallant who sought to bash me over the head with the cooking kettle?"

The memory brought a tightness to Rowena's jaw. "He would."

Gareth finished one braid and started on the other without a pause. "Tell me, Rowena—has your dearest betrothed ever touched you in an untoward manner?"

Rowena snatched her braid out of his hand. "Indeed not! I'd have cracked his skull if he had."

Gareth bared his white teeth in a smile. "Pray do not crack my skull for asking. You are of an age to marry. 'Twas an honest enough question." He pried the braid from her hand and began to gently undo the damage she had done.

Rowena sniffed, disowning her braid as if it belonged to someone else. " 'Twas an honest enough question coming from you. Perhaps my kin have the moral fortitude your friends lack."

"Trust me, my dear. Moral fortitude does not run rampant in your family."

"I suppose it does in yours? Along with dicing, leaping out of trees at people, and abduction." She glared at the forest, waiting for him to cuff her out the window for her insolence. She flinched as he dropped her braid. Fortified by indignation, she drew in a deep breath and announced, "I am experiencing some confusion as to my purpose at Caerleon."

Gareth finished the braid and let it swing against her throat. His teasing tone stripped her of anger. "We cannot stand for that, can we? I assume everyone had a purpose at Revelwood."

"Of course," she replied, as if the thought of anyone not having a purpose was ludicrous to her. "I hunt. Little Freddie cooks and weaves. Big Freddie and the boys tend the crops. And Papa . . ." She fell silent with a puzzled frown.

Gareth's smile was bitter. "Papa squanders away his only daughter to a lecherous nobleman."

"Which returns us to the subject of my purpose here." Her bright blue eyes studied his face. "Am I to be your whore, milord?"

Gareth cleared his throat. He was a man accustomed to wasting a thousand words to arrive at one lucid point in his banter with women. Rowena's forthrightness disarmed him.

He crossed to the leather gauntlets on the table and began to work a leather thong from its lacings.

She stumbled on, " 'Tis just that I know more of hunting than whoring. I fear I should be a great disappointment to you."

Gareth bit his tongue as he snapped the thong in two with his teeth. He returned to wrap the ends of Rowena's braids, all laziness banished from his precise motions.

"It might amaze you, my dear, to realize there is an abundance of purposeless ladies—and noblemen—in this world."

It was a feeble comfort and not the answer she deserved,

but it was all he could give her. Rowena lowered her eyes before he could read the doubt in them. His fingers tightened for an instant on a silky wisp of hair.

He was still holding her braid when the door crashed open and Marlys burst into the chamber. "I heard no grunts, moans, or screams so I assumed it was safe to enter." Gareth dropped the braid. Marlys took in the motion with a bitter smile. "How sweet! Is he dressing you? As his squire, I thought 'twas your duty to dress him. Or does he prefer you to undress him?"

"A good morn to you, Marlys." Gareth rose from the window.

Marlys was unarmored and unarmed except for a dirk crammed into her belt. Her black tunic and breeches hung in disheveled folds as if she had slept in them. From the awkward patching, Rowena realized the garments must have once belonged to Gareth. Cracked leather gauntlets covered her arms to the elbows, incongruous against the radiant sunlight breaking through the fog to stream over the windowsill. Her hair hung in ratty hanks over her face.

She prowled the chamber like a hungry bear. She picked up Gareth's dagger, feinted twice at the air, then threw it down. Her foot scattered the furs beside the bed. "A bed for your new puppy, brother? A warm pelt and some scraps from your table and I'll wager she is at your feet like a bitch in heat, just begging to lap your—"

"Marlys," Gareth warned.

Marlys stepped up to Rowena. The corner of a naughty grin peeped out from behind her hair. "May we pat its pretty little head?"

Before Marlys could move, Rowena's hand shot out and grasped her wrist. A glimmer of doubt touched Marlys's eye. Rowena pulled Marlys's hand down between them before loosing it.

Marlys massaged her wrist under the gauntlet with a wounded pout. "Beware, brother. Your puppy has fangs."

Gareth lifted one eyebrow. "I thought you well warned of that after she knocked you over the head last night."

"Mayhaps the blow dislodged my memory."

"Not overmuch, I hope. I have a task for you, and your memory will serve you well." He threw open a chest and drew a plain black tunic over his head. He scrounged deeper in the chest and came up wielding a tiny silver flute. "What are your interests, Rowena? Music? Embroidery? Dancing?"

Rowena looked puzzled. She knew of no interests except the gallant pursuit of food for their table. Gareth waved a scrap of linen embroidered with dancing pheasants beneath her nose.

"Pheasant stew," she said suddenly. "That holds my interest."

The scrap of fabric went limp. Gareth's eyebrows drew together in a forbidding line. He returned to the chest. "You mentioned Irwin telling you tales. Are you fond of the chansons, the romances?"

She raised her palms in a shrug. She adored tales of monsters and heroes but did not realize that was what he had asked her. Gareth gave an exasperated snort. "Are you fond of anything you cannot eat?"

Marlys muttered something under her breath, which earned her a searing glance from her brother. He pulled forth a creamy sheet of parchment, a cow horn, and a feathered quill. "You may put your impertinence to good use, sister. You will teach Rowena to write."

Marlys gagged. "I detest writing. And I detest catering to your doxies. If you must consort with uneducated villeins, could you not hire a priest to undertake their education? I would have thought she'd already know everything necessary for the tasks you have in mind. Some things do come naturally, you know. If she can lay on her back and spread her legs, then she ought to be able to—"

"The lady Rowena is not a peasant. She is the daughter of a baron," Gareth interrupted, watching Rowena turn from pale white to pink to a mild shade of purple. " 'Tis no fault of her own that her education has been neglected."

Marlys crossed her arms over her chest, and her square jaw protruded. "Command the village priest to come teach her. He has been idle too long."

"You know 'tis impossible." Gareth slipped behind her and put his mouth next to where an ear should be. His words were audible throughout the chamber. "I suggest you follow my wishes. The next time you ambush me, I might forget you are my beloved baby sister and regrettably skewer you."

Marlys's fingers flexed in her gauntlets. Gareth buckled on a silver belt. He started for the door, whistling a jaunty tune. "If you are entertaining notions of his goodness," Marlys snapped at Rowena, "then beware. He may kill you with kindness."

Gareth stopped for a moment, his broad shoulders filling the doorframe. Then he continued on, and Marlys's low laughter flooded the chamber.

Rowena sidled around Marlys, trying to peer beneath the lank locks for the deformity the young girl hid—a twisted lip or a glimpse of the milky white of a cataract marring an eye.

Marlys bent her head. Her hair fell like a curtain over her anger. "You'd best break your fast," she muttered, "before Dunnla throws your porridge to the hogs."

A memory of snarling dogs tearing at the remains of Ardendonne's feast sent Rowena for the door, Marlys's face forgotten. She hesitated.

Marlys anticipated her question. "Left, right, down, north, left and east. Take care not to get lost. We still haven't found the bones of the last chit who lost her way."

Rowena's eyes widened. She stepped out the door and turned to the right. Marlys's laughter rang after her.

Rowena wandered for an interminable time. The castle corridors tangled around themselves. She trotted along, out of breath, but refusing to sit down and rest lest they find her bones months from now, crouched in defeat in some deserted corridor. She found herself at the door of Gareth's chamber twice before stumbling onto the wide stone steps curling downward into the heart of the castle.

Last night's impression of vast space was not cured by the beams of sunlight pouring through the arrow slits. The great hall of Caerleon stood at the base of a square tower three times as large as all of Revelwood. The vaulted ceiling loomed high above. A faint breeze stirred a crested banner suspended from the oaken beams. Rowena understood for the first time why Gareth's surcoat had contained no coat of arms. His family crest consisted of a bleating sheep with his tongue stuck out. The vapid creature bore no resemblance to its wolfish master. One of Gareth's ancestors must have had a wicked sense of humor.

Swallows darted like shadows between the massive beams. Ardendonne's hall seemed a cottage dwelling compared to this, and Revelwood seemed only fit for swine and dogs. Sunlight drifted through the open door. Carved chairs and tables littered the floor with no apparent pattern in their arrangement.

Rowena picked her way along the wall, dodging table legs and chair backs. Her foot caught in the foreign fabric of an Oriental rug. By the time she reached the kitchen, Marlys was cheerfully polishing off the last of the porridge.

"Too late, love," she said at Rowena's crestfallen expression. "Dreadfully sorry." A smile gleamed between matted strands of hair.

Rowena slid onto a bench and folded her hands on the empty table. A wizened man close to seven feet tall ducked through the kitchen door with an armload of wood. Rowena scooted backward as he dumped the wood on the table in front of her.

"Gridmore," Marlys grunted. "Dunnla's husband. He is as blind as she is deaf. If I were you, I should move. He

thinks you are the fire. You've probably been stoked well
enough after a night with Gareth.''

Gridmore turned on Rowena, poker in hand. His cloudy
blue eyes narrowed to menacing slits. Rowena ducked and
slid down the bench. He jabbed at the air a few times before
the poker found the hearth.

Marlys lapped at the inside of her wooden bowl. ''My
mind reels at the vision of their antics in the marriage bed.
Mayhaps she folds him up and slips him in the cupboard
each night.''

Marlys jumped guiltily as Dunnla shuffled up behind her
and bellowed, ''Eating again, Lady Marlys. I see you've
finished yesterday's porridge. Sir Gareth ordered some fresh
made for the Lady Rowena.''

Dunnla clunked a bowl on the table in front of Rowena.
Marlys's visible eye glared at her. Rowena dipped a spoon
into the steaming goodness, not caring if she burned her
tongue. She swallowed the creamy mush and licked her lips,
refusing to bite back a grin. Marlys slammed her spoon on
the table, sending bits of barley flying.

Throughout the next few days, Rowena came to regret
every spoonful of that porridge. Marlys proved to have a
long memory.

Her writing lessons consisted of Marlys pacing beside the
table while Rowena struggled to form the letters of her name
on scraps of parchment. Marlys would pause only long
enough to tweak Rowena's ear or poke her with the tip of
the quill when she thought Rowena stupid. Rowena fancied
herself terribly stupid. Her arms remained dotted with ink
and her ears bright red all the day long. Trying to peep
beneath Marlys's hair earned her an especially vicious jab.
Rowena always jumped when Marlys jerked out her dagger
to scrape another blunder from the page. Suppose the churl-
ish creature confused quill and blade and stabbed her?

One afternoon after Rowena had spelled her own name
Wenrona for the third time, Marlys boxed her ears and drove

all the parchments into the floor with a sweep of a gaunt-leted hand. "I'm weary of teaching a lackwit to write. The time has come for you to learn something useful."

Afraid to even speculate on what Marlys might consider useful, Rowena tripped after her charging path down the stairs and into the beckoning sunlight of the list. Marlys's hunched shoulders disappeared in a crude wooden chest set against the bailey wall. She rummaged through the chest, humming a melody of grunted curses. Rowena ducked as a rusty helm went sailing past her head. She picked it up, running her fingers over the crusted visor.

Marlys reappeared, wielding two long poles, their ends blunted by a conflict long forgotten. "These would never do for a proper joust, but they'll do for you. We'd best abandon the list for the forest. If Gareth finds me tilting instead of teaching, there will be a beating in it for both of us." She leered at Rowena through a matted cloud of hair.

"I've yet to see him lift a finger to you."

Marlys hooked a finger in the neck of Rowena's kirtle and shoved her face at her. "I suppose you think 'twould benefit me if he did?"

Rowena cleared her throat awkwardly. " 'Tis late in your life for Gareth to chasten you. Mayhaps your papa should have done it when you were but a babe."

"My father never had the time to beat me. He was too busy fawning over his precious son." Marlys slung her toward the barbican. "Onward, insolent puppy. We shall rout the Saladin's armies and spill the heathens' blood before this day is done."

Caught in the spirit of Marlys's playacting, Rowena marched forward, giving the sharpened wooden sticks implanted around the castle a wide berth.

The rain that had ushered Rowena to Caerleon marked the dying breath of summer. The nip of autumn sweetened the air. Leaves were beginning to crisp at the edges in flagrant hues of orange and yellow. Marlys led them to a fern-filled glade rich with the scent of damp earth and summer's decay.

Rowena gathered her kirtle between her legs and tied it around her waist. Marlys slammed the ancient helm over Rowena's head. She was lost in the salty tang of metal and old sweat. Before she could reach for the visor, a mighty buffet set her head to spinning with the hellish echo of bells. She sat down abruptly.

Her shaking hands jerked the helmet off. Marlys stood a few feet away, the lance turned across her body like a shield.

Her laugh was the low ripple of a deep flowing stream. "Did I truly look so stupid when you bested me from behind?"

Rowena rubbed her ears, glaring at Marlys with narrowed eyes. "Infinitely stupider."

With a snort of laughter, Marlys pulled on her own helm. The lance in her hands came shooting at Rowena. Rowena caught it in one fist. She banged the helm on the ground, loosening the visor before she donned it. She barely had time to raise the lance as a shield before Marlys charged her, knocking her flat. She rolled to a crouch and Marlys roared past again. The side of her lance caught the side of Marlys's, deflecting the blow. Marlys was on her again before she could drag in a heated breath.

The afternoon wore on with Rowena doing little more than dodging and falling. Triumph sang through her blood each time her lance slowed Marlys's charge for the barest instant. At Marlys's command, she jerked down the visor and peered through the narrow slits at a world divided into the dappled shadows of the forest and the dark figure of Marlys hurtling toward her. She was staggering to her feet once again, every muscle aching, when she saw Marlys freeze. The tilt of her head locked on the forest behind Rowena.

Marlys jerked off her helm. "Good day, brother dear. We thought you'd gone pillaging the peasants."

Rowena spun around and curtsied to the nearest tree.

Gareth's voice came from somewhere to the left. "I was forced to subdue my love of rapine and mayhem when I heard the clash of two mighty dragons in the forest. You've been up to mischief. I don't suppose 'tis Dunnla you've got under there?"

Gareth plucked off Rowena's helm, and her golden hair spilled around her face. Rowena bobbed another curtsy. "Good day, Sir Gareth. I pray we have not displeased you."

"God forbid," Marlys muttered.

Gareth tucked a strand of Rowena's hair behind her ear. His eyes sparkled beneath his dark brows. "Are you harmed?"

Rowena shook her head.

"Then you have not displeased me."

Marlys groaned into her helm.

Gareth's fingertips slid beneath the sleeve of Rowena's kirtle to probe a purpling bruise. A frown darkened his brow. He pointed a finger at Marlys. "You, on the other hand, have displeased me greatly."

Marlys sank into a mock swoon. "Pray do forgive me, milord. I tremble at the mere thought of your displeasure."

Rowena's giggle deepened into a cough as Gareth turned his frown on her. "You both ought to be sent to bed without supper for your dangerous play."

Rowena's face fell.

Marlys swaggered up to Gareth. "Don't you think I'm a bit old to be sent to bed without my broth? If you send Rowena to bed, she will have you to nibble on." She patted his beard with her cracked nails. "Why do you flush, brother dear? Do you resent your honeyed scabbard learning to pierce you back?"

Gareth caught her wrist in his hand. His expression did not change, but Rowena saw Marlys's arm go white. Her fingers curled into claws, then went limp. He dropped her hand.

"Damn you to hell, Gareth." Marlys's low mutter sent a shiver down Rowena's spine. "The devil take both of you."

She scooped up her lance with a vicious jab at the air and loped into the forest.

Rowena shook her head. "I fear your sister bears no fondness for me."

Gareth snorted. "Marlys has never been fond of anyone but me." At Rowena's quizzical look, he added, "Is her tender regard for me not obvious?"

They both laughed. Tension seeped from Rowena's spine.

Gareth's laughter faded to a rueful smile. "Marlys loves and hates me with equal passion. On the sixth anniversary of her birth, she cut off all her hair so as to look more like me. My father took no notice. He only patted her on the head and ordered her a new kirtle. She cut it into a kite and flew it from the highest tower." He shook away the memory. "Come. I shall walk you back to Caerleon. With that helm under your arm, you might be mistaken for a robber baron and carried to the lord of the castle for justice."

Rowena started down the path, unable to hide the half-skip the autumn day put in her step. "And is the lord of the castle a merciful man?"

"On the contrary!" Gareth exclaimed. "I hear he is a dreadful wolf of a man who would as soon roast a robber baron as hang him."

"And if that robber were a baroness?"

Gareth's voice lowered to a husky growl. "Why he'd gobble her up in a single bite!"

"Why 'tis just what Marlys said—" She spun around to witness the guilty slide of Gareth's gaze from her legs to her face. She had forgotten the immodest slant of the kirtle tied between her thighs.

Her cheeks burned as her fingers stabbed at the knotted skirt in what she hoped was a subtle effort to free it.

"Be still." Gareth's hand closed over hers. She stumbled to a halt. He knelt on one knee before her, his deft fingers tugging at the knot. "We shall have you garbed as a proper lady in no time."

If his open smile was an attempt to calm her, its effect

was the opposite. Her muscles contracted as his knuckles brushed her stomach, heightening the flames in her cheeks. She stared at the top of his head, counting two gray hairs amidst the shaggy black.

"How many years are you?" she asked softly.

"How many years do you think I am?" He leaned back, resting an elbow on his knee.

"I do believe you are older than Big Freddie."

Gareth's grin deepened the tiny crinkles around his eyes. "How old is Big Freddie?"

Rowena's blush disappeared in a frown of concentration. Gareth crouched patiently at her feet as she counted on her fingers. Finally she said, "Older than all of us. So how many years does that make you?"

With one finger, Gareth dislodged the knot. The skirts of the kirtle came tumbling around his hands. "Too old, I fear. Thirty-three."

Rowena flitted forward on the path. Gareth cupped his chin in his hand, watching her. Sunlight burst through the uneven branches of an ancient oak, gilding her hair into waves of coarse gold. She skipped from one side of the path to the other. Her hands darted out to caress the rough bark of a walnut tree. She crumpled a thinly veined leaf between her fingers, then spun around, smoothing her skirt in a fit of demureness.

Her question came to him on the wings of a cooling wind. "Thirty-three years, Sir Gareth. Is that dreadfully old?"

He dropped his eyes before she could read the expression within them. "Sometimes, Rowena, it feels it."

She waited for him to rise, then danced on, her exuberant flight defying the deepening shadows as determinedly as the last fall of sunlight warmed the top of Gareth's head.

In the days following the jousting lesson, neither Marlys nor Gareth sought her company. Rowena threw herself into a life of leisure. Despite boundless enthusiasm, she did not excel at it. She would start out for a gentle meander in the forest and return mud-stained but grinning. Dunnla looked the other way as she thumped a skinned hare on the hearth with a sheepish grin. Gareth lifted an eyebrow at the freshness of the meat on days he did not hunt and murmured something about the "prevalence of poachers in his woods." Dunnla only smiled and nodded, feigning blindness as well as deafness, while the serving girls exchanged knowing giggles. Rowena took to tagging after Gridmore, who was too blind or too polite to chasten her.

She knew little of noble life. Papa had squandered away her mama's fortune long before she was born. But she could sense the unnatural isolation of Caerleon. There should have been knights and squires and pages and servants enough to meet all of Gareth's needs. Instead, he dressed himself, armored himself, and made do with a score of servants in a castle that should have had a hundred.

As her loneliness deepened, her thoughts turned again and again to Revelwood. She sat by the fire in the solar one night, hugging her knees and thinking how Little Freddie would have enjoyed the steaming blancmange Dunnla had served for supper. A fraction of the rice and milk Gareth had left unfinished on his manchet would have filled the boy's stomach for a week. Angry tears stung her eyes. She was nothing at Caerleon but another mouth to feed. As little attention as any of its inhabitants paid her, she might run away and not be missed for days.

She lifted her chin, forgetting to dim the dangerous glitter of her eyes. Sir Gareth stood in the doorway, his long frame propped casually against the timbers. His eyes assessed her coolly. Rowena had the maddening sensation that he could read her mind. He had just returned from his fields. His immaculate surcoat was thrown carelessly over one shoulder. He was stripped down to tunic and chausses, dusted with chaff and dripping sweat like a peasant. The happy glow of exhaustion bathed him. His eyes sparkled in the firelight. Rowena inclined her head, struggling to reconcile the vision of the knight who had threatened to slay her family with the laughing man who had tossed honeyed raisins in the air for her to catch on her tongue. She supposed to him she was only a pet, and according to Marlys, not a very clever one.

She wanted to shake him, demand answers to questions she'd never dared to ask, claw away the mask that hid the man.

But the answers might be worse than the questions, and the man more dangerous than the mask. She rose and brushed past him without a word, answering his murmured good night with a stilted nod. She had promised Papa she would stay for a year, and stay she would. Gareth's dark eyes bored into her back as she climbed the winding stairs.

As fall waned, daylight grew shorter, each hour bringing Rowena nearer to nightfall when she would curl into the bed of furs at the foot of Gareth's bed. She knew now the furs had not been careless cast-offs from Gareth's bed, but had been artfully arranged for her comfort from the first night. She waited for a suggestion for her to move into Marlys's chamber or sleep huddled in the great hall. It did not come. The pattern of the first night was never repeated. She was always snug and dreaming before Gareth came to bed. Some nights he did not come at all. Once an entire week went by without his presence at Caerleon or in his bedchamber.

Rowena started awake one night, her heart heavy with nameless longing. She rubbed her cheek against the soft fur but did not find the comfort she sought.

She tossed back the furs and padded to the window. The shutter creaked open at the touch of her fingertips, and pallid moonlight streamed into the chamber. A cool breeze poured over her. She shivered, knowing the wind blowing cool at Caerleon would soon blow cruel at Revelwood. The silver glaze of the moon burnished the cobblestones to the color of Little Freddie's hair. She lay her cheek against the shutter with a sigh.

Gareth's voice came out of the dark, as warm and intimate as a touch. "Are you saddened, Rowena?"

Rowena lifted her head. "I knew not that you were here, milord."

"Why do you sigh? You are well fed and warm and no longer have to toil from dawn to dusk."

"But I have no Irwin to tell me tales and no Little Freddie to comb my hair." The words came out more bitter than she intended. Gareth would think her an ungrateful wretch. Tonight she did not care.

Gareth rose from the bed, slipping his chausses over his naked form. Rowena turned her face to the night outside the window. He reached for the comb on the table, then paused. His callused fingers crept upward. He stared at his scarred nails. They seemed suddenly broad and common, unworthy of touching the silky mass at his fingertips. He buried his fingers in the coarse softness of her hair, drawing them downward in a gentle motion.

"You've grown wan and pale in the past weeks. Do you pine for your betrothed?" His teasing tone masked the huskiness in his voice. He reached around and touched what he knew to be a cheek newly flushed with good health. Wetness bathed the back of his fingers.

He froze. Before he could command any semblance of restraint, his arms slipped around Rowena's waist and pulled her against him.

Rowena stood barely breathing in his embrace. The cool wind flooding the chamber fled before the warmth of his hips pressed to her back. His head bent to hers. His lips touched her throat.

"You don't have to be lonely, Rowena," he whispered.

Rowena melted against him, letting his warmth envelop her in a cocoon of safety. His lips brushed her ear. She shuddered, his invitation a more compelling temptation than if he had made the choice for her.

See how he charms.

The words came from nowhere, an ugly whisper fraught

with accusation. Rowena stared down at the arms circling her waist. The dark hair that furred them stood out stark and foreign against the whiteness of her bliaut.

A bitter knot tightened in her chest. She stiffened. She was no Lady Alise to warm a nobleman's bed for a night.

Her voice was an octave lower than normal. "And what price your company, milord?"

Gareth's arms dropped. He took a step backward and the wind blew very cold indeed.

Rowena bowed her head. "Could you not send me home?"

"I could. But I won't."

Rowena spun around. "Then send word to my papa that I am well. Not starved or"—she briefly dropped her gaze —"sorely abused. You have it within your power to ease my family's torment. You are a man of power. Surely you could grant me such a small boon."

Gareth turned away from her, able to face anything but her pleas. 'Twould be far easier to deny her if she stamped her foot with petulant demand like the pampered bratling he had hoped to find. Little did she know his whole life these long weeks had been consumed with sending word to her father. Through malicious gossip spread among the villeins, an offhand remark to a neighboring lord, a casual leer in the village. Word of Rowena's captivity and brutality at his hands was spreading like wildfire through all of England. He was likely to bring down the wrath of King Edward himself before Lindsey Fordyce mustered enough courage to confront him. A part of him blanched before the stories he had spread, but another part of him recognized them for what they were—the product of his own dark fantasies.

Rowena touched his bare arm. "I beg you, milord . . ."

He recoiled as if she had wounded him. His fist came down on the table, shattering the shell comb. "Nay! If your father wants word of you, then let him come to me."

Words of anger died in Rowena's throat when she saw the

fire that smoldered in Gareth's dark eyes, not yet banked. She could not hold his gaze, and her lashes swept down to veil her eyes. The door slammed with a mighty crash, and she was alone.

Gareth's shin slammed into an immovable wooden object. He bit off a curse that reverberated from the rafters.

"My, my," came Marlys's voice, low and taunting in the darkness. "Such curses in the presence of a lady."

Gareth's eyes adjusted to the dim light of a dying fire. Marlys had draped her stomach across a wooden lounge next to the door. Her feet swayed in a childish rhythm.

"Show me a lady, and I will beg forgiveness," he snarled, jerking on his gauntlets as he walked.

Since the door was the obvious goal of his ragged path, Marlys jumped up and sat down, pressing her shoulders to it. "Does your whore displease you so?"

Gareth halted before her. His brows drew together in a glare that would have sent most men cowering in fear. "Stand aside."

Marlys studied her ragged fingernails. "I think she does not displease you at all. But she does not please you, either."

Gareth caught Marlys's tunic in his hand. He lifted her until her nose touched his. "You may not know as much as you think you do, little sister." He dropped her as if she were a sack of apples and flung open the door.

"I know if that sweet morsel in your chamber was warming your bed, you would not be storming out of Caerleon at midnight."

Gareth stopped.

Marlys's tone lost its mocking edge, leaving it flat in the echoes of the hall. "Why, Gareth? She is only a pawn in your game. Surely her papa has had word of the golden-haired angel imprisoned in your bedchamber. Even the peasants whisper of it. Is that not what you wanted? Why not finish it and send her home?"

Gareth turned on his heel, his eyes darker than the midnight sky. "If I send her home raped and with child, what have I gained?"

"Revenge."

"Revenge on whom? Her? Me? Nay, Marlys. I want the truth more than I want revenge. And I am willing to wait for it."

Marlys reached for his hand but he was gone, his shoulders hunched against the bitter wind.

Rosy dawn slipped through the shutters. Rowena flung herself over and tossed away the furs. She lay still for a moment, feeling hot and vexed, then jerked the furs back until only her nose protruded. She rolled to her side with a disgusted grunt and glared at the dust balls under Gareth's bed. She threw herself over again, jerking her eyes closed as the door to the chamber glided open.

Gareth's steps were heavy and stumbling. Rowena heard the solid thwack of a foot striking wood, followed by a slurred curse. Silence followed. She did not dare open her eyes. The smell of him wafted down to her—sweat and ale and the ridiculous scent of lilacs overlayed by an earthy tang she did not recognize. His footsteps moved away.

He fell to the bed without bothering to disrobe. Only when his even breathing filled the chamber did Rowena open her burning eyes. She dressed in silence and slipped out of the chamber.

Marlys was leaning against the post at the bottom of the stairs. She lifted her head. Dark eyes gleamed from somewhere beneath her mop of hair. Without a word, she scooped up the helm and lance and tossed them to Rowena. Rowena caught them. They started into the chill dawn, pausing in the list to divide the steaming barley bread Marlys had stuffed in her pockets.

CHAPTER 6

Marlys charged through the open door of Gareth's chamber.
Her roar nearly sent Rowena tumbling out of her chair.

"He comes! He comes at last! I saw his flags from the
north tower. May I ambush him? Please, say I can. Gareth,
I beg you. Do let me give his pride a damnable whack!"

To demonstrate the whack she would give, Marlys
slammed her mace on the table. The parchment Rowena
had been studying split and rolled into two halves. Rowena
reached for the torn parchment, only to have the precious
paper flutter into the air and out the window on the chill
draft Gareth invited when he pushed open the shutters.

Gareth swore under his breath.

Marlys joined him at the window. "By God, there he
comes! Do let me ambush him. I know just the tree."

"He left us in peace longer than I thought he would,"
Gareth said. "The torture of his curiosity must have bested
him."

Rowena stood on tiptoe behind them but could see nothing but the broad expanse of their shoulders. She elbowed
her way under Marlys's arm only to have her cheek smashed
against the shutter when Marlys turned.

"Why, look at his retinue! He must have brought half of
England with him."

Gareth sighed. "The scoundrel is determined to see us
civilized. He has never forgiven me for dismissing Father's

knights. He makes no secret of his contempt for our country life.''

Rowena dropped to her knees. Gareth glanced down at her with a lift of one eyebrow as she wiggled between his legs and knelt at his feet. She absently leaned her cheek against his hand, all of her attention captured by the spectacle rolling over the hills toward Caerleon.

The festive party flowed away from Ardendonne, dotting the landscape with splashes of purple and crimson against the gray earth. Chariots and hand-carried litters mocked the barren land with their gaiety. Prancing horses followed, decked in hangings of yellow and emerald satin tasseled in gold. Rowena breathed a sigh of awe, hearing in her mind the steady flapping of the pennons affixed to the litters, the snort of the magnificent steeds blowing clouds of fog into the chill air, the heady laughter of the ladies being coiffed in the litters.

"One good thump," Marlys pleaded. " 'Tis all I want to give him.''

"Nay," Gareth replied.

"I shall free him after one whimper. I swear it.''

"Nay," Gareth repeated.

Marlys's lip protruded through a tangle of hair.

Gareth wagged a finger at her. "I forbid it. Blaine hasn't the fondness for you that I have. He would welcome any excuse to poke his lance through your black little heart.''

Marlys sniffed. "Blaine has been striving to poke his lance in me in one fashion or another ever since I disdained his suit.''

"He might have forgiven you for disdaining his suit. 'Twas knocking him off his horse in front of his father that gained his disfavor. Sir Bryan had finally knighted him. He was a proud lad.''

"A foolish lad to lay his lips on me.''

Rowena shivered in excitement. Gareth glanced down at the golden head resting on his hand. Her eyes were misty, her lips parted in dreamy perusal of the color-splashed meadows. Gareth's hand tightened on the windowsill as he wondered what effect it would have on him if she ever looked at him that way. Rowena felt the almost imperceptible movement. The wiry coil of hairs on the back of his hand pricked her smooth cheek. She shifted, suddenly conscious of the gentle pressure of his thighs against her shoulders. She lifted her gaze past the neat folds of his hose, past the silver threads embroidered in the hem of his tunic, to meet his dark eyes. In the guise of a casual gesture, his fingertips stroked her cheek. A shiver that had nothing to do with Blaine's retinue lifted the tiny hairs on the back of her neck. Confusion flooded her in a wave of heat.

Marlys smirked as she watched the exchange. Gareth stiffened and gave Rowena's cheek a fatherly pat. "I'm off to the village for more servants. If we are to sup tonight, we will sup in style or not at all. If I know Blaine, he hopes to be trapped by the winter snows and forced to spend the winter feasting on our beef and ale."

"And our maidservants," Marlys added as Gareth left them. Her speculative gaze dropped to Rowena's head.

Moments later, Rowena cupped her chin in her hands, the resplendence of Blaine's procession forgotten as Gareth mounted Folio in the list below. Folio pranced as Gareth gave their window a jaunty salute. Rowena lifted her hand. Gareth squared his shoulders and sent the horse cantering through the castle gate and into the forest.

"You don't hate him nearly as much as you'd like to, do you?"

At Marlys's gentle question, Rowena swung around. Marlys swiped a strand of hair out of her mouth. A smile of terrifying sweetness appeared. She extended a grimy palm to Rowena.

"Come, Lady Precious. If I am to be denied my ambush, I've time to find you some garments for the feast. If you go down wearing that silly rag, you'll quite fade in the presence of so many ladies and duchesses. 'Twould not be your desire, would it?"

Rowena reluctantly took the hand Marlys proffered, half preferring a cuffing to this unexpected kindness.

The door creaked open on iron hinges. Rowena clutched Marlys's hand and peered around the taller girl's shoulder. Marlys moved forward into the shadows of the chamber, her normally exuberant footsteps muffled to silence.

The chamber was not in total darkness. The afternoon sun touched the sheets of velvet spiked over the windows, casting a pall of blue gloom over the shrouded furniture. A delicate mingling of rosemary and mildew wafted to Rowena's nose, making it itch. Marlys's hand slipped from hers. Rowena pinched back a sneeze.

"Everything's the same," Marlys whispered.

Cobwebs draped the candle sconces in elaborate falls of gray and white. A canopied bed frame larger than Gareth's sat in the center of the chamber. A single sheet of linen covered it. Rowena half-expected the shapeless mound beneath to rise and float toward them.

Marlys shook her head as if to clear it and crossed to an oaken cupboard in the corner. "I daresay we'll find a kirtle for you here."

Her matter-of-fact words spoken in the undisturbed quiet were both comforting and irreverent. Rowena started as the door of the cupboard crashed into the wall. While Marlys dug through the cupboard, Rowena sidled toward the bed. She reached out a tentative finger and poked at the lump in its center. The straw tick erupted in a frenzy of squeaking and skittering, and she snatched her hand back.

"Mice," Marlys pronounced without turning around. "There would be, you know. The cats don't come here. Keep an eye out for rats."

Rowena peered around nervously. The sheer size of this chamber unnerved her. She sat down on the corner of the bed frame. Her toe glided over the dark stain spilling over the stone floor beside the bed.

From beneath the bed came the faint skitter of claws on

stone. Rowena jerked her feet up. Marlys paid her no heed; she had crawled into the cupboard. Only the soles of her boots were visible. Her voice was muffled. "Used to hide in here when I was little. Goes clear through the wall. Big enough for a family of ten."

Rowena leaned over the side of the bed and gingerly lifted the sheet. In the eerie light, she could barely make out the faint outlines of a cradle. She ran her hand along the beautifully carved surface. Her finger came back furred with dust.

She dropped the sheet guiltily as Marlys rose from the chest with a hiss of satisfaction, unfurling a mound of peacock blue trimmed in ermine. In the eerie blue light, the crushed velvet seemed to hover above the floor with a life of its own.

Marlys lifted one trailing belled sleeve of the matching undertunic. "What do you think? Perfect for you, is it not? Blue to match your eyes."

The rich blue was not near to the color of Rowena's eyes, but she did not say so. " 'Tis a lovely kirtle. But I dare not wear another's garments without their leave."

Marlys snorted. "The lady who would mind is long gone. My stepmother has been dead for nigh on twenty years. You have my leave. 'Tis all you need."

She piled the dress in Rowena's arms, then dove back into the cupboard to pull out a wimple and girdle. Marlys muttered to herself, "Stand up straight, Marlys. Comb your hair, Marlys. Don't slouch like an ape, Marlys. Silly bitch thought she'd make a lady of me."

"Silly, indeed," Rowena said softly. A veil came sailing over to land on her head. Rowena swept the gauzy softness from her eyes. "Was she pretty?"

Marlys threw back her head in a bay of assent. "God, she was beautiful! With raven black curls that tumbled to her waist and flashing blue eyes."

Rowena touched the cradle with her toe. "Did she and your papa have a babe?"

"She brought her bratling with her when she came. Never had time for it though. Kept it swaddled all the time. I used to hide in the cupboard and sneak out to untie the fat little thing when she left it unattended. Used to drive her batty. She never could figure out how the creature wiggled its way out. She was blessed with beauty but no brains." Marlys slapped a comb in her hands. "Much like yourself."

Marlys crossed the chamber, her strides quick and sure. She swept back the linen covering a table, carelessly knocking a pine box to the floor. Rowena bent to retrieve it. Her finger traced the sloping wing of a bird carved into the pale wood, and she started to open it.

Marlys snatched the box from her hand. "Gareth spent days carving this for her when Father sent word he was bringing home a new mother for us."

"How did she die?"

Marlys lifted her gaze from the box. Her lips quirked in a strange smile. "She had a bad heart."

Rowena flinched as Marlys flung the box behind her. "Don't stand there gaping at me, Ro. We've work to do."

Rowena gave a secret smile, thinking how pleasant it was to be called Ro instead of Puppy and wondering what Marlys hoped to gain with her kindness.

Sir Blaine of Ardendonne conquered Caerleon without the fall of a single sword. By nightfall, the castle was ablaze with light and laughter. Music rang from the rafters. The swallows darted into the night, seeking any surcease from the raucous merriment. Burly villeins with sleeves pushed up over hairy forearms dragged the furniture along the wall to make room for dancing. Dunnla shuffled in and out from the kitchens, bellowing commands that sent more than one lady into a genteel faint. Gridmore followed her commands by putting plates of cold partridge on the hearth and loads of firewood in ladies' laps. Blaine supervised the chaos with hands on hips and a proprietary smile. He single-handedly rescued a squealing midget from the oven where Gridmore had tossed him after mistaking him for the roast boar.

In a deserted chamber at the top of the keep, Rowena heard the faint piping of bells and a heated squealing as if a herd of pigs had laid siege to the feast below. She stared into a mirror of hammered silver. A stranger blinked back at her. Her chest rose and fell in shallow rhythm. She touched her cheek with two fingers. Her skin was as cold and foreign as the polished surface of the mirror.

Two brilliant slashes of crimson stained her cheeks, matching the lavish red of her lips. A thick line of kohl rimmed her eyes. With each blink, her eyelids clung, and she feared they would be stuck forever closed. Darkened with ashes and stiffened with oil, her lashes swept upward like rebellious spiders to meet the darkened arch of her brow. A golden crespine net confined her hair. A blue wimple flowed from it, hiding her sturdy neck in folds of plush velvet.

Count to one hundred. Then come down and join the feast.

Rowena began counting aloud as Marlys's words returned to her. She got as far as eight before forgetting the next number Marlys had taught her and being forced to start again. Her hands fumbled nervously with the exotic jars of ashes and berries spilling from the teak box to the table. "Fourteen," she mumbled. "Sixteen, forty-four, sixty-eight, twelve, one hundred."

She leaped out of the chair, tripping over the sleeves of the undertunic. By holding her arms at stiff angles in front of her, she maneuvered the door open. The golden girdle resting on her hips caught on the iron handle as she tried to slip through. She tugged herself free with a curse learned from Gareth and perfected by Marlys. If things proceeded in this alarming manner, Gareth would not fail to notice her. She would be the only lady in the hall laying flat on her face.

A sweet tenor drifted to Rowena's ears. A nasal bray of

laughter followed. Her steps slowed as she entered the open gallery leading to the stairs. Entranced by the flood of colors and lights sweeping through the hall below, she sank to her knees, clutching the balusters in her sweaty palms.

The candles had been replaced by a blaze of torches. A fire roared along the length of the wide fireplace, banishing the drafts to the deserted corners. A line of ladies clasped hands and wound among the men, leading their perfumed sleeves and wimples in a seductive dance of shimmering silk. Gareth was nowhere in sight.

A handful of dice clattered on the stones in the center of a kneeling circle of squires. Their hearty shouts rose above the din. Rowena was not surprised to find Marlys among them, her only concession to the celebration a shiny black pair of gauntlets newly pilfered from Gareth's chamber. Her rusty scabbard clanked on the hearth as she swaggered to the other side of the group.

Her dark eyes lifted to the gallery. Rowena ducked behind a wooden column.

"You do seem to turn up in the most remarkable places."

Rowena looked up as the smooth voice poured over her.

Sir Blaine leaned against the opposite wall, arms crossed. The corner of his mouth lifted in a smile. "Sleeping in my hall. Crouching behind pillars. You are a lady of mysterious pursuits. I've been asking Gareth where you were all evening. He simply replied, 'About' in the most infuriating manner. His habit of babbling all the time is one of his more endearing traits." He extended his hand to Rowena.

She took it, her eyes narrowed. He gently pulled her to her feet. "Ah, you have not forgotten me, either." This with a sheepish grin that must have gotten him far with his nurses. "I swear to you I have no intention of ravishing you here in the gallery. I mistook you for a different sort of lady at Ardendonne. There now. Do stop yelling at me. I can see you've acquired Gareth's loquaciousness in your stay at Caerleon."

Rowena opened her mouth and closed it. She had not said one word.

"That will be quite enough," he went on. "I will not tolerate that sort of talk from such a charming damsel. You should be ashamed."

Rowena found her tongue. " 'Tis you, sir, who should be ashamed. Regardless of the sort of lady you mistook me for, you had no right to force your attentions on me. Knights are supposed to stand for something kind and good. Would you not give even a lady of low birth a choice? Have you no respect for chivalry?"

Blaine applauded. "How your eyes sparkle when you chasten! More, more! Don't stop now."

"I should think—" Rowena paused, realizing she had been baited into berating him. Her glower collapsed into a reluctant smile at the mischievous sparkle in his brown eyes.

"You see, my fair lady, I was not only besotted with your beauty on that night, I was besotted with ale. I awoke the next morn with pounding head, aching chin, and cringing with mortification at my ill-mannered treatment of you. I humbly beg for the boon of your forgiveness."

Before she could answer, he had taken her arm and led her to the rail of the gallery.

Directly below them, the minstrel Mortimer bent over his lute, his mop of blond hair hiding his face. A lady clad in scarlet from wimple to slippers plopped down on his lap. He pushed her away with a sour note from his strings. A laughing squire took her place, and Mortimer's music took wing. The hall rocked with laughter.

"Gareth has always told me Caerleon was my home as well as his," Blaine said.

"You take his words to heart, do you not?"

"Not as I take yours to heart. What does the merriment put you in mind of, dear lady?"

Rowena rested her chin in her hand to relieve the weight of the wimple from her aching neck. "An undignified siege."

"A charming thought! A siege not of blood and battle, but of music and laughter, wit and pleasure. Does it not make your blood sing?"

Rowena shrugged, ignoring the husky note which edged his voice. He rested his elbows on the rail, leaning nearer as if they had been friends for years.

"What would you do if it were a real siege disguised beneath the cloak of hospitality? Mayhaps I've only hastened abovestairs to carry away the lady of the castle while the master is distracted."

"Marlys is the lady of Caerleon."

Blaine's smile tightened. "Marlys is no lady."

Rowena edged away from him. Her gaze darted over the hall. "Where might the master be?"

"Probably in the bailey discussing some of the duller aspects of knighthood like tournaments and horses."

"Those are not the aspects you prefer?"

"I prefer ladies to mares, if that is your meaning."

"Ladies who throw themselves at your feet, no doubt, to beg for your attentions."

"I prefer ladies who throw themselves at my chin. And quite effectively, I might add." He rubbed his smooth chin as if the memory still stung.

Rowena bit back a smile. His winsome grin was hard to resist. "I shan't beg forgiveness if that is what you await."

"I would wait an eternity for one plea from you."

He would have to wait, for at that moment Gareth entered the hall from the bailey. He came not with the laughing group of knights Rowena had expected, but alone. He stood head and shoulders over most of the men in the hall. His demeanor was not that of the jovial host but of a stranger, his stiffened shoulders defensive to the point of arrogance. Was it Rowena's imagination or did the laughter grow shriller and the silences more pointed? The strumming of Mortimer's fingers against the lutestrings took on new violence as if to fill the void of talk with music. Gareth took the goblet offered from a lady's hand and raised it in a mocking toast to the minstrel.

After he drank, Gareth raised the lady's hand to his lips. She curtsied as he kissed her palm. Pale blond strands of hair escaped her silver wimple. Rowena recognized the Lady Alise.

Gareth's dark head blurred before her eyes. A knot of unfamiliar hunger tightened her belly. This hunger was subtle and piercing, twisting like a thousand tiny daggers in her gut. Blaine watched her face, his caramel-colored eyes dispassionate.

Gareth lifted his head and glanced up at the gallery. Rowena threw herself behind the column, pushing her back to it as if she might sink into the wood and disappear. She squeezed her eyes shut, thinking she must be mad. How could she have let Marlys dress her like some mummer's dummy to gain Gareth's attention? Gareth's attention was the last thing she needed.

She gathered her skirts to flee, but Blaine's hand caught her wrist. "Shall we dance, milady squire?" Before she could protest, he had raised her palm. He lifted one eyebrow in a challenge, his lips warm against the racing pulse in her wrist.

Rowena snatched her hand back, and for a gratifying instant she thought Blaine was going to duck. Instead, he turned his dip into a mocking bow, the sweep of his hand motioning her toward the stairs.

The ballad swept Mortimer's voice high enough to escape its nasal tones. A lady in the corner wept prettily at the bittersweet tale of a peasant girl taken and forsaken by a philandering knight. The roast mutton and boar spread on the table against the wall were increasingly ignored for the casks of warm ale tapped on the hearth. A pall of fashionable sadness held the crowd rapt as Mortimer's voice soared in a triumph that would be lost in stupor by morning.

Gareth gently dried Alise's tears with a corner of her train.

As the last notes echoed through the sniffs and applause, Rowena glided down the stairs. Her sleeves flowed behind her like a separate entity. Blaine held her arm with a carefully achieved expression of delight and guilt.

A curious murmur filled the silence. Marlys took two steps toward them, then stopped, her long arms hanging loosely at her sides. At the foot of the steps, Blaine faced Rowena with a sweeping bow. She sank to a curtsy at his feet.

When Gareth drew away from Alise, the sight that greeted him was a regal figure kneeling in a billowing cloud of velvet at Blaine's feet. The peacock blue of her dress stained his vision. His goblet clanked to the stones, spattering burgundy wine over the lavender train of Alise's gown. He rose as if drugged, not realizing every eye in the hall was locked on him.

His hand closed on an ermine-trimmed sleeve, finding the arm within. His fingers dug like steel into warm flesh. Gentle blue eyes smothered in a sultry outline of kohl filled his vision.

"What in the name of God are you doing?" he demanded, his voice harsh in the sudden silence.

Caught in his grasp, Rowena bit her lower lip between her teeth. "Milord, I came to the feast. You did not forbid me to attend."

He shook her. "Where did you find these things?"

"I—we—" Rowena's eyes found the shadow of Marlys against the wall. Marlys was staring at her boots. The bile of betrayal rose in Rowena's throat. She stared into Gareth's eyes, choosing silence as her only plea.

Gareth released her arm. She felt Blaine's hand supporting her back as her knees betrayed her.

Gareth's face was suffused with red. "You look ridiculous." He snatched the wimple and coif from her head and hurled it to the floor.

Rowena paled as if he had struck her. Her hair fell to her shoulders, lank and dull from the weight of the wimple.

She looked around her, taking in at a glance the ashen brows and unadorned eyes of the ladies. The back of her hand lifted to her cheek. Crimson smudged her knuckles like a bruise of blood. Into the silence fell a nervous titter of laughter. Then another.

With spine straight, Rowena lowered her eyes and curtsied to Gareth. "Forgive me, milord. I have lived too long outside the realm of current fashion. I will not trouble you again."

Her skirts felt trimmed in lead as she gathered them in her hands. The crowd parted to let her through, their snickers dying, leaving Gareth to face Blaine's smirk. Blaine took a goblet from a servant's tray and pressed it into Gareth's hand.

"Drink, my friend. 'Tis your feast, after all."

The heat of the goblet warmed Gareth's hand. He swirled the amber liquid around the rim before draining it and reaching for another.

CHAPTER 7

Rowena broke into a run, ignoring the curious glances of the stragglers in the bailey. Her feet thumped down the drawbridge. The steady strum of Mortimer's lutestrings leaped into song, pounding out a rhythm for her flight to follow. Bursts of laughter chased her through the courtyard. Tears streaked her cheeks, staining the pristine blue of the dress with crimson rivulets. Her train caught on a stray stake, and she ripped it loose, taking a perverse satisfaction in the shredding of the velvet.

"Rowena!" came a cry, hoarse and breathless behind her.

She threw herself against the castle wall, impaled in a slanting beam of moonlight. The cry came again, nearer this time. She flung herself forward, her feet caught in the lilting cadence of speed, propelling her without a beat of hesitation through the blocks of shadow cast by the towers. She passed into the list. Three more strides, and the forest would be hers.

"Rowena!"

The note of unfamiliar pleading weighted her feet. She stumbled to a halt, resting her hands on her knees.

Moonlight bathed the deserted list. Footsteps crunched on the dying grass, the only sound except for the muted nickering of the horses in the stable. Marlys stood just inside the gate. Her eyes were veiled by a web of hair as she took a step toward Rowena. Rowena danced toward the darkness of the forest as smoothly as a doe poised for flight.

Marlys raised one hand. "Please. Don't." She straightened, blowing out a breath through pursed lips. "I never intended—"

Rowena's voice had the cutting edge of flint. "What did you intend?"

Marlys shook her head. "I don't know. Not that." She sank down on the chest against the wall, dragging a hand through her hair. " 'Twas a bit of mischief—a prank."

"Your brother did not find your humor to his liking."

"Gareth has found little humor to his liking for a long time." Marlys absently rolled the balls of her feet over the lances piled in the grass below the chest.

"Why did he look at me that way? Did he bear your stepmother no fondness?"

Marlys threw back her shaggy head to the moon with a harsh laugh. "He bore her all fondness."

Rowena crept nearer. "Then it pained him to be reminded of her?"

"When Gareth was twelve, my father brought our new mother to Caerleon. She was younger than Father—always laughing and gay. Like a vivacious angel sent to sweeten our lives."

Marlys gave the lances a vicious kick, scattering them in the grass. Rowena was too lost in Marlys's story to heed the painful thud of a lance against her ankle.

Marlys's voice lowered. "Her sweetness held only poison. Gareth was barely out of the first flush of boyhood. She was captivated by his smooth skin, his innocence. When my father was called away to help King Edward fight the Welsh, she begged him not to send Gareth to Blaine's father for fostering as was the custom. Instead, she had Blaine sent here. She undertook their training as pages herself." Marlys met Rowena's gaze with uncompromising candor. "She taught Blaine courtesy. She taught Gareth everything."

Rowena held out a hand to stop the torrent of words that

threatened to come spilling from Marlys's lips, but it was too late.

"So at the tender age of fourteen, my brother knew the guilt of loving his father's wife. When Blaine's father brought word of my father's death from a poisoned arrow wound, Gareth went to her to tell her he had begged the priest for forgiveness for both of their souls. He found her in her bower in the embrace of one of my father's knights. My father still lay on a muddy Welsh battlefield, his flesh not yet cold." Marlys jerked up one of the lances and paced the list like a caged wolf.

Rowena sank down in the grass, fingering the comforting contours of the lance beside her. "What did Gareth do?" she asked softly.

Marlys spun around. The gleam of one eye shone eerily triumphant through a mat of hair. "There's the question. You see—no one knows. They found her the next morn with Gareth's sword through her heart. Elayne's fingers still lay in the pool of blood she had drawn from to trace Gareth's name on the bedclothes beside her."

The broken words of a haunting melody tore through Rowena's brain:

> The fair Elayne
> Unfairly slain
> Her faithless hand
> Stilled by a name.

Elayne. Rowena rested her forehead on her palm. Her brow felt cool and clammy. Her fingers plucked fretfully at the velvet skirt as she raised her head.

"You put me in her garments," she said calmly.

Marlys stood in a shaft of moonlight, leaning on the lance like a staff. "I did not intend—"

"You put me in her garments," Rowena repeated, louder this time. She stood in one fluid motion, the lance finding a place in her sweating palm.

"Ro, I would not have—"

"You made him look at me and see her. How he must hate me . . ."

The pain of Gareth's censure amazed her. A twin fury swept the dazed curtain from her eyes. Marlys barely had time to bring the lance across her body as a shield before Rowena charged her. The solid thwack of wood meeting wood echoed through the deserted list. Marlys stumbled backward, keeping her footing by the barest of chance. Rowena did not dare to question the source of this terrible anguish. With a roar of rage more animal than human, she lunged forward, hurtling all of her weight into the charge. Marlys's lance splintered beneath hers with an echoing crack. Marlys fell backward, her body trapped beneath Rowena's weight, her breath paralyzed by the pressure of Rowena's lance laid across her windpipe. The fall had flung back Marlys's hair, baring her face to the merciless moonlight.

Rowena had never stopped wondering why Marlys took such care to keep her face veiled. Her imagination had provided scores of romantic stories involving terrible burns or disfiguring scars. The truth was far worse.

Marlys was beautiful.

The rugged imperfections of Gareth's features had been smoothed and refined in his sister. Square of jaw and high of cheekbone, Marlys glared at Rowena, her dark eyes sparkling like chips of obsidian in the moonlight. Her full lips tightened to a proud line. The tangled fall of hair hid a woman that made the Lady Alise appear an insipid imitation of what God intended a woman to be. Rowena's eyes shifted to a bewildered blue as the lance hung limp in her hands.

"Why?" Rowena whispered, unsure herself of the question she asked.

Marlys gave her a shove, and Rowena rolled to the side without protest. Marlys sat up, scooting around so her back was to Rowena. Once again her hair hung in a lank curtain over her face. By the time she could speak without her voice cracking, Rowena was gone.

Rowena tore off the dead woman's kirtle as she ran, shedding layer after layer of velvet sodden with the blood of years. She clawed at the embroidered bodice until it ripped beneath her nails. A bush shuddered beneath the weight of the camlet undergown. She flung aside the golden girdle as heedlessly as the silken kerchief. Stripped to her thin linen chemise, she flew through the forest, dodging the tree trunks with a flawless accuracy born from the wings of freedom. She was free. Free as she had been before Gareth had come to Revelwood. Nothing could stop her now. Not Gareth, and not even Papa. No threats. No promises.

Ignoring the twigs slapping her face, she fled deeper into the forest, leaving behind the dying leaves for a stand of pine. Cone-laden boughs admitted the moonlight in dappled patches. She stopped, feeling the chill of the November air against her heated skin for the first time. Gooseflesh prickled her arms at the eerie creak of branch against branch. Caught in the whisper of the wind, the thin trunks swayed to and fro in the ghostly moonlight.

She jerked off the satin slippers and sprang forward. Her bare feet crunched on the prickly needles. Only when she came to the edge of the copse did she stop, her arm flung around the rough bark of a pine. A rumble deeper than the wind warned her. Rushing out of the ground and into a pool silvered with moonlight flowed a fresh spring.

Without hesitation, Rowena plunged down the hill and into the chill water. She dove deep, then broke through the surface, sending water shooting from her hair in a sparkling spray, baptizing herself free of the dark stain of Caerleon.

Marlys watched Gareth approach through a veil of hair that colored the world dark. He sauntered through the list, his grace so deliberate that she knew he had been drinking. She leaned back on one elbow and tucked a hollow tube of grass between her teeth. She blew softly. A haunting whistle drifted into the night. Gareth stopped in front of her, legs planted firmly apart.

"Have you seen her?" he asked. His diction was flawless.

Marlys blew a short blast on the reed. "She's gone off."

"Gone off to sulk?"

Marlys wadded the grass in her jaw and spit it at his feet. "She's not given to sulks, in case you haven't noticed."

"Then where is she? She is not in the kitchens. She is not in my chambers."

"You've hardly given her a reason to stay there, have you?"

Gareth stared blankly at Marlys. "Do you know where she is?"

"I told you. She's gone off."

Gareth squatted beside her. He crooked his thumb in her hair and gently lifted it from her face. For the second time that night, searing moonlight bathed the slanted planes of her cheeks.

"Gone off where?" he said softly.

Their dark eyes met. With a short jerk of her head, Marlys indicated the forest. "She's gone off for good. Why don't you leave her be? Can't you get it through your thick skull that her papa's not coming? Or do you even care anymore?"

Gareth stood with a frown, leaving Marlys in darkness once more. "She is a stranger to the forest. She could be lost. She could be attacked by wolves or bears."

"And eaten?" Marlys volunteered. Her smile was a grimace.

Gareth's frown deepened. He spun on his heel and strode toward the stables, sobered by purpose. He tightened his gauntlets with efficient jerks.

As she watched him, Marlys rested her cheek on her knee. Her eyes narrowed as Blaine slipped out of the shadows and caught Gareth's arm.

"Gareth, I heard. Give me leave and I will summon the knights and organize a search."

Gareth jerked his arm free. "Rowena is already helpless prey for one sort of boar. I'd rather not expose her to your kind as well."

He disappeared into the stables and reappeared leading Folio. As Gareth mounted, Blaine had to dance sideways to avoid the horse's flailing hooves.

"Gareth, you've made it clear you bear the girl no fondness. You won her in a wager. Let us wager together. Give me a chance at her."

Gareth wrapped the reins around his hands, bringing the prancing horse under his control. The corner of his mouth lifted in a cold smile. "What sort of contest would you prefer? Hazard? Chess? Tilting?"

Blaine took a step backward and raised his hands in surrender. Gareth pushed Folio past him, and the thunder of hoofbeats rolled through the long courtyard, fading into the night.

Blaine glanced back to the list. Moonlight spilled over the empty grass. A pebble rolled against stone on the wall above. As he glanced up, a helmed figure grasping a splintered lance came sailing over the roof of the stable. It crashed into his shoulder with a victorious screech.

The castle with its lights and laughter seemed a world away as Gareth picked his way through the primeval silence of the forest. Night sounds came to him in crackling spurts: the flutter of unseen wings against a branch above; the indignant croak of a frog drowned in a splash as Folio's hooves grazed the dry grass; the whisper of a leaf surrendering its embrace of a twig and drifting down to brush Gareth's cheek in the darkness. In places where the leaves still clung in dying bunches to hide the moonlight, he guided the horse forward more on instinct than sight, his eyes blank and shining like the eyes of a blind man free of the encumbrance of sunlight.

He was deep into the forest when he stopped and called
her name. His voice rolled back to him on a hollow echo,
jarring him with its hoarseness. Beneath his knees, Folio's
sleek flesh quivered. The lonely cry of a nightjar spilled
into the silence. He urged the horse forward through a tangle
of vines. Folio balked and tossed his head as nettles caught
at his fetlocks.

Gareth dismounted. Unsheathing his sword, he cut at the
web of underbrush, clearing a path for Folio to follow.
The horse nickered softly, blowing a musty breath against
the back of his neck. He paused. His fingers closed around
a scrap of velvet dangling from a low-hanging branch. He
stared at it for a long moment, then touched it to his cheek,
rubbing its softness against the prickle of his beard. He
raised his eyes to the light that came streaming through the
bushes ahead, then parted the branches. Moonlight bleached
the pine needles in a wash of silver.

Sword hanging forgotten in his hand, he moved toward
that alluring absence of color with a sleepwalker's gait. The
shadows fell away as the crisp scent of evergreen filled his
nostrils.

At the bottom of a treeless hill, a figure in white lay
sprawled beside a spring. At first Gareth thought she was
dead. Her limbs were so pale, her chest so still. But as his
heavy steps drew him closer, he could see life coursing
through her, coloring her cheeks with its rose hues, parting
her lips with its nourishing breath. She lay on her back, her
legs parted in the unconscious innocence of a child.

The chemise, so shapeless when dry, clung to her damp
skin. Gareth's gaze raked her, searching the teasing demar-
cations of shadow and light beneath the linen. His groin
tightened and he swore softly, his oath more endearment
than curse.

She must be cold. To lay so exposed to the cooling winds
and not shiver seemed unnatural. Then Gareth remembered
the grim keep of Revelwood and the winters she must have

known. The autumn wind must be no more than a passing breeze to her.

He was not cold. On the contrary, his skin prickled with heat as if he had taken a sudden fit of ague. He opened his mouth to awaken her, then closed it. He half turned away. Folio watched him curiously from the top of the hill.

She nestled her cheek into the damp tendrils of hair that pillowed her head. The sight of her made Gareth bite back a groan. She belonged to him. A wager was a debt paid in honor. She was his for a year. He could work her in his fields or his kitchens or his bedchamber if he so desired. No man could condemn him as a scoundrel for his actions. No man could stop him from kneeling at this moment between her parted thighs and making her his own. Rowena stirred. A wince furrowed her smooth brow.

He stood over her, barely breathing. A part of him still wanted to hate her, had longed to find her cosseted by an adoring father, bred for charm and deceit as Elayne had been. 'Twould have made it easier to break her then, to punish Fordyce by sending her back, ravished and shamed, her pride torn, her conceit in shreds. But there was nothing of Elayne in this girl. Bred in the poverty Fordyce had sunk to since the night he'd fled Gareth's sword, she had a spirit devoid of conceit, as bright and shining as the sun. What right did he have to stain her with his darkness?

His possession of her did not have to be cruel. He could make her life pleasant enough in the year she spent at Caerleon. He could give her comforts and luxuries she had only dreamed of at Revelwood. And at the end of the year, he could find her a worthy husband or send her on her way with a weighty sum of gold and a future free of poverty and hunger.

A future with men like Blaine waiting to snatch up your scraps.

The voice in his head was Marlys's and he hated it. With a curse, he drove his sword into the damp earth. He unbuckled his scabbard with shaking hands. Rowena moaned softly as his shadow fell over her.

The sun beat down like a hammer. A warm wind rippled the tall grasses into a swaying symphony of green and gold. A dot on the horizon grew larger as it hurtled toward her. Rowena's heart swelled with joy. The sun glinted silver on Little Freddie's hair as his childish sprint drove him closer to her arms. Her heart thudded in her ears. She lifted her knees higher, exalting in the clean, sweet beat of the run. Her steps faltered.

A dark shadow loomed behind her brother, closing the distance with the inevitability of a hawk swooping down on a mouse. Rowena screamed a warning, but her throat closed with a gurgle. Little Freddie ran toward her, oblivious to the menace sweeping down on him. A grin lit his face. His gray eyes sparkled.

A knight, armored all in black, pounded across the moor, the silky white mane of his mount rippling behind. A gridded helm hid his face. The knight bore down on Freddie, his lance outstretched, its carved tip aimed straight for the small of Little Freddie's back. Rowena's scream finally came. The thunder of hoofbeats drowned it out, and she fell to her knees, clapping her hands over her ears. When she opened her eyes, the moor was empty and silent, except for the lonely whistle of the wind.

She was crouched in a sea of peacock blue, her hands spread in a plea in front of her. Gareth stood over her, his blade lifted. Tears trickled down her cheeks as her pleas filled the merciless silence. She had not meant to run. She had forgotten his threat, forgotten Papa's wager. Shame flooded her. Her eyes dropped to the twisted clothes, but she could not remember why she should be ashamed. Gareth's dark eyes flicked over her. His lip lifted in a sneer of contempt. The fire sent shimmers of red across his blade. She clasped her hands to beg for his forgiveness. The blade descended in a flash of silver.

Rowena turned her head and opened her eyes, tasting the salt of a single tear in her mouth. A blade silvered with moonlight filled her vision. She stared blankly at the sword, awaiting the horror of another nightmare.

Warm lips brushed her throat, saturating her senses with a spicy breath of ale. She lay without moving as a mouth glided up her throat. Sharp teeth caught her earlobe in a tingling embrace. She was being eaten by a wolf, she thought vaguely. A slow, enticing wolf with meticulous table manners. He nibbled the tender flesh of her shoulder. Only when his teeth gently dragged down the top of her chemise so his mouth could claim the swell of her breast did Rowena turn her face. The wolf lifted his shaggy head. She stared into eyes that were dark and dangerous and sleepy. Gareth's eyes.

Her gaze flicked back to the sword, then back to him. The weight of his body poised above her, impaling her to the ground more effectively than the sight of the sword driven into the soft earth. Yet except for his mouth, not an inch of him touched her. A pine needle pricked her thigh. She was not dreaming. Her lips parted as the dreams came flooding back. She trembled inside, but not a muscle jerked. She turned her face away, but it was too late.

Gareth caught her chin between his finger and thumb, his grip none too gentle. Rowena met his steady gaze. She could still feel the imprint of his fingers when he rose and paced away. He stood with his back to her, hands on hips.

"Marlys told you," he said flatly.

Rowena sat up. "How did you know?"

"I've seen that look before in a woman's eyes. Fear. Doubt. Morbid curiosity."

Rowena bowed her head, hoping he'd misjudged her. "Were you brought to trial?"

Gareth spun on his heel. "What would have been the use? I was judge and juror after my father's death. They preferred to condemn me with their whispers and their looks. I would never have become a knight at all if Blaine's father had not fostered me.''

"And if the king had not knighted you," Rowena murmured. She lifted her head. "Your villeins seem loyal enough.''

His nod was untouched by mockery. "They are. I am their lord. I hold their fiefs. 'Twas they with their primitive sense of moral justice who were the first to whisper that the lady of the castle needed killing. That she got what she deserved. But the village priest still refuses to pander his prayers at Caerleon.''

"You could force him to, could you not?''

"Why bother? Whether I am a murderer or not, I am an adulterer. Any of the nobility feasting in my hall as we speak would be overjoyed to proclaim me both.''

"How do you silence their whispers, milord?''

He came and knelt beside her. He reached for a tangled strand of her hair, the caress as soft as his voice was hard. "I challenge the men. I bed the women.''

Rowena dropped her eyes. The sight of Gareth's scabbard and gauntlets laid neatly on the ground hardened an unfamiliar knot in her stomach. " 'Tis most unsporting to fall upon an opponent while they are sleeping.''

"I was not aware you were an opponent.''

"I stand corrected. I am a possession—akin to your sword or your mount.''

He twisted her hair into a curl around his finger. "You are.''

"But far more trouble than a sword or a horse, I would wager. Dragging you away from your feast, sending you on a merry chase.''

His hand slipped beneath her hair to cup her neck. "Swords must be learned. Horses must be broken.'' Before she could retort, his lips grazed hers with a teasing stroke of his tongue. He drew back and stared into her face, his arrogance bridled by curiosity.

"Shall you break me, milord?'' she queried softly.

Gareth could find no trace of accusation in her eyes. He stood and whistled softly between two fingers, and Folio came trotting down the hill. The stallion nuzzled Gareth's cheek. Gareth entwined his fingers in the horse's forelock and gently tugged. Folio ducked his head and sank to one knee in a pretty bow. Rowena applauded.

Gareth's teeth gleamed through his dark beard. He met Rowena's gaze over the stallion's head. "Before I could break Folio, I had to teach him to trust me."

Rowena picked at a black patch of sap on her chemise to hide the effect of a smile that held no mockery. Gareth gathered his belongings and sheathed his sword. He mounted. She stood awkwardly, wondering if she was to be left alone in the vast forest as punishment for her flight.

Folio pranced forward under the invisible rein of Gareth's control. Rowena held her feet steady, refusing to flinch.

"Gareth?"

She looked up at him without realizing it was the first time she had said his name without prefacing it with "milord" or "sir." To Gareth, it held the ring of music.

His knees tightened. Folio tossed his head. "What is it?" Gareth said harshly to hide her effect on him.

"God does not fight on the side of the guilty. If you have won every challenge to your honor, does that not mean you are innocent?"

Gareth stared down at her, the well of silence deepening between them.

He held out his arm to her. Rowena clasped his forearm and found herself mounted on Folio, sitting sideways behind Gareth.

The nearness of his warmth lent a dangerous edge to his soft words. "Don't be so quick to exonerate me, Rowena. I've killed men who've done nothing but accuse me of being a murderer."

"And bedded their widows?"

He did not reply. He urged the horse up the uneven ter-

rain of the hillside and did not betray himself with so much
as a shiver when Rowena's arms crept around his waist.

Blaine was sitting in the bailey with his back to the wall
when Folio came walking into the courtyard. The merriment within the castle had long ago died to broken snores.
He lowered the damp rag from his split lip and squinted
through the eye that was not swollen shut. Rowena's cheek
lay against Gareth's back. Her eyes were closed. She murmured a sleepy refrain as Gareth slid off the horse with one
arm held behind him to keep her from falling. Then his
hands caught beneath her arms and drew her to her feet.
She opened her eyes. The untarnished emotion within
their blue depths sent a thrill of pure lust shooting through
Blaine. He climbed to his feet, the ache of his battered knee
forgotten in the harder ache of his groin. Rowena's eyes
drifted closed again, and she swayed in Gareth's embrace.
Blaine started forward, but Gareth's furtive glance around
the bailey stopped him in the shadows. Rowena never felt
the brush of Gareth's lips against her temple. Blaine sank
against the wall as Gareth scooped Rowena into his arms
and carried her into the castle.
Blaine rolled his eyes skyward with a groan. A yellow
stab of light flickered in the tower on the other side of the
bailey. His eyes narrowed, fixing on the unshuttered window
where a dark and shaggy head loomed behind the flame.
With a crash, the shutter slammed, and Blaine threw back
his head and laughed aloud until blood from his torn lip
trickled down his chin.

CHAPTER 8

The first snowflakes of winter came spinning out of a sky laden with gray. They darted and spun on an icy wind to be captured by the castle walls and sent drifting into the bailey. The doors of Caerleon were flung open. Knights and ladies bundled in wool and ermine spilled into the courtyard, their laughter ringing like bells in the crisp air as they turned their faces skyward. Brittle bits of snow tapped their flushed cheeks, and they opened their mouths hungrily to catch the flakes on their tongues.

As the snow frosted the brown grass, then carpeted it in white, the men snuck up behind one another and shoved handfuls of snow down tunics. Someone found the chest of lances in the list and soon mock tournaments were being held with the men sliding on the slick grass beneath the snow.

Rowena slipped out of the castle behind the others. She pressed herself to the wall, wondering if the nobility were not tinged with madness. Snow had never meant joy to her. Snow had meant a winter trapped inside a dark castle with drifts piled so high against the doors that they could not be opened from December to March. Snow had meant one rag of a coverlet spread over nine people and nothing but a raw turnip and Irwin's tales to nibble on through the short days and endless nights. Snow had meant bowls of soup flavored more with water than barley.

As Gareth had predicted, Blaine and his retinue settled

themselves at Caerleon and proceeded to eat up the stores
of years. Dunnla ordered about villeins summoned from the
village, frightening them into fits with her bellowing. Gridmore led an alarming number of pages into stone walls and
onto window ledges before they could be rescued. Blaine
lounged around the castle, posturing like a satisfied cat,
ever hungry for new entertainment.

Traveling troupes, quick to hear rumors of Blaine's lar-
gesse with gold coins, flocked to the castle. Mummers were
followed by puppeteers, acrobats by rope dancers, and trou-
badours by a sword swallower.

The snow brought with it a fresh entertainment and
infused the courtyard with joy. Rowena hugged herself, stifling a shiver. She wore no mantle, but only a shapeless
cotte of white wool. She had learned well the value of simple garments on the night of the first feast. She had no
desire to fuel the whispers spoken behind the sleeves of the
ladies. They knew she shared Gareth's bedchamber.
Whether she was his leman or a glorified maid kept to stir
the fire, no one knew. Gareth treated her with nothing but
distant courtesy in front of them. Or alone with her.

The only time Gareth showed any interest in her at all
was when Sir Blaine approached. Then he would spring
from the very walls to inquire about her writing lessons or
ask if her porridge had suited her that morn. It confused
her and infuriated Blaine, whose courtesy grew to terrifying
proportions when he was angry. She would stammer a reply
with all the grace of the village idiot and stumble over her
own feet to escape them both.

The snow billowed down in a deepening curtain of white,
frosting beards and capping the turrets in a pearly blanket.
Across the bailey a spray of snow shot into the air as Marlys
tusseled with a chubby squire. His howls for mercy drew a
smile from Rowena. Snow caught on her eyelashes and
melted like tears down her cheeks. She had been watching
Gareth for several minutes with growing disquiet.

Lady Alise knelt at his feet. She scooped a swath of snow

into her satin gloves. Her ferret-trimmed pelisse was spread around her in rippling elegance. She lifted her face to Gareth, her delicate features aglow with laughter. He offered her his hand, and she took it. He ducked as she leaped to her feet, blowing snow like sparks of moondust in his face. Then she gathered her skirts and dodged behind a squealing lady as Gareth started after her with a growl. Across the bailey, his gaze met Rowena's.

He straightened and lifted a black-gloved hand in greeting. Rowena managed a wince of a smile, then slipped back into the shadows of the keep. Her feet carried her to the kitchen, where she plopped down on the bench and rested her chin on her hands.

"Half frozen, are ya?" Dunnla wailed in her ear.

Rowena didn't even jump as Dunnla slammed a bowl of lentil stew on the table. Rowena stared into its bubbling depths, then pushed it away. She had seen Gareth's smile fade when he saw her. Why did he keep her around if he detested her so? She folded her arms on the table and rested her head on them. She did not see Gareth pause in the doorway or Dunnla shake a spoon at him. When she lifted her head, the doorway was empty, and Dunnla was bellowing a tune about the gruesome end of a lusty knight.

Rowena huddled on the lowest stair, wrapped in a musty pelt. Icy gusts rattled the shutters against the stones. When the shutters resisted the battering siege, the wind went wailing around the ramparts in furious protest. The eerie wail rose to a howl, and Rowena signed the cross on her breast beneath the pelt. At last the wind sated itself by shooting blasts of cold through the arrow slits. Even the richness of Gareth's keep could not halt the attack of England's winter.

A week ago the sky had begun to spill new snow. Rowena had gathered on the parapet walk with the others to marvel at the size and beauty of the snowflakes. Within minutes every tower carried a frosting of white until the castle itself looked as if it had been fashioned of snow by a giant child

with an artist's hand. The lash of the wind drove them inside. The men escorted the women down the winding stairs
with forced jocularity, but beneath their smiles, Rowena
saw the strain of frowns. The murmur of "blizzard" passed
between them like a dreadful incantation.

By dawn of this, the seventh day, Rowena could see no
more than a hand's length in front of her from any window
in the castle. The world darkened to whirling white as the
invisible sky dumped snow into the merciless hands of the
wind. Snow billowed around the ramparts, rolling into ice-
capped drifts at every wall. Gareth's guests wandered to
the great hall without being summoned, trying to ignore the
sharp gestures and raised voices of Gareth and Blaine at the
hearth.

Finally Blaine lifted a finger for attention. His smile was
deadly sweet. "Our host has wracked his mind for a way
to relieve our tedium and provide us an entertainment on
this grim day. Every man in the castle is to join in a hunt
to bring back meat for tonight's feast."

A halfhearted cheer went up from the men. The Lady
Alise pressed a kerchief to her trembling lips. Gareth's face
was set in grim lines.

Woolen greaves and fur vests were fetched by the arm-
loads and tossed in a heap on the rugs. The men shifted
from foot to foot like restless children as the women bundled them into cloaks and wound their capuchins into hoods.
They tossed challenges and taunts across the hall to keep
the silence from closing in. Shrill laughter rang out as the
women pressed kisses of luck on clammy brows. A matronly woman patted her husband's rump as he turned to
go. A freckled girl no older than Rowena pressed her kerchief into a knight's hand.

"Have you no favor for me, sweet Rowena?" Blaine
whispered. He had crept up behind her as silently as a cat.
A fur cap hung jauntily over one ear.

"What might these favors indicate?"

Blaine placed a hand over his heart and blinked winningly. " 'Tis a pledge of my eternal love to a lady I adore."

Rowena glanced down. Her simple cotte was unadorned by girdle or kerchief. "I fear I have no such favor to give."

"I beg you. Mayhaps a kiss then, one memory of your soft lips. Pray do not send me to an icy grave with naught."

Rose stained Rowena's cheeks. She swayed backward as he leaned forward.

"Stand aside, Blaine, or I shall give you the favor of my lance against your brow." A bear with a muffled growl came clumping down the stairs between them.

Blaine leaped backward, giving the shaggy giant a wide berth. A woman screamed, and all eyes turned to the bottom of the stairs. Bound in ragged pelts from ankle to nose, Marlys stomped into the hall wearing what could only be kitchen trays strapped to her feet with leather thongs.

Gareth crossed the hall to meet her, and a hissed but heated exchange followed. Marlys ended it by hurling her lance across the hall. A page ducked, his face ashen as the lance thumped to a quivering halt in the oaken beam he had been leaning against. Rowena flinched as Marlys proceeded to tell Gareth loudly and explicitly what he could do with his hunt. She grabbed a flagon of ale and stomped out of the hall, her curses ringing behind her.

Blaine shrugged his wiry shoulders into a vest as he tripped down the stairs. "What does he expect? He lets her run like a beast. A good thrashing would cure that."

A squire below them chortled. "Or a good—"

Rowena cleared her throat. The squire met her level gaze and slunk away. Rowena had no idea why she should be defending Marlys, though she supposed Marlys and Gareth were the only family she had now.

At Gareth's signal, two men wrenched the doors open. The silence everyone had feared fell over the hall.

A solid mound of white covered the doorway. The muffled scream of the wind behind it shielded the nervous beat

of a hundred hearts. The men stood as if frozen themselves
until Gareth's cry flung them into movement.

"Lances! Bring all the lances you can find."

Lances were brought amidst excited jabber. The women
stood back with clasped hands as the men stabbed the snowy
beast. The snow collapsed in a powdery avalanche. A cheer
went up. A rush of arctic wind and blinding snow shot into
the hall. Last embraces were exchanged. Then, with Gareth
in the lead, the men climbed over the crumbling hill in the
doorway and disappeared into the white.

Rowena turned and ran up the stairs. She flew down the
long corridors, through a squat hall, and up a narrow spiral
staircase she thought would never end. Her harsh breathing
sent puffs of fog into the stale air.

She burst into the north tower and stumbled to her knees
at the bottom of a narrow window. Her stiff fingers tugged
at the shutter latch, but the latch held. Too cold to feel her
knuckles tear against the rough wood, she rammed both
fists against the shutter. With a crack of protest, it flew
open.

The burst of cold air and the dizzying height of the tower
knocked Rowena backward. Icy flecks of snow blinded her,
melting to tears beneath her eyelids. She rubbed them away.
Gripping the icy stone windowsill with both hands, she
leaned into the blizzard. Her eyes narrowed against the
wind, and her fingers went numb. Squinting, she could
make out blurred shapes like tiny shadows crawling down
the drawbridge far below. The shape at the head of the hunting party held all of her attention. The wind whipped from
north, south, east, and west, hiding him from her view for
an agonizing second. Then the straggling line reappeared.
Rowena leaned out farther, her hungry gaze following Gareth until her hair hardened to icy strands and the last dark
shape disappeared into the crystalline forest.

She pulled the shutter closed with a shiver. The broken
latch dangled, and the shutter banged wildly as she left the
tower, pulling the door shut behind her. Her slippers made

no sound against the stones. She drifted to the bedchamber she shared with Gareth. The morning's fire had died to embers. She spread her palms over their glow to capture a hint of warmth. The snow trapped in her hair and kirtle melted and dripped into her kid shoes. She scooped a pelt from her nest of furs, then let it roll from her fingertips as her eyes locked on the bed frame that dominated the chamber.

She dragged one of Gareth's pelts from the bed and buried her face in it. The fur tickled her nose. She closed her eyes as the sweet, musky scent of him filled her senses. Her lips moved wordlessly against the fur. She threw the heavy pelt over her shoulders and went to the stairs to wait with the rest of the women for their men to return.

As the afternoon waned to dusk, the chatter of the women sharpened, honed by the passing of minutes and the increasing frequency of glances at the door. The snow had been swept outside by laughing maidservants, and the door had been shoved closed against the wind. Only a dark puddle remained to mark its passing.

Hours passed. The silences grew longer and the laughter lower. The ladies bent their heads to their embroidery and pretended not to start at every sound. Dunnla shuffled between them, offering lark pasties and mead, but her platter remained untouched.

In a silence broken only by the howl of the wind, Mortimer hefted his lute and plucked gently at the strings. He was the only man left behind, except for a handful of smooth-chinned pages. Mortimer stroked the beginning notes of first one tune and then another, playing absently, more to comfort himself than to amuse the women. Rowena's head flew up as she thought she heard the haunting notes of a ballad she had never thought to hear again. The lyrics circled unsummoned in her mind, then Mortimer's fingers shifted to the chorus of another tune. Rowena dipped her nose into Gareth's pelt, seeking a musty comfort to soften the sharp edge of despair.

When she raised her head, the Lady Alise's gaze rested on her, curious and cold. Rowena met her gaze unblinkingly until Alise bent her head to the cambric in her lap.

Marlys paced the hall like a caged wolf. The ladies drew in their feet each time she passed and tried not to flinch.

A plump woman encased like a sausage in ocher wool gave a bright, false smile. "Was it not clever of Sir Gareth and Sir Blaine to organize a hunt? Men do so hate to be confined."

Marlys spun around. The deliberate grace of her swagger carried her back to the woman. She leaned forward, resting her hands on the arms of the carved chair.

The caress of her voice could be heard at every corner of the hall. "You silly bitch. Believe it or not, freezing to death in a snowdrift is a worse confinement than being locked up with a ninny like you. Your fat little belly might crave meat ere this blizzard ends. My brother took your men out there so the villeins would not find a castle full of noble bones come the spring thaw."

The woman stared into her lap, lips quivering. Her needle stabbed the linen kerchief and sank into the tender pad beneath her thumbnail. She burst into tears. Marlys backed away with a glare of contempt.

An uneven melody rose from Mortimer's lute. There would be no more idle chatter to hold the fear at bay. Marlys strode to the stairs where Rowena huddled and sank down beside her, cracking knuckles stiff with cold. Rowena raised herself to loose the pelt beneath her and dropped it like a cape over Marlys's shoulders. It enveloped both of them easily.

Without a word, Marlys scooted against the warmth of Rowena's body. They sat wrapped together for a long time before Rowena's head nodded against Marlys's shoulder in a fitful doze.

Rowena awoke to a silence so profound she thought she was dreaming. She opened her eyes to meet Marlys's dark, waiting gaze. Not a murmur or a whisper of wool broke the quiet. This was more than silence. It was a terrible absence, as if the beat of their own hearts had stilled. Marlys threw back the pelt, and they peered upward. The shadows under the rafters surrendered no answers.

"The wind," came a choked whisper. "The wind has stopped."

"Has it?" The lady who spoke was the freckled girl who had pressed her kerchief into the young knight's hand. "Has it really stopped, or are we just deaf to it?" Her voice rose with an edge of hysteria. "Perhaps we are buried alive and can hear nothing. Perhaps the men are behind the snow right outside that door, begging and pleading for us to let them in and we cannot hear them. Perhaps their bodies stiffen and die even as we sit and sew. Perhaps—"

"Stop it." Marlys crossed the space between them in two strides. Her slap rang out in the silence. The girl sank into the arms of a matronly woman.

The woman glared up at Marlys. "I told my husband we never should have come here. All of England knows your brother is a madman. Dismissing all his fiefs. Living like a hermit with no one but cripples and villeins to serve him. Letting you run wild like an animal instead of shutting you in a convent as he should. Caerleon is cursed. Damned by the dark deeds of its master."

A dull flush darkened the back of Marlys's neck. The Lady Alise kneaded her cambric between her thin fingers. Rowena stepped between Marlys and the woman, and those who had never heard her utter a word strained to hear her soft voice.

"You have no right to speak so."

The woman's virulent gaze shifted to Rowena. "Who are you to defend him? We know where he keeps you at night. Chained to his bed. Forced to satisfy his darkest and most unnatural desires. You should wish his death with your every breath." The woman's hand absently patted the hair of the sobbing girl in her lap.

Rowena fought an absurd desire to laugh, but the cruel words coupled with a jolting realization of her true feelings suddenly did not seem very funny.

Even to her own ears, her voice sounded faint and far away. "You will owe Sir Gareth an apology when he returns."

Marlys's voice was strangled with bitterness. "*If* he returns."

Her voice was joined by a distant sound, as deep and rolling as the ocean. Rowena cocked her head to the side with a frown. The Lady Alise came to her feet. Voices. Male voices, lifted in song, rumbling with vibrancy. And followed by each swelling chorus was an echoing slam as if of a gong sounded deep underwater.

The auburn-haired girl sat straight up. "Holy Mother of God preserve us. They are dead. We hear their angels."

Mortimer threw aside his lute. "If angels sing a song such as that, 'tis not in heaven they reside."

The ghostly chorus swelled:

> Me Jenny is a fiery lass
> Whose love is ne'er too cold
> With her sweet thighs to sheath my sword
> I ne'er shall grow too old.

Rowena's lips curved in a smile. The massive door shook in its frame as the battering ram broke through the ice and thundered to a halt against the sturdy wood.

"Do our fair ladies deny us entrance?" came a voice that was unmistakably Blaine's.

Mortimer's wiry arms knotted with the effort as he swung open the door. "They might, but I never would."

He was trampled as the ladies surged forward in a mass of squeals and tears. The men swept in to meet them. Ice and snow clung to every fiber and hair, rendering them crackling mountains of white. Suspended on poles between every two men hung wild boars with blood caked and frozen on their carcasses. Cheers rocked the hall.

Rowena stood alone amidst the furniture. Tears misted her eyes as Marlys flung herself on the neck of a snowy giant just inside the door. When he could disengage himself from her embrace, he lowered her, shaking snow from his dark hair. His cheeks glowed with good health. His teeth gleamed through his frosted beard in a smile that held no hint of bitterness as he accepted the embraces and salutes of both men and women. His dark eyes sparkled as he swept Lady Alise under his arm.

Rowena's stomach churned as her feelings for Gareth broke over her like a storm. Believing herself invisible in the joyful chaos, she crept up the stairs, dragging Gareth's pelt behind her.

Dunnla's knock came twice upon the door, then came again in another hour. Each time, Rowena answered the same way. "Go away. I am ill."

How could Dunnla have missed her in the revelry below? Snatches of music and cries of joy drifted up through the stone floor to Rowena's ears. She snuggled deeper into her pelts and stared into the deepening shadows. The snow had stopped. The wind wailed a rising tune against the latched shutter.

Rowena *was* ill. Self-contempt curled like a fist deep in her gut. How could she have been such a fool as to let herself be won over by a pair of somber dark eyes and a fine set of muscles? She was no better than Lady Alise. She drifted into sleep more than once, but always awoke with the restless shivering of one fevered and the wetness of tears on her cheeks. She would have a long time to nurse her shattered pride. Gareth would no doubt be celebrating far into the night, first in the great hall, then in the Lady Alise's bedchamber.

She did not roll over when the door creaked open.

"I beg you, Dunnla. Go away," she said crossly. "I am ill. I am not hungry."

" 'Tis no wonder you are ill with no fire on the grate. I can see my breath in here."

Rowena rolled over and sat up, her hair tumbling over the fur drawn to her chin. Gareth leaned his weight against the closed door.

He held out a white bundle. "I brought you some hot pastries. Peach. Your favorite."

Rowena sniffed. "Nay. I do not want them." She rolled away from him.

There was a moment of puzzled silence, then the gentle thump of logs being tossed on the grate. The rhythmic snap of a fire followed, making a pretty noise but doing little to warm the icy air. Rowena waited for the slam of the door. It did not come.

She peeked out of her hiding place. Gareth paced in front of the hearth, chafing his arms. "I cannot seem to get warm."

She watched in surprise as he pulled his tunic over his head. Howls of laughter and voices raised in song floated up from below.

" 'Tis poor manners for a host to abandon his own feast, is it not?"

Gareth shrugged. "I tire of their toasts. Fickle lot, are they not? Stuff them with roast boar and they drop their suspicious glances and lift their goblet to you. I came up here to seek a warm bed. I fear I've come to the wrong place."

His words were more ill chosen than he realized. Rowena's lips tightened, and she jerked the pelt over her head. Gareth shoved two more logs on the fire, ate one of the pastries he had brought for Rowena, and dove into the center of the bed. He spread the pelts over him.

Even as the fire roared upward, the chill in the chamber deepened. The wind whistled with joy at the plunging temperature. The shutter trembled as stubborn drafts pushed themselves through the narrow slats. Soon Rowena could feel the cold emanating from the stones beneath the thick fur. A shudder wracked her. She wrapped her arms around her back but found little comfort in her own heat. A heap of pelts could not compare to the warmth of nine bodies curled under a single coverlet. She had no Little Freddie, snug and sweet-smelling, to throw her leg over.

She crawled toward the fire, dragging the pelts behind her. She arranged them at the base of the hearth and crawled inside, shivering in the scant warmth. The shadows dancing on the wall cast an illusion of warmth, all the more cruel for its cozy perfection. Cold seeped through Rowena's skin into her bones. Her teeth chattered. She wrapped the pelts around her and climbed to sit on the hearth itself, pressing her cheek to the warmth of the stones.

With a crash, the wind slammed the shutter open, and Rowena started. Cold wind poured into the chamber, sending the snow piled on the windowsill into a sparkling whirlwind. Gareth jumped up and forced the shutter closed with a curse. He turned, stomping his feet on the stones, to find Rowena huddled on the hearth. Only her eyes and a thatch of golden hair was visible over the dark fur.

He climbed back into the bed. "How am I to sleep with that infernal chattering?" he growled.

"I humbly beg your forgiveness, milord," Rowena choked out between clenched teeth. "You may banish me to Marlys's chamber if it displeases you. I am not accustomed to sleeping alone in the winter."

"I am. But not with half my pelts. This is absurd. There is no benefit in both of us freezing to death within five feet of each other." He threw back his covers in an unmistakable invitation.

Rowena's eyes grew round and large. The tip of her reddened nose poked over the furs, but she hugged the pelts tighter.

Gareth rolled his eyes. "Your hesitation is flattering, but

I can assure you any part of me amenable to molesting you is frozen solid at the moment.''

Rowena looked at him sideways, still uncertain. He puffed out a fog of breath in exasperation. She screwed her eyes shut and made a mad dash for the bed, bounding next to him with a leap that shook the bed frame. She snuggled deep into the feather tick, her back to him.

Gareth stared at the graceful curve of her back beneath the cotte and wondered if he had spoken in haste. He tucked the combined pelts around them both, then rolled to his side and closed his eyes.

A steady rustling seized the tick. Gareth opened his eyes and rolled over. Shivers wracked Rowena's slender spine.

"Good God, woman! If your teeth don't make a racket, your bones do.''

Rowena erupted from the pelts in a flurry of gold and sable. "Pray do forgive me, milord.'' Her talent for mockery found the precise words she sought. "Mayhaps you'd care to chain me to your bed and force me to satisfy your darkest and most unnatural desires.''

Gareth rubbed his already tousled hair. The words she hurled at him were his own, whispered to a lecherous old duke from London whose lady could be counted on to spread the malicious gossip to the four corners of the known world.

His mind keened a warning, but his hands ignored it as they cupped Rowena's neck and pulled her forward until only her palms pressed to his bare chest kept them from colliding.

" 'Tis a tempting invitation, milady, but we both know there would be no need of chains between us.''

Rowena quailed before the devilish light in his eyes, wondering what idiocy had prompted her to taunt him. He was twice her opponent out of bed and even more her master in it. His hateful Elayne had trained him well. She dropped her gaze. Her hands looked stubby and ungraceful against the sleek fur of his chest.

Gareth's fingers tightened on her neck. Her meek accep-

tance of his bullying angered him more than rebellion. To
him it spoke of a lifetime of acceptance of whatever foolish
excuses her papa had chosen to offer. Had that been the
way? He wanted to shake her. To urge her to speak up for
herself, or even to strike out at him. He wanted to stir the
spark of spirit glimpsed so briefly in her complacent gaze.
His hands itched to lay her back among the furs and slowly
and patiently stir another spark into roaring flame. His own
flame threatened to consume him as he buried his lips in
the ethereal softness of her hair.

His harsh words echoed against her skull. "A peaceable
sleep is all I desire. Is that so unnatural? Do I have to chain
you to get it?"

"Nay, milord."

"Then roll over."

Rowena rolled over as if she half expected to feel the
sting of his palm against her rump. With a silent groan,
he slipped his arms around her waist, and she sank into the
warmth of his embrace.

Long after Rowena's shivers had stilled, she lay curled
like a statue against the hard length of his body, basking in
his nearness but afraid to stir lest she betray herself with a
caress or word of folly in her sleep. Exhaustion finally
steadied her breathing to the gentle rhythm of slumber. Gareth stared at the shadows of leaping firelight against the
wall, his chin resting on her silky head, fearful of moving
lest she realize he was not as frozen as he had believed. If
Lindsey Fordyce did not come soon, 'twould be he who
would need to be rescued from the silken snare of her embrace.

CHAPTER 9

Somewhere in its colorless sky, winter found its mercy and sent a reprieve with the melting of the snow. Beneath the vanishing snow, the land waited, silent and sleeping. Black branches stood naked and stark against the gray sky. Winter stripped of snow was an ugly creature, plain but habitable. Several of the guests at Caerleon took their polite leave, including the woman who had pronounced the castle cursed. Others followed Blaine's obstinate example and stayed on, filling their days with wagers over chess and draughts and their nights with Gareth's endless supply of ale.

The first day the list was no longer a sea of mud found Rowena and Marlys tilting at a battered quintain. Marlys flung herself on the back of her piebald mare and charged the scarred shield nailed to the post.

Her lance grazed the wooden shield, and the quintain went spinning. Rowena jumped up and down, clapping her hands, as Marlys guided her mount around the post before it could swing back and strike her. From where he sat on the gate, Blaine applauded dryly, though his eyes were not on Marlys.

Rowena's blond hair spilled over the stark black of garments that had once been Marlys's after they had been Gareth's for a very long time. The tunic hung well past Rowena's knees. Uneven patches dangled from tangled threads. She should have looked ridiculous, but her slender figure endowed the garments with an awkward grace like that of a regal jester, funny and heart-catching at the same time. Each time she jumped up and down, Blaine caught a milky glimpse of one knee within the torn hose. He shifted his weight and crossed his legs.

Rowena grabbed the shaggy mane before Marlys could finish dismounting and dragged herself on the horse's back.

"Suit yourself, Lady Precious." Marlys gave Rowena's rump a hearty shove, then jerked her tunic down. "Beware creeping garments. Blaine's tongue has wrapped itself around the fencepost."

Her words were just loud enough to carry across the list. Blaine waited until Rowena was facing the quintain before giving Marlys a friendly smile and an unfriendly gesture. Marlys slapped a lance in Rowena's palm. Rowena lowered her head with a frown of concentration. Her booted feet dug into the mare's sides. The horse surged forward. The shield flew toward her as if she were standing still and the quintain moving. Her lance struck the shield on the red heart painted in its center with an enviable thud.

She raised the lance in a salute of triumph and cantered around the quintain. She was a hoofbeat away from being clear of the careening post when she saw the dark figure standing behind Blaine. Her knees tightened convulsively, and the mare came to a dead halt. The quintain slammed into her back, neatly unseating her.

Blaine leaped off the fence, but it was Gareth with his long strides who reached her first. His hand gently cupped her neck, feeling for lumps beneath her hair. She tried to draw in a breath but could not; her lungs had gone hollow and empty. Only a squeak passed between her lips. She blinked up into Gareth's eyes, unable to speak or stir. Two other pairs of eyes joined his.

"Knocked the breath out of her," Marlys pronounced from somewhere above. "No need for the last rites yet. If the priest would come to Caerleon, that is. The vicious bastard's done it to me many a time."

It took Rowena a foggy moment to realize Marlys was

referring to the quintain, not the priest. Marlys struck the shield a savage blow of revenge.

Blaine's eyes burned an indignant brown next to Gareth's. " 'Tis your fault for letting the child amuse herself with this hoyden.''

"Safer for her to amuse herself with Marlys than with you,'' Gareth retorted.

His hands caught under Rowena's arms, and he lifted her to her feet. By that time she had gathered enough breath to speak and enough humiliation to wish she hadn't any breath at all.

"I am all right,'' she rasped. Her head ached and her mouth tasted like old blood, but she would not have confessed it for the world. She jerked out of Gareth's grip. She brushed herself off with jerky motions.

Gareth frowned. Blaine hid a smile behind his hand. Gareth's voice was gruff. "I came to inform you all that I've planned a feast for the morrow.''

Blaine snorted. "*You've* planned a feast?''

"Aye, my gallant friend. Since certain guests whose names will remain unmentioned show no sign of taking their leave from my castle, I've decided to invite some civilized folk of my own. I will expect to see each of you in the great hall tomorrow night.''

Gareth's sweeping gaze ended its sweep on Rowena. For a moment, she thought he would speak, but he did not. She turned to the mare with a motion that was an insult in its sharpness. She stroked the horse's quivering withers, hiding her blush. Gareth turned on his heel without another word and strode out of the list. Rowena led the mare into the stables, murmuring soft words into her mane.

Marlys squinted into the sunless sky. "Those two creep off to bed earlier than anyone else at Caerleon. How is it they awake with such foul tempers and dark circles under their eyes?''

Blaine growled at her under his breath. Marlys ducked his slap with a laugh that was almost girlish.

• • •

A rap sounded on the door. Rowena dropped the braid she was tidying. A vision of the hand on the other side of the door quickened her breathing. Powerful knuckles, laced with pale scars and dusted with dark hair. The knock sounded again.

"Enter," she said.

She rose. Gareth's dark presence filled the doorway. Their eyes met, and Rowena's cheeks flooded with a heat she despised. There was a difference to his gaze tonight. The cool distance was gone, replaced by something assessing and almost predatory. His smile did not reassure her.

He hefted an object of shimmering gold in one hand. "I brought you an adornment for your kirtle."

Rowena stood mesmerized by his bright, dark gaze as he approached. The strange excitement that touched him was almost palpable. He slipped behind her. Her lashes swept downward as his arms moved around her waist without touching her. She caught her breath at the sight of emeralds and amethysts sparkling up at her from a girdle of the finest gold. As he prepared to lower it to her hips, she caught his wrists in her hands.

"I've no need for such finery, milord. I have none of my own and would prefer not to wear someone else's."

Gareth paused. His warmth emanated to her back. His lips brushed the nape of her neck in a gesture as unconscious as the emotion that prompted it. Rowena shivered.

"This girdle has belonged to no one but you." Without awaiting her protest, he lowered the gilded weight to her hips. His deft fingers brushed the small of her back as he hooked the clasp. Rowena wondered if he was lying.

Warm hands grasped her shoulders. Gareth turned her around to face him. She stared up into the shadows of his face, finding an uneasy heat in his tightened jaw, his arched brows. Without a word, he untied the thongs binding her braids. He dragged his fingers through each plait until her hair lay in a shining curtain around her shoulders. Rowena's scalp tingled.

"Wear your hair loose tonight." His words were soft, but the tone of command was unmistakable.

He turned at the door with a frown, then closed the door behind him. Was it a shadow of regret she read in his eyes?

Rowena tripped over a silver chain stretched taut across the lowest stair. She followed it to its source and clapped a hand over her mouth, stifling a shriek. A toothless bear sat beside the stairs, furry legs spread on the stones like a child playing ball. A wimple fixed with a flowing veil sat atop his shaggy head. At second glance, the bear did not look nearly so fierce—only mangy and somewhat embarrassed. A dwarf cavorted on the other side of the stairs. He held the chain up so a line of ladies could pass beneath its links, then dove under one of their skirts. They scattered with delighted squeals. Mortimer's steady strumming drowned out all but the most determined shouts of laughter.

As Rowena passed a trestle table laden with food, she plucked a dripping honeycomb from a bowl and tossed it to the bear, remembering what it felt like to be alone and hungry at such a feast. He caught it between his clumsy paws and sat happily sucking the honey from its combs.

Rowena tucked her fingers in her mouth and lapped at the sticky sweetness. She met Gareth's gaze across the teeming hall. A shock as warm and brilliant as lightning passed between them. Warmth flooded her body. The word she had sought for the change in him rose unbidden to her mind.

Possession.

It was written in his eyes, in every elegant line of his being. For some unknown reason, Sir Gareth of Caerleon had chosen to play lord of the manor that night.

He sat at the end of the hall with one foot propped in a massive carved chair Rowena had never noticed before. The thronelike seat would have dwarfed a lesser man, but its lines and curves only enhanced the edge of dangerous masculinity held in check by Gareth. He was garbed all in black threaded with silver. The king of the underworld himself could not have looked more regal and striking than Gareth at that moment. When he cocked his head at her, she floated to him as if she were his Persephone, bound by an invisible chain.

Rowena felt other eyes on her as she picked her way among the dancers. She curtsied before Gareth and felt the shimmering weight of her hair on her shoulders. He brought her hand to his lips. Instead of kissing her palm, his tongue curled between her fingers as he licked the last vestige of honey away.

"My sweet," he murmured. Rowena pulled her hand back, as shocked as if he had bitten her. Most nights went by without one word of acknowledgment from him.

A cushion spread with furs lay at Gareth's feet. He indicated it with a mocking nod and Rowena sank down, fearing him for a new reason. Her pounding heart confirmed that she would never have the strength to survive a genuine attempt at seduction.

Afraid to turn and meet his gaze, Rowena studied the faces she did not recognize. Two very familiar faces danced to a halt in front of them. Blaine bowed. The Lady Alise gripped his arm as if he might somehow slide out of her grasp.

"You have outdone yourself, Gareth," Blaine said with an admiring glance around the hall.

"Nonsense. I've outdone you. 'Tis what truly vexes you," Gareth replied.

Blaine lifted a hand in a masculine salute. "Look. There by the door. Sir Martain, the Duke of Gloucester giggling with Marlys. And there is the Earl of Medford prowling around the pudding. I half expect the door to fly open and the king to stroll in."

"Edward is in France. He sent his regrets." Gareth plucked a goblet off a passing tray. "However, you will find the Prince of Wales in the midst of the hot cockles game."

Blaine paled in envy. The lines around his smile deepened. Their gazes followed Gareth's to find a willowy young man with his head resting on a lady's lap. Nothing was visible beneath his blindfold but a mass of frizzy blond curls. Black and white squares checkered his surcoat, making Rowena dizzy to look at him.

"The lad resembles a chessboard," Alise said. "Pray tell, is he your mysterious guest of honor?" Her nose was tilted so high in the air Rowena could see nothing but the delicate flare of her nostrils.

Gareth shrugged. "Perhaps Bartholemew the Bear will take the seat of honor."

"Bartholemew is a fine fellow, is he not?" Rowena chimed in. "When I first came down the stairs, I thought he was Marlys, but his melancholy eyes showed me I was mistaken. My heart went out to him. A fine fellow like he must be mortified to be wearing that ridiculous wimple." She giggled. "I would cower under the stairs myself if I had to wear such a silly structure on my head."

There was a beat of silence. Too late Rowena realized the flowing tower perched on Alise's head was identical to the one Bartholemew wore. Alise's nostrils flared large enough to swallow her. Blaine cleared his throat.

Gareth lifted a strand of her hair, and it flowed through his fingers like liquid gold. "Very observant of you, dear. Bartholemew is a fine fellow. He eats far fewer guests than Blaine's fish."

Rowena bowed her head, wishing the bear would trundle over and eat her. A florid man in a feathered cap paused to exchange pleasantries with Gareth. As the glib conversation went on above her, Rowena tired of studying Alise's slippers and began to arrange her own skirt in neat folds. She had the soft camlet laid out in a perfect fan when the door swept open again, and a line of colorless shapes slumped into the hall. Rowena's heart started an uneven rhythm.

"What might this be?" Blaine murmured. "A peasant revolt?"

"Revolting indeed," Alise said.

The new guests slunk around the hall as if their colorless rags might allow them to fade into the stone. But at the end of their unobtrusive parade walked a slender figure whose straight shoulders and cap of silver-blond hair would not let him melt away like the others.

Rowena had half risen when Gareth's hand slipped beneath her hair and tightened on her neck. She shot him an agonized look. His face revealed nothing, but the subtle bite of his fingers forced her back down.

Lindsey Fordyce, Baron of Revelwood, strutted into the hall behind his seven sons and one nephew, his plum chausses and yellow tunic marking him as a garish peacock to their sparrows. His eyes darted from side to side. His hands twisted one against another. When Mortimer broke into the violent chorus of a *chanson de geste*, he jumped straight into the air. Little Freddie's gray eyes slid over the crowd. It was he who spotted Rowena sitting at Gareth's feet. His nudge went down the line, rocking his brothers like a wave until it exploded against Fordyce with a thump on the skull from Big Freddie.

Papa's eyes lit with benevolent welcome. Before Rowena could raise her trembling hand, Gareth tilted her chin between his thumb and forefinger, forcing Rowena to stare up at him. Bewilderment lit the darkest corners of her eyes. He leaned over and touched his mouth to hers. His moustache tickled her nose. The warm smoothness of his lips brushed the corner of her mouth in a teasing caress. Too surprised to resist, her lips parted beneath his. He turned his head from side to side, drawing a feathery threat with his tongue as a weapon until he felt the tiny, white ramparts of her teeth part to draw him inside to some moist, sweet part of her that had never been touched.

A shudder twisted Gareth's gut. He tried to pull away, but a fragile thread of tenderness and longing held him fast. When he finally freed her, it was he who had to look away. He sank back in the chair. He snatched a goblet off the tray Dunnla offered, drained it, then took another.

Rowena felt the dig of his knee against her shoulder blade. She plucked the last goblet off the tray to occupy her shaking hands, splashing ale heedlessly on her skirt. Blaine led Alise away, his smile as fixed as her grimace. Papa stood frozen by the door. Rowena waited for him to cross the hall to her, to come and bid his only daughter a greeting. He glanced over his shoulder at the arrow slits set high on the walls as if expecting a feathered plume to shoot backward and embed itself in his back. Rowena watched in amazement as he shooed the boys toward the overflowing tables and bowed to a plump woman sitting along the wall. They joined the dance, the woman's cheeks patches of scarlet at his flowery prattle.

Rowena's brothers cleared three tables of all but bones in a matter of minutes. Dunnla shuffled in, shook her head in exasperation and went back for more food. Gareth's dark eyes brooded over the hall. He stroked his beard with one hand, ever conscious of the blond head bent at his knee and the faded gold of her papa's bobbing across his hall.

It took Papa two flagons of ale, six galloping turns at the dance, and a bawdy ditty to gather his courage and three of his kin and approach Gareth's chair.

Rowena followed Little Freddie's path toward them as if his shining head were a beacon. She would have risen again had not Gareth chosen that moment to gently cup her cheek with one hand in a proprietary gesture that reminded her oddly of the way he handled Folio.

The crowd cleared before Papa's strut. The foot he dragged behind him only served to put more bounce in his step. The ladies murmured behind their sleeves at the hulking creature that followed him.

Behind Big Freddie trailed Irwin with a nervous chorus of, "Pardon me. Pardon me. Do pardon me. I beg your forgiveness, milady. 'Twas not my intention to trod upon your train. Do forgive me." He kept this up until he stumbled into Big Freddie's back and Little Freddie stomped his shin.

Fordyce gave Gareth a sweeping bow. Irwin stared down at Rowena from a height she did not remember. From this angle, his legs looked less like sausages. But his rapt gaze held the familiar adoration that still turned her stomach.

Papa ignored her. "My dear Sir Gareth," he began, his voice cracking. He coughed, spat on the floor, and continued. "I cannot begin to express our honor at your kind invitation. We feared the snow would detain us, but God has been kind and carried us unscathed to Caerleon."

"I always said He had a wicked sense of humor," Gareth replied. His fingers stroked Rowena's cheek with the expertise of a diabolical minstrel. Her heart skipped more beats than it hit.

Papa tittered and wiped spittle from his moist lips with the back of his hand. "Not as wicked as yours, kind sir."

By poking her foot out from under her skirt, Rowena was able to touch Little Freddie's ankle with her toe. Her kid shoe was as white as snow against the bound rags that served as his excuse for shoes. A quick, bright glance was his only betrayal of her touch.

"Do you still find Caerleon to your liking, Fordyce?" Gareth drained his goblet and let it fall to the stones with a thump.

Rowena's father peered around with the jaundiced eye of a potential buyer. "A bit large for my tastes. I prefer a more cozy abode for my lads. Keep 'em humble, I say."

Big Freddie shuffled his feet as if pondering the charms of humility.

"Do you find Caerleon as you remember it?" Gareth added.

Fordyce cleared his throat. " 'Twas many years ago I served your father. My memory fails me."

Rowena gave a quizzical frown. "You served Gareth's fath—"

Gareth's fingers tightened imperceptibly on her cheek. He turned his hand, and the back of it glided down her throat.

Papa's eyes dropped for an instant to the seductive motion.
Rowena stared into her lap. Little Freddie swallowed hard.

Gareth leaned forward, impaling Papa with his dark gaze.
His other hand caressed the silver hilt of his sword. Irwin
took an involuntary step backward.

"Mayhaps there is need I refresh your memory," Gareth
said.

Papa looked wildly behind him as if a horde of knights
were going to rush out of the crowd and skewer him.
Mortimer's lute fell silent for the first time that night. The
minstrel pretended to tune it, watching Gareth through a
limp curtain of hair.

Fordyce rubbed his head, fluffing his scant hair into tufts.
"Before my unfortunate accident, I sold my services to
many men. Your father was only one of them. I cannot be
expected to remember everything, can I? Caerleon is but
the shadow of a memory to me. What difference does it
make? Did I mention our gift? We've brought you a gift to
show our honor." He clapped his hands together. "Gifts,
Freddie, bring on the gifts!"

Big Freddie and Little Freddie struggled over a burlap
sack. Papa boxed Irwin's ears for standing there with his
mouth open and snatched the bag. He waved it with a flourish. The rusty goblet from the mantel at Revelwood rolled
into the folds of Rowena's skirt. In her embarrassment, she
forgot the havoc Gareth was wreaking with her heartbeat.
She reached to throw a corner of her kirtle over the goblet,
but Gareth's boot came down neatly beside her fingers.

"Charming," he said dryly, nudging the relic with his
foot. "But not nearly as charming as the other gift you
provided me."

Before Rowena could do more than gasp, Gareth's hand
slid into the bodice of her kirtle. She felt the shock of his
warm hand cupping her bare breast; his fingers fondled her
with crass familiarity. Papa's eyes widened. Irwin's face
went as plum as Papa's chausses. But worst of all was the

steady motion of Little Freddie's fists clenching and un-
clenching.

Rowena flushed scarlet, and her hand came up in an in-
stinctive gesture of outrage. She intended to strike Gareth
but had forgotten the goblet in her hand. As it passed in
front of her eyes, she hurled its contents straight into his
face. He blinked stupidly at her, ale dripping from his brow
to his chin. Then his lips tightened and he snatched her up
by the hair, dragging her between his knees until all she
could see were eyes darkened to jet by burning rage. Her
jaw was set in an anger as deep as his own.

Someone coughed, and the sound echoed clearly in the
silence of drawn-and-held breaths. Gareth tore his gaze from
Rowena to find a hall of eyes filled with sly satisfaction.
They had waited for this moment for almost twenty years.
Waited for his iron control to snap. Waited for a glimpse of
the man who had murdered Elayne of Touraine in her bed.
And Rowena had given it to them.

His hand slowly relaxed its grip in her hair.

"Begone," he said between clenched teeth. "To your
chamber."

She held herself rigidly against his knees to keep from
falling. For a moment, he thought she would defy him, then
she bowed her head and said softly, "As you wish, milord."

Every neck in the hall craned to follow her path through
the crowd and up the stairs. Her head was modestly bent,
but her back was painfully straight.

It was Marlys who broke the silence with a round of
mocking applause. "Now, Mortimer. Can you give us any
entertainment as grand as that?"

"I think not. Perhaps you'd best turn to Bartholemew the
Bear. He is a better man than I."

"Marlys is a better man than you," someone called out
to the accompanying hoots of the crowd.

No one dared look at Gareth as he wiped away the last
traces of ale with his sleeve. Lindsey Fordyce backed into

the crowd, dragging Irwin and Little Freddie by their collars. As the dwarf led Bartholemew into the center of the floor, Gareth took the goblet Blaine offered him and drained it. His burning gaze followed Fordyce's blundering path through the hall, but he found his eyes powerfully drawn again to the top of the stairs.

CHAPTER 10

Gareth stumbled past the door of the chamber he had occupied since he was a boy, then backed up. He groped for the handle. His head rapped the door frame as he ducked through the door. With a groan, he kicked the door shut. He stood with head down like an ox ready to charge. The ale he had consumed to blunt the edge of his anger might as well have been water as his fury churned at the sight before him.

Rowena did not pace before the fire wringing her hands. Nor did she cower at the window, her brow darkened with the fear of their confrontation. Instead she lay sleeping, nestled in the center of the vast bed like an angel in a cloud of fur. Her golden hair roamed untrammeled across his pillow. Her brow was smooth and sweet, untroubled by even the hint of fretful dreams. The sheer audacity of it dragged a growl from deep in Gareth's throat.

With one hand, he grasped the edge of the furs beneath her and jerked. Rowena rolled rudely onto the floor.

"Ha!" Gareth hoisted the pelts like a flag of triumph.

Rowena sat up, blinking and rubbing her elbow. The sight of Gareth would have quelled his staunchest adversary. He stood with feet slightly apart, his usually impeccable garments rumpled and stained. His hair stood out in wild tufts, untamed by fingers or comb. The scent of danger rolled off him with the scent of ale.

"My bed," he snarled through bared teeth.

He pulled his surcoat and tunic over his head. The pelts went sailing back toward the bed. Without removing his hose, he threw himself after them. The bed rocked with his weight.

Rowena sat in wide-eyed silence for a moment, pondering his timely disappearance. She shrugged and curled up on the stones with no pelt to cushion or cover her. Shivering, she rolled to her back. She had never realized how many sharp edges the stones possessed. A solid lump poked at the base of her spine. A perverse calm claimed her.

"You had no right," she said softly.

She was hardly aware she had spoken aloud until Gareth's incredulous face appeared over the edge of the bed. "What did you say?"

She met his gaze with perfect serenity. "I said you had no right. To touch me that way in front of my papa."

"No right? *No right?*" Gareth climbed off the bed knee over knee. Rowena scrambled backward, but his hands caught in the wool of her bliaut. Her feet left the floor as he picked her up and slammed her to the feather tick. "I had no right? Let me inform you of a few facts about my rights, sweet Lady Rowena Fordyce."

His eyes were very close to hers. Only his elbows resting on either side of her head kept his weight from falling against her.

"I won you in an honorable game of chance. Your bastard of a father wagered you as any decent man would a cow or a parcel of land. You belong to me. I have the right to do whatever I please with you, and I've had that right from the first day I laid eyes on you. If I care to drag you down those stairs and spread your legs at your precious papa's feet, 'tis my right. Not a man in the hall would dare condemn me for it."

Her aching pride made Rowena careless. "They condemn you for other things, do they not?"

Gareth's eyes narrowed into the eyes of a stranger. Rowena tried to turn her face away, but he caught her chin in one hand. "Watch your tongue, girl. I've quaffed enough ale tonight to ravish five maidens before dawn without a qualm of conscience."

"If you've quaffed that much ale, you're probably not able," she retorted.

"Try me."

He lowered his lean warrior's body with a deliberate motion, and Rowena felt an unfamiliar hardness graze her abdomen. Her eyes widened. It was a cruel thing to do, but Gareth never went into battle without showing his weapons. Her skin shrank from the crude caress. The wool and linen between them was suddenly like so much parchment.

Rowena bit her lip and blinked back tears. "Do you seek to make me what you would have Papa believe I am?"

Her tears were as sobering as a dash of cold water. Gareth buried his face in her hair to hide their effect on him. "I know what you are. I've known your kind before. All soft and sweet and as deadly as poisoned honey. If your father only knew what restraint I've used . . ." The heat of his lips brushed her temple.

"Do not mock me," she choked out. "The only thing you've used is me. You invited my papa here so you could humiliate the both of us in your little game. You dragged my family here in the dead of winter, half-starved and freezing, knowing they could be trapped by a snowstorm at any time."

"Why do you defend your papa?" he murmured against her hair.

"Why do you hate him?"

Gareth made no reply. His mouth glided over the tiny hairs at her temple and down to the corner of her mouth.

"Have you lodged my family in the next chamber?" She was desperate to stop him before she tasted the ale on his tongue. "The better to hear my pleas and screams? Nay, Gareth, if you will make a whore out of me, you shall do it in silence, for I swear not one whimper will escape my lips."

He caught her hands in his and held them captive on each side of her head. "If you think I could not make you cry out, you are wrong." A dark hint in his eyes warned her that it was not pain he threatened.

Rowena caught half a breath before his lips descended on hers. She steeled herself against his kiss, preparing herself to be punished and hurt. But she had not prepared herself for the tenderness of his assault. As his mouth met hers, the violence left his body with a wracking shudder, to be replaced by a gentleness as disarming as it was potent. His tongue tasted her lips, then dipped inward in a leisurely exploration of the sweetness within. When his fingers laced around hers, Rowena held on, clinging to the one thing of substance that kept her from drowning in a luxuriant sea of fur and sensation.

He lowered his body against hers, thigh to thigh, belly to belly, balancing his weight perfectly to keep from crushing her. His dark head glided downward, pushing her bliaut away until his mouth tenderly grazed the peak of her breast in a caress that had no relation to his crass pawing in the great hall. Her skin shivered and contracted beneath his tongue. She moaned softly as pleasure and shame quickened within her.

The low sound brought Gareth's head up. Rowena's eyes were clenched shut. He freed her hands and cupped her chin in his palm. She opened her eyes. A cloud of tears could not dim their brilliance. The trust with which she had met his kiss in the great hall still shone within, battered and bruised but unsurrendered. He had seen that look once before in blue eyes welling with tears. Her trust was a formidable enemy. It had conquered death and poverty and betrayal with a dignity he could barely understand. Now it would conquer him. If he had been a man who begged, he might have pleaded with Rowena then and there to open herself and let him slake his bitterness in her healing warmth.

She snuffled softly.

He rolled off her without a word and sat on the edge of the bed.

A terrible coldness pricked Rowena where his body had been. She hugged her bliaut to her neck and sat up, biting a lip that felt tender and swollen.

Her fingertips touched one of the rigid scars on the smooth plane of his back. "Gareth, please . . ."

He flinched as if her touch had scorched him. For her to beg now was more than he could bear. "Go away, won't you? Leave me be."

If Gareth could have guessed what Rowena's plea was going to be, his response might have been very different. She had opened her mouth to beg for any kindness, for a hint of his smile, for the courteous attention he had waved before her like sugar before a starving child. She was willing to pay any price to stop him from turning his back on her. At his words her hand fell away from him like a dying flower.

Silence followed, then the soft pad of her feet against the stone. The door creaked open.

Gareth did not have to turn to sense the straightness of her spine, the hurt pride locked in her voice. "I may not be able to spell my own name, but I am not so foolish as to be blind to the truth. There is only one man in all of England you would hate so well. The knight you caught with your precious Elayne."

Gareth wanted to turn and shout the truth at her. To cross the chamber and shake her until she opened her eyes and saw her father for what he was. Instead, he stared at the back of his hands.

"Despite your feelings for Papa, you've treated me with nothing but kindness since bringing me to Caerleon. Why you would have him believe otherwise, I do not know. I cannot fathom what I've done to make you hate me so." The door sank into its frame with a final thump.

"I don't hate you," Gareth said to the empty chamber.

The words that followed were only a whisper in his mind as he buried his aching head in his palms.

Rowena wandered the endless corridors, deaf to all but the sputter of the ebbing torches. The snores and moans that drifted out from behind the closed doors held the cadence of unreality in the darkest morning hours, like echoes from a time long past. The shadowy corridors grew longer and longer.

"Holy Mother of God," she swore as Marlys erupted from the darkness of a doorway. The oath coming from Rowena's lips stopped Marlys in her tracks. "Spare me your offended glare, Marlys. Did it never occur to you that I am sick to death of you stalking me like the grim reaper? I weary of it."

Marlys stepped in front of her, but Rowena shoved past her easily. "Leave me be." She echoed Gareth's words without realizing it.

"Wait." Marlys caught her arm. "There is someone you must see."

Rowena glanced over Marlys's shoulder where a heavy door stood ajar. She shrugged Marlys's grip away. "Another of your twisted jests? Have you Blaine lurking inside to ravish me? Or mayhaps the ghost of Lady Elayne cowering on the bed with a sword through her breast?"

Beneath dark strands of hair, Marlys paled. "Rowena, please."

Begging did not suit Marlys. Rowena slid her hand under Marlys's hair and flipped it back. Marlys flinched. Rowena could find no trace of laughter or mockery in her face. Surprised by her own cruelty, she freed the hair, then gave a curt nod. Marlys gripped her arm and drew her forward.

Her nose twitched at the odor of stale rosemary. The blue pall of daylight was gone from the chamber. In its place were the flickering shadows cast from a tallow candle shuttered by translucent slices of horn. Rowena strained her eyes to see. The door slammed. The cupboard door creaked open, and hot, wet lips sucked at her cheek. For an instant, she believed once again that Marlys had betrayed her. But even Blaine at his crudest could not compare to the lack of finesse in this kiss.

Her hand curled into a fist and crashed into the head attached to her cheek.

"Aaaargh!" Irwin reeled backward, clutching his ear. "Gads, Rowena, no need to deafen me, you know. I had hoped you had abandoned your violent ways for a gentler demeanor."

"That scene in the great hall should have warned you differently," came a boy's voice rippling with laughter. "If she'd toss ale in an earl's face, I shudder to think what she'd do to you."

Rowena glanced wildly around the chamber. The pale sheen she had been searching for glided into view. Little Freddie found his way into her arms.

"There now," he said, patting her back awkwardly. "No need for tears. We've come to make it all better."

Rowena's tears soaked his shoulder. She knew the time when things could have been cured by optimism had long passed. Irwin stole a pat but jerked his hand away when she turned her watery glare on him. Big Freddie shuffled forward. Cobwebs draped his ducked head.

Rowena sat on the edge of the musty counterpane, smothering the last of her sniffles in a rag torn from Big Freddie's sleeve. Marlys stood leaning against the door with arms crossed.

"This familial display of devotion is touching," she drawled, "but I must remind you that haste is of the essence. Gareth's stupors are short and his temper fierce when he awakens."

Rowena was hard pressed to imagine his temper any more fierce than it had been moments ago. Irwin knelt on one knee at her feet. He *had* grown taller since she had seen him last. His innate plumpness was betrayed by the round fingers that clasped Rowena's own. The beginnings of a moustache fuzzed his lip.

He beamed up at her. "We have come to rescue you."

"You mean Papa regrets his wager? He has come to carry me home?"

Irwin cleared his throat. Big Freddie glared at his feet as if he found them offensive.

Little Freddie stepped forward, loving her too much for kindness. "Papa is tucked under a table in the great hall, snoring soundly. He wants no part of our plan."

"But surely if you told him—" Rowena started.

"We did," Little Freddie said flatly.

"I see." Rowena tried to withdraw her hand, but Irwin held it fast with a strength that surprised her.

His eyes devoured her face. "I'm not sure that you do. I am still your betrothed, Rowena. We have been betrothed since we were but children. I hold fast to that oath. I care not what that beastly wretch has done to you. I am willing to overlook any defilement, any breach of innocence you bring to our marriage bed."

Marlys's cough sounded more like a shout of laughter. In that moment Rowena hated her. She resisted the urge to plant her foot in Irwin's chest. Her gaze dropped. He was kneeling in the center of the dark stain that spread from the bed to the stones—the last trace of the life that had dripped away on that night so long ago.

"How kind," she said faintly.

She rose, slipping out of his grasp like a wraith. She brushed past Big Freddie. More by instinct than sight, her hands found the heavy velvet folds draped over the windows. She drew them back and slipped into their shelter. Her hands fumbled with the shutters. Fresh, cold wind poured past her and into the chamber, sending the drapes into a lashing dance. Her hands clutched the stone wall. Before the voice could sound low and pervasive in her ear, she knew who it would belong to.

"Did he whisper sweet endearments to you? Murmur of marriage? Plight his troth?"

That picture was so far from the truth of their encounter that Rowena had to close her eyes.

The voice went on. "He will use you if you stay. The winter nights are long and cold. Even a monk would be sorely pressed to resist a chit as convenient as you. He might even be kind to you. When he tired of you, he would send you on your way with a few trinkets, a family brooch, a brotherly kiss."

Marlys's diatribe died on a hiss. Her voice softened. "I shield my face because I have no desire to be a man's chattel. Every time my father looked at me, he saw nothing more than a future alliance with Blaine's father. Be it whore or wife in merry old England, a woman is still a man's property—his toy. Is that what you wish for your life, Lady Precious?"

Rowena opened her eyes. Every line of the courtyard below was drawn with painful clarity. Beneath the empty boughs of an oak, four horses milled on their tethers. All she wished for was yesterday when the tenuous thread between she and Gareth had not been laced with revenge.

Marlys's gaze dropped to Rowena's stomach. "What if he should get you with babe? Gareth does not fancy children. He despised Elayne's babe."

The courtyard blurred. Rowena brought a strand of hair to her lips. She kept her tone light, refusing to betray the cost of a question that had been niggling at the back of her mind for weeks. "What became of the child when Elayne died?"

Marlys gently pulled the hairs from Rowena's lips. "No one knows. The child disappeared on the night Elayne was murdered. Some say Gareth strangled her and buried her in the orchard."

Rowena's fingernails dug into the stone. The chestnut mare in the courtyard tossed its head with a soft nicker. Rowena gripped Marlys's hand. "Will you help us?"

Marlys nodded.

"Papa . . ." Rowena began.

"I shall get him free of Caerleon before Gareth can kill him. He deserves no more."

"And what of you?"

White teeth flashed in a grin more carnivorous than human. "Gareth cannot kill me. He loves me."

Little Freddie was standing outside the curtains. Rowena knew he had heard every word. He extended an arm to her. "Shall we go home?"

"Home," Rowena repeated. "To Revelwood."

"Keep off the main roads," Marlys commanded. "Stay away from Revelwood for at least a week. The bread will last if you are sparing. Eat only when you are hungry." This gained her a dubious glance from Irwin.

"Must we steal the mounts?" Rowena said from the back of the chestnut mare.

"Would you care to be run down by Folio?" Marlys arched one eyebrow. "Or hunted by Gareth's wolfhounds? Most of them are trained to kill, you know." Rowena did not know and wished she had not asked. "Anyway," Marlys added with a smirk, "I'd never allow you to steal our horses. These mounts belong to Blaine. Even if he catches you, a flutter of those eyelashes would probably save you from the hangman."

She jerked Rowena down by the neck of her woolen kirtle. Her eyes nervously scanned the horizon. Between the stark branches of the trees, the black sky melted to gray. "Heed my words well. Don't let him find you. Gareth hates to lose anything that belongs to him."

Rowena straightened in the saddle. "Soften the blow, won't you? Tell him I never belonged to him at all."

Marlys nodded with an approving smile. Rowena had to grab the bridle with both hands as Marlys smacked the mare's rump with a hoarse cry. The mare bolted. The other horses followed, stretching their long legs in an exuberant canter toward freedom. The damp, chill air filled Rowena's lungs but failed to drive out the oppressive heaviness in her breast as she left behind the shadow of Caerleon and its master forever.

PART II

Western wind, when will thou blow,
The small rain down can rain?
Christ, if my love were in my arms
And I in my bed again!

—*Anonymous*

CHAPTER 11

Marlys tumbled into bed with a groan. The flat, pale sun had done little to warm her chamber. She thought of reaching to the end of the bed to drag the coverlet over her, but the contemplation of such motion after finally laying down her aching bones drew another groan from her throat. She threw herself on her face and burrowed deep into the feather tick.

"Marlys!"

The bellow warned her before the thunderous rapping exploded on her door. With a last spurt of energy, she flopped over and dove headfirst into the counterpane bunched at the foot of the bed. The door crashed open. She curled into a ball, knowing the inert lump she had become had little chance of fooling her brother. She was right. The flat side of his sword smacked into her rump with a twang that sent the blade vibrating into song.

She popped up with a growl. "Suppose you had inadvertently whacked the wrong end? You would have brained me."

"Methinks there are as much brains in one end as in the other," Gareth shot back. He faced her like a savage twin, his hair tangled in a dark web around his face, his eyes red-rimmed and wild. "Where are they?"

"Who?" Marlys sank back on her knees and gathered the coverlets around her shoulders like a shawl.

"You know who. Fordyce and his damnable litter of pups."

"How should I know? I was abed as soon as Dunnla gave me my milk bath and coiffed my curls."

One eye fluttered prettily at him. Gareth plucked a twig from her matted hair. "A new fashion, I suppose?" His gaze dropped to the feet poking out from under the blanket. Their soles were as black as the grubby tunic she wore from yesterday. She jerked them back. He grabbed her big toe and twisted.

She howled.

"Where?" Gareth demanded.

She pounded on his shoulders with open palms until he freed her toe. "What do you care of Lindsey Fordyce's comings and goings? You could have tossed him in the dungeon last night if you were hoping for public confession. 'Twas you who chose to torture Rowena instead of him."

He had the good grace to color. " 'Twas Rowena's insolence that demanded my attention. Fordyce had enough ale in him to keep for a few hours. He was fair pickled 'ere I went abovestairs."

"As were you."

Gareth chose to ignore that. "If not for your cursed interference, the fool would've slept till I was ready to conclude our dealings."

"He has no dealings with you. You heard him. He barely recalls holding Father's fief."

"We both know he lies." His shaggy head bent over her as his voice lowered. "If you do not tell me where they are, I swear I shall see you married to Blaine yet. The priest may not come to Caerleon, but I shall have you dragged before him. 'Twould suit Blaine's sadistic streak to finally have a chance at taming you."

Marlys gave an injured sniff but Gareth knew her well enough to duck before her hand whistled past his jaw. He caught her fist in his. "Shall I have the joyful banns of your

upcoming nuptials read in the village? Or would you prefer
to tell me what you've done with Fordyce?''

Marlys glared up at him. ''The bandy-legged little rooster
has gone scampering for home.''

Gareth loosed her and started for the door. Marlys buried
her mouth in her knee, muffling her words. ''Let the puppy
go, Gareth.''

Gareth stopped. ''What did you say?''

Marlys lifted her head. A woolen fuzz from the coverlet
clung to her tongue. Gareth turned. His face had gone white.
Marlys realized she had made a terrible mistake, but it was
too late to bite back the words.

A pained bewilderment twisted Gareth's features. ''You
let him take Rowena?''

Her brother's vulnerability was more than Marlys could
bear. She summoned a smirk to her lips with an effort he
would never see. ''She begged I give you a message. 'Soften
the blow,' she said with that tinkling little laugh of hers.
'Tell him I never belonged to him anyway.' ''

Gareth's breathing was suddenly the only sound audible
in the chamber. With mingled relief and regret, Marlys
watched a cold mask of fury slip over his features.

His hands balled into fists. ''When I get my hands on
her, I shall leave no doubt in her mind as to whom she
belongs to.''

Marlys stretched out her long limbs and rested her head
on laced hands. ''You should have thought of that before
she fled from you. A dark-eyed bastard in her belly would
have kept your memory fresh.'' She watched him through
slitted eyes, expecting a curse, or maybe even a blow. The
speculative gleam in his eyes frightened her. She rolled to
her side with an indifferent yawn. ''Tell Dunnla if she dis-
turbs me before nightfall, I shall cut off her head.''

''Aaaah, the sleep of the innocent. Free of any unsightly
twinges of conscience.''

''I told you long ago. I have no conscience.''

''For once,'' Gareth said, ''I must agree.''

The door softly closed and Gareth was gone. Marlys jumped out of bed and stumbled to her knees before the window. A moment later, Gareth appeared far below leading Folio out of the stables at a run. Without slowing, he flung a long leg over the stallion's back and drove him through the castle gates.

"Ride hard, little one," Marlys murmured. "Ride as if the devil himself were on your heels." She knelt there as if in prayer until her knees went numb. Her callused knuckles dashed away her tears before they could splash on the stones.

Lindsey Fordyce swore under his breath as he slid off the nag for the third time. His bad leg throbbed. He lay on the frozen dirt like an amiable cherub swaddled in scarves from toe to brow. The illusion was shattered when he opened his mouth and a new string of curses spewed forth. His sons loped to his rescue, tugging him to his feet and dusting him off with hamlike hands. Two of the boys rewound a scarf over his pink-tipped nose and across his eyes.

He clawed at the scarf. "God's nightgown, why don't the lot of you just throw me on the ground and smother me? Are you in that much haste to gain your inheritance?"

The boys looked at each other blankly, then broke into grins. They nudged the dirt with toes poking out of their rags. Fordyce shook his head. "Scold you and you grin. If I thrash you, will you laugh?" He shook his fist at the shuffling circle of giants, then thought better of it.

He satisfied himself with kicking the nag in the knee. The beast rolled its eyes but did not flinch. "I cannot fathom where that chit found such a creature. 'Tis not fit to feed the vultures. More carrion than horse, I say. But the chit was more man than woman if you ask me. Wouldn't surprise me if she were hiding a healthy moustache beneath all that hair. She was a beastly little girl, too, always tagging after that arrogant brother of hers. You there—William. Nay, Phillip. Whatever the hell your name is, hasten over here and help me mount."

The hulking lad he pointed to got down on hands and knees. Fordyce trundled up on his back, heedless of the dig of his heels into his son's ribs. He laid across the horse with a solid "oomph." His rounded gut fit neatly into the hollow of the horse's spine. The other four boys pushed him into place as their brother lay gasping for air.

The ribbon of road unfolded through the massive trunks of trees scarred with winter's grayness. The ancient forest had lost none of its menace with its leaves. An aura of stillness and decay hung over it like the pall of the sun pasted in the gray sky. Fordyce rubbed his dripping nose on his scarf, his temper unimproved by the memory of the warm hall he had been forced to desert as dawn had claimed the skies.

He might still be languishing there now if that hairy creature had not thrust his tunic in his hand, hissing of danger and flight. His regret sharpened with the chill in the air. He had so hoped to deepen his acquaintance with that ample widow he had danced with the night before. Images of pleasant days spent living off de Crecy's food, ale, and hospitality rolled before his eyes to be obliterated by the narrow road leading back to Revelwood. He considered sending the boys on and braving a return to Caerleon. His squat trunk followed the direction of his thoughts, pivoting on the horse so he could peruse the ancient Roman road they had traveled from Caerleon.

Rowena had done well enough for herself there. She had sat like a princess on a throne of furs at Sir Gareth's feet. Why should her father be responsible if she had thrown a tantrum and ran off to sulk? Surely a man as reasonable as Sir Gareth would not blame him for the folly of a woman. Rowena had probably trotted back to the castle at first hint of dawn and was even now cuddled in the knight's arms, begging prettily for his forgiveness.

If he returned to Caerleon, he and Gareth would raise a mug around the fire and toast the stubbornness of women. A smile played around his lips. 'Twould not be the first time they could ruminate one with another over the fickle heart of a woman.

He was still lost in this pleasant reverie when a nightmare garbed in black rounded the bend and hurtled down the long stretch straight for him.

Ignoring the open-mouthed mutters of his sons, he slammed his heels into the nag's flanks. The horse did not betray itself with even a breath. A frantic glance over his shoulder showed the dark shape looming larger, riding as one with a white beast whose heels skimmed the earth as if winged.

Fordyce bounced up and down to jog the horse into motion. The nag shuddered and leaned backward. For one terrible moment, Fordyce feared it would sit down, dumping him onto the packed earth for the fourth time. The nag swayed but held firm. He wrested a rusty dagger from his waistband and drew the blade neatly across the nag's hide. With a bray of pain, the horse lurched forward in an uneven canter Fordyce would have thought impossible seconds before.

He heard the cries of his sons and dared a look back to see them trotting after him, arms upraised. Almost upon them was the thundering shadow. With a chuckle of glee, he humped over, his heels beating a sharp staccato against the nag's ribs. His next look back showed the boys staring after him, limp-handed and open-mouthed. He twisted around, gripping wisps of mane to hold his seat. The stretch of road between them was empty. The dark rider had vanished.

A flash of pure black out of the corner of his eye warned him. His pursuer was no longer behind him. He wheeled around with a choked squeal as a muscled arm shot out and curved around his windpipe. The nag galloped on without him, finding a grace it had forgotten in the freedom of his bulk. The sun went purple before Fordyce's eyes. For a moment, he thought he would simply hang there, finished by that merciless arm with no noose, no gallows, no noble speeches of farewell. When Sir Gareth launched himself off his stallion without losing his grip, he knew he would not be so fortunate.

They hit the ground with an impact that had to hurt Gareth as much as it hurt him. The thought gave Fordyce satisfaction even as his lungs sucked in on themselves; there was no air to be found. Their momentum sent them rolling off the road into the dead underbrush of a ditch. A twig dug a shallow trench in his forearm. The pain was a welcome reprieve to the numbness in his chest.

Gareth straddled him. Fordyce dragged in a breath as the arm at his windpipe was replaced by the silvery tip of a misericord. ''What have you done with her?'' Gareth rasped. Blood trickled from a corner of his lip.

Fordyce started to say ''Who?'' but wisely refrained. He satisfied himself with blinking owlishly until he could summon enough breath to answer. He made a decision he would not make often in his life. He told the truth. ''How many lads do you see?''

Gareth looked at him askance, wary of a trick. Neither the misericord nor the hand that held it wavered as he raised his head. ''Five. And if they are lads, they are overgrown indeed.''

Fordyce gave a fraction of a nod as if that settled the matter. ''Five. Then mayhaps you should pursue the other three and ask them what *they* have done with her.''

The five shaggy shapes crept nearer, hands shoved deep in flaps that were once sleeves. A frown of consternation touched Gareth's brow. Fordyce bit back a smile.

Gareth settled back on his heels. Dirt smudged his cheek, making him appear as sinister as if he had been driven from hell itself, trailing sparks and ashes. ''The silver-haired boy has her. And Irwin—the one who tells the stories. They are the ones who carried her off? Where might they be?''

Fordyce took advantage of Gareth's relaxed posture to fill his lungs in the guise of a shrug. ''How should I know? They came to me last night, blathering of some preposterous plan to rescue Ro.'' He embellished the tale with typical dramatic flair. ''Irwin told me how she came to him on her knees, weeping piteously and begging her rightful betrothed to free her from your monstrous bondage.''

Gareth opened his mouth, then closed it. The hand holding the misericord went limp. ''And you refused to help her?''

Fordyce sniffed. ''I made a wager. I am an honorable man.'' He nudged aside Gareth's blade with one finger and sat up, plucking dead leaves from his scarf.

Gareth's gaze traveled frantically from Fordyce to the road. His brow furrowed, the weight of decision obviously paining him. His words were more for himself than Fordyce. ''There is no telling what those fools will lead her into.''

He stood, towering over Fordyce. The baron climbed to his feet to find himself glaring at the center of Gareth's silver hauberk. When had the lad grown to such monstrous stature? He threw the ends of his scarf over his shoulders and started up the ditch bank. ''To be so accosted! There are laws to protect innocent travelers. England is a civilized land. Why, if the king had any inkling—''

His words died on a gurgle as Gareth caught the ends of Fordyce's scarf and wound them around his fist. He was jerked against a body as hard as iron.

Gareth's breath was hot in his ear. ''You haven't seen the last of me yet, Fordyce. I'll be back for you. And if I find her with you—if I find out you lied—neither law, nor Edward, nor God Himself will stop me from killing you. Do you understand?''

Fordyce managed a cough that Gareth blessedly took for assent. The knight freed him. He scrambled out of the ditch, heedless of the dirt and leaves he scattered on Gareth's head. Fordyce's nag was nowhere to be seen, and he eyed Gareth's stallion wistfully. The beast rolled its eyes and pawed the dirt. Mustering the remnants of his dignity, he limped down the narrowing road, his eyes darting from side to side in search of his own dismal excuse for a mount. The boys followed in a bedraggled parade.

He was well out of arm's reach and almost out of earshot when he called back in the tones of a benevolent papa, "Don't fret about the girl, Sir Gareth. She is in good hands. Little Roddy is a responsible lad."

"His name is Little Freddie, you idiot!" Gareth's cry was filled with such virulence that Fordyce began to march in double time and the lads had to lope to keep up with him.

Rowena should have grown accustomed to the cold. Her numb fingers uncurled from the reins. The prick of it stung her anew. The fingerless gloves swathing her palms hung in tatters. The air was different today—lighter somehow, and sparkling with an airy iridescence that rendered its raw chill all the more cruel. Rowena felt giddy, as if the air burning her lungs lacked substance. The sun hung like a flat yellow disk in the sky, mocking them with its illusion of warmth.

A harmless ribbon of gray clouds unfurled themselves on the horizon. She glanced at Little Freddie. After a week of huddling in the forests, nibbling on what berries or acorns they could scrounge, his cheeks had taken on a sunken look she hated. Sensing her somber gaze, he swiveled on his pony and gave her a heartening smile.

They sat on the hill overlooking Revelwood. An unbroken stretch of gray swelled behind the castle, resembling more a vast sea than the moor it was.

Without wanting to, Rowena saw another castle transposed over the crumbling ramparts of Revelwood. She blinked to dispel the image, knowing she might as well imagine her hands cupped around a steaming bowl of barley stew or her hair untangled by hands that mocked her with their tenderness. Below them, nothing stirred but the wind. Irwin's bay snorted nervously.

"No reason to dawdle now." Irwin chafed his palms. "Home awaits us."

But none of them moved until Rowena clucked softly to her mare to guide them down the hill. They dismounted clumsily, their limbs stiff with cold. Big Freddie took a step toward the frozen moat.

"Wait!" She caught his arm.

They all looked at her, then at the door of the castle across the moat. The splintered planks that had served as a drawbridge were gone. Between them and the iron-banded door lay a ditch fifteen feet wide, ten feet deep, and mottled with water frozen to a grimy dun.

Big Freddie dropped to hands and knees to peer into the abyss he had almost walked into. Little Freddie paced along the moat, his gaze trained to the ground. His smooth forehead puckered in a frown.

Irwin hugged himself and stamped his feet. "Hullo," he called out.

The cry echoed, then went drifting over the moors. A rising wind whipped tears into Rowena's eyes. The impassive stone walls blurred through her watery gaze. She shivered with a chill that had nothing to do with the cold as she remembered Gareth's long-ago threat. Perhaps even now the bodies of her papa and brothers littered the great hall, their eyes frozen in sightless horror, a single line of crimson marking where their throats had been cut.

Irwin blew into the cup of his hands. "How we reached Revelwood before they did I do not know. This beastly week has gone on forever. Did Uncle remove the planks when we left? I cannot recall it, but he must have."

"He did not." Little Freddie straightened. His lips were compressed to a thin line. "Do you see any planks? The ground was soft from the melting snow when we started out. Do you see any ridges or marks where the planks might have been dragged away?"

Irwin gave the ground a halfhearted sweep. "Well, nay, I suppose not . . ."

"Of course you don't," Little Freddie said. "Because the planks were not dragged away. They were—"

Rowena finished the sentence with him. "—dragged inside."

They raised their gazes to the weather-beaten stones, seeing their home as an impenetrable fortress for the first time. The empty eyes of the arrow slits stared back at them.

Big Freddie ambled to his feet, scratching his head. "The ice is solid enough. I could climb down and cross it."

"How would you reach the door? Spread your arms and fly?" Little Freddie shook his head. "Nay. 'Twon't be necessary." His voice cracked as it rose to a roar. "Whoever locked us out can bloody well open the door and let us in!"

Something in Rowena snapped to see her brother's even features contorted with rage. Her voice joined his in a mindless cry of anger. Irwin bellowed. Big Freddie scooped up a handful of stones and pelted the castle door. Their cacophony should have woken any dead Gareth might have left.

Rowena's cry died on a hacking cough as icy air paralyzed her raw throat. One by one, the others lapsed into silence. The air itself seemed to be waiting. A muted click from the door echoed with the resonance of a bell. Rowena held her breath as an iron panel slid open, driven by the chubby fingers curled around its edge.

"Begone," came a petulant voice. "There is no one home."

The panel slammed shut.

CHAPTER 12

Rowena slumped against Little Freddie. Bittersweet relief softened the remnants of her strength.

Irwin was the first to master his voice and his senses. "Uncle," he called. "Uncle, dear, 'tis your nephew and children come home. Do let us in, won't you, sir?" He mumbled in an aside to the rest of them, "Must not know 'tis us," then bellowed cheerfully, "Hullo! 'Tis Irwin, sir. We are not beggars or robbers come to loot your castle. We are your kinfolk. Open up and let us warm ourselves at your fire."

Big Freddie stared at Irwin, his mouth hanging open.

"Mayhaps Papa does not realize . . ." Rowena said faintly.

"He realizes." A cold gray light burned in Little Freddie's eyes. "You try, Ro."

Rowena's first cry came out in a croak. She swallowed and tried again. "Papa, 'tis Rowena. We need your help. We have been hiding in the forests for over a week. But now we are home and ever so hungry and cold. I've fled Caerleon. I've come home, Papa. To Revelwood and to you. I beg you . . ." Her voice trailed into silence. Little Freddie's hand slipped into hers. Anger deepened the edge of her voice as she drew herself up straight and added, "Papa, open the door. We are exhausted and chilled to the bone. How long must we stand out here and beg for entrance to our own home? You must open the door. You must—"

Little Freddie tugged her hand. The icy wind bit at the tears wetting her cheeks.

With a click, the panel slid open. Papa's face appeared like a bright moon in a square sky. "Foolish child."

His words were all the more jarring for being spoken softly. Rowena knew instinctively that he was referring to her. Her eyes widened. Papa had never once rebuked her.

Irwin started toward the moat. A grin stretched his full lips. "My dearest uncle, we've rescued Rowena from a ghastly fate and brought her home. Are you not pleased?"

"Get back!" Papa's spat words erased Irwin's grin. "Foolish children, all of you. Begone. Go as far away from Revelwood as you dare. We do not want you here. None of you."

Little Freddie's features hardened to a mask. "Tell me, Papa, was it a well-worn sack of gold that won your loyalty to the dark knight? Or mayhaps thirty pieces of silver?"

Papa sniffed. "You wound me, lad. Do you truly think no better of me than that?"

Little Freddie's sneer was answer enough.

"Twasn't gold or silver, was it, Papa?" Rowena cried. The wind sent her hair streaming across her face. Papa's face blurred and crumpled like a pudding in the rain.

"Not gold. Nor silver. But murder, Rowena. Murder in his eyes when he attacked me like the madman he is. He swore if he found you here, there would be no hope for any of us." Papa continued in more chiding tones. "By fleeing him, you have dishonored my good name."

Little Freddie muttered a word that would have done Marlys proud.

Papa's voice sank to a whine. "I beseech you, child. Save yourself and your kinfolk. Return to Sir Gareth on your knees. Beg for his mercy and forgiveness. Surely you can use your feminine wiles to win your way back into his heart and bed. Your papa cannot allow you to return to Revelwood in disgrace."

Rowena lifted her head. "I understand. If I go on alone, will you open your door to the boys?"

Irwin and Little Freddie broke into protest, but it was Big Freddie's baritone that silenced them all. "Nonsense. You'll go nowhere alone. I'll not be having it." Rowena stared at him and he ducked his head, his shy smile revealing a row of broken teeth.

When she turned back to the door, the panel had closed. All was silent within the castle. The pale blob of a gate-keeper was gone.

Rowena fought to keep the note of pleading from her voice. "Papa, we are starving. Can you not spare us some food to ease our journey?"

The panel slid open. Rowena ducked as four dark bulbs came sailing across the moat. A bruised turnip rolled past her feet and bounced into the crusty edge of the moat. Irwin dove to his hands and knees, trying to save the other turnips from meeting a similar fate. Then the panel slammed shut.

Rowena sat down with legs crossed and chin propped in her hands. Out of the pale sunshine and borne on the airy wind came tiny flakes of ice that cut like daggers against her skin. She tilted her face upward and licked a snowflake from her cheek.

"Wonderful. Papa has forsaken me. I could be hung for horse thievery. A madman is pursuing me. And now God sends us snow to brighten our journey."

Little Freddie knelt in front of her. "Papa forsook each one of us with his cry of pleasure when our seed left his loins."

She studied his face. Tiny cracks spread along the borders of his lips. His gray eyes were huge and eerie above the shadows etched in his fair skin.

"Perhaps Papa is right," she said. "Perhaps I should return to him. Throw myself on his mercy."

"From what I've heard of him, he has no mercy. Do you believe otherwise?"

Rowena's eyes darkened as she felt again the tender stroke

of Gareth's fingers against her cheek. She had been a heart-beat away from surrendering to those hands when his cold words had stopped her. *Leave me be.* Could those same hands have used their diabolical expertise to end a child's life? She shivered at the memory of his caress. If Gareth ran her through, her pain would be over. His mercy might prolong it indefinitely.

" 'Tis what frightens me the most. I do not know."

"Then we go on." He offered her his hand, and they rose in one motion.

"Where shall we go on to?" Irwin asked. Rowena flinched as his teeth crunched through the skin of the turnip.

Without wanting to, she remembered Dunnla's stew, steaming thick with beef and barley. The world wavered before her eyes as if seen through a haze of smoke. When Irwin offered her the turnip, she snapped a large bite of it. Its bitterness was somehow heartening.

She tossed the turnip to Big Freddie.

"I've never had my own horse before," he said.

She lacked the heart to protest as he held the turnip in front of the horse's nose without taking a bite of it. The sorrel swallowed it whole. Irwin's face fell. His hand darted to his sleeve to massage his other treasures.

"Horses are nice," Rowena said gently. "But we cannot eat them." She cuffed Irwin as he gave Big Freddie's horse a speculative look.

It was beginning to snow in earnest. Feathery flakes settled in Rowena's hair. Above them, the sun dissolved behind a veil of low-hanging clouds.

Rowena mustered a smile as she mounted her mare. "We shall go wherever we choose. The world is ours and we shall make our way in it as any travelers would do. What is hunger compared to the thrill of adventuring?"

"Damned inconvenient, I say." Irwin rolled onto his horse. "Pardon me, Ro. Shouldn't have sworn in front of you. Though I daresay you've heard worse living in that nest of noble vipers."

Rowena started to protest, then remembered she had heard much worse from Marlys's lips. She inclined her head in a regal nod. "I shall grant my forgiveness this time, Irwin."

"Frightfully benevolent of you," Little Freddie whispered with a smirk.

She nudged his pony with her foot. Of one accord, they circled the castle and started across the cold, gray expanse of the moor. Dead bracken crackled beneath the horses' hooves. The wind, unbroken by even the bones of trees, whipped flecks of snow into their pores. Rowena huddled deeper into her mantle. She took a perverse comfort in the bleak emptiness of the landscape. There were no ancient trunks waiting to spill a dark shadow armed with silvery sword onto their heads. There were no dark blots of doubt on a barrenness that was a vast shadow in itself. In the most wintry, desolate season, the moor had become her friend again.

Her optimism lasted until a nightfall which found them huddled behind a moldy hillock. They lay in the same heap they had slept in for years. Little Freddie's back fit to her stomach like a spoon. Rowena's leg was thrown over his waist. Little Freddie pillowed his head on Irwin's bulk and Big Freddie curled around their feet like a faithful hound.

The snow had stopped after laying a feeble blanket on the ground. The sky had cleared. The stars winked like cruel diamonds against a pelt of sable as impenetrable as Gareth's eyes.

"What ever shall become of us?" Rowena said to no one in particular.

Irwin burrowed into the dirt like a groundhog. "If we freeze to death, we shan't have to worry about it."

Little Freddie shrugged. " 'Tisn't much colder than Revelwood. 'Tis Rowena that frets me. She has grown accustomed to a warmer bed."

Irwin sniffed. "I daresay she has."

Rowena was too addled from hunger to retort. "We could become a traveling troupe of entertainers," she mused. "Wealthy wastrels like Sir Blaine tumble over one another to hurl them pouches of gold and silver. We could sing for our supper."

Little Freddie poked Irwin. "Can you sing?"

"Well . . . nay. I can play the trumpet and hum a little."

"How about you? Can you sing?"

Big Freddie shook his shaggy head.

He lifted an eyebrow at Rowena. "You?"

"I fear not, but perhaps I could learn to rope dance. And you could tumble. And Irwin . . ." her smooth brow furrowed, "Irwin could juggle. Aye, 'tis a fine thought. Refrain from eating the turnips, Irwin. You can juggle them."

"Can you juggle two turnips?" Little Freddie rolled to his back and cushioned his head on Irwin's belly. "The nobility are looking for oddities to amuse them. They tire of their own perfect flesh."

"Nothing odd about us," Irwin mumbled.

Rowena giggled. "Shall we strap a bundle on your back, Little Freddie, and bill you as a hump-backed dwarf?"

Irwin flung himself on his side. "Can the two of you not freeze to death in silence and let a man sleep? Cease your musing. We have no coin, talent, or gross deformities to make such a venture worthwhile. If a dancing bear should happen by, you may awaken me."

Rowena looked at Little Freddie. They propped themselves up on their elbows.

Little Freddie's finger stabbed beneath Irwin's ribs, and Irwin lifted his head with a groan to find them grinning like idiots. He followed their gazes to their feet where Big Freddie had thrown out his limbs in a shambling stretch. He pillowed his shaggy head on Rowena's ankle. His mouth fell open in a snore deeper than a growl.

Irwin frowned thoughtfully. "Can he dance?"

"As well as you can juggle, methinks," Rowena replied.

• • •

Rowena bent low over the mare's neck. A stone slammed into her shoulder. She cried out at the throb of pain and dug her heels into the horse's flanks. The ground unrolled beneath pounding hooves. The others were a blur of shadows racing beside her. Some distance from the village the shower of stones striking the hardened ground lessened, then ceased. Relieved, Rowena drew up the reins and the mare shuddered to a halt. She collapsed into the tangled mane, her breathing as ragged from fear as if she had outrun the bellowing mob on foot. A paroxysm of coughing wracked her chest.

A hand gently drew her hair back. Little Freddie peered into her face. "Are you ill?"

She shook her head with a feeble smile. "Winded."

Irwin's horse pranced in a circle, spurred by the restless bouncing of its rider. Irwin's cheeks were flushed an indignant red. "You would think we were murderers or child-stealers. 'Tis the third village we've been run out of in as many days. I had no inkling that people took their entertainment so seriously."

"Mayhaps the humbler art of begging would be a more profitable pursuit." Little Freddie put out a hand to stop Irwin's horse from trodding on his pony.

"Nonsense," Irwin snapped. "Not with our talents. I found it quite amusing when Rowena fell off the rope we had strung between the church and the stable."

Rowena looked at him askance. " 'Twas not supposed to be amusing. 'Twas supposed to be rope dancing. Even the village idiot knew that."

"But the way you hung there by your knees with your kirtle over your head . . ." Irwin chuckled at the memory. Rowena gave him a look that would have cut a diamond only to have its effect ruined by another fit of coughing.

Little Freddie slipped off his pony and unstrapped the bundle of rags from his back. He straightened with a moan. "Quarreling amongst ourselves won't put bread in our stomachs. We are as poor and hungry today as we were a month ago. We've had to beg or steal every crumb we've laid in our bellies. Not one ha'penny did we gain from that village today.''

''Them folks had no coins. They were poor like us.''

. They all turned to look at Big Freddie. He scratched the top of his mangy head, forgetting he had two of them. A stuffed bear's head had been shoved back from his own lank hair. The stolen pelts trailing from it were bald in spots, thickly matted in others. Dark, sightless eyes stared back from the bear's head. Rowena blinked, forgetting for a moment which face belonged to her brother.

Little Freddie sighed. ''Out of the mouths of bears . . .''

''He makes his point well.'' Irwin twirled the drooping ends of his moustache, an annoying habit he had adopted since they had grown long enough to droop. ''The nobility seem to be eluding us. Where do all the rich folk go in the winter?''

''Winter is yet another toy for them.'' Bitterness laced Rowena's voice. ''They proclaim it charming and pretty till it wets their woolen gloves. Then they weary of it and creep inside to languish before their fires and gobble their Christmas puddings.''

Little Freddie ran his hands down the bony flank of his pony and gave her a curious glance beneath half-lowered lashes. Her callused hands kneaded the mare's mane.

''If the nobility will not come to us, then we shall go to it.'' Irwin smiled as if he had said something profound.

Rowena lifted an eyebrow. ''Shall we ride to Londontown itself and demand an audience before the king?''

''We must stop spurning the castles. Let us play before those who would appreciate our talents,'' said Irwin.

Little Freddie mounted. ''Barring you, that leaves only the blind and deaf. Castles are dangerous for Rowena. We have discussed this before.''

Irwin sniffed. ''She is being selfish. If she would accept my generous offer and allow the next village priest to marry us, she would no longer find herself in danger. Surely even this grim knight would hesitate to abduct a woman married before God and king.''

''God and king mean nothing to him. Nor would you, if you stood in his way.'' With those words, Rowena nudged her mount past his and into the shelter of the woods. Big Freddie shrugged the bear head over his own and followed.

Irwin shook his head. ''When did she become such a shrewish creature?''

''Don't be a pudding,'' Little Freddie said. ''If she cared naught for you, she would wed you and let Sir Gareth whack off your head.''

The boy stared back into the forest, wondering if Rowena had caught a glimpse of the man who had cantered into the village as the mob began pelting them with stones. A mantle of the blackest fur had veiled his features. He shook away a shiver and urged his pony forward as the first snowflakes slipped from the sky.

By nightfall, their horses waded through the dim forest in a sea of white. Round flakes drifted downward to mesh in a seamless pillow that muffled all but the gentle click of flake hitting snow. The wind blew deceptively gentle. Rowena's cough ceased. The beast in her empty belly curled tightly into her lungs and began to scratch. As a heated flush followed a tooth-chattering chill, she wanted nothing more than to sink into the seductive blanket of snow and sleep forever.

The snow masked all traces of a path. They wandered silently and without purpose over the dreamlike terrain. When a castle came looming out of the darkness, Rowena was too numb to be startled.

They halted their mounts at the edge of the wood.

'' 'Tis smaller than Revelwood,'' Irwin said, subdued for once.

''Like an abandoned toy,'' Little Freddie mused.

''Not a toy. And not abandoned.'' Rowena pointed. The

orangy glow of a torch threaded its light through a shuttered window.

"Not abandoned indeed." Irwin's horse quivered as his knees went taut.

His gaze had found another structure harbored against the outer wall of the castle. It was a makeshift stable, open on one wall, with smoke pots scattered along its length to cast warmth and feeble light on its occupants. A dozen horses shared the stable.

"Pretty," Big Freddie murmured.

It took no connoisseur of horseflesh to recognize the magnificence of the beasts. They were all stallions or destriers, more than half of them marked with the sleek powerful lines of the Arabian. Even in the smoky light the emeralds and rubies encrusted on their bridles sparkled brighter than the snow impaled in the glow from the castle window.

Rowena shivered. "We should not tarry here."

"Hold your tongue, Ro," Irwin said sharply. " 'Tis a godsend. A castle of bored knights and ladies trapped in a snowstorm. Why they'll be tripping over one another to surrender their gold for a bit of entertainment."

Rowena bit her raw lip. The sharp retort Little Freddie expected did not come. " 'Tis too charming," she said softly. "Like one of those enchanted castles you told us of. Suppose we enter and can never leave?"

"Pshaw! You are too fanciful. If I recall, most of those enchantments involved excesses of food and drink and a beautiful maiden or two. Would you rather we all freeze to death to humor your womanly foreboding?"

Rowena gave him a dark look. There was no courtyard, no moat and no drawbridge between them and the castle door. There was only a deep blanket of snow, unruffled by human or animal prints. Her eyes searched the stable. None of the stallions was pure white.

"Rowena, Irwin may be right this time. I don't know how we can go on in this snow. If we try to sleep, I fear we will . . ." Little Freddie's voice trailed off as he rubbed raw knuckles over his dripping nose.

Irwin did not wait for Rowena's approval. He dismounted and trundled toward the door. The others followed with Rowena hanging behind Big Freddie's mangy pelts. Irwin pounded on the door. Little Freddie slipped in front of him. They were engaged in a polite shoving match when the door slipped open.

Rowena's fears were greatly relieved at the sight of the face appearing in the halo of light. No ogre or goblin this, but a man's face, smooth of chin and pleasant of expression. It was a face Rowena would have considered the height of handsomeness prior to meeting Sir Gareth. He could not have been much older than she, but a trim blond moustache and a gleaming pair of golden spurs marked him as a knight. A burst of hearty male laughter rolled out from the hall behind him.

"I say," he said, "did someone knock?"

Little Freddie stopped squirming in Irwin's grasp. "We did, sir. We are humble beggars in need of charity. Can we offer you some tricks and songs for a bowl of porridge?"

Irwin hefted Little Freddie into the snow by the seat of his braies. He bowed deeply and twirled his moustache. "Our tumbler speaks in haste. We are a troupe of international fame fresh from the province of Anjou."

The knight's eyebrows swooped upward. Rowena groaned silently.

Irwin swept out his arm. "Allow me to present Petit Frederick, tumbler extraordinaire." He jerked Rowena out from behind Big Freddie. "And the charming Mignon, whose array of tricks will astound you." Rowena hissed at Irwin from the corner of her mouth and curtsied sweetly to the knight. "Most amazing of all—Freddie the dancing bear."

Big Freddie peered stupidly at him. Irwin jerked the bear's head down and slammed his fist on it. The knight glanced politely at Big Freddie's perfunctory shuffle, but Rowena bore the brunt of his smile. She smiled back, warmed by its welcome and the scent of roast pheasant wafting out the door. Her hunger returned with a ravenous growl.

The knight leaned against the doorframe and stroked his chin. His slender hips and broad shoulders were outlined against the light. "How fortunate. My companions and I were weary from boredom. It seems the fates have favored us with rescue."

"All we ask," Irwin said, "is a chamber to prepare in, a little meat, a little gold—"

"And a little feed for our horses," the bear growled.

The knight made a gesture behind his back, and a squire scraped past them. Rowena watched their mounts being led toward the stable with a tiny thrill of trepidation. She forgot her fears as the knight threw a friendly arm around Irwin's shoulders and ushered them into a hall whose warmth hung in the air as palpable as an embrace.

Handsome young knights ringed them, their curiosity held in check by good manners. After a month spent fleeing one peasant mob after another, Rowena found one quality most entrancing. The knights were clean. There was none of the stench of unwashed flesh so lethal to an empty stomach. A kettle bubbled cheerfully on the hearth. The scent of cinnamon wafted through the cozy hall to mingle with the crisp cleanliness of breath flavored with nothing but spiced ale. A sudden fit of horror washed over Rowena. Had it been today she had washed or yesterday? She slipped her nose into her kirtle in the guise of scratching it. Friendly young faces bowed to plant genteel kisses on her palms.

The knights clustered around as the blond knight introduced his new guests one by one. When he bowed to Rowena with a special mention of her "array of tricks," the men's smiles broadened. Several of them clapped the knight on the back with a general murmur of, "Jolly good, Percival" and "Array of tricks, eh? Simply grand."

Rowena barely had time to give the half-eaten slab of

meat on the table a longing glance before they were whisked
into a tiny cell to prepare for their performance.

She slipped out of her ragged boots and smeared rouge
on her cheeks in circles of plum. After smoothing her tattered kirtle as best she could, she raked her fingers through
Big Freddie's pelts.

Little Freddie mumbled something to himself as he pulled
on a hole-ridden pair of blue hose. He was frowning
thoughtfully.

Rowena knelt beside him. The door thumped open and
they were swept into the hall. The knights had propped
themselves up on benches and tables in various states of
repose. Most of them were closer in age to boys than men.
Rowena's mouth watered at the sight of a turkey leg dangling carelessly from aristocratic fingers. She inched toward
the fire.

Percival led the knights in a round of applause. Irwin
stepped into the center of the hall. He pivoted on his heel
and threw kisses all around. Rowena grimaced.

"Welcome to our grand exhibition. For our first entertainment of the evening, I should like to introduce Freddie,
the dancing bear."

Big Freddie shambled out, overturning a chair and
sweeping a goblet from a knight's hand in his blindness. He
had barely made two graceless turns and a clumsy kick before the hall erupted into thunderous applause.

"Marvelous!"

"Bloody brilliant!"

"What a dance. Give us something else now."

Irwin frowned, bewildered, and gave Big Freddie a shove
toward the wall. One of the knights caught him before he
fell into the table.

Irwin shrugged. "If it pleases you, I call forth Petit Frederick, master of the tumble and fall."

Little Freddie danced forward with a smile pasted on his
lips. His act was more fall than tumble, and after the first

genuine flip, Percival caught him in midair and neatly set him aside.

The hall rocked with cries of admiration and more applause. Rowena was baffled. She had never seen an audience so easily satisfied. She blinked and shook her head. The heat from the fire against the blush of her skin was making her giddy. Against the wall, Percival kept a friendly grip on Little Freddie's shoulders.

Irwin coughed and sputtered. The gleam of a trumpet hanging over the hearth returned his composure. "May I?" he asked.

Percival nodded shortly. His open smile seemed less open now. There was an unpleasant twist to his lips that reminded Rowena of a sneer.

Irwin climbed on a stool and took down the trumpet. His lips touched its tip and a sputtering note escaped. The trumpet was snatched from his mouth by a genteel hand. The arm that had taken it remained fixed around his neck in a jovial embrace.

Rowena's sense of foreboding came flooding back too late. Faces that had been boyish and friendly hardened as they turned toward her. Chins tilted at arrogant angles. Tongues darted out to moisten lips. The barest shift of a stance or posture and she was at the center of a ring of men who had been born to privilege and denied too little in their short lives. She backed toward the hearth. The heat at her back was no longer a welcoming warmth. Sweat trickled between her breasts.

"Any one of you that touches her is a dead man!"

The cry was Little Freddie's. Its shrill, broken note deepened the cold smiles. He struggled in Percival's embrace. Percival ruffled the boy's hair and passed him to a red-haired knight who pinned his thin arms behind him.

Firelight cast gold lights in Percival's cap of hair as he swaggered toward Rowena. "Stifle your whining, wee one. We only wish to see what we were promised—the charming

Mignon's array of tricks. There will be gold enough in it for all of you."

Rowena was rewarded by the sight of Irwin's face going pink and then white. A moment later Percival blocked her view as the back of his hand gently brushed her cheek. His thumb cut a teasing path across her lips.

"Do not tremble, sweet Mignon. We only wish you to perform for us. We shall make it well worth your time."

Rowena made a pretty moue and rubbed the floor with one bare toe. Percival's breath quickened. His other hand lifted to her hair. He yelped as she jumped, planting both of her feet on one of his. His sword was half out of its scabbard in her grip when the side of his hand came down in a chop that deadened her wrist and flooded her eyes with tears. From the corner of her eye, she saw Big Freddie go down under a glancing blow.

Percival spun her around and twisted her arm behind her. "Foolish wench," he bit off. "You shall not tease us with promises of entertainment and then try to cut our throats."

"You misunderstand," she said as he shoved her toward the table. "Those were not the kind of tricks he meant. I am not a whore."

"You're not the Holy Virgin, either, or you wouldn't be traveling with this motley troupe. How else could they earn their living but from the sale of your sweet flesh?"

Rowena was fighting in earnest now. His smooth limbs were like steel. She glanced frantically around the hall. "I beg you. I am innocent. Is there no decency here? You are knights. Is there no chivalry amongst you?"

Hard, young faces stared back at her. One man unbuckled his scabbard with a deliberate motion and let it fall to the floor. Percival jerked her back to thrust her on the table. A dark-haired man stepped in front of them. When Rowena stared up at him he grinned at her with a wink of one green eye. Hope stirred in her breast.

His voice rang in the sudden silence. "If she speaks the truth, then the stakes are much higher."

A thoughtful murmur rose. Percival's fingers dug convulsively into her wrist as a rumble of thunder rolled through the hall. Rowena thought she was going mad, then she realized it was not thunder but the pounding of a dozen fists on wood as the knights chanted in one demanding chord, "Wager! Wager! Wager!"

Percival flung her from him in disgust. Rowena caught the edge of the table to keep from falling.

The voices throbbed to silence. Percival sneered. "If you care to put your faith in the word of a barefoot light-skirt, bring on the dice. The winner can take her upstairs and find out what a fool he has been."

Bone dice clattered on the stones in front of the hearth. Irwin, Big Freddie, and Little Freddie were bound and tossed in a heap in the corner. The knights clamored with excitement as they knelt around the game. Those in the back craned their flushed faces to watch. They seemed to have forgotten Rowena altogether in the thrill of the wager.

She backed away, not daring to breathe. Her shoulders came up against an unyielding chest. She had not been left unguarded. Green eyes flashed a greeting as she looked back over her shoulder.

A silky smooth voice poured into her ear like honey. "I could not bear to see you pinned on that table like a lamb for the slaughter."

Rowena stared straight ahead. "You would help me, sir?" she said with no change of expression.

"I would." His arms slipped around her waist. "Come away with me while they play. I swear to be gentle with you. When I am done, I shall help you escape before they can take their turns on you."

Rowena closed her eyes. Why did the kindest words she had heard that night have to be the cruelest? "The others? The rest of my troupe? Will you see they escape with their lives?"

"For you, little one—anything." One of his hands glided

under the worn linen of the kirtle to cup her thigh. Smooth lips nuzzled her throat.

Rowena's mind raced. What would Marlys do with this lecherous man-child offering to politely ravish her?

She would take him upstairs and kill him.

The answer came with such haste that Rowena gave a pained yelp of laughter. Green Eyes groaned softly, taking her start as one of pleasure. His hand drifted between her thighs.

In the center of the circle, Percival's long fingers danced on the dice. He gave a nasty grin. Perhaps he was winning. Rowena made an awkward hop to avoid the probing fingers and turned in the knight's embrace, better to keep both of his hands in view. Green Eyes took it as a gesture of assent.

Before she could speak, he laid his lips across hers. Oddly enough, his was the kiss of a whore, not hers. Teasing and practiced, with an undertone of passion held leisurely at bay in the exploration of his tongue. With another man, Rowena might have wondered what came after such a kiss. But Green Eyes was a stranger. How would Marlys kill him? Would she bash him on the head? Run him through with his own sword? Marlys would appreciate the irony of that. His roaming hand dipped down the neck of her kirtle, and Rowena squeezed her eyes shut in resignation. Unbeknownst to him, he was a dead man, anyway.

Lost in the throes of plotting the knight's imminent demise, Rowena heard the crash of the door as if it were a mere echo of her heartbeat. Icy wind poured over her. A beat of silence lasted too long, and the knight pulled away. Rowena raised her head. The faces at the hearth were all fixed on the door, frozen in expressions of boyish guilt Rowena should have found amusing.

Too late, she turned.

A snowy giant stood in the doorway. Snow whipped around his broad shoulders and into the hall, lingering for an elusive instant before being sucked into the void of warm air. The wind whistled an eerie refrain. Rowena clung to the knight's forearms to keep from swaying as black eyes darker than night and colder than ice froze the blood in her veins.

CHAPTER 13

Gareth stood in the doorway like a snow-covered Thor fresh from besting the frost giants. So riveting was his dark gaze that Rowena could not have ducked if a lightning bolt had come hurtling from his fingers to fry her where she stood. Snow frosted his dark hair. Tiny icicles clung to a beard that had lost its trimmed edges. He was shrouded in a mantle of fur so black and lush it could have been hours old instead of years. For one terrible moment, Rowena fancied the dark drops falling to the stone were not melting snow, but beads of blood from a fresh kill. Her hands uncurled their clawlike grip on the knight's arm. An awkward cough broke the silence.

Gareth swaggered forward, shedding snow with each step.

Percival rose from his kneeling position to meet him. "Sir Gareth! What a surprise! What brings you to Midgard?"

"Snow." Gareth reached down and tweaked the younger man's nose. "Does your father know you're here, Percival?"

Percival grimaced. "Nay, but I fear he will."

How could Rowena have thought Percival handsome? His classical features faded to pallid prettiness in Gareth's rugged shadow. His walk was little more than a strutting imitation of a man's.

Gareth's gaze swept the hall, taking in the kneeling figures at the hearth, the heap of bound and gagged bodies against the wall. His eyes passed over Rowena with the merest flick of an eyebrow. She stepped away from Green Eyes, putting her hands behind her back like a naughty child.

Gareth jerked his head toward the squirming heap. "They alive?"

"Hardly fit to be," Percival sneered. "But they are."

Gareth dropped an arm over Percival's shoulder and steered him toward the fire. "Then they're no concern of mine. Have you no warm ale to offer on such a treacherous eve?"

The knights leaped up, falling over one another in their haste to polish a goblet and pass a flagon down their ranks until it reached Gareth's hand. He bared his teeth in a growl of thanks. The knights ducked their heads, throwing covert glances at the massive broadsword hanging at his waist. The tip of his scabbard scraped the floor as he moved into their circle.

A foot moved to kick the dice under a table, but Gareth's boot came down in its path. He scooped the dice up, weighing them in his gauntleted palm like chips of gold.

"Wagering your father's castle again, Percival?"

"Nay, sir. I learned my lesson last time."

"Well you should have. You almost lost an ear to Marlys that night if my memory serves me well."

"Aye, sir. 'Twas fortunate you came home when you did."

Gareth leaned against the table and tossed first one die and then the other into the air. "What might you be wagering tonight?"

Percival shuffled his feet and fumbled for words. "Nothing of any import, sir. Just a whore." Gareth's gaze passed over Rowena with polite interest. Percival pointed. "Those fellows over there—the ones wiggling about—tried to sell her to us, promising us she was well versed in an 'array of tricks.'" Gareth cupped a hand over Percival's ear and whispered. In response, Percival gave a shout of laughter.

"That, too, I'll wager. She has got the mouth for it." Fresh heat flooded Rowena's cheeks. Percival shrugged as if explaining away a boyish prank. "She claims to be an innocent. So we thought a toss of the dice might decide who would be the first to take her abovestairs and prove her a liar."

Gareth rubbed his beard and sidled off the table. Green Eyes melted back into the crowd of knights, leaving Rowena alone. She placed her feet in a wider stance but still swayed when Gareth's shadow fell over her. Her jaw clenched, she stared at the silver links of the hauberk beneath his mantle. When he did not budge, she was forced to lift her eyes to his face. His scathing gaze assessed her from head to toe, taking in her bare, dirty feet, her shredded kirtle, her tangled hair.

"Is she worth your gold?" he called over his shoulder.

Rowena's eyes narrowed in a look of genuine dislike. Murmurs of assent came from the hearth.

With a smile as sweet as any of Marlys's, Gareth shrugged. "So be it. On with it then. Don't let my presence hinder your game."

He turned away. Trembling with disbelief, Rowena tangled her fingers in the chain links of the hauberk and jerked him back. Her action was shielded from the others by the folds of his mantle.

"Gareth, please," she hissed, a more coherent plea deserting her.

His fingers gently untangled hers, and he pushed her hand away as if it had dirtied him. He stared down at her, his eyes narrowed and his smile compressed to a hard line. If Rowena had been versed in the art of begging, she would have let her round, blue eyes fill prettily with tears. Since she did not know the effectiveness of this trick, she blinked hard to smother the tears and sniffed twice with her reddening nose.

With a sweep of his mantle, Gareth turned away. "Mayhaps the chit would prefer to take a man abovestairs instead of a boy. The night is cold. I, too, might wish a soft, young body to warm my bed. Throw my wager in with the rest.''

A distinct bleating sound floated out from Rowena's pile of kinfolk. The knights exchanged nervous glances.

Percival cocked an eyebrow. ''I had not heard such sports were to your taste, Sir Gareth.''

Gareth loomed over Percival. ''But you've heard other things about me, haven't you, Percival?''

Percival studied his immaculate fingernails. ''Your wager is as good as the next man's, of course.'' He exchanged an uncomfortable glance with the others. ''But do not misunderstand our intent. The man who takes her upstairs will only be the *first* man to do so.''

Gareth's hand brushed the hilt of his sword in a loving caress. ''If I win, I will be the first. And the last.'' His sweeping gaze dared any man in the hall to contradict him. None did.

'' 'Tis because he is going to strangle me when he is done,'' Rowena murmured. No one glanced at her but Gareth. If looks could kill, he would have been spared the inconvenience. She sank into a chair.

With chin propped in hands, she watched Gareth kneel in the circle of men. He received their thumps on the back and good-natured jests as if they were long-lost brothers. Not once did he glance at her.

Her eyes devoured him with all the fatal curiosity of a doomed man pondering his gallows. He shrugged away the mantle with his first toss of the dice. His hair had grown long and shaggy. Ebony tendrils curled over the broad shoulders beneath the silver hauberk. Rowena watched, barely breathing, as he scattered the dice into the folds of his mantle. He retrieved them with a smirk of apology for his clumsiness. The dice flew once, twice, and a third time in a graceful arc that wrung groans of disappointment and leering well-wishes from the other men.

She was still sitting with chin in hands when he thrust his gauntleted hand in her face. She ignored it.

"Come abovestairs with me, sweet Mignon. I am eager to sample your array of tricks," he said heartily.

She gave him a withering glance. The knights laughed.

Percival doused his goblet with a consoling dose of ale. "Shall we help you get her up? We've rope if she's quarrelsome. We'd be delighted to hold her down for you if that suits your tastes."

"I do hope that won't be necessary." Gareth knelt in front of her. His words were forced out between teeth clenched in a frozen smile. "Shall you accompany me, or shall I leave you here to be ripped apart by these arrogant whelps?"

"Are those my choices?"

"They are."

He held out his hand again. Her world narrowed to the soft beaten leather crowning his knuckles. "Bully," she said, taking his hand.

"Your opinion matters not to me." Gareth pulled her to her feet.

"Has it ever?"

She gave him no resistance until they passed the bundle of tangled arms and legs. Little Freddie's eyes stared bleakly up at her over an egg-stained gag. She stopped, and Gareth's hand tightened in a crushing grip around her fingers. She refused to look at him.

He stared at her bent head, then jerked a commanding thumb at the pile of bodies. "Feed them. But keep them out of my way."

The warning in his voice was palpable. The knights galloped around in a flurry of haste to do his bidding. This time when he squeezed her fingers, Rowena followed him meekly up the stairs.

Gareth dragged her into the first chamber with glowing embers on the grate. Without freeing her hand, he splintered a stool against the hearth and fed its spindly legs to the gasping fire. Rowena hung back, half-expecting him to heave her into the fire with his next motion. He puffed into the embers like a dragon. Sparks flew. The fire sputtered, igniting the dry wood into a snapping flame that filled the chamber with the heady scent of woodsmoke.

She stumbled after him as he threw open the door of the heavily carved ambry, kicked a chest until the latch broke, and popped the shutters open with his elbow. Snow swirled into the chamber. He leaned out, peering below the window at the unmarked quilt of snow. He was forced to free her to latch the shutters.

Then he turned on her, and she backed away as each word shot at her on a sharp puff of fog. "If so much as one brother, one uncle, or one twice-removed third cousin pops out at me, brandishing hoe, sword, or trumpet, I swear I shall cut off his head first and ask questions later. Do you understand?"

She nodded. The back of her knees came up against something solid, and she sat down. Gareth strode to the door and slammed down the slat of wood that served as a bolt.

He leaned his back against the door and jerked off his gauntlets finger by finger. "Spare me the crestfallen look. I beg pardon if I am not the knight of your choice."

Rowena's eyes drifted away from his mocking gaze. The stone walls of the chamber were gently rounded to mark the interior of a miniature tower. A bed smaller than Gareth's sat in the center of the floor. On the wooden ceiling above it, fixed in entwined hands of gold, hung a mirror of hammered silver. Rowena frowned, pondering the disastrous effects if it should fall on the occupants of the bed. Her fingers absently toyed with the silken ribbons dangling from the arm of her chair.

"Do you know what sort of place this is?" Gareth's features were set in a stony mask.

Rowena squinted at the dim images in the tapestries that draped the walls. She had a fleeting impression of creamy flesh, contorted faces. "A castle," she said faintly. "Mayhaps a hunting lodge of some sort."

Gareth crossed the space between them. He leaned forward, imprisoning her with a hand on either arm of the chair. "Aye, Rowena," he said softly. "A castle. A lodge. Have you ever seen a mirror such as that?"

In a corner of the mirror Rowena caught a watery reflection of the burnished gold of her hair against the dark of his. She shook her head.

"A chair like this?" He trailed the backs of his fingernails over the plush red velvet of the chair arms. Rowena's arms prickled as if the caress had been made against her skin. She shook her head again. "This chair, my dear, was pilfered from an Arabian harem, probably by some devout Christian knight who brought it back for his mistress. 'Tis very costly and very rare. You see, these ribbons were fashioned to slide around your wrist." She sat paralyzed as a scarlet streamer was looped gently over her hand. "And these ribbons can be brought around like this." His broad fingers circled her slim ankle, parting it from her other ankle and pressing it toward the chair leg.

Her leg jerked convulsively. She realized too late that he had not secured any of the ribbons. Her foot slammed into his thigh. He caught it in an iron grip.

"Aye, Rowena. A castle. A hunting lodge. A dozen bored young knights. And their quarry? A lusty young widow mayhaps. Or an innocent peasant girl abducted from a village. If you will study the tapestries, you will get some idea of what sort of place this is."

He caught her chin and forced her gaze to the wall. Even a blur of tears could not disguise the arch of a swanlike neck as a maiden was forced to her knees at the feet of an armored warrior.

Rowena sniffed hard. Her voice was barely audible. "But they are knights . . . chivalry . . ."

Gareth knelt between her knees. "Welcome to the real world, Lady Precious. 'Tis no romantic tale of Irwin's. I

hate to be the first to tell you, but the Pendragon and the
Lionheart died long ago. Chivalry belongs to those wealthy
enough to afford it.''

Her eyes narrowed to suspicious blue slits. ''How did *you*
know of this place?''

''Blaine brought me here once when we weren't much
older than those belowstairs. Did you think it was a place I
would frequent?''

Rowena shrugged.

''How depraved do you think I am?''

She stared into her lap without answering.

Gareth caught her cheeks in his hands with a curse that
gave new weight to her opinion. She jerked in a half-sob.
He lifted his hands. Two bright circles of plum stained his
palms.

''Sweet Jesu,'' he murmured.

His hands claimed her face again, chafing mercilessly
until the pallor of her skin shone through the carelessly ap-
plied berry ash. Flesh that had been round and smooth with
health lay against her bones like melted wax. Her eyes glittered with unspilled tears.

She ducked out of his grasp with a yelp. He shoved her
back into the chair and squatted in front of her. Rowena
waited for the wrench of one knee away from another, the
bite of a ribbon around her ankle.

''When was the last time you ate a full meal?'' he demanded. Her face went blank. He shook her. ''When did
you eat last, Rowena?''

Her lips moved as she counted. She held up four fingers.
''Three days.''

Gareth's expletive was short and descriptive. He strode to
the door. Throwing back the bolt, he leaned out and bellowed, ''Bring me food. Make haste.''

A chorus of ''Aye, sir'' floated up the stairs, followed by
a symphony of banging and clashing. Gareth slammed the
door and resumed his position at it, glowering at her.
Rowena was spared from the niceties of conversation by the

crash of a knight against the door. Unaware that Gareth's bulk was on the other side, he had slammed into it at full tilt. Gareth jerked the door open, and the knight reeled into the chamber, balancing a full tray on one hand. He shot a quizzical glance at the fully clothed Rowena sitting with hands folded demurely in her lap. Gareth snatched the tray and sent him stumbling out. Gareth dropped the tray on a small table. Rowena gasped as he lifted her, chair and all, and dropped her in front of the table.

He turned the chair across from her and straddled it, glaring at her over folded arms.

Beneath his piercing stare, the beast of hunger in her stomach rolled over with a whimper and quietly died.

She stared glumly at hunks of salted boar meat smothered in brown dollops of gravy. "I should eat."

"You should."

"I shall need all my strength tonight."

"Well thought, milady."

A shiver that had little to do with cold ran through her. She speared a bean with her knife and began to eat. The food lay like ashes in her mouth, but she ate every bite of it. When her lips closed around the last bite, Gareth snatched away the tray, leaving only a flagon of sweet wine and a goblet on the table. He disposed of the rest by throwing it out the door. The tray clattered to a halt against the wall. The door slammed. The bolt dropped home.

Rowena's head jerked up as she heard the clunk of his boot against the stones. He sat on the edge of the bed; his other boot fell.

"Proceed," he said. "Let the entertainment begin. I want to see your tricks."

"Tricks," Rowena repeated stupidly.

Gareth tugged his hauberk over his head. Dark fur erupted from the neckline of his rumpled tunic. "Tricks. The ones Irwin sold so freely. Is he the one who taught them to you?"

"Some of them."

The hauberk clinked to the floor with more violence than

was necessary. Gareth's smile was strained. "Then show me. As you well know, I am not a patient man."

Rowena mumbled something unintelligible, then stood with a curtsy. "As you wish."

Gareth's eyes darkened. He leaned back on his elbows, watching the play of the firelight through her threadbare kirtle. Her painful slenderness was broken only by the gentle swell of her breasts. She dropped to her hands and knees. Gareth sat up straight, his eyes widening. She rested the top of her head on the floor and balanced her knees on her elbows. Her shapely legs flailed wildly at the air. She held that pose, heedless of the fall of her skirts, for nearly a minute before toppling to the side with a grunt of exertion. She sprang to her feet with a graceful bow. Gareth stared at her as if she'd gone mad.

Her hopeful smile faded. "You did not fancy that trick? I have others." Her gaze darted around the room. "If you would call for some rope, I could string it from the mantel to—"

"Rowena."

"Sir?"

"Those were not the tricks I had in mind."

She met his gaze evenly. "They are the only ones I know, milord."

Gareth rose in a smooth motion. Rowena took a step backward. "I had something more in mind of the tricks you were showing that green-eyed whelp when I walked in."

He sauntered toward her. Her shins hit the Arabian chair; she leaped sideways as if scorched. What use would it be to explain that Green Eyes was as good as dead when she kissed him? Her eyes made an unconscious sweep of the chamber, finding Gareth's sword propped against the hearth. She would be hard-pressed to murder Gareth with his own sword. Even Marlys would take a dim view of that. Her search for something to bash him over the head with proved as futile. She realized too late that he had backed her into a circle. Her trembling knees fast approached the bed.

His voice lowered to a husky whisper. "I had thought to sample some of your tricks, and then show you a few tricks of my own."

Rowena smiled brightly. "Do you juggle, milord?" When her words did not slow his advance, her smile faded. Her knees locked against the mahogany bedstead. She put out one hand as if its fragile weight could stop him.

"Gareth, if you believe my family has taken to selling me and I to whoring to earn our bread, now would be a good time to admit you are sorely mistaken."

He gave her a long look from beneath his smoky lashes. "Mayhaps morning would be a more apt time to admit it. When I can kiss away your wounded tears and beg sweetly for your forgiveness."

She tilted her face to his, determined to award his honesty with her own. "Such ploys might work on the lady Alise. They will not work on me. I will not forgive you."

"It might be worth it." He bowed his head. His hand brushed her tangled cloud of hair. His fingers found a loose strand and brought it to his lips. "Why did you flee Caerleon?"

The truth was too dangerous for Rowena to admit, even to herself. "Because you asked me to leave you be."

His snort could have been one of laughter. "If I had asked you to stay with me that night, you would have done my bidding?"

"I would."

His head flew up. The strand of hair slipped from his fingers and fell across her face in a silky web. She blew softly and it drifted upward. His hand slipped beneath her hair to cup her neck, his fingers warm against her skin.

"If I bid you to lay with me tonight, would you?"

"The choice is yours, is it not? Yours is the strength, the will. There is no one to answer my cries for help. Percival and his cohorts would only delight in them."

Gareth's thumb toyed with the feathery softness of her earlobe. " 'Tis not rape I speak of, Rowena."

"The knight speaks of little else, be it rape of the man less fortunate than he, or rape of the woman he chooses to subject in the guise of chivalry."

His fingers tightened. Her pulse raced beneath the silken sheath of skin. His voice held an edge of bitterness. "Well spoken, milady. Marlys would applaud your newly found politics. You've become quite the learned woman beneath my tutelage."

"If you have your way, I fear I shall become more learned before this year is done."

His powerful fingers spread into her hair, cupping her skull with taut restraint. "I have lost a month of that year chasing you in bitter cold all over England, one step ahead of a mob that wants to stretch your pretty little neck on the gallows. I could have better spent the time curled in my warm, cozy bed at Caerleon."

"With the lady Alise?"

His voice deepened. "With you."

Rowena dropped her gaze. She longed to nuzzle her face into the soft folds of his tunic. The sating of her stomach had left her exhausted and terribly vulnerable to this dark-garbed man. His fingers lost themselves in her hair, stroking her scalp with hypnotic rhythm. She was so weary of taking care of others. To be taken care of by a man as strong and capable as Sir Gareth of Caerleon was a formidable temptation. To sway forward into his arms, to be carried to the ermine-trimmed bed and tucked beneath the warmth of his body. She knew instinctively that surrender would be as painless as he could make it.

Surrender.

Her eyes flew open at the glint of firelight off steel. Between Gareth's raised arm and rib cage, she had a perfect view of the window. Inching upward between the latch and shutter was the thin blade of a hunting knife.

"God's blood!" Rowena screeched as the latch went clattering up and the shutters flew open.

"Whatever is the matter?" Gareth's brows drew together

in a puzzled line as she flew around him and across the chamber like a woman possessed.

"Whatever is the matter?" she parroted. "Whatever is the matter? Can you not even latch a shutter properly? I've spent the past month clambering around in the ice and snow. I should hardly have to put up with it in my bedchamber, should I?"

She grasped the edge of the shutters. A desperate glance out the window showed her a pair of eyes as silvery-gray as the blade held between clenched teeth. Little Freddie stood on Irwin's shoulders, his foot in Irwin's ear. Irwin teetered on Big Freddie's back. Little Freddie's wiry fingers caught the shutters and tugged. Rowena tugged back with a grunt, steeling herself against his pleading gaze. Gareth's vow to kill first and ask questions later echoed through her mind. It was only when she heard his curious footfalls behind her that she found the strength to slam the shutters on her brother's fingertips.

She whirled around, clapping her hands together to muffle the yelp of pain and solid "Oomph" that came from below the window. "There now. Where were we?"

Gareth came toward her, his steps slow and measured as if he was afraid she might bolt out the window. "I understand that you are afraid, Rowena. But there is no need for hysterics. I am not a brute. I can be kind."

She gave him a brilliant smile. "Of course, you can." A timid scratching came on the shutter behind her as if they were besieged by an obstinate rat. She shot forward and grasped Gareth's forearms with a strength that surprised even her. She propelled him backward into the arms of the Arabian chair. "Are you comfortable, sir?" She peered into his face with the tenderest solicitude.

A flush of color had risen to her cheeks. Tangled curls tumbled over her brow. She could not know what an enchanting sight she made leaning over him in that manner.

"I should be more comfortable in the bed," he growled.

Rowena's tongue darted over her lips. She was at a genuine loss for words. The scratching against the shutter deepened to a persistent rattle.

Gareth peered around her shoulder. "The wind has risen most fiercely since we arrived."

Rowena's heart hammered. Her gaze danced around the chamber, seeking for some weapon to hold his attention away from the window. Her gaze lit on one of the provocative images embroidered in the tapestry.

She smoothed her skirts as if they were the finest satin, then sat gently on Gareth's lap. His legs went rigid like cords of iron. Before Rowena could lose her nerve, she cupped the satiny roughness of his bearded cheeks between her hands and pressed her lips to his.

His lips flattened beneath hers as his tongue succumbed to the temptation of a mouth opened like a rosebud to the nourishing rays of the sun. His arm slipped around her waist, crushing her against him with a hunger that put her own to shame.

His roughened knuckles slid beneath the kirtle to graze the fluttering pulse behind one knee. Rowena shifted her weight only to realize she was trapped like a butterfly against his lap. Gareth's hand glided up her thigh until the worn linen of her undergarment was the only thing that separated his greedy fingers from the soft warmth of her. Beneath her palms, his throat vibrated with a deep groan. His hand cupped her, pressing her down until she feared not even the sheath of their garments would stop him from satisfying the appetite she had so heedlessly whet.

Drunk with the taste of Gareth's tongue against her own, mad with the rough caress of his beard against her throat, Rowena forgot her reason for provoking his tender onslaught. She thought the hammering of angry young fists against wood was only the slam of her heart against her rib cage until the shutters gave way in a shower of splintered wood and a silver-haired sprite came spilling into the tower.

CHAPTER 14

Gareth slammed Rowena to the safety of the floor as an instinct bred deeper in him than bone or blood sent him diving for the hearth and his scabbard. He unsheathed the broadsword with both hands and crossed the tower in three strides. He drew the sword over his head, prepared to plunge it into the heart of the assassin who had burst through the window. The blade quivered, then froze in its downward motion.

Steel gray eyes glared up at him. Little Freddie lay on his back, knees akimbo, weight propped on his elbows. A scarred hunting knife spun on the floor a few feet away. He regarded Gareth's blade without a hint of a plea in his silvery orbs.

"You," Gareth breathed.

The plea absent from Little Freddie's drawn features came tumbling into view as Rowena tripped over her brother's foot and sprawled across his thin body.

She tossed her head back. Her gaze traveled from Gareth's straddled legs to his poised blade to his features, which hardened as if someone had set them in stone.

Her voice was low and urgent. "Gareth, please. Don't chop his head off. I beg you. Don't hurt him. I shall do anything you ask."

A dull red flush suffused Gareth's face as he realized the reason for her sweet subterfuge of passion. His eyes raked her in a wordless insult, taking in the mop of tangled gold falling over her face, the slender curve of her hip where her skirt had ridden up, her parted lips.

"Anything?" he heard himself reply coldly. A mercenary song strummed to life in his groin.

"Anything," she repeated. Her eyes met his boldly even as she clenched her jaw to stop it from quivering.

"Rowena!" Little Freddie squirmed beneath her with an agonized croak. "Make no bargains with the devil." His foot shoved at the small of her back.

"Be still, boy!" Gareth brought the sword down with a roar. The blade sank six inches into the wooden floor between Rowena's knees.

"I would have driven it through your hearts," he hissed, "if I thought either of you possessed one."

Two pairs of wide eyes blinked at the vibrating blade. Rowena swallowed audibly.

Gareth strode across the room and splashed wine into a goblet. "Mummers, indeed. If you could have extracted such a winsome performance from your sister at any one of those villages, you would be choking on gold by now."

Pink stained Rowena's cheeks. She and Freddie jumped as Gareth slammed the goblet down and paced back to them. He rocked lightly on the balls of his feet, locking his hands behind him. An unpleasant light glowed in his eyes.

"Let me insure that I understand you, Lady Fordyce. To spare the head of this brash stripling, you offer me anything I desire from you."

Rowena met his eyes over the sword hilt. She nodded, ignoring the vicious pinch Little Freddie gave the back of her arm.

Gareth crossed his arms. "No remorse. No rebuke. No mewling tears of recrimination on the morrow."

"None," Rowena said softly.

"You heartless bastard!" Little Freddie shoved himself at Gareth, but Rowena caught his neck neatly between her elbow and ribs, squeezing until his string of protests was smashed into garbled grunts. Her gaze never left Gareth's.

A cold smile flickered across his face. "All I must do is leave your brother's head attached to his shoulders."

She nodded solemnly, then stopped. A thoughtful look crossed her features.

Gareth started to turn away. "Your offer is accepted."

"Nay," she said suddenly.

Beneath her arm, Little Freddie collapsed in relief. Gareth pivoted on his heel, arching one eyebrow. "Nay?"

"Nay. Little Freddie's life is not enough. I want more. You must promise him your protection. Your nourishment. Even after my year is done and you've banished me from your company, you must find him a place in your household or in another. As a squire. When he comes of age, you will help him win his spurs."

Little Freddie's squirming began anew, intensifying with each word. His foot inched toward the hunting knife. Rowena drove a merciless elbow into his stomach, and he doubled over with a grunt.

Gareth's gaping mouth snapped shut. "Lindsey Fordyce as I breathe and speak! I thought your greed only extended to your charming little gut. You are a gem with many facets, indeed, milady."

Rowena did not flinch at his mocking tone. Gareth's cynicism warred with amusement in the face of her stony reserve. A muscle twitched in his cheek. He turned his face to the fire, trusting the leaping flames to hide his features in a silhouette of shadow.

"Your price grows steeper with each passing second. I should make haste to acquiesce before I am forced to foster your entire family and make your papa my page. What makes you think I wish to be saddled with this stubborn whelp for all eternity? He has proved himself painfully imprudent with a hunger for martyrdom that makes even myself skittish."

"He is bright," Rowena said quickly. Little Freddie's fingers curled like claws toward the knife. She caught his hair and gently rapped his head on the floor until his eyes fluttered shut in groggy surrender. She cradled his head in her lap and stroked his brow. "He is brighter than all the rest of us."

Gareth stroked his beard. "I'll grant you that."

"He would have had his chance to be a knight if Papa hadn't been lamed. 'Tis his birthright, you know. 'Twas not his doing that robbed him of it."

"That it was not. But 'twould be your doing that restores it. How noble." Gareth's tone implied the opposite. "Mayhaps he is too young to be a squire."

"Mayhaps I am too young to be your leman."

His lips quirked to acknowledge her hit. He ran one finger lovingly over the hilt of the sword embedded in the floor. "Are you worth it, Rowena?"

Rowena tossed her hair back boldly. "You will have to be the judge of that, won't you, sir?"

Gareth felt his groin tighten as his eyes followed the arch of her throat down to the gentle swell of one breast. "Very well. This devil accepts your bargain."

Rowena stood to face him in one smooth motion. Little Freddie groaned as his head was dumped from the cushion of her lap.

"Swear it."

Gareth stared at her. "My word is not generally suspect."

"Swear it."

"By God, you push me. As you wish. I give you my oath as a knight of—"

"On your knees."

With a growl, Gareth dropped to his knees at her feet, straddling the blade. His eyes burned up at her like live coals. For the first time, Rowena was glad to have the cold steel between them. He gritted out a guttural oath between clenched teeth, promising Little Freddie his protection and nourishment as long as he should live. The boy moaned, his eyes still shut. Rowena nodded, satisfied.

Gareth's hand shot out and encircled her wrist like a band

of iron. His words were clipped. "You may make your oath to me in private, milady. On your knees."

"As you wish, milord." Her eyes held a steely light Gareth did not recognize.

He climbed to his feet and plucked Little Freddie off the floor by the scruff of his tunic.

Rowena caught his sleeve. "You swore you would do him no harm."

Gareth shook her away as if she were no more than a bothersome flea. "I am doing him no harm. I am showing him out." He strode purposefully toward the window, stepping over shards of splintered shutter. Little Freddie's eyes popped open. "He can damn well leave the same way he came in."

Rowena flung herself on Gareth's back, wrapping one slender arm around his throat. "You mustn't. You shall kill him. You promised."

Gareth straightened with a sigh. Rowena's feet dangled a foot off the floor. "Woman, you try my patience."

Without bothering to unhook her, he leaned out the window, Little Freddie still in tow. Two dark shapes milled nervously below the window.

"Who goes there? Irwin, is that you?" he called.

There was a moment of silence broken by nothing but the murmur of the falling snow, then a faint, "Aye, sir."

"I've something for you. Hold your arms out."

Rowena slid off Gareth's back and sank to the floor, covering her eyes with her fingers as he dropped Little Freddie out the window. She waited for an agonized scream. A muffled grunt was followed by a timid, "Thank you ever so much, sir."

"My pleasure." Gareth leaned farther out the window. The firelight from the tower burnished his black hair to blue. He glared down at the pale, worried circle of Irwin's face.

Irwin cleared his throat. "We must be going, sir."

"No farther than the stable, please."

''Of course not, sir.''

Gareth dug his fingers into the snow crusted on the windowsill as the two dark shapes shuffled away, bearing their awkward burden between them. A hysterical giggle drifted back to them. Rowena crossed herself, mumbling a prayer of thanks that Little Freddie was not dead or maimed.

She watched as Gareth pried his sword from the floor and used its hilt to pound a tapestry over the yawning window. A cozy orb of color wreathed them. Rowena's eyes shied away from the sly winks and knowing leers of the faces frozen in the tapestries. Gareth knelt before the hearth and fed the planks of the hapless shutters to the waning fire.

Without turning around, he said, ''Tell me, Rowena. How many men have you offered yourself to in order to save your hapless kinfolk?''

''One. Only you.''

He gave the flames a vicious poke with the last plank. ''If you're lying, I am about to find out.''

Rowena picked at her cracked fingernails and studied his broad back beneath lowered lashes. He went to the table and poured himself another goblet of wine. His motions were painfully deliberate. When he came for her with his hands so cold, Rowena wondered how she would stop herself from pleading. But she had sworn not to. She had sold herself as basely as any whore, forfeiting any tenderness he might have offered.

He sank into the Arabian chair. The goblet dangled from his fingertips. Without looking at her he swished an inch of amber around in its bottom. ''Where were we? Shall I set the stage? I was here, and you were sitting in my lap, seducing me very prettily. Pray do continue.''

Rowena's heart sank. She crossed the chamber and slid onto his lap. His empty hand lay open and limp on the chair arm. He stared straight ahead, his features as impenetrable and pale as marble.

Drawing in a short, jerky breath, she pressed her lips to his. Her kiss was inexpert, amateur, and she knew it. She drew back. His lips had not moved beneath her caress, but his gaze had shifted to her face. He was studying her through narrowed eyes. This emboldened her to kiss him again. She cupped his neck in her palms. The powerful muscles were as rigid as steel. Gareth remained unmoved by her softness, as unrelenting as a statue in her embrace.

She drew away. Heat flooded her cheeks, and she hated herself for it. "You mock my inexperience, sir. I am not versed in the arts of love as you are."

The goblet rolled to the floor with a heavy clunk. Gareth caught her wrists in his hands. " 'Tis you who mock me. I know nothing of love. Nor do I care to learn."

Buried in Gareth's eyes, Rowena found a fear both deeper and more permanent than her own. She felt the warning prick of his words like a dagger at her throat. But she would gladly impale herself on such a weapon to storm the wall he'd built so well around himself. Her hands laced around his own, disarming him with their surrender. She leaned forward and drew her small tongue gently along the seam of his lips, feeling them part beneath the coaxing motion. His smoky lashes veiled his eyes as he returned her kiss, his mouth spreading beneath hers, his tongue sweeping out to possess hers. His broad thumb probed the center of her palm, sending an eerie rush of blood to her belly. She moaned softly against his lips.

He threw back his head with a laughing shudder. His knuckles rubbed the curve of her spine. "Do you seek to shame me with your surrender?"

"I swore not to beg or mewl, did I not?"

"And you are a lady of honor." Gareth's words held a strange note as if it were he and not she that he mocked. He gently pried her face out of his beard and cupped it between his hands. He looked down into her eyes. "If I gave you leave to beg, what would you beg for?"

"That if revenge on my papa was all you sought from me this night, you would throw me to Percival or one of the others." Her gaze did not waver.

Bewilderment touched his eyes. "Sweet Christ, I think you mean it. Do you hate me so well?"

Rowena lowered her gaze. "I could bear their cruelty better than your own."

He pulled her into his chest and rested his chin on top of her head. "Fickle child. Whose touch would you prefer to mine? Mayhaps that green-eyed fellow you kissed with an enthusiasm denied me in the simplest greeting? Or your dearly betrothed?" His hand rode the curve of her rib cage around to gently cup her breast. His thumb circled, caressing its small, tautening tip beneath the coarse linen. "Is it Irwin's fumbling hands you would have touch you this way?"

Rowena's mouth opened in a soundless gasp as a heat spread from Gareth's fingertips to her flesh. She nuzzled against him, pushing his tunic down with her nose until she could bury her face in the soft fur of his chest.

"Irwin offers me an honorable union blessed by God." Even to her own ears, her pious words rang with lack of conviction.

Gareth tilted her face, studying her features in the gentle glow of the firelight. He punctuated each word with the brush of his lips down the purest curve of her cheekbone. "What do I offer you? A slow ride to hell?"

His lips came to rest against the thundering pulse in her throat. Bewitched by the lingering heat of his mouth, Rowena's head fell back in languorous surrender as if her neck had grown too lazy to support the weight of her hair. Spurred on by the ceding of her ivory throat to his dominion, Gareth dared to slip his hand into the neck of her kirtle. Her breast fit neatly into the cup of his hand. With a tenderness he had forgotten he possessed, his fingertips stroked and teased the hardened bud pressed to his callused palm until a shudder wracked her slender frame.

Rowena's head was thrown back, her sandy lashes pressed to flushed cheeks. With her legs parted slightly so her skirt fell into the valley between, she looked ripe for his taking.

Gareth was not prepared for the trembling that seized his
hands. His other hand cupped her cheek. She opened her
eyes. They gleamed like stars in a sky that had known night
for too long.

"I've been so cold and hungry without you, Gareth."
Her fingers traced his lips as if memorizing their contours.

His lips parted. He bestowed upon each fingertip a tender
kiss. The hand that had cupped her breast slid downward
over the grooves between each rib, teased the smooth, flat
plane of her belly. Her blue gaze held him fast.

It seemed his whole life had brought him to this moment.
He held the power in his hands to release her from a bargain
made in wounded pride. But the time when Gareth could
have stopped his hand's descent had passed. It slipped between her skin and the rough folds of her undergarment,
finally coming to rest in the exquisite softness of the curls
between her legs. Gareth lowered his head, partly to earn
him time to steady his breathing, partly to hide the flush
that bathed his cheeks like the flush of a youth in the first
throes of manhood.

He pressed his lips to the delicate bell of her ear. The
kittenish softness of the tiny hairs there tickled his nose. "I
am going to fill you, milady. I am going to fill you so you
will never have to go hungry again." His husky words died
on a groan as one of his fingers dipped into her, touching a
warm, moist promise of ecstasy he had hardly allowed himself to dream of.

She slung an arm around his neck in a strangely fierce
embrace. He slipped an arm under her knees and shoulders
and carried her to the bed.

He laid her back on the goose-down coverlet. Her nervous
fingers plucked at the ermine trim. Gareth stood over her.
The dancing flames threw his shoulders into silhouette.
Wind gusted through the shutterless window until the tapestry billowed out in a graceful bell. Rowena shivered, more
from fear than cold.

Gareth knelt on the bed and gathered her in his arms like

a child. "You'll not go cold again. If we are going to burn, then we shall burn together."

His fingers curled around the nape of her neck like a band of velvet. His mouth found the silky softness of her lips and parted them for a leisurely pleasuring. Rowena returned his kiss with a newfound ardor. She eagerly pressed her young body to his muscled frame until the suggestive rhythm of his tongue taking the deepest corners of her mouth became impossible to ignore.

He broke away with a groan, tugging her kirtle off her shoulders as he went. Her hands caught his shaggy hair as he bent his head to her breast, gently teasing its coral peak with lingering strokes of his lips and tongue until an exquisite knot of longing tightened low in her belly. She stared with wonder at the coarse threads of silver woven through his dark hair. The feather tick rustled as he pushed her to her back. She lifted her hips obediently as he slid the kirtle down and followed it with the linen drawers.

A rosy blush crept in a charming pattern over her breasts and throat as she lay exposed to the hungry heat of his gaze. But her eyes remained open and trusting, and it was she who caught his hand and brought it to her lips. Her teeth gently nipped his thumb.

"Come, milord," she said with a tremulous smile. "You promised me a respite for my hunger."

He drew his tunic over his head and bared his teeth in a wicked grin. "I misled you. 'Tis I who would feast on you."

Rowena was reminded once again of the wolf as he lowered his head to her throat. A playful caress from the roughened softness of his tongue was followed by the scrape of his teeth against her flesh. His mouth glided lower, following the valleys and hills of her smooth flesh with teasing determination. Rowena choked back a giggle.

Gareth lifted his head with a throaty growl. "You make sport of me, lady. I daresay a good tongue lashing would curb your impudence."

He proceeded to prove his point, devouring her with his

mouth and hands until she tangled her fingers in his hair
and begged for a mercy she did not want. His dark curls
slipped like the silkiest pelt between her fingers. Pleasure
spread its fingers through her body like an exotic net, trap-
ping her in the web of her own need. His broad hands
cupped her buttocks, then slid lower, coaxing her thighs
apart with elaborate tenderness. She closed her eyes and
turned her face to the coverlet with a wordless murmur as
his fingers and lips made melody on her until every muscle
of her body arched into song.

She fell back to the bed, breathing as if she had been
running for a very long time, her eyes huge and misty with
wonder. Gareth met her gaze across the length of her body.
She knew instinctively that the time for play had passed.
His eyes were narrowed in dark slits of desire. A thrill of
fear and anticipation shot down Rowena's spine.

Gareth climbed to his knees and began to unwork the
points of his hose. His hands trembled. Rowena pressed her
fists to her eyes.

She kept her eyes clenched shut when he tugged one of
her hands into his.

"Rowena?" he said softly.

"Hmmm?"

He drew her hand to him. Her fingers uncurled and she
was touching something that had the resilience of steel
sheathed in velvet. Her hand explored its length in curious
wonder. A hoarse sound escaped Gareth's throat.

Rowena jerked her hand back. "I cannot," she moaned,
". . . you would surely slay me, milord . . ."

Gareth collapsed against her neck with a shaky laugh.
"You flatter me, my dear." He raised himself on his elbows
and stared deep into her eyes. " 'Tis passingly normal. I
swear to you, I have not slain anyone with it yet."

The briefest of shadows passed over his features. Rowena
could not bear to see it. She cupped his face in her hands
and drew his lips to hers. His mouth parted hers. His tongue
gently penetrated her, soothing and slaking as if to prepare

her trembling body for a deeper invasion. She relinquished the fear that held her muscles rigid. Her knees fell apart and she felt Gareth's groan of pleasure like a purr against her palm.

At first the hardness of him was like an unrelenting blade driven with merciless slowness into her tenderest flesh. She muffled a whimper of pain against his lips. Gareth felt it, though he did not hear it. His heavy frame shuddered, and she realized what the effort of his patience was costing him. He was a man accustomed to charging violently into every challenge life offered him. And now he was holding his own desperate need at bay to ease her pain.

Rowena tore herself away from his kiss and pressed her lips to his ear. "Fill me," she whispered. "Now."

She did not have to ask twice. Gareth drove the length of his hardness into her, tearing away the last fragile protest of her innocent body. He was still for a long moment, basking in the miracle of her warmth surrounding him. Her breath came in short pants. He studied her face, waiting for the abatement of pain that would tell him she was ready. His tongue lapped a single tear from her sweat-sheened cheek.

She blinked quizzically up at him. "Is it over?" Her crestfallen expression melted his heart.

"Nay, my sweet. 'Tis only beginning."

With those words, he began to move deep within her. Her eyes fluttered closed. Her head turned from side to side. Her moist, swollen lips caught threads of gold on them. Gareth smoothed them away, deepening and lengthening his strokes until Rowena learned there was a deeper more insatiable hunger than that for food. Her hands caught his shoulders, feeling the smooth play of the muscles sheathed beneath rigid scars, urging him on as he rode her to the edge of hell and back until she swore she could see the exploding stars of heaven itself.

A gust of wind sent the tapestry billowing behind Gareth like a cloak of darkness. A chunk of wood on the fire breathed its dying gasp in a brilliant sputter of light; the mirror above the bed gave up its secrets. Rowena watched mesmerized as Gareth's back went rigid. He arched his neck, his muscles cords of tension. A guttural cry escaped his throat before he collapsed against her, his weight no more a burden than her own.

She stared up into the mirror at the pale blond stranger trapped beneath the sated body of a man. She watched the stranger's fingers tenderly comb through the man's sweat-tangled hair. An enigmatic smile curved the stranger's mouth. Rowena closed her eyes, the faint half-smile still on her lips.

CHAPTER 15

Gareth clattered down the steps two at a time. His head spun with thoughts centered on the sleeping angel he had left curled in the bed. He did not realize he was singing until he rounded the last step and his rich baritone burst into the dead silence like an unwanted gift.

Three glum faces surveyed him. For an instant, Gareth saw himself as they did—hair tousled, tunic rumpled, hose furred with dust where they had been tossed heedlessly on the floor. Irwin shoved away his trencher as if he had suddenly lost his appetite. Thrown over his shoulders was the mantle of lush fur Gareth had discarded the night before. Big Freddie turned a sullen jaw to the fire. Little Freddie glared at him, gouging a pit in the oaken table with the blunt end of a knife.

Gareth's song subsided to a hum which ended on a faint questioning note as he surveyed the cozy hall.

"Confess, lads. Have you vanquished the knights of Midgard? Do they be bound and gagged in the stables?" Gareth deliberately made his voice cheerful and booming.

Big Freddie snorted. "Knights indeed."

"The knights have fled." Little Freddie's words were laced with contempt. "Irwin blundered into telling them what Rowena was to you. They scurried like rats to their holes, fearful you might awaken in a cranky temper."

Gareth whistled as he hooked an iron pot over the fire.

He stuck a finger in its contents and brought it to his lips. "Not much danger of that, now was there?"

"None at all. Savagery and treachery bring out the best in some men."

Gareth's fist swung around on Little Freddie, but the boy ducked. Gareth rumpled his hair. "Curb that tongue of yours and we'll make a knight out of you yet, my lad."

Little Freddie's fair skin blushed a becoming pink. His hand reversed its grip on the knife, and Gareth knew he was one smirk away from getting it in his gullet. The knight's smile did not waver. The boy satisfied himself by stabbing an errant roach scuttling across the table.

Irwin flinched and snuggled deeper into Gareth's mantle. He drew the wooden trencher close to his chest only to have it plucked out of his hands as Gareth paced behind him.

Gareth poked at the salted fish and cheese with interest. "Where did those cheeky bastards get fresh grapes this time of year? Is Rowena fond of grapes?"

Irwin opened his mouth to answer but it was Big Freddie who said, "Never had them. There were no grapes at Revelwood by the time Ro was old enough to taste them."

Gareth pursed his lips as if deep in thought. "What think you, Little Freddie? Would grapes make your sister happy?"

Little Freddie leaned back on the bench and crossed his arms. "Do you care?"

"Deeply."

Their eyes locked in silent battle.

"Water's boiling," grunted Big Freddie.

"So it is." Gareth bustled to the hearth. He wrapped a rag around his hand and unhooked the pot, leaving it to cool on the hearth. He plunked the trencher down on Big Freddie's thighs.

"Watch those grapes, won't you?" he whispered with a sidelong glance at Irwin. "I must see to my mount."

"No need," Big Freddie replied. " 'Tis been done."

"Many thanks. Would you do something else for me?" Gareth could almost see Irwin's ears perk up. He leaned closer to Big Freddie's ear. "Make ready the mounts for the journey to Caerleon."

Big Freddie stared straight ahead. "Yours and Rowena's and Little Freddie's?"

"*All* the mounts."

"Aye, sir."

Gareth tucked a small log under one arm, latched the kettle over one finger, and held out his palm. Big Freddie laid the trencher across it. Gareth gave Irwin an infuriating wink as he started up the stairs, balancing his treasures with elaborate care. It was not until he rounded the first curve of the enclosed staircase that his throat warbled into song.

Rowena hugged the pillow to her stomach, murmuring Gareth's name into it. The pillow made no response. A sound like ivory chittering against ivory brought her tousled head up and her bleary eyes open. It took a long, puzzled moment before she realized it was her teeth chattering. She rolled over and sat up on her knees, bearing the brunt of her shrieking muscles with a grimace. She peeked beneath the coverlet, searching her body for some cryptic sign of Gareth's possession of it.

His crest was not emblazoned upon her chest. His brand upon her was an invisible chain binding her to him by the faint tenderness between her legs, and the quickening of her breath as scenes of the night flashed through her mind in a dazzling procession. Her teeth stopped chattering abruptly. She fell forward, burying her face in the coverlet with a shriek of laughter.

A growl of hunger tugged her upright. The curve of her hollow belly seemed to be touching her backbone. She pulled the coverlet up around her shoulders, suddenly chilled to the bone. Had Gareth forgotten his pledges already? He had promised to banish both hunger and cold from her life. Had they only been pretty words designed to satisfy the lust that had driven him to take her again and again in the night,

sometimes tenderly, sometimes savagely, until they had collapsed into each other's arms in stuporous slumber? What
did he promise Lady Alise for a taste of her favors? A bag
of gold? A cluster of pearls? How he must be laughing at
her, won by only the promise of a basted ham and a stoked
fire.

Despair darkened her eyes as she surveyed the abandoned
chamber. Only a handful of embers glowed orange on the
hearth, and the shards of splintered wood on the floor were
dusted with a light blanket of snow the wind had swept
beneath the tapestry. Perhaps the dark lord had already fled
his handiwork of the night, leaving her at the mercy of the
next randy group of knights who might stumble upon Midgard. Her brow folded with consternation. She could almost
hear their bawdy ditties like the echo of ghost songs far
away.

The bawdy ditty grew louder. Her bleak musings consumed her so neatly that when the door flew open with a
kick of Gareth's foot, she blinked at him as if he himself
were a ghost. The smile that curved her lips was like the
sun breaking through a bank of thunderheads. She held out
her arms to him. Gareth stopped, his song dying on an
indrawn breath. A look crossed his face that Rowena could
not interpret. She had the eerie feeling she was seeing the
ghost of a younger Gareth, shy and uncertain of his welcome.

When he did not move to accept her embrace, a wave of
answering shyness washed over her. She pretended to
stretch, surveying him beneath lids still swollen with sleep
and the lack of it.

"The color suits you, milord," she said lightly, referring
to the length of fine wool draped over one brawny shoulder.
"The shade complements your hair."

"Conduct yourself well," he replied, "and I might let
you borrow it."

Gareth shoved the log into the strangling fire and dumped
his other burdens on the table. He crossed to the bed and

dangled a kirtle of the most exquisite shade of rose in front of Rowena's freckled nose. She reached for it. He jerked it back with a smirk, his gaze dropping as the coverlet slipped off her creamy shoulders.

Rowena pulled the coverlet all the way up over her nose, her eyes mischievous slits of blue. "Conduct yourself well and I might let you borrow it," she said, her voice muffled.

The kirtle slipped to the floor in a pool of softness as Gareth dove on her. Feathers flew as he rolled over, pulling her on top of him. As they settled into the hollow his body molded in the tick, the coverlet enveloped them both. Gareth's hands were warm against her bare waist.

His eyes sparkled. "Such insolence. Little do you know what dangers I braved to procure these treasures for my lady. Three dragons I faced, breathing fire and retribution down my neck."

Rowena lifted her hips in a halfhearted attempt at escape. "Might the dragons have been christened Irwin and Freddie and Freddie once again?"

"They might." Gareth took advantage of her struggles to slide himself into a position that would have been worse than compromising were it not for the soft sheath of his woolen hose between them.

Rowena grew very still. "You did slay these said dragons with your mighty sword?"

"Alas! I was unarmed. I was forced to bear the brunt of their surly looks and dastardly mutterings in the most sheepish surrender. My mighty sword was spent, sorely taxed by a winsome damsel who mocks my meager gifts with the cruelest of jests."

Rowena flattened her palms against his chest with a tantalizing wiggle. "Your mighty sword shows signs of life."

Gareth's eyes narrowed into lazy slits of passion. "You, winsome damsel, could stir a dead man to life."

He cupped her head in his hand and drew her face down to his. When she finally straightened, her hands were trembling and her breathing unsteady. "Is that the only gift you brought me? Or are there others?"

The corner of Gareth's mouth lifted in a wry twist. "Ever the pragmatist."

He shoved her heedlessly off him, sending her tumbling to her rear with a squeal. She crouched in the folds of the coverlet as he crossed to the table to fetch his offerings.

With a bow, he set the iron pot beside the bed, pretending to struggle beneath its weight. "Your bath, milady."

Rowena frowned. "A trifle small, is it not?"

"Whine not or I will put you in it myself."

Rowena studied the ten-inch pot and wisely shut her mouth.

He presented the trencher to her with a flourish. A spark of interest lit her eyes.

"These gems were wrested from a ravenous dragon, indeed, with flapping ears and a most indignant stare."

"Indignant no doubt because you pilfered his cheese."

Gareth sat down on the edge of the bed and caressed her hair. "And his betrothed."

"No doubt you were paralyzed with shame." Rowena shuffled through the slabs of fish and cheese.

"Only when the smallest dragon pierced me with his stare. Had it been a blade, 'twould have severed my lecherous head."

"As you were wont to sever his own last night." Rowena's fingers squeezed a grape until it squished out of its skin onto the bed.

"Hardly. I find myself growing quite fond of the lad. He is a foe to be reckoned with when armed with kettle or knife."

Her mouth fell open. "You had no intentions of killing him?"

Gareth popped a grape in her yawning maw. "None whatsoever."

Her mouth snapped shut. "You tricked me."

He sighed. His fingers toyed with the silky flesh of her

cheek. "Must we flog this point to death? How many times must I win you to convince you that you belong to me?"

Rowena swallowed the grape whole. "You did not win me last night." She calmly pushed his hand away. "You turned the dice in your mantle. You cheated."

Gareth stood, his features hardening. "The last man that said that to me got a lance in the throat."

"For what? Questioning your honor or telling the truth?"

Gareth's foot lashed out, overturning the pot. "So I cheated! Would you have preferred I let that nasty wretch Percival carry you abovestairs? Or killed him for even daring to look at you?"

"But how do I know you did not cheat Papa out of me to begin with?"

Her serenity only infuriated him more. "Contrary to your high opinion of me, I am not given to cheating idiots. Or murdering boys."

"Are you given to murdering women?" The words slipped out before Rowena could bite them back.

Gareth's head fell back. He stared at the ceiling, his effort to control himself as visible as the rigidity of his stance. A stricken look slacked his jaw, and Rowena gazed upward to see what he saw.

Bloodstains in the mirror. Her shattered innocence staining the linen sheets. And next to the bed, the dark pool of the spilled water running in rivulets, lapping hungrily at the sodden kirtle in its midst—a rose-colored kirtle that loaned the water its hue in the torchlight. Gareth lowered his gaze to her.

A strange smile quirked his lips. Rowena shivered as he ran his forefinger down the length of her nose, then kissed its tip. "Only time will tell, my love. Only time will tell."

He left her then, still steeped in the echo of his careless endearment. She sat with her cheek against her knees, pondering his words and aching for his touch until Irwin banged on the door and gruffly announced the horses were ready for their return to Caerleon.

CHAPTER 16

Marlys swung from bough to bough like a graceless ape. At the top of the ancient oak, the branches grew more fragile and farther apart until she was forced to scuttle up the trunk. The rough bark tore a chunk of flesh from her knee, but she hardly felt it. The last slender branch she reached for came away in her hand. A few years ago she could have scaled the top branches with no more than a creak to betray her. With a mutter of disgust, she hunched into the thin lacing of branches, hating the weight of her womanhood.

The tree cradled her like a nest, its naked branches shielding her black-garbed figure almost as well as summer foliage. A balmy wind shivered a leaf that still held its tenacious grip on a twig. Marlys lay her cheek against the damp bark, loving winter because it made no promises it could not keep.

The morning's gentle rain had washed the snow into muddy patches. Land and sky curved into a bowl of unremitting gray broken only by the faraway towers of Ardendonne. Blaine's scarlet pennons rippled in defiant splendor against the meek sky. If her father had lived, Marlys knew she would have been mistress there by now. Even now, only her own stubbornness and Gareth's grace saved her from that fate.

As a child she had fled often to this tree, escaping the rebukes of a nurse who would chasten her to ''act more like a lady and less like a wild thing,'' escaping the mild dis-

appointment in the eyes of a father who had wanted only
sons, escaping the inescapable allure of a brother who could
displease no one. In its branches she found a grace unbound
by the fetters of childish clumsiness. When the hawks
skimmed past on invisible sheets of air, she would dream
of going with them, soaring away from Caerleon, gliding
over the meadows to a place where no one chided or yelled
or tweaked her nose to tenderly bait her as her brother was
wont to do.

The sky was empty on this day. The hawks had sailed to
that better place without her. A cramp tightened her ankle.
She rubbed it absently, and lifted her head. Black dots crept
across the meadow in the distance. Her pulse quickened.
She counted under her breath. Five horses. Four riders. Nay.
As incongruous as Folio's prancing gait against a quilt of
dun came a splash of yellow hair against a field of black.
The black was her brother's chest. The yellow hair,
Rowena's. Marlys's nails dug into the tree bark, driving cold
black silt beneath them.

She could not see Rowena's smile, only the tilt of her
head toward the man who held her. Marlys wanted to throw
back her head and howl. She watched them cross the meadows, her eyes hot and dry, until the riders disappeared into
the shadows of the forest below.

She shimmied down the tree trunk. Near the bottom, her
heel caught a branch near its tip. The sharp crack warned
her too late. She fell backward as the branch gave, not recognizing the frightened cry as her own.

She lay in the leaves for a long time, feeling their wetness
seep into the back of her tunic. When her breath returned,
the sobs came with it, deep and shuddering with an edge
that sliced her gut, making her want to vomit. When they
were spent, she sat up and scrubbed the tearstains from her
face with her hair. The rain beat over her in windy sheets
as she sprinted toward Caerleon to welcome her brother and
his lady home.

• • •

Rowena sank into the linen-lined tub with a sigh. Warm water lapped at her chin. A faint smile curved her lips as she remembered her first bath at Caerleon. This night there was no Dunnla to scrub her skin raw. The beaming old woman had tactfully disappeared after filling the tub and booming something that sounded like ''bacon home'' in Rowena's ear. This time she bathed not in the kitchen but in the privacy of Gareth's chamber. Irwin's face had fallen with disappointment when Gridmore had dragged the wooden tub past him and up the stairs.

A fire roared on the hearth, its warmth ballooning through the chamber. Rowena dragged her fingertips lazily through the water. Her eyes fixed on the great bed, remembering the nights she and Gareth had lain like statues, afraid to touch one another for fear they could not stop. Only when exhaustion had claimed them had their bodies sought out the warmth of one another. They had awakened most often with their limbs entwined, the sweet smell of sleep an intimate bond between them. Tonight would be different. When Gareth returned from his tour of Caerleon, he would find her tucked between his furs, damp and clean and waiting.

The nights since they had left Midgard had been passed beneath the watchful eyes of her brothers and cousin. Little besides their hands and gazes had touched. Only once had Gareth drawn her away while the others were taking down the tent, pulling her into a copse and pinning her against a pine with his kiss until she thought he would take her then and there, quickly and secretly. But he had pulled away, driving his fingers through his hair with a groan. They had returned to mount with the others, her silly grin matching the one on Gareth's lips. Beneath the fur mantle he had wrested from a reluctant Irwin, his hands had roamed shamelessly until her giggles became small moans and she begged him in a tight whisper to end his exquisite tortures. Tonight would be very different indeed.

Rowena held her breath and ducked beneath the water to

rinse away the soap. She emerged and flipped her streaming hair out of her eyes. Marlys stood at the end of the tub, arms crossed and one booted foot propped on its rim.

Marlys's hair hung in damp hanks. Her tunic was beaded with moisture. In the heat of the chamber, she smelled like a damp hound. Rowena crossed her arms over her chest, remembering their last meeting—Marlys's kindness in helping them flee. After too many sleepless nights on earth frozen to icy lumps, Rowena now wondered if it was kindness or malice that had prompted Gareth's sister.

"Welcome home, pup."

"Hullo, Marlys. 'Twas hardly a homecoming without you leaping out of a tree at us." Rowena reached for the soap, keeping her face carefully expressionless.

Marlys scooped up the slippery ball and tossed it in the air. "I was around."

"You always are, are you not?"

"Only when you need me." Marlys circled the tub.

Tears stung Rowena's eyes as Marlys grabbed a handful of hair near the scalp and jerked her fingers through a tangled strand. Rowena bit her lip to stifle a shriek.

"How many weeks has it been since you combed this mop?"

"I could ask you the same thing," Rowena retorted.

"It wants untangling badly."

Rowena snatched her hair out of Marlys's implacable grip. "I have no desire to be bald by the time Gareth returns."

Marlys tossed the soap in the water and took an ivory comb from the table. Her smile was a flash of startling white behind a fall of dark hair. "Trust me."

As Marlys approached, Rowena fished the soap out of the water and cradled it in her fist like a rock. Marlys knelt behind the tub and gathered a handful of hair. With surprising gentleness, she began to work the comb through its length. Rowena's scalp tingled as the languid strokes drew her head back. The rim of the tub cradled the nape of her neck. She closed her eyes. The grainy soap slipped from her hand and drifted downward in a cloudy path.

Marlys's voice was as soft and soothing as her hands in Rowena's hair. "Where did you spend your nights on your return to Caerleon?"

Rowena did not open her eyes. "Fields. Copses. Once the snow began to melt, 'twas pleasant enough."

Marlys abandoned the comb and curled the damp tendrils around her fingers. " 'Tis a pity he could not lodge at the keeps of his friends. I suppose his reputation is black enough without carting a bright-eyed whore all over England."

Rowena's shoulders heaved in a weary sigh. The last time she had thought herself a whore in this tub she had dissolved in tears. But then it had not been the truth. She could hardly lash out at Marlys for putting her new status into words, however cruel their intent.

Marlys gathered her hair into a knot. "You were a fool to let Gareth catch you."

"Do you see any scars marring my flesh? Your brother did not flog me. He did naught but warm and feed me."

Marlys's laugh was low. "I daresay he did. The way his hands lingered when he pulled you off Folio, I thought he was going to warm you right there in the bailey."

Rowena's eyes were as opaque as the cloudy water. "Why did you send me away?"

"You were losing your heart to him, were you not? Like all those others before you." Marlys's hands tightened into fists, tugging the tender hairs at the nape of her neck. "Is that how you would choose to spend your life? Simpering over a man who could never return your love?"

" 'Tis how you have chosen to spend your life, is it not?" Without warning, Marlys slammed Rowena's head under the water. Rowena came up, sputtering and spitting, only to be shoved under again. The next time she came up swinging, and Marlys caught a soapy fist in the mouth.

Water flew as Rowena shook her hair out of her eyes and leaped to her feet. "Shall you drown me?"

" 'Tis more compassion than Gareth will show when he tires of your mewling." Marlys jammed her hands into her sleeves and paced to the window. She threw open the shutter and turned her face to the rain.

Rowena sat down abruptly. "The truth of your jealousy stings, does it not? I've heard the things you say to him. As long as you keep him obsessed with the past and make him feel unworthy of another's love, he belongs to you. You can keep him at Caerleon, cut off from society, in virtual isolation. He will venture out to fight his tournaments, to bed his women, but he will always return to you because you will insure he believes you are the only one who loves him, despite the past."

Marlys slammed the shutter. "Of course I love him. Everyone loves Gareth. I heard it as a child until I thought it would make me ill. My mother loved him. I tore open her womb fighting to be born, but 'twas Gareth's name she whispered with her dying breath. My father loved him. He was every hope my father had. And we both know how well Elayne loved him."

Rowena stood. Pride stiffened her spine. Refusing to show a trace of shyness, she climbed out of the tub and crossed to the linen towel draped in front of the fire.

She bent to dry herself with the stiff warm folds.

Marlys's arms hung loose at her sides. "Not one mark did he leave on you." Her voice tightened. "Unless he put a babe in your belly." Rowena straightened, mesmerized by the venom in Marlys's voice. "You'd best hope he failed at that, lest it meet the same fate as Elayne's babe."

Rowena's towel hung forgotten from her fingertips. The door swung open. She was unaware of the portrait the flames painted of her in shades of peach and gold and stricken blue.

"Begone, Marlys." Gareth stood in the doorway, a steaming cup cradled in his hand. "Now."

His expression did not invite argument. Rowena shielded herself with the towel, suddenly shy. Marlys gave Rowena a mocking bow before sweeping out the door. Gareth slammed the door behind her.

Rowena turned all of her attention to drying between her toes. She could not meet Gareth's gaze with Marlys's words still spinning through her head. Elayne's cursed babe again. She kept her head bent, praying her hair would hide her flush of confusion.

The cup clinked as he laid it on the hearth. His hand brushed the naked curve of her spine. "Was she taunting you?"

"Sometimes I think she must hate me as much as she hated your stepmother."

Gareth's eyes darkened. "On the contrary. She worshiped Elayne. Followed her everywhere like a puppy. I suppose she tired of following me."

Rowena shivered, more from Marlys's lingering miasma of doom than from cold. Gareth held up a finger for her patience. He wrested two pelts from the bed. One he spread at Rowena's feet. The other he held like a cloak in front of him.

She arched an eyebrow. "My bed, milord? I had hoped I was done sleeping at your feet."

"Impudent wench. One bath and you fancy yourself fit for my bed." He threw the fur over her head. His arms circled her. Her feet left the floor. He sank down, dragging her into his lap. The soft fur tickled her nose, making her sneeze. He poked around in the top of the fur until a golden head emerged. "Look what I found! A stray beastie among my pelts." He ruffled her damp hair. "What a lovely pair of gloves these locks would make! Or mayhaps a muff for my lady."

"Your lady would be cursed indeed at such a perverse muff. She might stuff her hands in and never retrieve them."

Gareth brought her palm to his lips. "We must avert such disaster, for her hands are precious to me indeed."

Rowena's hand lingered at his face, her fingertips tracing warm lips through a prickly beard. When enfolded in the warmth and nearness of him, the doubts stirred by Marlys's icy words seemed a world away. She leaned the back of her head against his shoulder as one of his hands began a leisurely quest beneath the fur for something more substantial than her palm. Warm earthenware brushed her lips. The cozy scent of cloves and cinnamon wafted to her nostrils in a curtain of steam.

"I almost forgot," Gareth said. "Drink this."

Rowena recoiled from the cup in his hand. "What is it?"

"Poison, of course. What else would you expect of me?"

Rowena giggled, not sure if she should. She took a sip. Spiced cider flavored with ale slid down her throat.

"How sweetly you would drink poison for me." At his pensive tone, Rowena twisted to see his expression. He dug his chin into the top of her head to prevent it. " 'Tis a sobering thought."

" 'Tis a pleasant poison."

He gently boxed her ears. " 'Tis only a posset Dunnla brewed for you. I bade her go heavy on the ale in the hopes you would lose your wits and I could make merry on your body all the night long."

This time Gareth failed to hold her still. Rowena's struggles rocked the cup, and he was forced to set it aside. She wiggled in a circle and threw herself against him, driving him to his back. The fur slid off her shoulders. She leaned forward, dragging her bare breasts across his tunic in a tantalizing motion.

"I've already lost my wits. I need no posset to prove it."

Gareth murmured an agreement as he cupped her head and pulled her mouth to his. Their lips lingered in a touch of flame, bound together by the inextricable sweetness of warmth and cinnamon.

After a breathless moment, Gareth wrapped her hair around his fist and pulled her head up. "Rowena, these stones are rather lumpy."

Her smile was crooked. "Suffer, sir. You've had no bath. You are not fit for my bed."

She pressed her sweet-smelling body to his. Rain pattered against the shutters as Rowena proceeded to make him forget about the lumpy stones and every other thought that had ever entered his mind. She shuddered as his velvety hardness deepened the ache within her. She squeezed her eyes shut against the tears that would come, and for a timeless moment cared naught if he had murdered a hundred treacherous women and their mewling babes.

Marlys stood with her back pressed to Gareth's door. A groan so deep it was almost a growl was followed by a tinkling bell of laughter.

"Aye, my sweet puppy," Marlys said softly, burying her face in her hands. "Jealous."

A soft moan, throaty with the exquisite agony of pleasure, drifted through the door. Marlys clapped her hands over her ears and fled down the corridor, trying to escape the bright edge of light the lovers cast. It left her in a shadow so deep she was afraid she might disappear forever. She threw herself on her own bed and stuffed the coverlet in her mouth to muffle her sobs.

PART III

Silly boy, 'tis full moon yet, thy night as day shines
     clearly;
Had thy youth but wit to fear, thou couldest not
     love so dearly.
Shortly wilt thou mourn when all thy pleasures are
     bereaved;
Little knows he how to love that never was
     deceived.

                 —*Thomas Campion*

CHAPTER 17

An early spring blew in on the winds of March. Rowena's shrieks filled the great hall one lazy afternoon as she ran, skipping down the stairs with Gareth in pursuit. Her hair swung out in a golden arc as she danced across the hall, putting a wooden table between them. Gareth stumbled after her like a rumpled ogre with tunic wrinkled and hair uncombed.

"Milord," she cried, leaning her hands on the table and fighting to catch her breath. "I swear to you. I thought them flowers. Did you not see the tiny blooms?"

Gareth's brow furrowed in a thunderous frown, yet his eyes sparkled with amusement. "The blooms were not visible from the angle I saw them while plucking them out of my flesh."

Rowena gave an impish grin. "I offered to help you . . ."

Gareth growled and lunged across the table. Rowena squealed and darted away. Her hair drifted across his palm, an elusive softness, then was gone. She scampered toward the patch of sunlight before the open door, the dove-blue wool of her cotte caught in her fists.

"Thistles!" Gareth bellowed. "The wench puts thistles in my bed!"

Rowena vanished into the halo of sunshine. Her words floated back to him on the wind. "But Little Freddie swore . . ."

"How many times have I warned you not to listen to Little Freddie? The lad despises—"

Gareth burst into the empty courtyard. The sun winked mockingly at him. He scanned gray walls covered with dead lichen but heard only the rustle of the wind until a haunting giggle drifted back to him. He scaled the wall with a small leap and sat perched on its ledge with chin in hand. At the bottom of the hill, Rowena's pert rump was all that was visible as she rolled onto a low stone wall. With a graceful kick of bare ankles, she propelled herself over and went skipping into the orchard.

Her laughter floated back to him as she twirled among the apple trees like a drunken pixie. Gareth shook his head, wishing he could preserve forever her childlike abandon. His smile faded. He had wanted to preserve her once before but had failed miserably. Her skirts billowed around her ankles in a cloud of blue. Gareth lifted his eyes to a sky of the same color. White-puffed cotton clouds lay across its crisp edges. The sun touched his face in pleasant warmth.

But he knew that, too, would fade, bringing a night marred by darkness and doubt. Rowena spun on one foot until she collapsed in a dizzy heap. Gareth would not have been surprised had she vanished before his eyes, taking, too, the boyish joy born anew in him. The only time he truly felt he possessed her was when she lay beneath him, her supple body spread to accept whatever tenderness he could offer. Then he reveled in the wondrous feel of her, the hair tangled in his fingers, the salty-sweet taste of her skin against his tongue. He slept each night with one arm locked around her waist and his other hand gently resting over her heart.

He was a fool to think he could hold her forever. If she knew the truth, she would hate him. And as long as Lindsey Fordyce was alive, the truth might bumble into this hall at any moment. It shook him to realize he hadn't even thought of the wretch in the last month. All of his dreams of justice faltered before the tender light in Rowena's eyes. He dreaded seeing her trust turn to loathing upon discovery of his deceit.

Perhaps God had not put Fordyce in his path for revenge. Perhaps instead God had laid Rowena in his arms, giving him one last chance to make amends for his mistakes. To be the kind of man his father had bred him to be. But his own selfish desires threatened to defeat him just as they had with Elayne. 'Twould be better to begin cutting the ties that bound before he and Ro grew even more deeply entwined. He should find her a husband and send her far away before summer's end. But how would he ever sleep when she was gone?

An apple, long dead and shriveled by winter, sailed past his ear. Rowena peeped at him from behind a weathered trunk. Pushing his dark thoughts aside, he scooped up the apple, slid from the wall, and loped down the hillside. He vaulted over the stone wall. Rowena started for the shelter of another tree. His arm shot out to circle her waist before she could take two steps. He swung her around in a wide circle, ignoring the futile scissoring of her feet.

"Thistles. A woman who would mistake thistles for roses would surely find beauty in such fruit." He waved the apple, dotted with wormholes, dangerously close to her nose and sang in a loud and lusty baritone, "My apple is rare and beyond compare." He dropped the apple so that his fingers could find the delicate ridge between her ribs where he knew she was most ticklish.

Her body went limp, and she collapsed over his arm. Her mop of hair swept the fruit-littered ground.

"Mercy, milord. I beg of you." She blinked up at him prettily.

He eyed her charming rump. "From this position, I would petition King Edward for England itself if you asked for it."

"Hmmmm. A tempting prospect."

He swept her up and around into his arms. He plucked a twig from her hair and gazed down at her, the laughter disappearing from his eyes. "Not nearly so tempting as this one." His mouth brushed the succulent fullness of her lower lip.

Gareth kissed her gently, coaxingly, until her slender arms circled his waist and he felt her sigh of surrender against his lips. The musky scent of decaying apples wafted around them. His eyes opened against his will. Tiny green buds of spring unfurled against the blue sky. He slammed his eyes shut at the sight. He dragged Rowena against him as if he could somehow stop the passing of the seasons with the onslaught of his body. Was he protecting her or deceiving her? His mind dismissed the question callously as answers that required no questions flooded his body in a molten stream of want.

The sun slid slowly into a pocket of rose as Gareth lifted Rowena over the orchard wall. They ambled toward the castle, his arm draped over her shoulder, her arms hugging his waist. He pushed open the iron gate to the courtyard with his free hand. The shadows of twilight drifted over the trees. A cozy hiss and sputter emanated from the great hall as Gridmore lit the flambeau. A pool of light spread from the open door. Rowena turned her face to Gareth's for a lingering kiss while the shadows of impending night still sheltered them.

A majestic burst of trumpets shattered the peace.

Rowena drew back from Gareth's kiss. She clung to his forearms, her eyes misty. " 'Tis the first time *that* has happened when you've kissed me."

Gareth grinned. "You do my ego well, but I fear 'twas not my doing." He kissed the tip of her nose. "Wait until tonight," he whispered. "I shall give you trumpets and lutes and tabors enough to make your heart sing."

The trumpets sounded again. Gareth and Rowena pounded through the great hall and out the main door like children. Marlys straddled the courtyard wall, grinning like a feral cat. Irwin stared at the men before him as if they were angels. The steely eye of the falcon was emblazoned on their breasts.

Gareth snorted. "I should have known. Only Blaine would send three trumpeters with a single herald."

The grim-faced men in their voluminous surcoats lifted their trumpets again. Irwin's face fell as Gareth snatched the creamy parchment from the herald's hand before they could blow. He slit the waxen seal with his dagger.

"He wants us to come for Easter. To break the Lenten fast with him. What say you, Rowena, shall we . . . ?"

His question went unfinished. Rowena was gone. Without her golden head, the courtyard seemed darker somehow, more fraught with shadows. He lifted a puzzled smile to the herald.

"Come, all of you. Sup with us. You may carry my answer to your lord at the dawn."

The men's stern faces relaxed as he ushered them into the beckoning light of the hall. Marlys sat in the deepening darkness until a single candle flared to life in Gareth's window.

Well after midnight, Irwin tapped on Rowena's door. "Sir Gareth wishes to see you in the solar."

Summoned. To a chamber Gareth used to discuss with his seneschal the fate of pregnant heifers and blighted wheat crops. And thieves. Only last week the seneschal had recommended an old beldame who had stolen a wheel of cheese have her hand cut off. Rowena had not lingered to hear Gareth's verdict.

She crept downstairs. The heralds lay wrapped in their cloaks before the fire in the great hall. She pushed open the door of the solar without knocking. Gareth sat on a stool before his desk, bent over a carved box. His scarred knuckles caressed the object beneath them with immeasurable tenderness. Rowena caught a glimpse of ivory silk.

At the creak of the door, he slammed the box and shoved it into a cubbyhole, his dark-fringed eyes shooting her a look as guilty as if he'd just shoved a woman under the desk.

"No need to look so distressed, milord. If there is naught you can do to remedy my fate, I understand."

He arched a tentative eyebrow. "You do?"

"Aye. I expected it sooner. I can only thank God that Sir Blaine gave us this brief time together before sending his writ of arrest." She gave a light shrug. "I seem destined for the hangman's noose. I suppose there is more dignity in being hanged for horse thievery than for bad comedy."

Gareth came around the desk. His hands touched her slumped shoulders. "Silly goose. Do you think I'd let Blaine hang you? Those horses you took were bought and paid for with my own gold."

Rowena turned in his arms. "The men did not come for me? I am to stay with you?" She could not dim the emotion that leaped in her eyes.

Gareth gently set her aside and returned to the desk, avoiding her gaze. He toyed with a feather quill. "The men came for both of us. My household has been invited to Ardendonne for Easter."

Something in his tone made Rowena wish it had been a writ of arrest instead of an invitation. "Must we go?" She clutched the edge of the desk. "We could celebrate here at Caerleon. I could gather eggs and bring them to you." She would lay eggs if it would preserve the fragile happiness they had found.

"We should not insult him by refusing his invitation."

"How courteous you've become," Rowena murmured. "Why did you not wait to speak of this when you came to bed?"

He gave a feeble laugh. "I fear you and a bed are not conducive to the clear thought necessary for what must be said."

A queer pit opened up in Rowena's stomach. She sat down on an oaken bench.

"I have decided 'twould be best if you and I did not share

a chamber at Ardendonne. I see no need in tarnishing your reputation further.''

"What reputation? No one had ever heard of me until you carried me away from Revelwood.''

"I am speaking of your future reputation. You have a life to think of when this summer's done.''

There would be no life without him. Rowena bit back the words with a hollow laugh. "A life of running on the moors and digging turnips requires no reputation. Rabbits are not snobs.''

He met her gaze across the desk. "I owe you more than that.''

"You owe me nothing.''

He shuffled a sheath of parchments with methodical hands. "A woman alone is at the mercy of any man. And don't give me that reproachful look. One word of how your papa will take care of you and I shall box your ears. If I send you back to Revelwood, how long do you think it will take him to sell you to another man? A year? A month? A week?''

Rowena wrapped her leg around the bench leg as if she would root there.

Gareth took a deep breath before continuing. "I wish to find you a husband this spring, Rowena. Not some boyish lech like Sir Blaine but a real man. A good man who would treat you well and not leave you at home while he is out lifting another's skirts.''

Some childish hope had stopped Rowena from preparing for these words. She inclined her head. "I fear I have little to offer a good man.''

Gareth pressed the quill into the desk. The tip splintered. "Nonsense. I have a castle in southern Scotland that came into our family with my father's second marriage. 'Tis not a large holding but 'twould make a fine dower.''

Rowena's voice was musing. "Marlys told me you'd send me on my way with a brotherly kiss and a sack of gold. And you offer me a castle and a husband.'' She stood. "Was

I that good, Gareth? If I pleased you so well, why have you tired of me so quickly?''

Gareth looked as if she had struck him. He had steeled his aching heart against Rowena's meek acceptance of his will, the gentle reproach he knew he would find in her eyes. But Rowena in rebellion stirred something deep within him. With the pain of anger etched on her features, she looked half-child and half-faerie, caught but not tamed.

Angry tears sparkled in her eyes. ''At least Papa would make a profit from me. You would give me away. Tell me, milord, is a castle payment enough for a good man to welcome another man's whore to his marriage bed?''

Gareth stood. Rowena broke into a sob and fled for the door. Before she could reach it, Gareth reached around her and slammed it in her face. His broad hands splayed on the door; his muscled arms on each side of her held her fast.

''What would you prefer, Rowena? Would you have me offer you my marriage bed? Is that what you wish for? To be the bride of the Lord of Caerleon. To languish beneath the sidelong glances of those who would watch your every move? To know each time you smiled at a squire or offered Blaine your kerchief as a favor, they would be wondering if that night would be the one when I would murder you in your bed?''

She pushed her aching forehead against the door as if she could stop his words from penetrating her mind.

Gareth's fingers dug into her shoulders. He pressed his body to hers. ''Is that what you want, Rowena? To start from slumber each night, never knowing when the shadow of my blade might fall over you. To share your life with a murd—''

Rowena turned. She tangled her hands in his hair and pulled his lips down to hers, damming up his dark torrent of words before they could sweep her away. Her kirtle was trapped in a sheath of softness between them. He groaned more in agony than pleasure as her mouth opened in an invitation to soften his ruse of cruelty. His lips swam from her mouth to her throat to the ethereal softness of one ear-lobe. He dragged her against him, his gesture robbed of violence by her tender capitulation. He pressed himself to her, finding a plush hollow to match every straining angle of his body.

His mouth took hers again, finding within a wet, honeyed promise that tightened his groin until he thought it would splinter if he did not find release.

Rowena stared deep into his eyes with a gaze as fierce as his own. "Gareth, I love—"

He laid his hand over her lips. "Nay, Rowena. 'Tis a word for other men, not for me. Don't say it. Never."

She buried her lips against his palm, kissing him everywhere her mouth could reach as he carried her to the rug by the warm stones of the hearth. He was ready to do away with words and take their battle to a place where he was secure in the potency of his weapons. The next time it was his mouth he lay over hers, muffling a cry Dunnla would have heard through three feet of stone as his body told her what words could never say.

The white mist of dawn seeped through the arrow slits. Rowena nestled against Gareth as he carried her up the stairs. She was awake but not yet ready to surrender the night. The coarse fibers of Gareth's hair brushed her nose, addling her so she was not sure if she was awake or asleep. She lay limp and pliant, her body a separate entity, enjoying sensations that required no thought or response. He slipped her beneath the downy softness of a pelt, fluffing the pillow behind her head. He brought her wrist to bear against the softness of his beard.

She watched him dress from beneath her lashes, marveling at his animal grace as he stood naked, silhouetted against the hazy light. He cleaned his teeth with a cloth rubbed in soap and trimmed his beard with the razor edge of his misericord. He cast a last smoldering glance at her humped form under the pelt.

After he slipped out, Rowena rose and padded to the window. A sky dipped in pink framed the castle walls. On the horizon a thread of blue slipped through the pink. A perfect breeze stirred her hair.

The Gareth that entered the courtyard might have been a different man from the one who cradled her across his lap in the orchard yesterday and slathered her nose with kisses. His dark beard was clipped close to his chin. A silver belt of braided chain encircled the black linen of his surcoat. With each step, the scabbard of his broadsword clanked against muscular calves sheathed in hose as tight and immaculate as a second layer of skin.

There was a hesitancy to his movements as he slipped a parchment from his sleeve and handed it to the waiting herald. The man and his companions mounted and rode through the bailey gate. Gareth lifted his hand. For a moment, Rowena thought he would call them back. Then his hand dropped. She took a step back as he lifted his gaze to the window.

Rowena crept out of Gareth's chamber, a small trunk cradled under her arm. She closed her eyes and touched the splintered surface of Elayne's door. With a creak it yielded to the gentle pressure of her fingertips.

The glow of the sun drifted through the shrouded windows. A faint demarcation in the dust marked where the carved coffer had been. The chamber felt as empty and barren of life as a tomb. It had been a tomb for one woman, she reminded herself. And whoever had made it so had left Gareth's name drawn in blood as a damning indictment of guilt. Her features hardened as she pulled the door shut.

She slipped down a back stairwell. The solar was empty, the fire's embers burned to ash.

She knelt before the desk. The coffer was where Gareth had left it. Her finger traced the delicate curve of a rose etched in the soft pine. Gareth's hands had carved it. A Gareth whose eyes were bright and clear, unshadowed by the past. A Gareth whose smile was genuine, whose lips had never known a sneer. Rowena would have given twenty years of her life to know that boy. She touched her cheek to the smooth wood.

She closed her eyes before lifting the lid, half prepared to find a nest of tiny bones nesting in the satin-lined confines. She swallowed hard before opening them. A scrap of ivory lay against the worn satin, forlorn and harmless. Rowena picked it up, fearful of finding a kerchief smothered in the delicate scent of Elayne's rosemary. Her curious fingers plucked at the fragile silk as her hand smoothed the garment against her lap. It curled of its own volition around her fist and she saw it was not a kerchief at all but a tiny coif like a baby would wear, yellowed and stained with age.

Her hands tenderly folded the garment. She started to drop it back in the box but after a moment's hesitation opened her trunk and tucked it within, letting the lid fall shut with a final thump before going to join the others on their journey to Ardendonne.

CHAPTER 18

The castle was deserted but the bailey roiled with life. Deciding a meager horse would not be sufficient to carry his trunks, Irwin had wheedled a rickety field cart out of Gridmore and heaped six trunks upon it. He straddled the topmost trunk looking more like a rotund jester than a squire in alternating squares of plum and yellow. Unlike Little Freddie, Irwin's affections had been bought with a maroon tunic, a silver buckler, and a fur cloak that was an exact replica of Gareth's. For a gold medallion and a signet ring, he would have traded Rowena and six more betrotheds had he possessed them. Little Freddie appeared to pluck Rowena's trunk out of her hand. She shaded her eyes against the morning sun but saw no dark-garbed knight amongst the chaos.

Dunnla waddled past with a tray full of buttery rolls, her skirt caught in the mouth of a gray-blue hound. Rowena grabbed a roll. Steam poured from the crisp crust as she sank her teeth into it. She tore it in two and tossed the other half to Little Freddie.

"Thanks," he mumbled, averting his eyes.

The sun kissed his cap of hair to silver. His braies and tunic were a silvery green that fit his willowy figure to perfection. The hollow caves had disappeared from his cheeks.

Her lips quirked at the sight of the jeweled hilt of a dagger protruding from his neat scabbard. She knew it had been a gift from Gareth. "Why are you not about your duties?"

"What duties?"

She took him by the shoulders, thinking how soon it would be that she would have to reach upward to do so. "You are a squire now. You should be seeing to your lord. Suppose he cannot gauntlet himself without your assistance?"

Little Freddie's jaw stuck out a dangerous angle. "For all I care, he can hang himself. Did I ask for this bloody education?"

"Nay. But you'll have it anyway, won't you? Because I paid for it."

A shadow fell over her. Little Freddie lifted his gaze over her shoulder, his eyes narrowing to silver slits. "Mayhaps the price was too high."

He stalked toward the stables. Rowena felt the possessive heat of Gareth's gauntleted hands before he laid them on her. He massaged her shoulders, his fingers bands of sun-warmed leather against her soft flesh.

"Do not rebuke the lad." His breath stirred her gossamer peach veil secured with a circlet of gold. "He may be right."

She did not resist as he eased her back against the muscled length of his body. Her rounded curves fit his hardness as well as his fingers fit the soft interior of his gauntlets. He rubbed his beard along her cheek, its teasing prick a caress that sent blood pounding from her cheeks, spinning to the nether reaches of her body. She was a breath away from feeling his lips graze the corner of her mouth when Folio's head appeared over his shoulder. The stallion butted his head against Gareth's cheek. Rowena shook herself as if awakening from a dream.

Her cheeks flamed as she saw Irwin gaping at them from the cart. Big Freddie drew a brush down his sorrel's coat, his face carefully hidden by the horse's flank. A rush of shyness flooded Rowena with the memory of her uninhibited response to Gareth's lovemaking in the night.

She hid her discomfort by stretching out a hand to caress Folio's neck. Black and silver ribbons had been lovingly entwined in the horse's flowing white mane.

" 'Twas your brother's doing," Gareth said.

The stallion nuzzled her palm, searching for a carrot. "Does it please you?"

"Not as well as you do."

Marlys cantered into the bailey. Her mare's shaggy hooves pawed the air, barely missing an oblivious Gridmore. A moldy knapsack was thrown over one shoulder.

"At this rate, Blaine will die of old age before we reach his keep, brother." Marlys nudged her mount forward. Rowena had to make a quick hop backward to keep from having her toes broken. "What's it to be, Gareth? Will you mount your bitch or mount your stallion?"

Before Gareth could reply, Marlys wheeled the mare around and shoved it between Dunnla and the hound.

Dunnla shook her fist at the air. "Keep that hairy beast away from me!" It was impossible to tell if she meant Marlys or the horse.

Rowena stared after Marlys's hunched shoulders. It seemed even their stilted camaraderie was a thing of the past.

Gareth threw one long leg over Folio and was astride.

He stretched out his gauntleted arm to her. "Shall we ride?" His eyes sparkled in the sunshine like wind-polished diamonds.

Rowena peered around the bailey to find Big Freddie and Little Freddie mounting their horses. "I had thought to have a mount of my own."

His arm held firm. "No need for it. Folio can bear us both."

Rowena slanted a look at him from beneath her lashes. "You would share your horse with me—but not your chamber?"

"Summer has not yet arrived." A wicked light danced in Gareth's eyes. She could not resist his challenge without looking a prim fool.

She took his hand and found herself astride Folio, her back pressed to his chest. He slapped the reins on Folio's neck, sending the bells along the stallion's bridle into a jingling carol. Irwin's cart trundled behind as they trotted through the gates, leaving Dunnla beating the hound with a spoon and Gridmore blissfully waving at the moat.

The world had awakened while they slept. A mist of green crept over the ancient forest, coaxing a tiny linnet into trilling song. Buds hung like beads in quicksilver branches. Unable to resist the yellow bells, Rowena caught a spray of wild forsythia as they passed. She rubbed the velvety petals beneath her nose, then sniffed back a sneeze.

Her pulse tattooed a warning beat as Gareth dropped Folio behind the others. He plucked the blossom from her hand and gently trailed it from her temple to her chin, then downward over her throat, leaving a trail of glittering pollen like fairy dust.

He pushed aside her veil and laid his lips against the velvety hairs at the nape of her neck.

Her voice dripped innocence. "Tell me, milord. Do your plans include marrying me to a man jovial enough to tolerate your continued visits to my bedchamber?"

Gareth stiffened. He crumpled the spray and let it fall beneath the horse's hooves. He cracked the reins on Folio's back and kicked the stallion into a gallop. Rowena slid backward and would have been unseated were it not for the unrelenting bend of Gareth's arm around her waist. They cantered past the curious faces of the others and were the first to burst into a sun-soaked meadow purple with a dusting of wildflowers. Rowena leaned the back of her head against Gareth's shoulder, lost in a relief colored by bewildering disappointment.

Unable to resist the sweet seduction of the sun-warmed wind, Rowena slipped the gilt circlet over her head and

freed her veil. Before she could get a grip on it, the wisp
of silk caught on the breeze and went fluttering upward,
sailing on the air currents like an elusive feather. Her cry
of dismay was drowned out by Gareth's guttural command
as he spurred Folio faster, flattening the greening grasses.
Her breath caught in her throat as he hauled back the reins.
The blue sky tilted. Folio's hooves flailed at the air. Gareth
shot out a hand and caught the veil in his fist.

Folio's hooves crashed down. At a cluck from Gareth,
the stallion folded his knees and sank into a bow with a
toss of his silky mane.

Rowena clung to the knob of the saddle to keep from
sliding down his sleek neck. "Methinks the horse has pret-
tier manners than his master, milord."

"Only when he has a comely lady to impress."

A shift of his knees brought the horse to a standing position. His gauntleted fingers smoothed the veil over the
back of his hand with infinite tenderness. The scrape of
leather against silk sent a shiver down Rowena's spine. She
reached for the veil.

He dangled it just out of her reach. "Nay, milady. I have
captured your favor. Contrary to what you believe, I do not
surrender what is mine with such ease."

With those words, he folded the veil into a pretty packet
and slipped it into the wrist of his gauntlet.

As the day wore on, Folio rocked like a cradle between
Rowena's thighs. When they stopped for water, Rowena
mounted behind Gareth upon their return to the horse. Except for a mocking smile, he had no comment. Gusts of the
sun's breath bathed her face in warmth. She flattened her
cheek against his broad back and let her eyes drift shut. The
hands that had clasped his flat abdomen fell into his lap in
trusting cups. Gareth brought one of them to his lips before
gently fastening it under his arm.

Rowena opened her eyes to a vision of arches and towers
shimmering beneath a veil of water. She blinked, half ex-

cting a dark-eyed merman to swim out one of the win-
ows, trident in hand. A giant white hoof, shod in polished
on, came down on the keep, obliterating the battlements
a swirling eddy of indigo.

Rowena lifted her head. Ardendonne itself loomed over
e lake, its delicate parapets and graceful arcades drawn
ke a mirage on the horizon. The afternoon sun slanted
ross the tiled roofs, etching shadows like bruises beneath
e arrow slits and conical towers. Rowena rubbed her eyes.

Gareth felt her slight movement. He reached behind him,
pping her back with a powerful hand.

She yawned and twisted around, puzzled to find them at
e edge of the lake with Folio standing knee-deep in water.
Why did you go around? Are there trolls beneath the
idge?''

"In a manner of speaking.''

The stone bridge bisected the pristine blue of the lake.
rifting toward its shadows was a silver-gilded boat, its
ow carved into the graceful neck of a swan. With the sun
her eyes, Rowena could not make out its passengers.
ippling pink satin topped a horned headdress that rivaled
y tower of Ardendonne's. As the boat drifted aimlessly
ward the shadow of the bridge, the woman ducked into
e bottom of the boat to keep her headdress and her head
om being swept off. Rowena watched for nearly a minute;
e woman's head did not reappear.

"Trolls on the bridge, too.'' Rowena followed Gareth's
nger to find Irwin's cart parked dead center on the bridge.

He was flanked by Rowena's brothers as they leaned
opefully over the other side of the bridge, waiting for the
wan-boat to reappear.

Rowena swallowed. "Curious trolls. It seems Little Fred-
ie's education is advancing faster than I'd hoped.''

"Indeed. We'd best reach him before Blaine does if we
ope to salvage any remnant of his innocence. Hold on.''

His golden spurs touched Folio's side and silver drops
hot like sparks from Folio's prancing hooves. Rowena's

hands wrapped around Gareth's waist. Beads of water caug
and hung like dewdrops in the sun's rays before splinteri
to mist her skin with their ebullient spray.

She caught a blurred glimpse of other boats skimmi
the lake, a circle of squires slamming each other to t
ground at the water's edge in a game of football, bursts
brilliant saffron and cherry as ladies strolled like roses alo
the green swath of lawn.

They galloped out of the lake and across the slopi
shore, reaching the small dock as the boat rocked gent
into its mooring.

Gareth reined up Folio. Rowena peeped out from behi
his shoulder. Blaine reclined in the bottom of the boat, t
back of his head resting on folded arms. His knees sham
lessly straddled the bow. A glow that had little to do wi
the sinking sun softened the sharp planes of his face.
slightly askew headdress popped up, perched upon a thro
as graceful but infinitely more flexible than the wood
swan's. The woman gently tucked pale strands of hair b
neath the horns. As her neck swiveled to include Gareth
her sultry stare, Rowena thought unkindly that a lizard mig
make a more apt comparison for the lady Alise.

Blaine shaded his eyes against the sun. "Hullo, Gareth
I thought you another peasant bearing eggs for Easter."

"I shudder to think of your uses for them. You give ne
meaning to the religious feast days."

Blaine flicked a long, blond hair off his clinging hos
"Is rapture not considered a religious experience?"

Gareth scowled at the sky. "No thunderheads, thank Go
I hate to be near any body of water when you blasphem
so."

Tiny waves lapped at Folio's hooves as Blaine climbe
out of the boat. "Lady Alise gives the best . . . ah, raptu
. . . that I know." Alise ducked her head demurely as Blai
helped her out of the boat. "But I don't have to tell yc
that, do I, Gareth?"

As Rowena met Alise's haughty almond gaze, she felt th

right armor of sophistication she had polished at Caerleon ll away like scales. How Gareth must have laughed at her wn feeble attempts to please him! No wonder he did not ant her in his chamber. Her hands loosened until they did ot touch him, but laced only in the links of his hauberk. laine's eyes softened as they lit on her.

His smile etched becoming crinkles around his eyes. "It eems you've brought me a gift more precious than eggs."

Without awaiting Gareth's approval, Rowena slid off Fo- o and into Blaine's waiting arms. One of her braids had ome unlooped and tiny wisps of hair escaped it. The cheek he had pressed to Gareth's back while she slept was as pale s cream while the other cheek had pinkened under the rays f the sun. She had no way of knowing she looked like a arlequin, half-woman, half-child, no less beguiling in her edraggled state.

Blaine ran his hands over her ribs, stopping wisely under Gareth's watchful gaze, his thumb a hair's breadth from the urve of her breast. "And as fragile as eggs, I do believe."

Rowena wiggled out of his grasp and dropped a curtsy. 'Your memory serves you poorly, Sir Blaine."

He stroked his smooth chin with a grimace. "Not as oorly as you might think. My jaw still aches when a storm rews." Gareth dropped between them on the balls of his eet, and Blaine fingered his chin, eyeing the taller man varily. " 'Tis aching as we speak."

"Not as much as it will be if you don't keep your hands o yourself," Gareth retorted. He looped an affectionate rm around Blaine's neck and pulled him toward the castle. 'Who knows where those hands have been?"

"Ask Alise." The mocking cry came from the bridge. Marlys sat on the stone wall, dangling her booted feet.

Blaine's eyes narrowed at the sight of Gareth's sister perched on his bridge like a vulture. "You said there were no thunderheads. Or did you say dunderheads?"

Irwin waved happily from the bridge. Gareth rolled his eyes skyward. "Neither."

Little Freddie appeared like a wraith at his side. Garet
slapped Folio's reins into his hands. They ambled up th
gentle slope with Blaine and Gareth in the lead, finishin
each other's sentences with the easy familiarity of ol
friends. Rowena kept a polite distance from Lady Alise an
tried in vain to tuck her braid back into its neat loop. Afte
it unrolled for the third time, she tugged irritably until th
other braid came tumbling down. She was beginning to fee
as invisible as she had on her first visit to Ardendonne. Pa
of her wanted to join Marlys on the bridge. At least ope
hatred was an acknowledgment of her existence.

They passsed beneath a line of budding oaks. "When ai
you going to build those flanking towers your fathe
planned? Ardendonne would crumble like a confection in
siege," Gareth was saying.

"Edward has bought us peace," Blaine replied. "Wh
waste gold on blocks and mortar when there are so man
other pleasant ways to spend it?"

Rowena lifted her gaze to the airy towers and flappin
pennons fixed on silver spires. There *was* something ethe
real and impermanent about the castle. Unlike the sturd
ramparts of Caerleon, Ardendonne looked as if a good rai
might melt it to sugary syrup.

She bit back a grin. "If I'd have thought the castle edibl
on my last visit, I would have devoured the barbican withou
a qualm of conscience."

Blaine and Gareth both turned around. Rowena blinked
hardly aware she had spoken aloud.

"A delightful prospect." Blaine's gaze dropped to he
lips. Gareth's face was impassive, but Rowena sensed some
thing less than pleasure in his eyes.

Blaine threw out an arm in a grand gesture. "Try to thin
of my castle as one gigantic sweetmeat concocted solely fo
your pleasure."

Rowena started at a trill of music from the tree abov
them. A willowy figure swung down from a low-hangin
branch and landed at her feet. "Beware. Blaine applies tha

philosophy to everything in life. Including his guests." The minstrel Mortimer thrust a long, slender pipe down the front of his hose. His gaze caressed Little Freddie. With a casual motion, he flipped a strand of hair out of the boy's eyes. "Charming. Who brought the hors d'oeuvres?"

Gareth fingered the hilt of his sword. "Keep your hands to yourself, Mortimer. Your fingers have probably been in more ungodly places than Blaine's."

The minstrel swept his own blond fall of hair out of his eyes. "Jealous, Gareth?"

Little Freddie colored, understanding the exchange better than Rowena would have hoped. She gave him a shove in what she hoped was the direction of the stables. He reluctantly went, craning his neck all the way. She half-expected Gareth to draw his sword and lop off the minstrel's head.

Instead he plucked the hautboy from the band of Mortimer's hose and lay its tip against the minstrel's thin lips. "If you would use your venomous tongue for the purpose it was intended, I might not be forced to cut it out of your head."

Spittle flew as Mortimer blew a hasty note. He skipped backward, disappearing behind a glossy hedge of hawthorn. Pink flowers bobbed in a dance of their own as his head popped up.

"Why, Sir Gareth, if I used my tongue for the purpose it was intended, you might not want to cut it out of my head." With a sly wink, Mortimer went sliding down the hillside. The smooth bowl of his instrument piped bell-sweet notes that lingered in the crystalline air.

Gareth's eyes narrowed. "He should thank God I am not armed with bow and arrow."

Blaine clasped his hands with a penitent look at the sky. "I add my prayers to his. Mortimer would look passingly stupid with an apple in his mouth."

Before Gareth could threaten to dismember a third person on their jaunt to the castle, Rowena danced forward and grabbed his hand. She swung it back and forth like an overexcited child. ''Did Sir Gareth tell you why we've come to Ardendonne, Sir Blaine?'' She ignored the warning pressure of Gareth's fingers. ''Sir Gareth is being kind enough to seek a husband for me.''

Blaine's eyes widened. ''Benevolent, is he not? 'Tis hard to picture him in the role of doting uncle. You mustn't duck your head, Gareth. Humility does not suit you.''

Gareth dropped Rowena's hand with a veiled look that clearly promised revenge. Blaine linked his arm in hers and inclined his head. ''What sort of husband might please you, Lady Rowena?''

Out of the corner of her eye, she saw Gareth fall behind, his hands clasped behind his back. Alise trotted forward to put herself beside him as they reached the drawbridge.

Rowena pursed her lips thoughtfully. ''Someone gentle and well-favored. Pleasant of speech and manners. Sweet of temper. Not given to brooding or crotchety behavior.''

Blaine cast a maddening grin over his shoulder.

''Kind to kittens?'' Gareth growled. ''Respectful of virgins?''

''That leaves Blaine out,'' Alise purred.

''How would you know?'' Blaine retorted. He lifted one of Rowena's braids and brought it to his lips. ''If you will throw in well-endowed with gold and generous of hospitality, I know just the fellow for you.''

Rowena blinked innocently at him. ''Did I mention faithful?''

''Damn.'' Sir Blaine dropped the braid. ''If a man did not meet one of your qualifications . . .'' He stroked his chin thoughtfully, ''. . . say, for instance, he bore no fondness for kittens, would you cast him out and break his heart?''

Rowena danced up the drawbridge. ''Is he handsome?''

''Very.''

''Sweet-tempered?''

''The sweetest.''

''Young?''

Blaine shrugged. "Thirty-three."

"Thirty-three?" Rowena cried in a horrified tone. "Why his muscles would be as soft as porridge and his faculties fading to dust! I want a man for a husband, not a doddering mummy."

She spun around to test the effect of her words. Gareth gave her a look that should have sizzled her braids off.

"Careful, milady." Blaine stretched out a warning hand as her train caught on a splintered plank.

She tugged the melon cotte with both hands, forgetting the satin was not as sturdy as her usual garments. The train ripped. The force of her tug sent her reeling toward the moat. Her arms cartwheeled madly. Her toes curled on the edge of the drawbridge in a last vain attempt to stop her descent into the murky blue water.

Leather-clad arms circled her waist and throat. She hung suspended over the water for a breathless moment, caught in the haven of those arms. Gareth pulled her back. It was a long moment before she realized that Gareth's face was buried in her throat and Blaine was as pale as parchment.

Alise's small, pink tongue darted out to moisten her lips. "The early warm snap allowed Blaine to stock the moat sooner than usual. Another step and you would have been the one gracing the table with the apple in your mouth. If we could have found more than your bones, that is."

Rowena's legs folded, and Gareth sank to his knees with her. She closed her eyes and rubbed her cheek against the beaten softness of his gauntlet. He caught her shoulders and pushed her away with an effort that would have been visible to a blind man.

" 'Tis a miracle my doddering steps reached you in time. My faculties are not as sharp as they used to be."

With that virulent reproach, he left her sitting on the edge of the drawbridge. She shrugged away the comforting hand Blaine laid on her shoulder. He and Alise disappeared into the castle, murmuring behind their hands. Rowena lay her head on her knee, content to watch the sun shimmer across the rippling lake.

A rough hand cupped the back of her neck. "C'mon, pup. Lest you want to sleep in the stables with Big Freddie, we'd best find a chamber."

"Why are you only nice to me when no one else is?"

Marlys caught both braids in her hand and pulled Rowena's head back. "I'm a fool for a stray."

"Mayhaps you are only a fool."

Marlys let that comment pass and helped Rowena to her feet. By the time they reached the castle door, she had Rowena smiling with a ribald and very exacting description of what had happened in Blaine's boat using Latin terms Rowena could only pretend to understand.

CHAPTER 19

Although Rowena had expected her flirtation with Blaine to goad Gareth into some sort of response, she had not expected it to be total disdain. They might have been guests in separate castles for all the attention he paid her that night. Gone was the seductive charm he had wielded so well on their departure from Caerleon. Gone the tender consideration for her comfort shown in the long ride. Gone the growling ogre with the jealous eye. His features had hardened like a diamond hewn from some exotic rock, arresting in its attraction but devoid of all human emotion. Rowena would have preferred surly condemnation to this total absence of feeling.

Every hour seemed to transform him back to the dark lord of Caerleon who had stolen her away from Revelwood. His mood had steadily worsened since arriving at Ardendonne. The more genteel the crowd around him the more savage he became. He answered every polite attempt at conversation with a curt reply or a sarcastic sally that left the other person bleeding before he even knew he had been cut. If offended feelings could kill, Blaine's great hall would have been littered with bodies.

At table he was seated near Blaine, above the salt cellar with the lords of the highest rank. Rowena was stuffed at the end of the table between a rotund lady and her leering son. She noticed miserably that Gareth was the only knight without a lady to share his trencher. The lady Alise divided

her time between drinking out of Blaine's chalice and plucking sugared raisins from Gareth's manchet. When Gareth's
glance did chance to graze Rowena, his eyes would linger
for a moment as if trying to place her. Then they would
move on as if not pleased with the memory.

Rowena toyed with her honeyed pear, mashing it with her
knife until the buttered honey ran into a lake in its center.
When Alise rose to join the dance, Rowena was only too
ready to slip into her seat.

"Good evening, Sir Gareth. I hope the partridge was to
your satisfaction."

His voice was cool. "At my age, I do well to gum the
wafers. I haven't found you a husband yet, if that's what
you're plaguing me about. Mayhaps that pimpled lad at your
side would suffice. He is probably not out of napkins yet."

Rowena's charming smile was belied by the words she
hissed under her breath. "Stop being cruel. 'Twas your idea
to pawn me off on another."

Gareth reclined on his elbow as if he hadn't heard her,
his grace as lethal as that of a snake. Rowena felt like a
dowdy mouse waiting to be swallowed. The curious glances
of the others at the table pricked her skin like invisible fingers. She had approached him. They both knew it would be
a crass insult if he did not offer her something from his
manchet. He bit off half a sausage with obvious relish and
held the other half out to her.

"May I tempt you?"

Rowena bit back the obvious reply. She reached for it.
He pulled it back. "Allow me. A lady should not soil her
dainty fingers."

He leaned forward, the sausage cradled between thumb
and forefinger. The succulent scent of the meat wafted to
her nostrils. Gareth was rewarded with a teasing rumble
from the beast she had thought tamed in the pit of her stomach. A mischievous grin deepened the lines at the corners
of his eyes. Rowena cringed inwardly.

The beast awakened another emotion and anger uncurled

its drowsy fingers. If Gareth wanted to play, then play she would.

Her lips parted in an artless smile. "How could I resist your kindness, sir?"

She took the tempting morsel between her teeth. Her lips closed around Gareth's fingers and lingered. She lapped away the juices of the meat like a lazy cat, taking his finger into her mouth all the way up to the second knuckle, tasting the tang of leather in the dusting of tiny hairs that furred his fingers.

His own lips parted but no words came forth. Rowena lifted a sultry gaze through her lashes. It was wasted. Gareth's gaze was locked on her lips, bewitched by the slaking spell of their coral softness against his flesh. A vicious triumph sang within her. Let him be caught in his own trap.

She drew back and inclined her head, granting him the flash of a dimple in the pure, peach line of her cheek.

"Delicious," she murmured. "Have you any cheese, Uncle Gar—"

He lay his moist fingers on her lips. "Don't."

The trap snapped closed with a sigh of its velvety jaws. Too late, Rowena realized her head was still inside. Curious onlookers forgotten, Gareth tugged her lower lip between thumb and forefinger and lay his mouth against hers. Her resistance melted like spun sugar beneath the exquisite pressure of his lips. His victory was sweet but fierce.

He freed her. Rowena dazedly put her elbow in his manchet. The wheat bread crumbled, sending honey dribbling into her lap.

Gareth rose with an impeccable bow. "Sleep well, milady." He started for the stairs. Alise made a hasty excuse from the dance and followed him. It was impossible to miss the triumphant look she cast back at Rowena.

Well after midnight, Rowena lay on the feather mattress, listening to Marlys's broken snores. A silvery orb of moon peeped in the narrow slit of a window.

She ached for Gareth with a physical pain that frightened her. Worse than the ache was the terrible fear that if she went to him now, she would not find him alone.

She threw back her thin coverlet. What would be worse? To lay alone in an agony of indecision? Or to pad her way to Gareth's chamber and push open his door to find him locked in a swirl of pale, blond hair? That was one question Rowena knew the answer to. So she lay there until the ragged rhythm of Marlys's snores lulled her to an uneasy sleep. She awoke only once to find that the coverlet had been drawn over her and tucked neatly under her chin. She rolled to her side in the cocoon of warmth, believing she had dreamed the soothing touch of lips against her brow. Marlys's bed was empty.

Blaine threw a long leg over one arm of his chair and pasted on a benevolent smile. His villeins shuffled past, one by one, bearing the traditional offering of eggs to mark the end of the Lenten fast and the beginning of the feast that would be Easter at Ardendonne.

He hooked a woven basket on one finger and peered within. "Gads, eggs! What an original thought! Did you come up with it yourself?"

The peasant gave a toothless grin and wagged his head in assent. Blaine reached into the leather pouch dangling from his belt. His slender fingers flicked a silver penny that went spinning through the air, catching the afternoon sunlight as it clinked to the floor and went rolling under a table. The peasant dropped to hands and knees and scrambled after it.

Blaine waited until the man had found it, gummed it a few times and backed out bowing all the way, before tossing the basket behind him to a smirking page.

"What smells worse? The peasants or the eggs?" he whispered to Gareth.

"The peasants," Gareth replied without hesitation, only half listening.

Gareth propped his foot on his chair as a bevy of giggling maidservants shoved a long table against the wall. Their giggles grew shriller as they peered over their shoulders at him, then buried pinkened faces in their linen aprons. In the quiet weeks with Rowena at Caerleon, he had forgotten the sting of their laughter. His fingers tightened on the carved arm of the chair.

Blaine's lips curved in a noble smile. Only the slight flaring of his delicate nostrils betrayed him as a wizened old woman with feet wrapped in cowhide limped forward. The instant she turned away, Blaine flipped her bag of eggs over his shoulder to another page who would take them outside and use them to pelt the unsuspecting squire who might make merry at his lower status.

A low whistle escaped Blaine's lips as a shy figure drifted toward them. Gareth sat up. The girl could not have been more than thirteen. Blond hair that had yet to lose its baby fineness hung over her face. Dirt smudged her nose. But there was still a promise of beauty in her slanted eyes and full bottom lip.

She curtsied awkwardly. Her tongue toyed with an empty tooth socket in her bottom jaw. "Eggth, Thir Blaine. Me mum thent them for the Eathter featht."

Blaine caressed the girl's cheek. "God bleth her thweet thoul." From the corner of his mouth, he said, "What do you say, Gareth? Would you care to join me in taking this one abovestairs and introducing her to a real feast?"

At one time Blaine's suggestion would have only annoyed Gareth. Now he felt a knot tighten in his gut. "However debauched your guests might think me, raping children bearing Easter eggs is not among my many vices."

Blaine gave an offended sniff. "Hypocrite. The girl is not much younger than what you've been dipping into. Besides, I've never resorted to rape. I've never had to." The girl looked from one of them to the other, not understanding a word of their rapid French. Blaine licked his finger and gently wiped away the smudge on the girl's nose. "Would you like a bath, child?"

"Nay. She would not." Gareth snatched three silver coins from his own purse and thrust them into the girl's grubby paw. He gave her a gentle shove toward the door. "Go," he commanded. "And keep your silly self away next year. And the year after that," he added as an afterthought. The girl obeyed, grinning sweetly over her shoulder at Gareth with a look that said plainly she had forgotten Blaine's existence.

Blaine flung the tiny basket behind him with enough force to crack the speckled eggs against the page's temple. "What ails you, Gareth? Picturing your own little charity child at the mercy of some lecherous liege lord? How do you expect to find a husband for her when the only wedding gift he can expect from you is a dagger across his throat?"

Gareth leaned back in the chair and closed his eyes. "You've been around Mortimer too long. You are turning into a genuine bitch."

" 'Tis a fine accusation from a man in the devil's own temper. Did you come to Ardendonne to terrorize my guests and cast your shadow of gloom over our joy? Your brooding visage may be attractive to the ladies, but I find its dubious charms beginning to pale."

Gareth opened his eyes. The shadow of a smile touched his lips. "You are only fussy because Alise came to my chamber last night before she came to yours."

"For all the good it did her. I am not a fool, Gareth. She did not bear your scent when she crawled into my bed."

"You would not have refused her if she had."

Before the words were out, Gareth wished he had bitten them back. Blaine stood. His mouth had a pale, pinched look about it that Gareth recognized from boyhood. Blaine's eyes lifted as Rowena came drifting down the narrow curving stairs in a cloud of purple velvet. His thin lips curved in a smile of ferocious joviality.

"Blaine, I—" Gareth started.

"Don't bother with an apology. I'd be cranky, too, if my leman was sleeping in my sister's chamber. Especially if my sister were Marlys."

With that parting stab, Blaine crossed the hall and offered a gallant elbow to Rowena. Gareth's knuckles whitened as he pushed himself out of his chair. His path was blocked as a ragged form came lurching into the hall, sending the page in the doorway sprawling.

The page climbed to his knees only to be knocked flat again as a bellowing figure came stumbling after the first. "Thief! Bring back me eggs, ya bloody thief!"

An ominous patch covered one eye of the pursuer. The other eye gleamed murder as he raised a hewn cudgel in a hand with only an ugly scab where his smallest two fingers should have been. Rowena took a step backward as the first man flung himself facedown at Blaine's feet, landing on the sack he was carrying with a sickening splat. His fingers clutched at the toes of Blaine's boots.

Wisps of hair trembled along with his voice. "Mercy, milord! I beg you. I sought only to honor you with gifts when this murdering miscreant fell on me outside your doors."

The second man skidded to a halt. Gareth grabbed his hairy wrist before he could bring the cudgel down and stain Rowena's skirts with the man's hapless brains.

The peasant twisted but, looking over his shoulder to find a knight restraining him, he lowered the cudgel with a respectful bob. "He is a lyin' wretch, milord," he said to Blaine. "I was standin' outside awaitin' me turn to be presented when the scurvy dog snatched me sack from me hand and darted past. I've known ye since ye were a lad, Sir Blaine. I'm given to wenchin' and robbin' meself, but I'm not no liar." He raised the cudgel. "Give me leave and I'll bash his skull in."

Blaine put out a restraining hand. "Nay, Jack. Leave this to me." He deepened his voice deliberately. " 'Tis a duty of your lord to mete out justice where it is due."

Gareth rolled his eyes. The man sprawled at Blaine's feet smeared kisses all over his boots.

"Begone, Jack," Blaine said soothingly. "Before we condemn any man to hanging, 'tis best to examine the motives that drove him to such desperation. Especially on Easter," he added with a benevolent smile at Rowena.

At the threat of hanging, the man began to grovel anew. Eggshells cracked beneath him as he crawled toward Rowena and began to kiss the damask hem of her skirts. Gareth was beginning to wonder if Blaine had paid the man for this stomach-turning performance.

"I beseech you, milady, intercede for me with your noble husband. I throw myself upon your kind and gentle mercy." The man clawed his way up Rowena's skirts and raised his head.

The change in Rowena's face should have warned Gareth. His eyes widened as she jerked her skirt out of the man's hands. Her booted foot came down on his fingers with enough force to elicit a strangled yelp. The man scuttled backward, a dark stain spreading down the front of his tunic where he had landed on the eggs. Blaine's mouth fell open as Rowena followed, stamping on whatever appendage she could reach as if the man were a spider that had crawled out of the wainscoting.

"I will give you gentleness," Rowena hissed. "I will give you kindness. I will show you the same mercy that you showed me when I crawled to you, half-starved and begging for sanctuary."

Gareth caught the man by the scruff of the collar and lifted him out of Rowena's reach. The man slowly twirled until he faced the knight. Gareth gave a chilling smile, all of his noble ideas forgotten.

As Lindsey Fordyce dangled between Gareth's smile and Rowena's flashing eyes, he choked out to Blaine, "Hang me, sir. Please."

CHAPTER 20

"Now, Rowena, are you not being a trifle bit hard on Uncle Lindsey?"

Rowena burrowed her face deeper in the pillow, her hands clenched into fists. Whose idea had it been to send Irwin in to cajole her? Either Marlys or Gareth was capable of such perversity.

"Leave me alone," she said, her voice thick from crying. "I hope Blaine hangs him."

Irwin lifted a strand of her hair and peered with concern at her reddened nose. "Not much chance of that with such a staunch champion as Sir Gareth. Why he has done everything but give him the clothes off his back! You should see your papa right now, garbed like a king, entertaining Sir Gareth with woeful tales of his misfortune."

"Then I hope Blaine hangs Gareth."

Irwin sighed and his hand stroked the nape of her neck. "Odd to think, if things had been different, you and I might have shared a bed like this."

That got Rowena's attention. She dove out of the bed and slid down the wall to a sitting position, crossing her arms over her scanty chemise.

Irwin shrugged. " 'Tis just as well. Since we are cousins, our children might have been cursed with four arms or been addle-witted."

"Or fat," Rowena added maliciously.

Irwin just smiled. "Listen, Ro. Listen to what you are missing."

He cocked his head. The rumble of distant laughter rolled up through the floor. A steady drumbeat swelled, intertwined with the piping of the hautboys and the siren song of a lute.

Rowena rubbed her swollen eyes. They felt as though she had salt beneath her lids. "I won't do it. I refuse to come down until Easter is over or Papa is gone, whichever comes first. I cannot bear to see him and Gareth with their heads together. 'Twas humiliating enough to have Gareth welcome him as if he was his own prodigal papa. Poor Papa. He won't know Gareth has severed his head until he's walking around with it in his hands."

Irwin laid across the bed and propped his chin on the heels of his hands. "Gareth was asking Uncle Lindsey a lot of questions. They were discussing your betrothal."

"Have they found me a suitably decrepit knight?"

"Several names were bandied about."

She stared at the floor. Emotions sifted like sand across her face. When she raised her eyes, there was more of slate in them than blue. "Perhaps I should go down and find out how sincere Gareth is about being rid of me."

Irwin gave her arm a friendly cuff. "That's my girl." He rolled off the bed. "If you decide to tell them all to go to hell in a handcart, I'll still marry you."

When he was gone, Rowena went to the basin and splashed cold water in her stinging eyes. Her face was still dripping when she knelt to unlatch the leather straps of her trunk. As she pawed through its contents, the silken coif fell to the floor. She stared at it for a long moment before tucking it into the bodice of her chemise. Gareth was not the only one who had questions on this night.

Gareth swirled his brandy in the bottom of his chalice, catching a glimpse of his own bored countenance in the amber mirror. He quirked his lips, experimenting with a new expression as Lindsey Fordyce regaled him for the fifth time with the tale of woeful luck that had brought him crawling to Rowena's feet. *Slithering*, Gareth amended under his breath. The forced smile only made him look sick. He abandoned it and drained the chalice, savoring the last sweet drop on his tongue. As Fordyce polished off his sixth chalice of burgundy wine, a sympathetic murmur or nod was all it took to keep him talking.

The round, blue eyes that had once reminded him of Rowena's were laced with fragile threads of red. Drops of spittle hung on his heavy lips. If the man was stupid enough to be taken in by Gareth's pretense of genteel concern, it was a miracle Rowena hadn't been born a drooling idiot.

And Rowena was no idiot. He could still feel the sting of the look she had given him when he had taken her papa under his wing.

Fordyce droned on, sputtering something about a rabid bear who had robbed him in the forest. He had only stopped at Ardendonne for a little food on his journey to Caerleon. Word of his daughter's good fortune had reached him, and he had hastened to rush to her side to share in her joy. Gareth's blunt fingers pounded out a rhythm on the scarred table as Mortimer's lutestrings soared into throbbing melody. He should have known it was Rowena's good fortune that would lure Fordyce, not her ill treatment. He had been a fool to believe otherwise.

Dancers clasped hands, sweeping past Gareth in a dizzying funnel of pastels and laughter. Marlys galloped through their lines, gleefully hurling both ladies and men out of her path. Irwin stumbled helplessly after her, vanishing into the twirling arms of the carol, a twitching tail to Marlys's kite. Blaine spun Lady Alise in their midst, his slender hands leaving hers only long enough to clap out a thumping cadence to match the drums.

Fordyce's bleary eyes focused on the hypnotic spinning circle of the dance. He slapped the table with his pudgy hands like a great overgrown baby. Fearful of losing his attention to the seductive swirl of color and music, Gareth grabbed the flagon and poured a stream of burgundy into the man's chalice.

The wine swelled over the rim of silver and splashed on the table as Rowena appeared on the stairs. The deep red of her high-waisted kirtle was gathered below her breasts and secured with a gold chain. Her hair fell away from her face in soft wheaten wings to be caught in a filigree crespine at the back of her neck. In contrast to the delicate lemons and dusty blues flitting about in the dance, Rowena glowed like a pale ruby lit by a fire from within.

Gareth jumped to his feet with a bitten-off curse as the wine found a crack in the table and dribbled onto his knee. He swiped at his hose. Rowena was a distraction he could ill afford if he hoped to wring any truth from her loquacious father.

"Rowena, my angel!"

Fordyce lurched forward, then recoiled and squinted at the stairs, his aching knuckles reminding him that her earlier greeting had held more violence than warmth. Gareth took the opportunity to shove him back in his chair.

"Papa!"

Eyes followed in shining curiosity as the charming minion of the dark lord flung herself down the stairs and toward the long table, trailing belled sleeves that rippled between the feet of the dancers like satin snakes. She sidestepped Gareth with tidy grace and threw herself into her father's lap.

Lindsey Fordyce huddled stiff in her embrace, but when she began to smother his fuzzy pate with the tenderest of kisses, he realized this was not some new attack and clutched her to his breast. Drunken tears unmarred by cloying self-pity spilled down his red-veined cheeks. Gareth realized with a jolt that whatever his myriad of faults, a part of Lindsey Fordyce loved his only daughter. His hands clenched into fists. He could not help but feel betrayed at the sight of them cheek to cheek, their blond heads tilted together in a single mist of gold. He half-expected Elayne's specter to appear behind them, jeering at his arrogance for believing he could ever break the bonds of their charmed circle.

The crowd murmured its appproval of the tender sight with a smattering of applause. Mortimer launched into a gentle ballad. The minstrel's eyes met Gareth's across the hall. A dark message passed between them. Mortimer's blond head lowered in imperceptible acknowledgment.

Blaine appeared behind Gareth like a mischievous gamin. " 'Tis not every day our jaded spirits are witness to such a tender reunion. Touching, is it not?"

"Dazzling," Gareth replied.

"Dear, dear, Papa," Rowena prattled. "I pray you will forgive me for my earlier tantrum. I was overwrought and quite beside myself." She smoothed his tunic and reached in her chemise for a scrap of silk to dry his tears with. "Once I had some time to examine my actions, I was appalled by their ferocity and unfairness. I am your child. 'Tis not mine to judge you. Say you will forgive me. I shall surely die for want of it."

Fordyce burped happily and patted her rump. "There now, lass, you know I've never been able to stay angry at my girl. There'll be no more talk of dying now. Life's a peach. We've each other and a full flagon of burgundy." He frowned into the flagon, mystified at finding it nearly empty. He mopped his forehead with the kerchief Rowena had given him. His sunny smile found an answering reflection in Rowena's face. "Best of all, child, your kind knight has offered me consolation and companionship this Easter feast."

Fordyce beamed up at Gareth. Rowena looped an arm around her father's neck. The tightness of her jaw betrayed her teasing tone. "Beware, Papa. His consolation is a rose with venom-tipped thorns, worthy of more caution than another man's enmity."

Fordyce waved the kerchief at Gareth. "Always was fond of the lad. Taught him how to dice, I did."

"I should have known," Rowena said smoothly.

Gareth frowned, his gaze fixed on the scrap of silk bouncing beneath his nose. He reached for it, hypnotized by the tantalizing motion. The sheen of the torchlight reflecting off the silk caught Fordyce's attention at the same moment. He pulled it back, smoothing it with reverent fingers.

With a lopsided smile, Fordyce dropped the scrap on Rowena's head. "There. It looks as lovely on your little curls as it did the day Dunnla stitched it for you." Before Gareth could stop him, he held up the wide goblet for her perusal.

Gareth watched over her shoulder as Rowena's gaze slowly shifted to her reflection. She reached out a finger and touched the polished silver. She ran a dreamy finger down the icy metal of her cheek. Blond hair. Blue eyes swollen to sultry fullness from crying. A ridiculous scrap of fabric on her head. The goblet threw back her reflection in painful clarity as she came face to face with Elayne de Crecy's daughter. Gareth held his breath, waiting for her to toss the contents of the goblet or mayhaps the goblet itself into his face.

Rowena hiccuped with the echo of a giggle, addressing her reflection. "Oh, God. At least he didn't bury me in the orchard."

Gareth wanted to take her in his arms but knew he didn't dare leave Fordyce tripping along the dark paths of his memory alone. He might not be given another chance. If he could clear the de Crecy name enough to give it to Rowena as his bride, there would be years and years to plead for her forgiveness.

Blaine stamped his feet impatiently as Mortimer's fingers flew over the strings in rollicking rhythm. "Come, milady, if it suits your papa, we shall celebrate this reconciliation with a dance."

Gareth snatched Rowena up and thrust her into Blaine's arms. She was as limp as a rag doll. "Her papa and I have not finished our dealings. Take her."

Blaine gave a wicked smile. "With pleasure."

Blaine swung her into the dance. Her blank face turned to Blaine and broke into a fiercely radiant smile. Gareth sank into his chair, stroking his beard.

Lindsey Fordyce patted his thighs absently as if surprised to find them empty. His gaze followed Rowena's golden path through the dancers with a wistful hunger undulled by ale or brandy. Gareth watched the man's face with something akin to pity, praying his own hunger for the girl did not show so blatantly.

There was a primitive grace to Rowena's dance, some tantalizing remnant of the moor creature untrammeled beneath the chains of satin and gold. She dipped in front of Blaine with a bow of her slender neck. Gareth's hands tightened convulsively as Blaine pressed his lips to the nape of her neck. His tension was not eased by the coy glance Rowena gave Blaine when they again came face to face.

Fordyce lifted the brimming chalice to his lips, his hands trembling as if palsied. "She puts one in mind of her mother, does she not?"

Gareth drew in a breath, not daring to move. The dancers reeled in a bewildering kaleidoscope of colors. At first, he believed that treacherous thought had come from his own mind, fallen from his own lips without his awareness. Fordyce was blithely nodding in time to the music.

"Does she now?" Gareth said lightly, the cost of the casual question betrayed by the rhythmic tic of his jaw.

Rowena and Blaine threaded through the dancers, hand in hand, spinning toward the arch of the stairway.

Fordyce thumped the chalice down. Burgundy sloshed over its rim and Gareth thought about communion for the first time in years.

"My Althea had not Rowena's spunk though. Her infernal delicacy prevented me from cherishing her as I might have desired."

"Althea?" Gareth echoed stupidly as his precious plans cartwheeled and came crashing down before his eyes.

Blaine drew Rowena into the shadows beside the stairs. From their gesturing hands and the toss of Rowena's head, they seemed to be arguing. She glanced back at the table, an unreadable plea in her eyes.

Fordyce rambled on. "Aye, my darling wife was sickly from the beginning. There were sacrifices to make. I kept her out of drafts and encouraged her to always pull her washtub into the nourishing rays of the sun. I gave her a few months respite between sons and resolved to seek out others to relieve those baser needs a man is prey to."

Gareth felt as if he were going to be sick.

"Now my Rowena has never had a sickly day in her life. I daresay she could bear the attentions of even the randiest knight." He nudged Gareth with a leering wink.

Rowena's slender wrists crossed behind Blaine's neck as she pulled him down to her kiss. Gareth stood, shoving his chair back with enough force to topple it.

Seeing Gareth start forward, Mortimer brought his tune to a crashing end. The drummers banged on their cowhide for a lost moment before lapsing into silence. The dancers stumbled to an awkward halt in a tableau of confusion.

The minstrel inclined his head, his limp hair gleaming in the torchlight. With a delicacy and grace that wrung a shiver from the hardiest of men, his long fingers stroked the taut strings, coaxing the first haunting notes of a ballad they had heard only once before.

Gareth froze in his tracks. With a toss of his head that sent his hair rippling down his back, Mortimer's voice rose in a sweet tenor unblemished by dissipation, plaintive with an innocence he had lost when only a boy at the hands of his father's most trusted knight:

The fair Elayne
Unfairly slain . . .

Even the flames dancing on the hearth seemed to quail before the melody. Shadows flickered on the walls, crowding in, tightening throats with their sudden proximity. Mortimer had lost his audience. All eyes were riveted on the tall, dark man in their midst.

Her faithless hand
Stilled by a name . . .

Gareth heard a metallic thump behind him. Burgundy splashed around his ankles like blood. He turned. Lindsey Fordyce's ruddiness drained from his cheeks. His face went deathly pale as the lies he had told so often and so well that he had come to believe them fell away like scales. His throat worked but only a meaningless moan came out.

A vicious song of triumph strummed through Gareth's blood. Across the hall, he met Rowena's stricken gaze and felt a brief moment of regret. But even that could not dim a burst of elation so intense it nearly blinded him.

He turned away from Lindsey Fordyce. There would be time enough for truth between them. He hid his smile behind a sneer and put a hand on his sword hilt. He had one more performance to make as the Dark Lord of Caerleon. After tonight, he would leave them to find a new player for their petty dramas.

With a snarl that would have struck terror in the staunchest of men, he shouldered his way through the dancers, not giving them time to flee before coldly shoving them out of the way. Mortimer continued singing as if oblivious to the thundering cloud about to descend on his head. A pale, dark-thatched squire threw himself in front of Mortimer, but Gareth pushed past him as heedlessly as if he had been a flea.

His fist closed around the strings of the lute. A last discordant note trembled in the air. The minstrel's song died to a silence so palpable that Gareth's harsh breathing was audible to everyone in the hall. Gareth snatched the lute. He lifted it above his head as if to smash it, saw Mortimer's imperceptible wince and hurled it to the squire behind him. One fist caught in Mortimer's tunic, driving the slender figure back until he slammed against the wall. His legs twitched helplessly.

"You fool! Did you not heed my warning the last time I heard that obscenity of a ballad pass your lips?"

Mortimer's attempt to shrug looked as if it were breaking his bony neck. " 'Twas a pretty tune, milord. My memory failed me," he rasped.

"I warned you that your life would fail you if ever again that melody fell from the strings of your lute."

"The people, sir. They hunger for new tunes. 'Tis my honor-bound duty to satisfy them."

The crowd gasped and took a step backward as Gareth dropped Mortimer and spun around. He hefted his sword. "I shall satisfy with my blade any man who requested such a song. Does any man dare to step forward?"

The broad blade shimmered in the torchlight. No one even dared to scratch their nose. Gareth turned back to find Mortimer crawling quietly toward the door.

He gave his rump a kick with his booted foot. "Flee, you knave and sing no more in my presence or any other this night. Another note from you will be your last."

Gareth fought an insane desire to burst into laughter as Mortimer dropped his head between his legs and gave him a wink hidden from the others by the hair around his face. His silk purse bulged with Gareth's gold as reward for his performance.

Gareth sheathed his sword with a growl and dusted off his hands as if contact with Mortimer's quivering flesh had dirtied them.

A magical path opened before him as he made his way back toward the table. For once, their sly looks of mingled excitement and condemnation amused instead of angered him. He would be free of them soon enough, leaving them with the truth of their lifelong mistake to wrestle with. Perhaps Mortimer would compose a charming ballad about it. He smiled without realizing it.

The smile faded as the path before his table cleared. The table was empty. The coif lay trampled among the rushes. Lindsey Fordyce was gone.

CHAPTER 21

Dragging Papa was like dragging a water-logged walrus. His squat body had gone boneless. His fleshy arms undulated beneath her touch. It had taken all of Rowena's strength to tug him out of his chair, to make him understand it was imperative they flee while Gareth was diverted. He still did not seem to comprehend her hissed pleas, the desperation that drove her.

They staggered through the courtyard past a circle of kneeling squires. Dice rattled like bones on the cobblestones. Her father went sprawling.

"If he can't stay up now, I daresay you'll not get him up later," called a pock-marked squire.

"Take me instead," cried a weasel-faced boy who couldn't have been much older than Little Freddie. "I am always up."

They cackled, their faces twisted into goblin masks in the fluttering torchlight. Rowena caught the back of her father's tunic and pulled, feeling every muscle in her back stretch like lute wires ready to snap. The squires shrugged and went back to their game. She wished for the comforting sight of Marlys in their group. How her sturdy strength would help! She shoved Papa forward. A narrow thread of spittle trailed from his lips as he gibbered in a ceaseless stream. Rowena had to fight the urge to box his ears.

Mumbling something about "sweet hoshpitality," he reeled to his feet. Their momentum carried them off the cobblestones and into the dew-slick grass. The cozy lights of the stable winked below. He fell again.

Rowena hooked her hands under his arms. "Come, Papa. We have not far to go."

"But I have come too far already," he mumbled.

Using her knees and trunk to support his weight, she steered him toward the stable. The stable door had been thrown wide to usher in the warm spring wind. Big Freddie and Little Freddie looked up from their own dice in surprise as Rowena and Papa burst inside. The horses nickered a welcome. The comforting smells of fresh, sweet hay and musty horses, untouched by the debauchery of the castle, brought tears to Rowena's eyes. She swayed. Big Freddie stepped forward and caught her in his arms. She buried her face in the burlap of his tunic, his honest sweat as sweet a fragrance as any flower or herb. Papa cursed as he stumbled into a pile of manure.

Her fingers clutched Big Freddie's tunic. "A horse. We must have a horse. I cannot take time to explain, but Papa must have a horse."

Big Freddie scratched his head. "He came on no horse."

Rowena shook him, helpless to stem the hysteria rising in her voice. " 'Tis of no import if he came on an elephant. I need a horse now."

Little Freddie caught her elbow. "Gareth?"

She nodded mutely and blessed the shining beacon of his mind as he ran from stall to stall, throwing open doors.

"There is no stallion here that Folio could not catch with Gareth astride him," he finally pronounced.

Rowena paused for a moment. "Then give me Folio."

Big Freddie blanched. "I cannot be giving away my master's horse."

"Would you rather see your father struck dead before your eyes?" A hard glaze descended over Little Freddie's face. "I know he is no prize. But he is our father. I cannot watch Gareth kill him in cold blood. It would kill me—" She stumbled to a halt.

Little Freddie flung open the last door. White forelegs pawed at the hay. The other horses milled nervously in their stalls. Throwing an exasperated look between the two of them, Big Freddie slipped a bridle studded with emeralds and onyx off a peg and tightened it over Folio's graceful neck.

Little Freddie lay a saddle across the horse's back with a tight smile. "There is a practical consideration, you know. Gareth will be spared killing Papa. Folio will throw and trample him before he can get down the drawbridge. The stallion does not know Papa."

Rowena's jaw tightened. "He knows me."

Little Freddie's hand froze on the saddle's pommel. "You are going with him?"

"Only until I can get him to a place where he will be safe. Then I shall bring Folio and return."

"To what? Boiling oil? The gibbet?"

Rowena lowered her eyes. "I shan't be afraid of Gareth. I have to believe he will not hurt me."

"I pray your faith is not misplaced."

"As do I." Rowena took the bridle with a firm hand.

Folio pranced out of the stall, casting a shadow on the wall that dwarfed them and dimmed the brightest torches. Rowena peered around, perplexed. Papa had disappeared. Big Freddie found him curled in an empty grain bin, snoring happily. He threw Papa over his shoulder while Rowena prepared to mount Folio.

Little Freddie laced his fingers together. Bracing one hand on his bony shoulder, Rowena hefted herself astride the stallion. She gave a weak smile and tangled her hands in the silky mane, struggling to hide from her brothers a fear bordering on terror. Free of Gareth's mastery Folio was a wild-eyed and quivering creature, like some monstrous unicorn out of a maiden's nightmare. She did not need the horse to remind her she was maiden no more.

Folio gave a dancing side-step as Rowena's brothers lifted

her groaning papa behind her. A sudden burst of drunken energy was nearly their undoing.

"That-a-way, girlie!" Papa jerked Rowena's hair out of its net and slapped it on her back like silky reins. He bounced up and down, driving his heels into the beast's sides. Folio surged forward, ready to make a new door in the planked walls of the stable. Big Freddie stepped in front of the horse with a grunted command that brought the horse to a trembling halt.

Rowena eyed her brother with new admiration. He grinned sheepishly.

As he steered the horse in a circle, Little Freddie caught her ankle. "Godspeed, love. I will hold up Gareth as long as I can."

Then the pressure of his fingers was gone and Folio was pointed toward the windy night. Without awaiting a command from Rowena, the stallion shot forward. The small remnant of sanity Papa possessed drove his arms around her waist with desperate strength. The courtyard passed in a blur of tattered images—the excited shouts of the squires as the phantom horse thundered past, a peasant stirring from his drunken stupor long enough to glance up, a knight clutching the silken shoulders of the lady on her knees in front of him, his eyes round with surprise. The courtyard wall loomed. Rowena pressed her eyes shut, waiting for the terrible sensation of weightlessness that would be hers when Folio leaped, the timeless moments before his forelegs caught on the top of the wall and sent them crashing down in a tangle of shattered bones.

The horse veered. She opened her eyes. They were through the first gate and heading for the drawbridge. Sparks flew as iron-shod hooves struck the bands that bound the drawbridge. Papa lost his grip and slid sideways. They went careening toward the oily black arms of the moat. Rowena threw herself to the other side until she clung by little more than the muscles of her thighs.

The stallion shot across the lake's bridge and toward the

beckoning meadows. With every hoofbeat, Rowena expected to slide beneath the horse's muscular girth and have
her skull split by the flailing hooves. Her hair whipped
around Folio's legs, spooking the horse further. As his
hooves struck the soft turf at the top of a hill, he reared.
Rowena said a silent prayer as the horse slipped out from
under them. She and her father went rolling down a gentle
slope in a tangled ball of skirts and grunts.

She ended up flat on her back, staring at a creamy belt
of stars scattered across a royal blue sky. She remembered
a night long ago, when she had lain cradled in the arms of
the moor, canopied by such a sky and blissfully innocent
of the lethal charms of knights and their intrigues.

She remembered toddling after the woman she had believed to be her mother. Tugging at her sun-warmed skirts
as she bent her slender back over a washtub. A back bred
for the comforts of nobility. A back her papa had finally
broken spewing out his sons in a desecrated castle while he
dabbled with whores like Elayne de Crecy. She closed her
eyes briefly.

Suddenly, she wanted nothing more out of life than to lay
in the wet grass forever and watch the clouds scuttle across
the pasty moon. Folio was doubtlessly gone now, and there
was really nothing left to do but lay there until Gareth came
and killed them. Papa chuckled.

"There now, Elayne, I'll have none of that teasing and
nuzzling. You always were a lusty wench when you caught
a man down."

A chill that had nothing to do with the damp grass shivered through Rowena. She looked over at Papa, expecting
to find a half-rotted specter poised over him, sword buried
in its bloody breast.

Folio nuzzled his throat, shimmering like mist in the
moonlight. Papa shoved his head away with a giggle. The
horse looked at her with such a curious, placid expression
that Rowena wanted to laugh.

She rolled over on her stomach and crawled on her elbows to Papa. Folio poked the back of her neck with his velvety muzzle.

"Papa?" she whispered.

"Aye, child?"

"Did you kill my mother?"

"Of course not. Little Freddie killed Althea. 'Twas not his fault. She just wasn't strong enough to bear another birth."

"Not Althea, Papa. My mother—Elayne."

His eyes cut to her in a moment of stark sobriety. He gave a defeated sigh. "I should have wrung her comely neck. But I could not. All I could do was shout and mewl and almost break my blasted neck fleeing that fool boy. Who could blame me, though? Lad or not, there was death in those eyes."

Rowena rolled to her back. They lay there like longtime companions watching clouds shift across the stars. She felt no surprise. He had only confirmed what she had suspected all along: Lindsey Fordyce, knight or no, hadn't the guts to kill a cockroach.

"What did you expect, Papa? He was in love with her. To walk in on such a tryst . . ."

Papa sighed. "No tryst. We were quarreling. She refused to come away with me. She saw no reason she could not stay and play lady of Caerleon twice over by marrying her husband's son. So I wanted you. I wanted to take you to Althea. She had wanted a girl child for so long. We were tugging on you like foul-mouthed harpies when the lad burst in." A long forgotten shame quickened in his eyes. "I dropped you."

"On my head, no doubt."

Her father gave her a reproachful look. "I dove out the window. I thought your cries would haunt me forever."

An idea split the darkness of her thoughts like the moon breaking through the clouds. "Papa, how did you get me? Who brought me to you?"

A murmur of vowels was her only answer. Papa had

lapsed into semiconsciousness and was softly singing. A cry
from the turret over the drawbridge shattered the chirping
serenity of the countryside.

Rowena straddled her papa's chest. "Papa, listen to me,
I must know. After Elayne was murdered, who brought me
to you? Think."

He winced in remembered pain. "Damned boy broke my
leg. Cut my rope while I was still fifteen feet off the ground.
I had to crawl to my horse. The farrier broke it again before
he set it. The butcher."

She shook him by the tunic. His head bounced on the
rich turf. "Papa, please! How did you come to bring me to
Revelwood? Who gave me to you?"

The bright clarion note of a trumpet brought Folio's neck
up. The stallion tossed his head; his mane rippled like a
cascade of satin.

Papa's belly heaved beneath her. Rowena realized with
horror that he was crying. "I could not believe my lovely
Elayne was dead. Hadn't the strength to get off my pallet.
Thrust the child into my arms." His trembling hand found
a loose curl and dried his tears with its softness. "I wanted
my little Rowena so. Had to take her away before the sins
of the mother were visited on the child."

Rowena lifted her head, her eyes flat disks of hatred.
"Who, Papa? Who told you such a terrible thing?"

She leaned forward, straining to hear his sibilant answer.

The clatter of hoofbeats on wood split the darkness. Folio
whinnied shrilly as a dark shape separated itself from the
castle above and came hurtling into the night.

CHAPTER 22

For years Rowena would remember the nightmarish contortions it took to get herself and Papa remounted. Sweat streamed down her face to be joined by tears when, after they were seated at last, Folio balked at her command. His ears pricked toward the approaching rider. His tail twitched. Rowena cursed in frustration and pounded on his back with her fists. The rider came at them, laid low over a charger's back, hell-bent and in no mood for conversation. Rowena knew the life of the limp, pathetic creature draped behind her hung in the balance.

The unkindest dig of her heels set Folio into motion. Some long forgotten memory of a coltish game flickered through his equine brain. He wheeled around and dashed away from his approaching master, swishing his tail in a teasing flash of white. Rowena clung to the reins with one hand, her other arm struggling with her father's dead weight.

Folio's long legs smoothed into the beat of the gallop. Wind stung Rowena's eyes. She dared a look behind her and saw in amazement that the distance between them and their pursuer was growing. Even with the weight of two riders, Folio possessed the speed and strength to fly through the thin spring grasses. They swept over a rolling knoll and Rowena thought the horse would surely soar up and into the sky toward the siren purity of the moon.

A seamless edge of black bordered the meadow. Rowena swung Folio toward the forest, unable to differentiate between the pounding of her heart in her throat and the pounding of hoofbeats on the turf. They plunged into the shadows. Rowena drew rein and Folio slid to a reluctant halt.

From far behind them came the parting of the crackling grasses before a tide as inevitable as the wind. They had little time. Rowena flung herself off the horse and stayed her father's leg when he would have followed.

"Papa, can you hear me?"

He slumped forward over the stallion's neck and opened one bleary eye. "Hmmmmm?"

Rowena grabbed his ears and pushed her face at him. "You must hold on. You must ride. Ride until you reach a castle or a village. Halt for nothing and no one. Do you understand?"

She released him. His head struck the pommel of the saddle. He groaned. His eyes crossed at the sight of the ground spinning far below. "Break my neck," he mumbled.

"You may. But Sir Gareth will sever it from your head if he catches you."

He made a supreme effort to straighten his spine. Rowena gave his thigh an approving pat. "There now. Make haste, Papa. Ride like the wind."

Lindsey Fordyce's lips curled in an echo of the sunny smile that must have once charmed Elayne. "I shall be back for you, lass. As soon as I make my fortune. I will bring you ribbons and gold as much as your little paws can carry."

His wispy hair and faded blue eyes swam before her gaze. "Aye, Papa, I shall be waiting."

Folio was as much in thrall to his master as she was. Rowena knew she must take drastic measures to stop the stallion from simply running in a circle. She fished beneath the tatters of her skirt until she came up with a headless pin, shiny and dangerous in the dappled moonlight. She lay her cheek against Folio's silky hide, snuffled an apology, then jabbed the tapered point in the tender haunch.

The stallion screamed and plunged into a rear. Rowena stumbled backward, pin in hand, away from the drumming hooves. Papa clung to the saddle with tenacious strength, caught in the burgundy haze of a drama more real than he guessed.

"Away, destrier!" he bellowed. "We shall slay those Arab heathens yet and return the Holy Cross to Jerusalem!"

A flash of white and they were gone. The thunder of approaching hoofbeats shook the earth. They slowed as Gareth met the thick bracken of the forest. Without giving herself time to think, Rowena scrambled up the widely spaced branches of a sturdy elm, wishing wildly for Marlys's helm.

Her sweaty palms caught a slender branch as a nightmare of black and silver came plunging through the underbrush. She squeezed her eyes shut and dropped, using all the force of her swing to slam into the rider. She wrapped her legs around his shoulders as they fell what seemed a hundred feet from the back of a gigantic midnight charger. She kicked at the beast's hooves as they rolled, spooking it into terrified flight back toward the way it had come.

A gauntleted hand caught her throat and slammed her to her back. A muscled arm drew back a sword. For one terrible moment, Rowena thought Gareth would not recognize her before that gleaming blade descended. For an even more terrible moment, she saw the cold light of recognition dawn in his eyes without stilling the descent of the blade. Ten inches of steel whistled past her ear as Gareth buried the sword's tip into the mulch beside her cheek with a cry of rage and anguish that threw the night noises of the forest into dead silence.

She lay there in his lethal grip, her fragile pulse cradled beneath leather fingers stripped of any semblance of mercy. A tear slipped out of the corner of her eye and traced a pale path down her dirt-streaked cheek.

Gareth's hand dropped to the bodice of her kirtle; he

jerked her up. "How could you?" He shook her like a doll, then hurled her back to the ground.

He stood abruptly, circling the trees, his head cocked, listening for any sign of horse and rider. The lonely cry of a nightjar mocked him. His heaving back was to Rowena.

"Gareth?"

He silenced her with a ragged gesture of one hand. "For twenty years, I've sought the man who dishonored my name. The man who cast his shadow over my father's every hope, dream, and ambition for me. The man who turned every countenance away from me, slammed every door in my face. I've spent half my life searching for that sniveling coward."

"And his golden-haired babe?"

He whirled around. "Aye. The babe Elayne brought to Caerleon, passing it off to my father as the legitimate off-spring of her dead husband. Her lover followed shortly thereafter, offering his services to Caerleon." He took a step toward her. Rowena refused to flinch at the bitter blackness of his gaze. "Marlys thought it would be revenge enough to send that golden-haired babe home to Papa raped and bloated with a bastard of her own."

The wind blew cool against Rowena's heated cheeks. "Too quick for you, eh? You preferred something slower and more diabolical," she said.

"I wanted the truth. I've lied my whole life to find it."

"Don't speak to me of truth. The word is a mockery on your lips. Nay, Gareth. 'Tis not the truth you seek." She climbed to her feet. "You want your name cleared. You want someone to blame for the murder they condemn you for. You want to punish someone for the pain you've endured."

"I suppose your jovial Papa convinced you he was innocent," he hissed.

"Papa broke his leg when you cut his rope. He could barely crawl to his horse much less return up those stairs to plunge a sword in Elayne's breast."

Gareth snorted. "Another Fordyce family fable. You lie as well as your mother." Rowena wouldn't have thought it possible, but his brow darkened further. "Tell me, then, my dear." He took a menacing step toward her. "If your precious Papa did not kill Elayne, then who did?"

A shaft of moonlight penetrated the clouds. Rowena had not prepared herself for that question. Gareth must not see her eyes. With the vicious cunning of a trapped animal, she spun around to flee, but his arms circled her before she could take two steps. Powerful bands of muscle pinned her arms against her body and pulled her back. She made no struggle. Gareth's heart pounded a mad rhythm against her spine.

The silky heat of his voice poured into her ear. "So he has convinced you that I am a murderer."

She leaned her head back against his shoulder, choosing silence for her shield. A hot tear squeezed out from between her eyelids.

His hands left her waist, slid slowly up her shoulders, and glided beneath the tangled weight of her hair to cup her throat. He curled his leather-clad knuckles inward, trailing them over her smooth skin with unbearable tenderness. Rowena flinched as if he had struck her.

He gave a low chuckle that sent fingers of fear down her spine. "Fickle creature. Now you shrink from my touch. Was it so long ago that you received it with eagerness? Was it only two nights ago that you lay beneath me, begging me to—"

"Gareth, don't . . ."

"Don't what? Don't continue? Or don't stop? Why don't you let me show you what an adoring stepbrother I can be?" His fingers grazed the swell of her breast then dipped into her kirtle until the beaten leather brushed the tender peak of her breast with a practiced eroticism. Fear and desire tightened her throat.

"Cease your torment!" she cried, shoving his hand away.

"I cannot bear you making sport of me." She twisted ou
of his grasp and backed away from him.

He followed her step for step, holding his hands out i
front of him. "Why do you shy away now, little sister
These murderer's hands pleasured you well enough when i
suited you. You cared not if they were dripping blood."

Rowena tossed her hair back. Her eyes held a wild gleam
Harsh bark cut into her shoulder as she came up against
tree. She forced herself to laugh, blinding herself to the
twisted pain she was causing him, biting back the truth be
cause she knew it would utterly destroy him.

"Shall you have me now, Gareth? Shall you bed me a
you bedded all those other women who dared to look at you
askance? Will you use your body as a weapon to silenc
me? Or will you close your eyes and pretend I am my
mother? Have you been doing that from the beginning?"

He continued to advance on her. His lip curled in a snar
meant to be a smile. "I've already had you. And I must say
you tumbled into my bed easier than most. I suppose you
cannot help it with the blood of a whore flowing through
your veins."

Rowena forgot she had been deliberately goading him
She forgot everything but the haze of red that drifted over
her eyes. Her fist came around, slamming into his jaw in
blow that staggered him and would have fallen a lesser man

Every knuckle ached as if it had been shattered, but tha
could not silence the perverse triumph singing through he
veins. The melody was sweet but brief. As Gareth caugh
her shoulders and pinned her against the tree with hi
weight, she began to ponder the consequences of her ac
tions. His face was scarcely an inch from hers. To her sur
prise, he was grinning like a naughty demon spurned from
the gates of hell. His face, stripped of light, was not the
face of a loving man she had known once in another life
time, but the face of a young man little more than a boy—
wild with infatuation, sick with jealousy.

"You golden-haired little bastard. I always knew you'd be more trouble than you were worth."

His lips closed on hers. He pushed his fingers through her hair, drawing her head back until her mouth was opened and helpless before the merciless assault of his kiss. The salt of blood stung her tongue where her blow had driven his cheek against his teeth. Rowena felt herself drawn into the maelstrom of his dark desire as if every moment of her life had brought her to this place to be held captive by her love for this man.

She moaned as his tongue feverishly stroked the deepest corners of her mouth. His knee slipped between her legs, nudging upward with crass finesse until her own fingers crept up to tangle in his hair. He drew back. There was no darkness on earth black enough to dim the luminous emotion in Rowena's eyes.

His breathing was harsh. "You are a fool, milady. You should have fled with your father." He caught her face roughly between his palms. "If I murdered your mother, do you not believe me capable of murdering you? Your fickle heart has cut me deeper than Elayne's ever could." His thumb reached out to stroke her trembling bottom lip like a creature with its own will.

Rowena laced her fingers in his and drew his hands downward. She pressed his palms to the thundering pulse in her throat and held them fast when they jerked convulsively.

"Go on," she said. "Murder me if 'tis what you desire. You hated me when I was a babe. You hate me now. You can tell them I fled with Papa. There are leaves enough to cover my body. No one will ever know. I shall try not to struggle. There. Would it be easier if I closed my eyes?"

Gareth's fingers tightened slightly.

Rowena kept her eyes closed, steeling her body against the trembling that threatened to seize it. "Why do you hesitate? You were going to kill Papa, were you not? Can you deny it? You were going to condemn him without benefit of questioning or trial, just as you were condemned. I set him free. So should I not take his place in the executioner's hands?'' Her arms crept down to her sides. She stood there, achingly passive in the power of a man who could snap her neck with a single flex of his broad thumbs.

Gareth's grip softened. Rowena's eyes fluttered open.

''Nay, sweet ladylove. The freedom of death will be denied you.'' His lips brushed her earlobe in a mocking caress. ''These executioner's hands can think of a thousand pleasant things to do to you that they could not do to your papa. You will serve me well enough alive. I will see to that.'' His eyes sparkled with an odd light.

Rowena inclined her head. ''If you take me tonight, I promise you 'twill not be a seduction. 'Twill be rape.''

''Do you think me incapable of such a heinous crime? Your faith in me is touching.'' He knelt at her feet and tore the hem from her skirt. ''Give me your hands.''

Rowena felt as if they were reliving a scene that had happened centuries ago. ''There is no need.''

''You've been running from me ever since you promised that the first time.''

Rowena held out her wrists, and he twined the length of brocade around them.

''If I try to run, you could just hit me over the head with something,'' she mumbled.

''I prefer my women conscious,'' he said in clipped tones. ''I hate for them to wake up tender and sated and not remember why.''

Rowena felt a flare of genuine hatred. ''An honorable nobleman, are you not?''

He jerked the bond, making her crash into his chest. He pulled her up until they were nose to nose. ''You stole any hope of honor for me when you freed your father. 'Tis time I started living up to my reputation. If you give me another of your speeches on chivalry, I swear I shall gag you.''

Rowena wisely bit back a retort. Her head ached with the effort.

They emerged from the forest to find Gareth's mount

grazing in the meadow. The destrier lifted his massive head. Despite his jarring size, he lacked the prancing nervousness of Folio and stood docile as Gareth secured a rope around Rowena's snug bonds and mounted. Without so much as a glance at her, Gareth nudged the horse into a sedate walk. Rowena supposed it was of no import to him whether she stumbled behind or lay down and was dragged back to Ardendonne on her belly. She prodded her feet into motion.

Ardendonne winked like a misty diamond studding a dusky crown, the parapets and towers drawn against the pitching clouds. She was shocked to find it so near. Folio's speed and her fear had led her to believe they had left it far behind. How could its lambent glow remain so serene when her whole life had shattered? The winds gusted, carrying over the rustling grasses a haunting note from a clarion, distorted by time and distance. She swiped a tear from her cheek with bound hands. When Gareth swung around in his saddle, she was plodding behind him, her eyes locked on the ground.

He snorted. "Such a charming picture of persecution. I daresay you would look lovely gracing a cathedral window. Your demure stance and blameless eyes would melt the heart of the staunchest sinner."

"If he had a heart."

Gareth's tone was deliberately light. "If such a sinner had any dealings with women, no doubt his heart was cut out and fed to his lady for supper."

"Then God take pity on her, for she would have starved on such meager fare."

Gareth doubled the horse's pace. Rowena stumbled after him, too angry to regret her impertinence. She gave a start of surprise as his voice rang out in a lusty baritone.

Mortimer would have never dared sing of these amorous adventures of a wench named Rosaleen in mixed company. Rowena did not understand half of the lewd verses. From the dark glances Gareth hurled over his shoulder after the most perverse lyrics, she had the discomfitting sensation that

she would before this night was over. When she could no
longer bear his gloating smirk, she joined in and bellowed
out the next chorus with such enthusiasm that Gareth lapsed
into brooding silence.

Her satisfaction was short-lived. The graceful arch of
Blaine's bridge clattered under the horse's hooves. Wind
and moon raked the lake into silvered peaks. Shimmering
waves lapped hungrily at the shore. The drawbridge loomed
before them like a black tongue poised to draw them inside
the yawning maw of the castle. Rowena shivered as they
passed beneath the arch, all that was grace in Ardendonne's
construction dying in the first stale breath of its debauchery.

The bailey reeked of stale wine, sweat and a potpourri
of earthy smells Rowena did not dare to name. As Gareth
dismounted, her gaze went of its own volition to the stable
cradled at the bottom of the hill. He tossed the reins to a
squire she did not recognize. The boy's eyes widened as
they fell on the rope which bound her to Gareth.

He led the horse away, looking over his shoulder until he
went sprawling over a trough.

Gareth jerked on Rowena's bonds, paying her no more
heed than if she had been a recalcitrant terrier on the end
of a leash.

"Have you . . . ? Where . . . ?" Rowena started but
could not find the words to finish.

"Did you expect to find your brothers' heads piked on
the gate? Sorry to disappoint you. I've decided to stop holding them responsible for the willful acts of their more
stubborn relations."

Rowena choked back her sigh of relief. The inner courtyard swallowed them. It was not nearly as late as Rowena
had imagined. The squires still rattled their dice on the cobblestones. The stuporous peasant had been replaced by a
stuporous herald.

The squires slyly nudged each other and muttered among
themselves. Those eyes that were not blind drunk with wine
or pleasure focused on Rowena and Gareth.

A knight spilled out of the door, dragging a plainly garbed maid into the hazy protection of the ivy shrouded wall. He thrust her to her knees in front of him, his hands fumbling with the points of his hose.

Rowena hastily looked away.

Gareth gave an ugly laugh. "Before this night is over, I shall remedy your shyness."

Rowena's feet froze. She did not feel Gareth's eyes on her as he turned to gauge the effect of his cruel words. She paled as her fragile illusions came crashing down around her. Somehow she had convinced herself that there was nothing he could do to her that she could not forgive. Somewhere in the back of her mind, she had even harbored the childish hope that he might forgive her, that he would laugh away her folly and draw her under his arm with a tender kiss. She felt faint at the realization that he could do unforgivable things to her. She swayed as a pain deeper than grief speared her heart.

Wrapping the rope around his fist, Gareth reeled her in like a fish.

He steeled himself against the lost eyes she raised to his face. "Come, Rowena," he growled. "I am in no mood for dillydallying."

Her gaze darted wildly around the courtyard. "I cannot bear them staring at me."

"You will learn to bear it soon enough. I did."

He jerked the rope, but her feet stayed rooted to the cobblestones. He jerked harder, and she dragged her feet, her lips set in a mutinous line.

Gareth's entire countenance dissolved in a sweetness so profound that Rowena was terrified. He caught her shoulders and drove her straight back into the shadows until the stone wall dug into her shoulder blades. One arm circled her waist. His hand cupped her head. He bent her over his arm in a kiss so darkly passionate that even the most astute observer would have sworn they were lovers too long torn asunder. A snicker among the squires was followed by a bray of laughter.

Gareth drew back. His arms stilled her frantic struggle with no visible effort. "I swear to you, my ladylove," he said between clenched teeth, "if you are so eager for my touch that you can go no further, then we will take our pleasure here like those others."

In counterpoint to his threat came a rustle in the ivy behind them, a man's groan thick with the muted agony of pleasure. Rowena's fingers uncurled and tugged on his sleeves, and she pressed her forehead to his breastbone in a wordless plea.

Gareth shoved her roughly into motion, the cost of his cruelty betrayed by his harsh breathing and the stiff jut of his jaw.

Gareth paused at the door to the great hall as his gaze fell on the rope that hung slack between them. The eyes he raised to Rowena were as black and calm as a sea before a storm.

His stride was sure and steady as he marched them into the hall. He ducked beneath the linked hands of the dancers in an unswerving path for the stairs. When Rowena faltered, he jerked the rope, ignoring the horrified gasps, the offended glares from those not draped insensibly over the tables or each other. Rowena knew she must look like a hoyden. She had lost her slippers. Her hair hung in tangled disarray down her back. From the corner of her eye, she caught a glimpse of something smudged with dirt, which she could only assume was her nose. The ruby kirtle hung in lank tatters around her ankles.

She shrank into herself, believing their disapproval was of her. The last plucked note of the psaltery wavered in the air. A dwarf's spatulate fingers stopped pounding the tabor and a steady murmur swelled to a hum.

"How dare he!"

"The poor child."

"Heartless wretch!"

"He may treat her like an animal on his own lands, but surely Sir Blaine will not allow it in the sanctity of his castle."

Gareth stared straight ahead as if he had been struck blind as well as deaf.

They had reached the stairs when Blaine broke from the crowd and stepped in front of them. His expression held such kind concern that Rowena felt tears sting her eyes. Alise hovered at Blaine's elbow like a nervous wren.

The crowd held their breath, straining to hear Blaine's soft words. "For once, they are right, Gareth. I cannot allow this."

No one had to strain to hear Gareth's booming answer. "She stole my steed and gave it to another man."

Even Blaine winced and recoiled from those words. A horrified murmur went up from the crowd. Alise smiled.

Blaine went down on one knee at Rowena's feet and caught her bound hands in his own. "Sweet lady, say it is not so! Did you not know what a mount means to his knight? What the stallion was worth?"

Rowena forced a wry smile. "More than me, it seems."

Gareth interrupted. "If you will cease groveling at the thief's feet, we will proceed."

Blaine stood, his slender form bearing more dignity than Rowena would have thought possible. "Gareth, I beg you. Surely for the sake of our friendship, you could show mercy to this sweet—"

Gareth's words fell like thunderclaps in the hushed silence. "Felon. She stole my horse. Do I take her upstairs or would you care to hang her?" He thrust the end of the rope at Blaine as if it were of no concern to him which course was taken.

Alise tugged at Blaine's sleeve. "Hang her, Blaine. Do let's hang her."

Gareth's nostrils flared as he shot Alise a look of pure contempt. She slipped behind Blaine, who stepped back from the swaying rope as if it might bite him.

Gareth pushed past them, and Rowena felt Blaine's sym
pathetic hand brush her shoulder as they passed. At the to
of the narrow staircase, Gareth came to a halt with a be
mused curse. Rowena stumbled into his back.

With a hand on her elbow, he drew her in front of him
"I've never had to face so many obstacles to get a woma
to my bedchamber. Have you the pope crouching under m
bed?"

Marlys squatted at the end of the corridor like a nestin
gargoyle. Between lank strands of hair, her face was star
white.

Her voice had lost its confident cadence. "I must spea
to you, Gareth."

His fingers lightly traced Rowena's collarbone. "Later."
"Now."

Rowena's eyes blazed a brilliant blue, narrowing in bot
a warning and a plea. She laughed lightly. "If you've com
to plead for me, save your breath. Blaine did a much prettie
job and his pleas fell on ears of stone. I fear it would tak
more than pleasantries to soothe your brother's wounde
vanity."

"Like a human sacrifice?" Marlys bit off.

"A charming one, at that," Gareth said pleasantly.

With a choked sound, Marlys leaped to her feet and fle
past them down the stairs.

In one fluid movement, Gareth had them secured behin
a chamber door with the bolt dropped home.

Rowena stood lost at the door while Gareth went to th
window. The moon cast his silhouette in wax.

"The remonstrances of your friends are touching, are the
not?"

"But ineffectual," she murmured.

Her heart plummeted as she saw the linen sheets humpe
and tangled on the bed. She would rather he kill her outrigh
than lay her beneath him on a feather mattress that only las
night may have held the mold of Alise's body beneath his

She spun around, a cry catching in her throat, and pressed her forehead to the door.

Gareth's head flew up as the piteous sound arrowed straight to his heart. He crossed to her. Rough hands cradled her shoulders as his husky voice rocked her with shivers.

"Your shyness would be more convincing if my body were not incensed with memories of your wanton surrender to me. I cannot sleep. I cannot eat. I cannot think without their visions rising unbidden before me. Your poison is sweet, but fatal. I can find no antidote except to partake of it again and again until I've purged it from my soul or died trying."

Rowena leaned her head back. Tears slid down her cheeks, wetting the silky heat of his beard. "What do you want from me, Gareth? Shall I scream so the others can hear me? Shall I drop to my knees and plead for your mercy?"

"Your knees would be as fine a place as any to begin."

He pulled her around and pinned her against the door. His lips harshly took hers. His tongue stoked the embers of want deep within her to hungry flames with a violence that warned her his desire was tinged with madness. His knee flexed between her legs, opening her to the brutal caress of fingers sheathed in leather. His palm rubbed the tatters of her dress against her, using leather against satin as a fiery conductor of his desire until her struggles deepened to tortured writhing. He scooped her up, one muscled arm cradling her hips, his other palm still cupping the hot, damp satin between her legs.

He lay her back on the bed, pulling her hips to its edge. Her legs dangled on each side of his thighs. He pulled his tunic over his head, revealing a dark mat of crisp fur.

"You are as spineless as your father," he snarled. "You'd give yourself to a man who hates you before you would fight for yourself."

His words were like ice water tossed on the flames of her

love. She lay stunned before their virulence and injustice. Gareth reached for the points of his hose. If his hands had not been poised there, he would have received the full force of her convulsive kick to his groin. As it was, his hand shot down in a reflex born of knighthood, catching her slender foot in his grasp.

He gave a low, taunting laugh. "There now, girl. I knew you had your mother in you somewhere. 'Twas only a matter of baiting her to life."

Rowena sat up, jerking her foot out of his hand. "The two of you deserved each other."

She scooted back on the bed, and Gareth crawled after her. "You've inherited her deceit, treachery and fickle heart. Perhaps 'tis time I taught you some of her other tricks."

"As she taught you?" Rowena shot back.

She rolled over, planning to launch herself off the bed and flee this vicious demon she had thought to be her lover. Gareth's arm snaked around her waist. He slid her face-down beneath his weight. She sucked in a sharp breath to scream, but before she could cry out his hand clapped over her mouth. She tasted leather against her teeth.

"If you scream, you shall summon Blaine and his minions," he hissed in her ear. "And if you think his chivalry possesses no price, you are mistaken. Do you want to be the whore of one man, or two?"

Rowena slumped against the feather mattress, defeat etched in the slender curve of her spine. When Gareth turned her over, her eyes were as dark with hatred as his own.

His knuckles brushed her cheek with a touch that was achingly tender. His lips grazed her temple, tasting tiny hairs like spun sugar against his tongue.

"How can I forgive you for this?" she asked.

His lips nestled into the hollow of her throat. "If I am a murderer, why should I care?"

Rowena ached to speak but held her tongue, painfully aware of the price of silence.

His hands undid the tiny buttons of her bodice. The satin

melted beneath his touch. Rowena lay malleable beneath his hands, holding back a shudder as he exposed her nakedness to his burning gaze.

She flinched at the unfamiliar graze of leather against the tips of her breasts. The delicate nubs tightened and contracted with a will of their own. Gareth lowered his heated lips to first one and then the other, taking them into his mouth and gently suckling until her hands caught in his hair. He lifted his shaggy head and met the ferocity of her gaze over twin peaks silvered with moonlight and frosted with the wetness of his tongue.

He pulled off his gauntlets.

She caught her breath as his blunt fingers slid between her legs, weaving an erotic spell with a delicacy that should have been impossible. Gareth watched her face, captivated by the fleeting glimpses of a pleasure she could no longer hide. Her body tensed and shuddered as he dipped one finger into her with a paralyzing gentleness, soothing the swelling membranes he found there with the silken fluids of her body. His finger ravished her with agonizing slowness, preparing her for the deeper filling that would come. Her lashes fluttered on her flushed cheeks. Her head rolled from side to side, the coral softness of her lips forming soundless words against the pillow of her hair. Gareth's fingers worked their magic in maddening rhythm until a shudder harder and deeper than the others rocked Rowena and held her fast.

Her throat arched and she fell back against the mattress, biting back a cry. Gareth felt the muscles of his abdomen tighten convulsively. Rowena opened eyes dark and misty with passion and bitterness as he withdrew his fingers from her and gently teased their dew over her taut nipples. He slipped his finger into her one last time. The pungent scent of leather assailed her nostrils as he gently drew it across her lips, pearling their softness with a glistening honey more potent than nectar. His mouth closed on hers, the taste and scent of her surrender fusing them together in a bond stronger than blood.

His knee nudged her thighs apart. He barely had his hose untied and down over his hips when Rowena felt the tip of a blade more lethal than any sword press against her softness, following the aching course his fingers had charted. She buried her face against his throat as he teased her, rubbing against her but holding back. Her teeth nipped his collarbone. Her moan reverberated against his ear in a plea that needed no words. His fingers laced around hers, pinning her palms in a prison of deceptive softness underlaid with a hardness as fine as steel. She clutched his hands as a matching hardness knifed deep within her.

Gareth took her, making her his own with tantalizing strokes, each longer and deeper than the last until Rowena shuddered, filled so deeply that she no longer knew where her body ended and his began. His breathing quickened as he rocked between her hips until the tenuous thread of his own control snapped and a guttural groan escaped his throat. Rowena arched against him as he poured his seed into her, impaling her like a spread butterfly against the bed.

The moon sank like a pale pearl into a black sea, casting its exhausted beams over a floor strewn with gauntlets, hose, and satin.

Gareth drew Rowena up in the center of the bed to face him. His fingers pushed through her tangled hair, his nails coming to rest against her scalp like tender blades. "I once swore an oath to you—on my knees." His hand tangled in her hair. She slid irrevocably down the merciless contours of his body until her cheek lay against the satiny heat of his thigh. Her hair sheltered her burning cheeks from him. He reached down and gently tilted her chin until she was forced to meet his gaze. "Now, sweet lady, you may swear your oath to me."

Rowena's eyes widened but the honeyed languor of their lovemaking still held her in its thrall. She was beguiled by the strength of his will. His hands and body guided her through this tender initiation until the sweet acquiescence of her lips and mouth wrung a groan of mortal pleasure from deep in his throat. He threw back his head, teeth clenched in a primitive portrait of esctasy. Exultation rolled through Rowena's veins like thunder as Gareth cried out a need for her that could find no words.

The moon fled beneath the clouds that darkened the horizon. Rowena lay with her face buried in the crook of Gareth's arm. His hand absently traced half-words and pictures on the flat planes of her sweat-sheened stomach.

"You will find me no husband, will you?" she murmured against his skin.

Gareth's fingertips paused in their gentle motion. He shook his head.

"And you will not let me go come summer, will you?"

She lifted her gaze. Gareth's arm tightened around her neck. "I will never let you go."

Despair darkened her own eyes at the tenor of those words. Once she had prayed to hear them, but not spoken like that, not thrown out like a black-edged threat laced with more hatred than love. She blinked back tears as he rolled her to her stomach and mated her with a savage intensity that left her incoherent and mercifully incapable of further thought.

Rowena stared blindly at the gray dawn creeping through the narrow window. The distant, lonely crow of a cock warbled to a pensive halt. She looked at the man beside her as if he were a stranger. A lock of tousled hair fell over his eyes. Sleep had soothed the lines etched around his mouth, but as she watched, a shadow of a grimace tightened his lips in a brief convulsion as if even the peace of sleep eluded him. Rowena did not want his pain. She had enough of her own. She nudged away the knee thrown over her thigh and scooted out from under his weight.

She dropped Gareth's tunic over her head. The heavy camlet felt rough against her nakedness. The garment cov-

ered her to the knees. She paused at the door and returned
to the bed to draw a linen sheet over Gareth's sprawling
form. He rolled to his side, pulling her pillow under his
chin with a slurred murmur.

Sleeping bodies littered the great hall like the victims of
some merciless plague of pleasure. Without a second glance,
Rowena stepped over the stained skirts of a spread-eagled
maid whose cheek was pillowed on the rump of a pock-
marked page.

As she passed through the bailey, Rowena filled her lungs
with damp morning air untainted by the stench of sour wine
and unwashed flesh. At the top of the drawbridge, she
stopped. Her bare toes curled against the splintered wood
as she gazed back wistfully at the cluster of wooden build-
ings that were the stables. She had come to seek the solace
of her brothers only to find that far more than the rich dirt
of the list separated them.

A chasm had somehow opened between them, a chasm
deepened by the long night when a merciless and coldly
inventive Gareth had used her love as a weapon to tame her,
using his dark cycle of pleasure to wring cries from her she
did not even recognize as her own. The courage that had
driven her to defy Gareth deserted her at the thought of
facing Little Freddie this way. Half-dressed with swollen
lips and tangled hair, she knew the evidence of Gareth's
possession was as plain as the lingering tenderness between
her legs.

She hugged her elbows, wishing she had thought to bring
a shawl into a morning that still held a breath of winter.
Clouds smothered the horizon, and the scent of rain drifted
to her nostrils.

Bracing herself against the castle stones, she crept out
along the narrow ledge overhanging the moat and sat down,
dangling her feet over the dark mirror of water. Mist drifted
across the lake in veils of white, obscuring the bridge. If
she started walking now, how long would it take her to get

to Revelwood? And how long would it take Gareth to come after her and drag her back?

I will never let you go.

His icy words echoed in her head. Gareth de Crecy was a powerful man. He could lock her away, keep her prisoner at Caerleon forever if he so desired. She imagined herself sitting in a lonely tower, watching from the window as he brought a wife to Caerleon, growing withered and gray while he fathered sons and slowly forgot the blinding passion that had once bound them.

She pressed her wrists to her eyes, praying the clean ache might erase her tortured visions. When she opened her eyes, something milky white was bobbing on the surface of the moat. She blinked, wondering if the pressure on her eyes had deceived her.

She climbed up on her knees and leaned over as far as she dared. A tantalizing edge of white drifted toward her. She hesitated before stretching out her fingers, having no idea if Blaine's vicious fish were an inch long or as big as whales. Drawing in a deep breath, she snatched at the scrap of white.

Her hand closed around a smooth cylinder and pulled it streaming from the water. She lifted it before her eyes. It was a bone, the long, slender web of fingers still tangled in the strings of a wooden lute. A shrill scream ripped from her throat, shattering the morning silence. Her scream went on and on until Blaine pried the thing from her hand and enfolded her in his arms, pressing her face into his shoulder.

CHAPTER 23

The seneschal's keys jingled wildly as he loped into the donjon. He cast the hearth a curious glance. Rowena returned it unblinkingly until he looked away. "Milord, milord, they set up a cry outside the doors. Whatever shall I do?" He trotted behind Blaine's pacing path, wringing his plump hands.

"Tell them to go to hell," Blaine gritted out from between his teeth.

The seneschal trotted faster. "They do not understand, Sir Blaine. First they were snatched from their sleep and tossed out of the castle like yesterday's cabbage. Half of them are still drunk. The mood is ugly and the rumors are getting uglier. The doors of Ardendonne have never been bolted against any man—knight or villein." He lowered his voice ominously. " 'Tis beginning to rain. I heard cries for a battering ram."

Blaine turned on the man, his patience frazzled to an end. He snatched him up by his tunic. "You are the seneschal, are you not? Pull up the drawbridge. Lower the cursed portcullis."

The man blinked. "The portcullis. Of course. I forgot we had one. I shall be at it right away. Mayhaps 'tis not rusted."

Blaine released the man, and he scampered off, happy to have a concrete task. Blaine blew out a long breath and ruffled his hair, looking more a perplexed thirteen than a self-assured thirty-three. Freckles dusted his pale cheeks.

A maidservant with eyes still swollen from the night's debauchery stumbled in from the kitchens. She cleared a scrap-littered table with one arm and dropped her tray. She managed a sloe-eyed wink at Blaine before turning to run into the door frame with a thump that made Rowena wince.

Blaine squatted in front of where Rowena huddled on the hearth and pressed a warm mug into her icy palms.

"Ale would serve you better. I shall have it mulled with cinnamon if 'tis the taste that plagues you."

Rowena cupped the mug gratefully, breathing in the steam. "Nay. 'Tis milk I wanted," she said through chattering teeth.

She blew the skin off the surface and took a deep draught. The creamy warmth spread like courage down her throat. Blaine pulled the edges of the blanket around her shoulders with an awkward pat.

Outside the chamber, a tremendous clanking of chains was followed by the throbbing groan of an iron pulley that had fallen into disuse before ever being used. The massive portcullis slid out of its mooring with a screech that set Rowena's teeth on edge.

"Careful with that crank now, Owen," came a wavery cry.

"I got it, mate. Oh, dear!"

"Stand clear!"

"Watch your feet!"

The muffled thump of bodies diving was followed by the crash of spiked bars striking stone. The echoing clang went on and on, dying with a finality that left Blaine's face as bereft as a child's.

" 'Tis not rusted," Rowena said in a vain attempt to cheer him.

Safe behind the iron bars of the portcullis, Blaine's seneschal and his hapless cohorts flung open the main doors. Rain pelted the cobblestones. Thunder cracked like a whip.

Rowena's face flushed as a roar of disapproval rocked the castle. She huddled deeper in the blanket as individual threads of sound unwove themselves from the bellowing tapestry of fury.

"Send out the murderer!"

"Justice for Mortimer!"

"Hang the dark lord!"

Blaine was across the chamber before she realized he had moved. "Close that door," he shouted. "And bolt it. If you open it again, the mob can have what is left of you after I've shoved you through the portcullis."

His men obeyed with a fawning chorus of, "As you wish, sir."

"Good God, Sir Boris, get in here." Blaine reappeared with a gray-haired knight in tow.

The man rubbed his red-rimmed eyes, finally bringing them to focus on Rowena. He was less disheveled than most of the occupants of Ardendonne, though he wore only one gauntlet and his tunic was on backward. Rowena curled her bare feet under the blanket, realizing she had no right to pass judgment while garbed in Gareth's tunic and Blaine's blanket.

"Is this the girl?" the man asked Blaine.

"It is," Blaine replied.

Sir Boris gave her a courtly bow Rowena hardly felt she deserved while dressed like some bawd escaped from the wharfs of London town.

Blaine did not stand on the ceremony of introduction. "I am at a loss, Sir Boris. What am I to do?"

"Being the oldest and wisest lech here, I suppose the burden of counsel falls on me. Can you summon your father?"

"I fear not. He is dead."

"Oh, dear, I'd forgotten. Hmmm." Sir Boris smoothed back gray hair peppered with black. "Unfortunate situation. Sir Bryan would know just what to do. He took care of it the last time Gareth got himself into such a pickle."

Resentment flared in Rowena. "Why does everyone have to assume Gareth got himself into anything? Mayhaps someone else got him there."

Sir Boris squinted at her as if seeing her for the first time. "Now, child, you must understand what the people believe, what they've believed for years. Everyone heard Gareth threaten Mortimer. 'Twas not the first time. His temper is as black as his reputation."

The knight's kind gray eyes and utter calm frightened her more than the rantings of the mob. She stood. The blanket slid from her shoulders. "Your temper might be black, too, if you'd lived your whole life under the shadow of gossip and innuendo."

"A minstrel's bones carry this beyond gossip, Rowena," Blaine said. "A man died last night."

Rowena turned on him. "And you believe Gareth killed him?"

Blaine's eyes clouded briefly. "I don't care if he did," he finally said. "I'll not turn him over to that clamoring mob."

"Good lad. My sentiments exactly." Sir Boris clapped him on the shoulder. "We shall have a trial before the rabble can hang him. We will send for some of the king's best knights."

"So *they* can hang me?" Gareth leaned against the door frame, his arms crossed in a study of casual arrogance. Rowena wondered how long he had been standing there.

Their gazes met. His eyes swept her in a velvet caress, a question stamped on his features Rowena was helpless to answer because she did not understand it. The night loomed between them, as dark and impenetrable as his eyes. Rowena had to look away. She forced herself to remember how he had used his body and her need as a weapon to weave a punishing net of pleasure. Steel threads garroted her heart as she fought the urge to run to him. She sat down and pulled the blanket around her shoulders like a mantle.

Gareth's mouth twisted in a bitter travesty of a smile.

"What good knights would you summon to my defense, Sir Boris? From my window, I believe I caught a glimpse of Sir Damien and Sir Leitchfield leaping about in a charming demand for my blood. Shall they head my tribunal?"

Blaine sank down in a chair as Gareth sauntered into the chamber and propped his hip on the edge of a table.

Sir Boris cleared his throat. "Gareth, you must try to understand their position. Mortimer was an extremely popular minstrel. A treasure of the court since he was little more than a lad. A pampered favorite of the king."

"And more of his dukes than I'd care to recount." Gareth smiled pleasantly.

"The man had his weaknesses. As we all do. But his follies were more than outweighed by his talents."

"As multifaceted as they were."

"Damnit, Gareth," Blaine erupted. "Stifle your flippancy. Sir Boris is trying to help you."

Sir Boris's hands trembled as he plucked the flagon off the tray and filled a goblet. For an instant, Rowena wanted to shake Gareth as badly as Blaine did.

Sir Boris grimaced at the warm goat's milk and set the goblet down without drinking from it. "The people feel Mortimer belonged to them. With his ballads and the spell he wove with words and music, he became the voice of their lives. They were willing to overlook his dalliances, his childish sulks—"

"His drunkenness?" Rowena added softly.

Sir Boris's head swiveled around to look at her. "The thought occurred to me, too, child. He may have simply stumbled into the moat." He shook his head as if to clear it. "But a hundred witnesses heard Mortimer sing his last ballad, heard Sir Gareth threaten him and saw the bard leave the hall never to be seen alive again."

Gareth applauded dryly. "Now that has the ring of a fine ballad. Such dramatic flair wasted in a knight!"

It was more to still Gareth's flagellating tongue than to

defend him that spurred Rowena to speech. "Sir Gareth could not have killed Mortimer. He was with me all night."

Sir Boris looked so pitying that she might have made the admission she had spent the night with a troll.

Her cheeks flamed as Gareth gave a short, ugly laugh. "Your loyalty is touching, milady, but there is no need to lie for me. Everyone saw me leave the hall alone. Just as everyone saw us return together."

Sir Boris chose his next words with care. "The less the young lady's name is bandied about, the better. There have already been some very—to put this delicately—distasteful rumors. Bringing them to mind will only blight your reputation further and fan the flames of outrage."

Gareth snorted. "What do those paragons of moral virtue dare whisper about Rowena?"

Sir Boris's gaze was uncompromising. "That you carried her off to Caerleon against her will. That you keep her chained to your bed, a slave to your dark desires."

Gareth's mask slipped as he realized the cost of the rumors he had spread himself to torment Lindsey Fordyce. Like a blind man he reached for a steadying corner of the table. The eyes he raised to Rowena were stricken with the knowledge that his anger of the night had turned rumor into prophecy.

It was he who had to look away first. "None of this is your concern. If they want me that badly, let them come lay siege to Caerleon."

Blaine sat up in his chair. "And if they bring Edward's armies with them? What then, Gareth? Civil war? You cannot fight everybody in England."

"Why not? I've been doing it all my life."

Boris laid a steadying hand on Blaine's shoulder and faced Gareth. " 'Tis with great regret, my son, that I suggest you be confined until the knights arrive. 'Twill satisfy even the most bloodthirsty of the lot outside."

Gareth swung around on the table. The threat of barely checked violence was written in every graceful line, making his powerful body seem even larger than it was. The suggestion of confining such a presence seemed as ludicrous as trying to harness the deep swell of thunder that rolled across the roof of the donjon.

He slid off the table, his swagger as deliberate as a taunt.

He stopped in front of Blaine's chair and held out his wrists. "Cart me off to the dungeon, friend. Have you any chains in this palace of pleasure?"

Blaine slapped Gareth's hands away, and Sir Boris had the good grace to look embarrassed. "Your chamber will be sufficient. I shall entrust my son with your safekeeping. He is young and not so easily swayed by the opinions of others."

Gareth's gaze fell on Rowena's bent head, and his lips softened in a smile more wry than mocking. "A marvelous and dangerous trait. Guard it well."

By the time Rowena had lifted her head, he had thrown a cheerful arm over Sir Boris's shoulders and was guiding the man from the chamber, leading him in a discussion of the latest tournament rules.

Blaine covered his face with one hand and cast Rowena a despairing glance between his fingers. Outside the hall, a cry of warning was followed by the thud of a heavy body striking the floor. The blanket fell away as Rowena sprinted for the door. She gave a cry of dismay at the sight of Gareth's form crumpled on the stones.

She flung herself to her knees and cradled his head in her lap. "What have you done to him?"

A bewildered looking young knight stood over him. He gave the broadsword in his hand a sheepish glance. "I saw his arm tighten around Papa's throat. So I hit him over the head."

"You knave. You might have killed him!" The young man quailed before the contempt in Rowena's voice.

She soothed the hair from Gareth's brow, crooning words of comfort he could not hear. His chest rose and fell evenly.

His dark lashes rested against his cheeks. He looked so peaceful, he might have been sleeping.

Sir Boris rubbed his throat with a convulsive swallow. "It was as the boy said. The lad did right."

"I suppose he was trying to kill you, too. Mayhaps he is in the throes of a murdering frenzy and is going to massacre us all." Rowena laid a lopsided kiss on Gareth's ear, daring the men to tear him away from her.

Blaine knelt in front of her. "Of course he wasn't going to kill Sir Boris. I know Gareth. He was going to escape and take his battle away from Ardendonne. I promise you, Rowena, if Gareth gets outside those gates, someone will die. And it might be him." The harshness of his words was tempered by the palm that gently cupped her cheek. "Let me protect him. From himself."

Rowena's arms fell to her sides. None of the three men met her eyes as they gently took Gareth from her and carried him down the dimly lit corridor.

A swish of Rowena's kirtle and a tremulous smile was all it took to convince Sir Boris's son that she must see Gareth. He watched her traverse the dim hall, admiration for her courage in the face of such trials written plainly in his besotted eyes. Perhaps he should examine his feelings about Sir Gareth. Any man who could inspire such devotion in so enchanting a creature could surely not be as wicked as they said. The memory of her eyes blazing brightly up at him over Gareth's prostrate form lent itself to daydreams where it was his own head cradled in her soft lap. He slipped around the corner to give her the privacy he had promised.

The best Ardendonne could offer for a dungeon was an isolated cell off the corridor from the kitchen wing. It was one of the few chambers in the castle with an iron lock placed to protect the salt and other precious spices. A grate of iron bars was set in the thick oaken door.

Rowena stood on tiptoe and peered through the bars. A tallow candle burned within the cell. It took a long moment for her eyes to adjust enough to make out the shadow of a man sitting on a barrel.

"Gareth?"

"Could you not wait to gloat at my hanging?" Gareth swung his long legs around. The candle threw his features into sharp relief as the shadow of a wince crossed his face. He rubbed the back of his neck. "Damned pup nearly killed me."

Rowena stuck her nose through the bars. Hulking crates and kegs were stacked along the walls. The pungent scent of ginger and cloves tickled her nostrils. "Folio came back."

"Was your papa's corpse draped across his saddle?"

"I fear not. He came back quite alone, stepping in high spirits and tossing his head in shameless pride at his independent jaunt." She peered around the shadowy cell. "Is it terribly unpleasant in there?"

"Not terribly. I've yet to find any skulls of former occupants, and Blaine has spared me the rack. You must find that a pity."

Rowena's fingers curled around the cold iron. "And you must think me a vindictive wench."

Gareth slipped off the barrel. The torch behind Rowena's head threw her hair into a halo of gold. Gareth laced his fingers around the chill bars, laying them lightly against her own. The soft heat of her skin seemed to be the only thing of substance against a world gone awry. He waited for her to recoil from his touch. She did not.

"Should you not be vindictive? I earned my reputation last night, did I not?"

Rowena knew he was not speaking of the murder. She could not offer him the comfort of denial. "Will you answer a question for me?"

"I owe you that much."

"When my moth—" Rowena could not bring herself to say the word. "When Elayne died, why did you defend

yourself to no one? There had to be those who would believe you. Sir Blaine's father? The priest?''

He bowed his head until they stood forehead to forehead.
His nose gently brushed hers. ''My father raised me to be
the best. I was to be the strongest, the wisest, the kindest
knight England had ever known. All of his dreams of honor
died in the breath of Elayne's kiss. The same night I lay
with her, my father died choking in his own blood. I felt as
guilty of murder as they claimed me.''

She gave his fingers a quick, hard squeeze, then stepped
back from the door. ''All will be well, Gareth.''

Gareth straightened. ''Of course it will be. They are going to hang me and you are going to be free.''

She shook her head with a wild glance at the end of the
corridor. Her voice dropped to a whisper. ''They won't hang
you. When I prove you did not kill Elayne, everyone will
know Mortimer knocked his own silly self off the drawbridge.''

Gareth went white in the sickly light. ''Have you gone
mad?''

She smiled happily. ''Nay. I am quite sane.''

Gareth lifted his head. The full import of her words penetrated the blackness of his heart in a ray of light that cut
as mercilessly as it warmed. ''You mean last night you did
not believe me a murderer? You let me believe . . . why I
could have . . .''

''What? Murdered me? Pshaw! You'd be hard pressed to
give me a good beating!''

Gareth flew at the bars. He tried to thrust his hands
through but got no farther than his fingers. They flexed
threateningly. ''Don't count on it. If I could reach you right
now, I would wring your pretty little neck.''

Rowena wagged her finger at him. ''Temper, temper.''

He rattled the bars with a growl, then spun around to
pace the narrow confines of the cell. ''Who, Rowena? Do
you know who killed her?''

''Not now. There will be time enough for that later.''

Gareth flung himself at the door, realizing her voice was a mere echo of what it had been. She was already fading like a wraith down the shadowy corridor.

"Rowena!" he bellowed. "Get me out of here. You little idiot. Don't you dare put yourself in danger."

Her voice floated back to him, its notes as melodic as a song. "No danger, milord. Only truth."

The pitter-patter of her slippers died away. Gareth threw himself at the door, kicking and beating until the stubborn oak gouged craters in his knuckles. His curses swelled to a roar. He battered himself against the door until his throat closed. His voice died to a hoarse croak. It was not until he lapsed into complete silence that his hapless young guard went to fetch Sir Blaine, fearing his prisoner had driven himself into an apoplexy.

CHAPTER 24

The sun broke through the clouds as Rowena strode across the bailey, paying no heed to the muddy goop sucking at her pattens. The clouds split asunder, revealing snatches of cerulean so brilliant they put a spring into Rowena's step, despite her grim mission. The sun painted streaks of silver and gold on the clouds' black underbellies.

After hearing of Gareth's imprisonment, the mob had broken up with a satisfied murmur. The gates of Ardendonne had been thrown open. A swath of lush green lawn rolled down to the lake. Abandoned raindrops sparkled like a thousand diamonds on every blade of grass and minty bud. Rowena was still blinded by their brilliance when she ducked into the tiny chapel and closed the door behind her.

A cobweb trailed its gauzy fingers across her face. She swiped at it wildly, fearful of a bloated, vengeful occcupant dropping on her head. The stone chapel clung stubbornly to the chill winter. Her eyes adjusted slowly to a darkness broken only by fragile sunbeams pushing their way through a stained-glass window furred with dust and set high above the altar. Her nostrils twitched at the rank smell of mold and disuse.

Mahogany kneeling benches were heaped carelessly against the wall. Rowena fought an irreverent desire to giggle, wondering if Blaine had shoved them aside for dancing. The archangel Michael, flaming sword raised high, frowned down at her from the window. A low growl came out of the shadows in front of the altar.

Rowena froze at the unholy sound. The hair on the nape of her neck bristled. She had heard a sound like that only once before, when rising out of a stream, she had come face to face with a rabid badger, spewing bloody foam from his nostrils and wounded beyond recognition. Pity had swallowed her terror as, with a deft flip of her wrist, she had dispatched it with her hunting knife. She cursed the soft kirtle she wore for having no pocket in which to hide knives.

The growl came again, followed by a terrible, heaving groan.

"God be damned!" A hoarse voice exploded into venom.

Rowena wiped her sweaty palms on her skirt and walked slowly toward the altar.

"God's nightgown!" A dark garbed figure sprang up from the floor. The dark shape writhed and heaved, sucking in a breath to let out an agonizing moan. Rowena ducked behind a pew. Another curse was followed by a ringing crash.

She peeped over the back of the bench. In the arc of sunbeams crossing the dust-sparkled air, an avenging har- ridan in black and silver railed at God and ravaged the dusty chapel. The creature shuddered, shielded by a mat of tan- gled hair. It emanated a musky scent deeper than that of fear. Rowena crept nearer. She flinched as the figure tossed the altar cloth on the stones and stomped it with both feet. A gauntleted hand shredded the thick webs that draped the altar.

Hands curled into claws reached for the golden cross.

Rowena straightened as her clear voice rang from the raf- ters. "You may surrender the relic. The undead do not walk at Ardendonne."

Marlys spun around, cross in hand, her eyes as wide as if she expected to find God himself, waiting thunderbolt in hand to rebuke her for her blasphemy. The defiant set of her chin did not relax.

" 'Tis what you think," she snarled.

Rowena slowly moved forward. "If you were expecting the Almighty, I fear to disappoint you."

Marlys's shoulders slumped as Rowena gently plucked the cross from her hands and returned it to its burnished base. What she had mistook for growls were only sobs, so deep and wracking it was as if Marlys's heart was being torn out by each one of them.

Rowena reached for one bucking shoulder, half afraid Marlys might turn on her like the wild creature she seemed and snap her hand off. Marlys froze at the touch, then flung her head back. Between dark strands of hair, Rowena caught a glimpse of eyes swollen to slits from weeping. She had to grit her teeth to keep from flinching before the malice within those eyes.

"What in the hell do you want? Have you come to tell me they've hung him?"

Rowena took a slow, measured breath. "I should hate to think you were here cowering in the chapel if they had."

Marlys brushed dust off her tunic in a crisp motion that reminded Rowena painfully of Gareth. "Would you prefer I don a white kirtle and weep prettily on Blaine's shoulder while my brother swings from the gallows?"

"Impossible. You do not own a white kirtle. And you do not weep prettily."

"I haven't had as much practice as you have." Marlys leaned one hip against the altar as a mantle of insolence seemed to fall across her shoulders. "What do you want?"

"I want to help Gareth."

Marlys snorted. "Want to help get him hanged most likely. Were it not for your noble little performance in the hall last night, the wrath of the people might not be so stirred against him." Marlys bit a crescent of dirt from beneath her fingernail.

Rowena toyed with the dust on the altar, absently tracing circles with her finger. "I know who killed Elayne."

A muscle in Marlys's cheek twitched. She shrugged.

"According to the mob out there this morning, so does everyone else."

Rowena gave Marlys a maddening smile. "But we know they're wrong, do we not?" She locked her hands behind her back and paced a few steps away.

Marlys's low-pitched laugh sent a chill down Rowena's spine. "So who do you think slew the bitch?"

Rowena arched an eyebrow in mild curiosity. "Why do you call her 'bitch'? Gareth told me you worshiped her."

"Gareth was wrong." Rowena was silent until Marlys grudgingly continued, "When there was no one else around to toy with, the pretty lady would call me into her chambers. She would braid my hair with her long, beautiful fingers until she got bored with it, then send me away when some new diversion presented itself."

"Like Gareth?"

"Like Gareth." Marlys gave a slow smile. "But sometimes I did not go away. She thought I did, but I did not."

Rowena bowed her head. "The hiding place in the cupboard."

Marlys nodded. "I would watch them. I watched her weave her web of pretty poison around him, teaching him courtly manners and music. He struggled at first, like any fly caught in the sticky syrup of a spider's trap. But he stopped struggling soon enough. Who could resist such sweetness?" Rowena closed her eyes briefly, not wanting to hear more but unable to stop listening. "As a student of lovemaking, my brother was an apt pupil, quick to learn and attentive to a fault. But I do not have to tell you that, do I?" Marlys turned her back on Rowena. Her hands clutched at the edge of the altar in some hidden emotion.

Rowena crept nearer. "Were you in the cupboard the night Elayne was murdered? Did you see Gareth come?"

Marlys's shoulders hunched. She gave a bitter laugh. "I saw everybody come. I saw your father sneak through the window and fly back out as if winged when Gareth stormed in. I saw Gareth raise his sword to Elayne only to drop it at her feet. I saw Elayne throw herself on the bed, weeping as if her black heart were broken.''

Rowena caught Marlys's elbows in a tight grip. ''And then?''

Marlys jerked out of Rowena's grasp. Her gaze fell on the tracings in the dust which had somehow twisted themselves into an awkward and misspelled scrawl of her own name. She swiped them away.

''You know, don't you?'' she said. Rowena would have sworn there was a note of wry tenderness in her voice. ''I was the last to come. I killed her, then I pried you out of her stiff and bloody lap and took you to your father.''

Marlys spun around. The abrupt motion flung the dark mop of hair out of her face. Rowena flinched, struck anew by the magnetic force of a beauty Marlys could never completely hide. Their gazes locked. Marlys gave a smile of sweet and terrifying proportions.

Rowena held her ground. ''You have to tell him. He has been punished enough. Last night, I was punished for my own silence. How long can it go on? You were only nine years old. You were a hurt little girl. He will forgive you.''

Marlys sneered. ''You're as bad as Mortimer. Always bringing back the old story, making it all new again.''

''Mortimer?'' Rowena breathed. She took a smooth step backward.

''Ro,'' Marlys said warningly.

Another step. Rowena's heel came up against an overturned kneeling bench. Rowena whirled and broke into a run. Before she could reach the door, Marlys's weight crashed into her, slamming her to the flagstones. Tears stung her eyes as Marlys wrapped a fist in her hair and jerked her head back with vicious strength.

''Chin up, pup. Your first whimper will be your last.''

Rowena's muscles went limp as she felt the icy bite of a blade laid across her throat.

CHAPTER 25

Marlys and Rowena strolled arm-in-arm through the bailey, chattering cheerfully.

"What shall it be, Marlys?" Rowena ground out between teeth clenched in a smile. "Will you stab me like Elayne or throw me into the moat like poor Mortimer?"

Marlys gave the chief porter a friendly wave as they passed beneath the arch of the main door. The sharp tip of her dagger poked beneath Rowena's ribs. "Mortimer never knew when to bridle his flapping tongue."

Rowena threw the stable a longing glance. There was no sign of a hulking figure or a cap of silver-blond hair. "You shan't get far without a mount."

She yelped as the blade slid through the thin linen of her kirtle and dug into her bare skin.

"It seems you and Mortimer share many traits."

They started across the drawbridge. Rowena kept her eyes fixed straight ahead, refusing to look at the oily sheen of the moat waters. She heaved a sigh of relief when they stepped off the drawbridge into the damp grass. Her relief was short-lived. Marlys doubled her pace down the slope and Rowena realized all of her hopes lay in the castle behind them. With each jog of Marlys's gait, the dagger blade jabbed beneath her arm.

Red and yellow pavilions were scattered along the lawn. Marlys gave a group of squires a careless salute, tugging Rowena toward the gentle arch of the bridge. The bloated lake shimmered beneath the caress of the afternoon sun. Rowena's flesh stung as the blade nicked her side.

"Sweet Christ!" she exploded. "Could you not grant me a quick death like the others? Must you torture me?"

With a nervous glance behind her, Marlys gave up the ruse of kindness and gave Rowena a hard shove. The slick grass slipped out from under Rowena's feet. She careened down the slope to land on her rear. From where she lay, there was nothing visible but an endless vista of rolling meadows and the crenellated edge of one tower peeping over Marlys's forbidding shoulder. Marlys sheathed the dagger. She stumbled down the hill, jerked Rowena up, and pushed her toward the open meadows. Her hands held the strength of a man's, all calluses and sinew.

Rowena whirled around, her back stiffened with rage. Her hair fell in a wild tangle around her face. Marlys drew a length of rope from her jacket.

The anger seeped from Rowena's body as a darker memory touched her. "You good folk of Caerleon are always prepared, are you not?" she said ruefully.

She stood stiffly while Marlys bound her wrists. Sweat beaded Marlys's upper lip. They started across the fields with Rowena trudging behind, bound to Marlys by the rope twisted around her captor's fist. They slid through a ditch. Marlys gave the rope a vicious jerk. Rowena stumbled, but straightened before Marlys could cast a mocking glance over her shoulder. The rope chafed her wrists, toying with the tender bruises left by Gareth. Rowena's irritation increased with each step.

"Why, Marlys? Whatever do you hope to accomplish?"

"Gareth cannot know," Marlys replied without turning around. "He would never, ever forgive me if he knew I let him take the blame all these years."

"Do you think he will forgive you for killing the woman he loves?"

Marlys whipped around and strode back to Rowena. She

slapped Rowena hard. The hand she raised to mop her own brow trembled.

Rowena did not speak after that. They traversed the long miles in silence. Marlys led and Rowena slogged behind until her feet felt as if they were mired in iron. She lost one of her pattens in the muck of a stream bank but refused to ask Marlys to halt so she could retrieve it. She limped along for several miles in one shoe, then kicked the other away. The soles of her feet had once been as tough as leather. After her sheltered life at Caerleon, she felt the bite of stones and the keen sting of the thistles with each step. The worsening slump of Marlys's shoulders revealed her own exhaustion. With a meanspiritedness that surprised her, Rowena hoped she would fall. Some gleeful sprite within her imagined pouncing on Marlys and choking her with her own rope.

She had been watching her feet for so long, entrenched in her pleasant fantasies, that she stumbled into Marlys's back without even realizing she had halted. The tangy fragrance of pine wafted to her nose. She lifted her head, surprised to find they had reached the top of a steep hill.

The sun splintered the clouds in a burst of lavender and pink. A twilight wind dried the sweat on her brow like soothing fingers.

They stood side by side like old friends. The rope hung slack between them.

Marlys's voice was husky and musing. "I found this place when I was a child. We spent each summer at Ardendonne. Blaine and Gareth were always play jousting or riding their new ponies. I was left to my own devices. I would lay at the top of this hill with my chin on my arms and imagine what it would be like to be a knight, to come thundering across that plain on a powerful charger."

"It must have been lonely."

Marlys shrugged. "I had the hawks and the wind for my companions. Some days those were enough."

"And other days?"

Marlys turned her face away. The impending night cast a shadow over her profile. Branches rustled as she ducked into the trees behind them. Rowena followed before she could be jerked along. A ring of low-lying pines made an almost impenetrable shelter. A perfect circle opened at the top. A handful of brave stars scattered their feeble light against the dusky sky.

Rowena peered beneath the shadowy branches. "Have you a privy pot tucked away somewhere?"

Marlys unsheathed her knife.

"Never mind. I can wait."

Marlys swaggered toward her.

Rowena backed away until she reached the end of the rope. "If you are going to sacrifice me, couldn't you at least find a rock to do it on? I am deserving of the same courtesy Moses showed to Joshua, am I not?"

" 'Twas Abraham and Isaac, idiot. How my brother fell in love with such a lackwit, I will never understand." The blade traveled down Rowena's throat in a tender caress. "Or maybe I do."

Rowena flinched as the dagger slid downward, leaving her hands bound but slicing the rope that lashed her to Marlys.

Marlys flicked a wheaten strand of hair out of her eyes with the gleaming blade. "Go find the privy pot, puppy, while I find supper."

After a few moments, Marlys returned, tossing a limp squirrel and an armful of brush in the center of the clearing. Rowena sank down cross-legged, muttering over her bound hands, while Marlys built a fire, skinned the squirrel, and roasted it on a clumsy spit.

Marlys tore the meat into hunks and squatted in front of her. Rowena glared at her. Her stomach betrayed her with an angry whine. She opened her mouth reluctantly. Marlys poked a bit of meat inside. The meat was tough but tasty. She had eaten much worse in her days at Revelwood.

"Why bother to feed me if you are going to kill me?"

Marlys grinned. "Have you not heard of the fatted calf?"

Marlys fed her until she would eat no more, then wiped the grease from Rowena's chin with a tender swipe of her own sleeve. She settled on the other side of the fire and tore into the meat with relish.

"Will you let them hang Gareth?" Rowena asked.

Marlys sucked grease from her fingers. "He will find a way out of it. He always does."

"But at what price, Marlys?"

"Why should you care?"

Rowena lowered her eyes to the fire.

Marlys set the meat aside. "I would have never treated you as he did last night."

Rowena met her dark gaze, realizing that Marlys had not bothered to veil her face since fleeing the castle. "How do you know how he treated me? Have you a hiding place in the cupboard at Ardendonne?"

"Nay. But I had a chamber next to his. And I had ears."

More than the heat of the fire warmed Rowena's face. "I am surprised we did not hear your shrieks of laughter."

"How could you? You were making enough noise of your own."

Rowena trembled with impotent anger. Marlys lifted a mocking eyebrow. "You are a fool, Rowena Fordyce. When will you come to understand that you are no more to my brother than any woman is to a man? You are a piece of property to be possessed, traded, won, stolen or sold to the highest bidder to make a desirable alliance."

"Is that what you were to your father?"

"I was nothing to my father. Only Gareth existed for my father. I couldn't even be bad enough to goad him into beating me. Lying, stealing, cheating, fighting. I tried them all but Gareth got more attention for one carved bird or a well-done turn at the quintain."

"So you tried murder?"

Marlys gave a chilling smile. "Father was stiff on the

ground by then. But no less loving toward me than he was
in life.''

A branch shifted on the fire, sending up a shower of yellow sparks. Marlys yawned and cracked her knuckles. She
stretched out on the bed of pine needles and closed her
eyes. The firelight scattered flickering shadows over her
face. Rowena flopped to her side, devouring Marlys's un-
veiled features with unashamed curiosity, searching for
traces of Gareth in the curve of a stubborn jaw, the mocking
slant of heavy brows against an ivory forehead. Marlys's
beauty was a dark and palpable thing, pulsing with substance and allure. Rowena understood why Blaine had pur-
sued her so heatedly in his younger days and had learned to
hate her with a passion equal to his lust when she mocked
his suit. What might have bloomed between them had Marlys not sought to retreat within the ugly shell she had fashioned for herself?

"I could have been your friend," Rowena said softly,
hardly aware she had spoken aloud.

Marlys opened her eyes. They stared at each other through
the shimmering firelight. "Not enough, Lady Precious.
Never enough.''

Rowena rolled over. She lay staring into the darkness
long after Marlys had lapsed into careless snores.

Rowena burrowed her nose into the nest of softness beneath her head, believing she was back at Caerleon, tucked
safe beneath the pelts of Gareth's bed. She rooted in the
soft linen, finding somewhere within a hint of Gareth's
clean, musky scent. Snow drifted down in her dreams, bur-
nishing her world with a fresh, sweet frosting of white.

"Wake up, you silly bitch. I haven't all day to coddle
your precious ass.''

Rowena bolted upright as a booted foot slammed into her
rear. She knuckled her eyes with her bound hands. Marlys
stood over her, snarling like a rabid harpy. The sky behind
her head was a startling blue as if God had dipped his brush

in a new vat and painted the world anew. The wrens chirped a cheerful morning song.

Marlys drew back her foot again, and Rowena scrambled to her feet. Before Marlys could snatch it up, Rowena saw that Marlys's overtunic had been lovingly folded and tucked under her head sometime in the night.

Marlys shoved her hard. "If you have any needs to take care of, do it now. We won't be stopping again until nightfall."

Rowena stumbled into the tentative shelter of the branches, her back to Marlys. She met her needs in an agony of embarrassment, hearing Marlys's short laugh as she struggled with her tattered skirts, her bound hands tingling to life. She straightened. Pine needles caressed her cheek. She lifted the curtain of branches, lured by the gentle wind stirring their limbs into creaking song.

Dawn was long past. The sun had started its arc through the morning sky. In the meadows below, the last tendrils of mist drifted into oblivion in the warmth of its slanting rays. Her breath caught in her throat.

"God's blood, Ro!" Marlys exploded behind her. "It should not take you half the morning. Am I going to have to—"

The voice died abruptly as Marlys burst through the foliage and saw what Rowena saw. "Sweet Jesu," she breathed. Her nails dug into Rowena's arm.

Far below them, a knight and stallion came charging across the meadows, melded into one like some mythical creature out of Marlys's fantasies. Gareth bent low over Folio's back, shifting the horse's path with the slightest tightening of his thighs. Rowena knew the power of those thighs. A shaft of sunlight struck the steed's golden bridle and split into a prism of amber. Folio's mane streamed behind him in the wind of his flight. Gareth's own dark mane whipped at the air, gilded to blue by the sun. Five horses poured over the horizon behind Gareth, but neither Rowena nor

Marlys paid any heed. They only had eyes for Gareth and his irrevocable drive toward their hill.

Marlys's grip changed, and Rowena saw that tears streamed down her cheeks. Her hand fell limply away from Rowena's arm.

Gareth plunged toward them. Folio's hooves blurred to white, showing no signs of slowing. Rowena thought he would charge straight up the steep hill. At the last possible second Gareth sawed back on the reins and Folio came to a rearing halt. The stallion's whinny rang in the air.

Rowena's eyes drank in Gareth's features, watching relief soften and then exasperation tighten the tiny lines around his mouth.

"You foolish little girls! What do you mean going off on such a harebrained quest? You almost got me killed."

The glance Gareth threw over his shoulder reminded them of the horses behind him, black shadows rolling across the meadows. Gareth slid off the horse and started up the hill.

"Gareth."

He stopped with a frown at the sharp note in his sister's voice. His gaze passed between the two women.

Rowena slowly raised her bound hands.

The puzzled expression in his eyes deepened. "What in the devil? I thought you went off to find a murderer."

"I did," Rowena said gently.

When Gareth started up the hill again without comprehending, Marlys's arm snaked around Rowena's waist. Sunlight glinted off the silver blade she pressed to Rowena's throat. Gareth froze, his hands on his knees.

His gaze lit on Marlys and stayed. Her chest heaved against Rowena's back.

"You," he said. It was not a question.

Marlys tossed her head back with a sneer that was answer enough.

"All those years you let them believe it was me."

"I had no choice," Marlys cried hoarsely. Her hand jerked. The blade bit into Rowena's tender flesh. "They

could not touch you. You were Lord of Caerleon. I wou
have spent the rest of my life chained up in a madhouse
cloistered in a nunnery.''

Gareth's mind was quicker than Rowena's. "And Mor
mer?''

"He was bent over fluffing up his hose. It only took
tiny bump. He didn't stay around long enough to hear n
beg his pardon.''

Gareth's eyes locked on Rowena's face. A thin line
blood trickled into the hollow of her throat. She pressed h
eyes shut.

"Free her, Marlys.''

Marlys's arm tightened around Rowena's waist as she du
her chin into Rowena's shoulder. "Why? Your sword bit
deeper than mine. You've spilled more of her heart's bloc
than I ever will.''

Gareth took a step up the hill. Marlys dragged Rowen
back until the pine branches quivered around their shou
ders.

He took another step. "How you must have hated me.'

Marlys's face crumpled. "You fool! Elayne hurt you.
could not bear to see you hurt. Don't you know? Don't ye
understand? You were the only one who was kind to m
Even when I left your life in ruins, not once did you los
your grace, your courage. You are everything I ever wishe
to be.'' The hand with the knife relaxed.

Hoofbeats bore down on them. Marlys cast a wild glanc
at the meadows.

Tears sparkled in Gareth's eyes as he stretched out h
hand. "Marlys. Love. Come to me. I shall take care of yo
I won't let them hurt you.''

Marlys's voice hardened. "Nay. Back down the hill, Ga
eth. Away from Folio.''

The blade touched Rowena's throat again. Gareth obeye
without hesitation. He spread his arms in surrender as Ma
lys shoved Rowena down the hill in front of her. The ar
around her waist did not relax.

Recognizing both women's scents, Folio twitched but did not flee when they stumbled against him.

"Your sword, brother," Marlys snapped.

Gareth unbuckled his sword and tossed it to the ground at her feet. Marlys clutched a handful of Rowena's hair in her fist as she draped the buckler over Folio's saddle and mounted. The sod trembled with the approach of Gareth's pursuers. Marlys leaned over Folio's slender neck.

For a fleeting instant, she buried her face in Rowena's tangled curls. Rowena felt the breath of her whisper against her ear. "I could have never hurt you. Never."

A careless shove. Gareth's waiting arms enfolded her.

Marlys straightened with a jaunty grin that cut through Rowena's heart. She fumbled in her sleeve, pulling out a tiny folded object. Gareth's fist shot out as it came sailing toward him. The fragile silk of Rowena's baby coif curled around his fingers.

"Take care of it, brother. If I hear you did not, you will answer to me."

With those words, Marlys wheeled the stallion in a circle and kicked the horse into a gallop, away from the approaching riders. She unsheathed the sword and lifted it in the air. Her battle cry floated back to them on the wings of the wind as she thundered toward the distant horizon as free as the knight she had always dreamed of being.

"Marlys!" Gareth's hoarse cry was caught by the wind.

Rowena gripped his arm. "Let her go, Gareth."

Gareth's legs crumpled. Rowena's hands reached for his tunic. He dropped to his knees in the soft turf as a hawk flew in front of the sun and went soaring in Marlys's path until both of them were only shadows against the swaying grasses.

CHAPTER 26

Rowena sank to her knees beside Gareth, nuzzling against his shoulder with a wordless murmur of comfort. He cupped her cheek with his hand, his thumb brushing the thin scarlet scratch marring her throat.

"Did she hurt you?" he said gruffly.

Rowena shook her head with a tremulous smile, remembering Marlys's last words to her—words that Gareth could not have heard. Gareth gave the scratch a tender kiss. His lips traveled upward, at first gently, then devouring hungrily her chin, her cheeks, her nose. She answered his kisses with her own, savoring the rough caress of his beard against her skin. His lips found hers. The tangy grit of their sweat bound them together in a taste more precious and infinitely more lasting than goblets of nectar. Gareth rested his forearms heavily on her shoulder.

His head dropped. "Whatever shall I do without her?"

Rowena pressed her brow to his with fierce strength. "You will go on. As she would want you to."

His lips quirked in a half-smile. "When you say it with such conviction, I almost believe it possible."

"All is possible, milord—"

The rest of Rowena's reply was lost in the thunder of hoofbeats. She threw herself at Gareth's chest, believing they were to be trampled. The thunder rolled to a halt. For a long moment, nothing was to be heard but the stamp and shuffle of hooves and winded snorts. Rowena opened her eyes. A circle of disapproving faces glared down at them. The most disapproving was Irwin's moon of a face glowering down from a dun palfrey. Little Freddie and Big Freddie rode nondescript chestnuts. Sir Boris shifted his bulk on his mount, a length of rope dangling conspicuously from his saddle.

Blaine gave a disgusted snort that would have done any of the horses proud and bounced off his black stallion. Gareth's arm circled Rowena protectively.

A pretty black ring around one of Blaine's eyes matched his horse perfectly. He flung out both arms. "Is this what you escaped for? To make merry in a meadow with this beleaguered child? Was it worth all the bodies you left littered across my hall?"

Rowena stiffened.

"Courage, child," Gareth whispered. "Unconscious, not dead." To Blaine, he replied, "You are only testy because yours was one of them."

"You're damned right I'm testy. 'Tis extremely bad form to render your host unconscious. 'Tis against all the rules of hospitality. The Prince of Wales would shudder."

" 'Tis extremely bad form to lock your guests in the spice cellar."

Blaine conceded that point by turning around and kicking a rock. He frowned at the horizon. "Where the hell did Marlys go?"

Rowena opened her mouth. Gareth gave her arm a warning squeeze. "My sister is no concern of yours. She made that clear at an early age."

"Painfully clear." Blaine rubbed his side at the remembrance. "Mayhaps she did not choose to see you strung over the nearest tree."

Little Freddie and Big Freddie exchanged a worried glance. Rowena pulled out of Gareth's arms, ignoring his warning glance. "Marlys did not flee to exile so you could go on bravely bearing the burden of her guilt."

Blaine whirled around. "Guilt?" He fixed Gareth with a

hard stare. Gareth climbed to his feet, fixing all his attention on dusting off his hose.

Blaine's eyes caught and held the horizon. He let out
slow breath, more of admiration than surprise. "So the can-
tankerous little bitch killed Mortimer."

"And Elayne," Rowena added. Gareth gave her a dark
look.

Blaine started for his horse.

Gareth was there with his hand on the bridle. "Going
somewhere?"

"To fetch a murderess."

"For hanging?"

Blaine arched an eyebrow. "I had a more private incar-
ceration in mind. With myself as caretaker, of course."

"You had your chance at taming Marlys. There won't be
another one."

Gareth's bulk was immovable. Blaine cast a hopeful
glance at Sir Boris. The elderly knight studied his fingernails. Rowena gave Gareth's arm a supportive squeeze.

Blaine bit off a curse. "I ought to hang you in her place
if only for your treatment of this sweet lady. And not nec-
essarily by the neck."

Rowena paled. Gareth neatly tucked her behind him. "As
I told you once before, Blaine, if you have any complaints
about my care of this sweet lady, you may challenge me to
a joust."

"I have a passel of complaints," Blaine hissed.

Gareth rolled his eyes.

Blaine shook a finger in his face. "You kept her at Caerleon against her will. You brought her to Ardendonne on
the end of a rope. Then you allowed her to be abducted by
a murdering madwoman. Your care, sir, leaves much to be
desired."

Gareth yawned. "So what is it to be? Shall you hang me
or challenge me?"

In one smooth motion, Blaine jerked off his gauntlet and

whipped it across Gareth's face. Gareth did not flinch. The leather left a reddened welt on his cheekbone.

"So be it," he said stiffly. "What are the rules of this joust?"

Blaine paced away, his hands locked behind him, then paced back. "The prize," he said, "is to be the Lady Rowena."

Rowena waited for Gareth's snort of laughter, his refusal of such a ludicrous wager. "Allow me to clarify that," Gareth said. "The prize is to be the *hand* of the Lady Rowena—in marriage."

"Why my hand?" Rowena mumbled. "Why not my head or my leg?" She tugged on Gareth's sleeve.

Gareth felt the fluttering motion and said out of the corner of his mouth, "Do not fret, my love. 'Tis not a bride Blaine seeks. He will withdraw his challenge."

Blaine shoved his fingers into his gauntlet. "Very well. A bride the lady shall be."

Another gauntlet came sailing through the air, striking Gareth on the temple. "Count me in." Irwin's face had gone as pale as snow, but his voice did not quiver. "She was mine to begin with."

Rowena peered around the circle of men with her mouth hanging open, wondering if they had all gone mad.

" 'Tis settled then," Blaine said. "A tournament tomorrow afternoon with Rowena sitting in the seat of the Queen of Love and Beauty. He who is unseated is lost."

Irwin swayed in his saddle. Big Freddie righted him with a punch to his shoulder.

They all turned to stare as Rowena backed away from Gareth.

Gareth's brow furrowed. "What is it, love?"

"Have you lost your senses? Did you learn nothing from Marlys? A woman is not a possession to be sold or won. Mayhaps if you could have ever convinced her of that, you would not have lost her."

They gaped at her as if she had sprouted horns and a tail. Big Freddie scratched his head.

Blaine looked genuinely puzzled. "You should be thrilled, Rowena. Most women would find it the highest honor to have a joust fought in their name." He looked to Sir Boris for help.

The knight nodded, a distant look in his eyes. "The Queen of Love and Beauty holds the seat coveted by every lady in the land."

Gareth stretched out a tentative hand as if afraid she might flee. His voice was low, meant only for her ears. "A knight cannot refuse a challenge and keep his honor."

She turned toward the open meadows, pushing her way past Irwin's horse.

Gareth strode after her. He caught her arm in a grip that was less than courtly. "I've lost everything, Rowena. I cannot afford to lose you."

"Nonsense, milord," she said softly. "You've gained that most precious thing you've sought your whole life—your honor. I hope it warms you at night."

With those words, she gathered her tattered skirts in her hands and marched away through the crackling grasses. Clutching a handful of mane, Little Freddie steered his mount in a circle.

He twisted around with an insulting dip meant to be a bow. An impish grin curved his lips. "With your leave, milord?"

Gareth shooed him away with a growl. Little Freddie trotted after his sister. Gareth did not take his eyes off Rowena until she mounted behind Little Freddie without relaxing the proud curve of her spine. Then he rubbed his pounding temples.

Blaine dug a sharp chin into his shoulder. "Women! Grand and mysterious creatures, are they not?"

"How would you like a black eye to match your other one?"

Blaine backed away hastily. At Sir Boris's tactful suggestion, they started back toward Ardendonne in a bedraggled parade. Blaine and Gareth shared the black stallion, struggling not to touch each other. Irwin trailed behind, praying and crossing himself in a sudden fit of piety.

CHAPTER 27

The slick waxed leather slipped from Irwin's hands. After the fourth try, he managed to buckle the cuirass only to discover he had the leather armor on backwards. Perhaps if he wore his helm backwards and walked backwards, no one would notice. He mopped his dripping brow, wondering what madness had possessed him to challenge Sir Gareth to a tournament. Damn Rowena's prettiness, anyway.

She had looked so soft and appealing clinging to Sir Gareth, her nose smudged with dirt, her skirt stained with grass. It had reminded him of the times they had wrestled as children. His mind had conveniently forgotten that it was always she who ended up on top and he who ended up squealing for mercy like a gutted pig. He had also forgotten the sharp lash of her tongue until she had flung Sir Gareth's pledge of honor back in his face with the force of a whip.

He stripped off the cuirass and wrestled with it until he got it turned around. He plopped down on the floor in a crackling heap. As his fingers fumbled with the laces on the chausses, he regretted chasing Big Freddie from the chamber. He could not bear for his cousin to see his shaking hands. And he could not bear to see the tears Big Freddie kept dashing out of his eyes when he thought Irwin was not watching.

The leather thong snapped in Irwin's hand. He hurled it away with an ineffectual oath. He hobbled over to the bench and lifted the coif-de-maille. The links of braided chain curled around his hand. He lowered it over his head, staggering under its weight, and silently cursed the fat-headed knight generous enough to loan it to him.

His neck craned forward like a turtle's as he groped for the silver helm, struggling not to lose his balance. He dropped the helm over his head as a cudgel came down against the side of his neck.

He straightened for an instant, then dropped like a stone. The helm struck the floor with an echoing clang.

He lay blissfully insensible as a pair of hands jerked off his helm and lowered his head gently to the floor. His coif-de-maille was stripped off, followed by chausses, cuirass, and short tunic until his pale mound of a belly rose and fell over nothing more than his linen slops. After a thoughtful pause, the narrow scrap of linen was unwound and added to the pile.

He rolled to his side, mumbling something about strawberries steeped in jam, and never hearing a bolt drop outside the door with a final thump.

"Come forth, knights, come forth!"

A shrill burst of trumpets poured into the air like liquid gold. Without rising from his stool, Gareth lifted a corner of the tent flap. A triangle of sunlight penetrated the hazy interior of the tent. The herald's cry was not an invitation to him. In a testament to his prowess as master host, virtually overnight Blaine had managed to arrange a series of minor jousts and melees to entertain his guests.

"Had Richard had such organized commanders, Saladin's hordes would have fallen in a single combat," he muttered.

"From laughter, no doubt," came a muffled reply.

Gareth grunted an agreement as jesters and tumblers garbed as knights streamed out of a striped tent, flipping and tripping over one another in gay abandon. He let the tent flap fall, content to sit in the scarlet gloom. A boy's slender form, apparently headless, was stretched out on his stomach at his feet.

Gareth yanked the boy's ankles, and Little Freddie's head appeared inside the tent with a disgruntled expression.

"No need to wallow about on your belly, lad. You may go outside and watch the proceedings in a civilized manner."

Little Freddie brushed himself off, the jut of his lip stopping just short of a pout. "I am to attend to you as your squire. 'Twas Rowena's command."

"Why? You dislike me nearly as much as she does."

"Not quite."

Gareth could find no answer for that. He stood and paced the tent. His chain mail hauberk clinked with each weighted step. He had been up and armored since dawn. Rollicking laughter filled the air outside the tent. He turned to pace the other way. Little Freddie placed the stool Gareth had vacated just inside the tent flap where he could peek out at the festivities. A snort of boyish laughter escaped him. Gareth stopped his hand short of patting the boy's cap of blond hair. His gauntleted fingers curled at the memory of gossamer blond strands cupped in his palm, and a frustrated despair flowered deep in his belly.

"What else did your sister have to say this morn?" His words came out more harshly than he intended.

Freddie shrugged. "She refused your request for a scrap of cloth or trinket to gird your lance with."

The screams of laughter died. An expectant murmur settled over the list. Gareth drew himself up straight. Little Freddie scrambled through the pile of Gareth's belongings in the corner. Gareth had left nothing in the castle. After this ridiculous tournament, he planned to claim his lady and go. He inclined his head. Little Freddie stood on tiptoe and slipped a black surcoat trimmed in silver over the knight's hauberk. Gareth stood motionless as the boy cinched a silver chain around his waist. He wore no sword. His only weapon would be the lance propped outside, its sharp tip blunted with a rounded coronal.

A trumpet sang out. A single, golden note lay its reverent hush over the crowd. Little Freddie hefted Gareth's helm in his hands. Even on tiptoe, his height was not sufficient. With an apologetic grimace, he clambered atop the stool and placed the helm on Gareth's head. The rosy light of the tent stained silver to blood. Gareth flipped the visor up.

His pulse quickened of its own volition as the trumpets trilled a mighty flourish.

Once again, the heralds cried in unison, "Come forth, brave knights, come forth!"

This time their cry was not followed by a rush of grinning jesters. Two men stepped out of tents set at opposite ends of the list. After the hot, still air of the tent, the rush of fresh wind ruffled Gareth's brain, making him giddy. The sun blinded him. For a long moment, he could make out nothing but dark shapes on a tapestry of velvet green. He mounted the black destrier Blaine had provided him, wishing for Folio.

The world came into focus. The hillside below the tilting ground was dotted with colorful tents. Canopied pavilions lined the grassy list, gaudy with scarlet and emerald hangings, undulating with the tense movements of those seated within. For a long moment, the only sound was the pennants fixed atop the pavilions flapping in the wind.

Then a mighty roar burst from the farthest pavilion and traveled like a wave down the list. Feet stamped in unison until it seemed the pavilions themselves might collapse in protest. The thunder of applause rocked the air. Little Freddie tossed the lance. Gareth caught it in a gauntleted hand. It was then that he realized every face was turned toward him. Every cry of approval was being sent to his ears. The crowd climbed to their feet, ignoring their slender host mounting his caramel destrier at the end of the field. They lifted their voices with one accord to cheer Sir Gareth de Crecy, the Dark Lord of Caerleon.

Word of his innocence had spread through this curious crowd like wildfire. With one voice, they sought to rectify the misdeeds of twenty years. At Gareth's sure command, the destrier trotted a few feet forward until the center gallery came into view. Brightly garbed ladies thronged the wooden rail. Kerchiefs and ribbons fluttered from delicate fingers.

Gareth had waited for this moment for twenty years. But now his peers' salutes were as empty to him as the gaping seat on the gallery, the throne of honor—the traditional place of the Queen of Love and Beauty. The crowd's colors seemed garish, their voices shrill. Gareth's head pounded as he wheeled the horse back to his end of the list, hearing beneath the heat of his helm a vitriolic whisper, *"You've gained that most precious thing you've sought your whole life—your honor."*

With a hunger that surprised him, he longed to see the golden flash of Rowena's hair in the sunlight. To find her slender figure leaning over the gallery rail to cheer him to victory. He had fought many jousts in his life—some to the death. In each, he had counted on his pride and his anger to carry him through, knowing within himself that right could make might whether they believed him or not. Knowing that beneath his grim facade lay the boy his father had born and bred to be a man of honor. Today, in the most important tournament of his life, he felt hollow and silly. He had nothing left to prove, except to Rowena, and he had the cross sensation that he was going about that in completely the wrong way.

Blaine drew his finger across his throat. Sir Boris, the appointed marshal of the tournament, trotted to the center of the list to a new burst of cheers. Sunlight glinted off gold as a row of trumpeters lifted the bells of their horns in the air. A melodious flourish sounded. Gareth's knees tightened on the satin blanket draped over his steed.

Sir Boris boomed out, "In the name of God and St. Michael, do—"

He stopped as Gareth raised his palm. The knight leaned down and whispered something in his squire's ear. Little Freddie ducked into the tent.

Blaine made a disparaging comment that Gareth could not hear but which drew a handful of snickers from the crowd. Little Freddie reappeared and handed him something. Gareth affixed it to the pole of his lance. A sigh of approval arose from the ladies as a veil of peach silk rippled in the wind. They could not know the veil had been captured from Rowena, not given freely. Rowena had never surrendered anything to him freely, except herself. He did not dare delve into the images that thought evoked. He signaled to Sir Boris that he was ready to proceed.

Sir Boris cleared his throat and began again. "In the name of God and St. Michael, do your battle!"

The heralds chanted in response, "Do your duty, valiant knights!"

They scattered, clearing the list for battle. Gareth slammed his helm shut. The world narrowed to a swath of green with his opponent at the end of it. He lowered his lance and raised his shield. His heart pounded in his ears.

Golden spurs touched destriers' flanks. The horses leaped forward in a rush of hooves. Chunks of turf flew as they thundered toward each other from opposite ends of the list. Gareth bent low over the charger's back, bracing himself for the blow to come.

For a fleeting instant before his lance struck Blaine's shield, he caught a glimpse of narrowed brown eyes through the slits of Blaine's visor. Lance struck shield with a mighty crack. Both lances held. The impact vibrated up the length of Gareth's arm and down his spine. He swayed but held his seat. The crowd roared its approval.

Gareth could not help glancing at the gallery as he galloped past. The lady Alise blew him a kiss. The seat of honor was still empty. His horse reeled around. A throng of peasants shoved against the ropes enclosing the far end of the field. Men shouted coarse suggestions on how to defeat their lord. A woman with a broad, sun-wrinkled face thrust a little girl in the air. A tiny hand tossed a bouquet of heather on the field.

Gareth's mount trampled the blooms heedlessly as he drove toward Blaine once again. He bent over his pommel. The horse's mane whipped at his helm. Wind whistled through his visor. The crowd disappeared. All that lay before him was the long, straight stretch and the falcon carved on the shield of the knight shooting toward him. Gareth fixed his gaze on the falcon's eye. He lowered his lance a fraction of an inch. He refused to think of the lance driven at his own shield. He refused to think of the weeks his muscles would ache from the impact. All he thought of was the brightly blinking eye of the falcon.

He closed his eyes on impact, knowing before Blaine's lance struck that he had won. Blaine's lance splintered with a terrible crack, folding in the knight's hand like a broken twig. The crowd gasped. Gareth pushed on. Blaine's stallion sank back on his haunches. The unrelenting force of Gareth's lance sent Blaine tumbling head over heels. He sprawled on the turf.

Blaine's horse wandered off to munch grass at the foot of the ladies' gallery. A laughing young maiden crowned his ears with a chaplet of gillyflowers. Blaine's squire trotted out to his master. Blaine waved him away.

Without dismounting, Gareth leaned over and stretched out a gauntleted hand. "Come, my friend, arise. Be thankful you did not wager your castle."

Blaine sat up and pulled off his helm. He glared at Gareth and rubbed his ringing ears. "What is a castle with no lady to crown it?"

Gareth grinned. "I've begun to ask myself that question."

The crowd whooped as Blaine took the hand Gareth proffered. Gareth hauled him to his feet. Applause filled the air. Blaine spread his arms and made a bow that would have done any jester proud. He staggered slightly as he straightened.

"The next time my friend and I will take our spats to the chessboard or the hazard dice," he called out to good-natured jeers and catcalls.

"Not hazard." Gareth shook his head emphatically. "Never hazard."

Blaine slapped his knee. "I hate to leave you like this, but I see a gallery of sympathetic ladies waving me forward. There is nothing like a wounded little boy to bring out their maternal instincts. I see several laps I'd love to recover on. Besides, you've another challenge to meet."

Gareth snorted. "I think not. If I know Irwin, he is halfway to Revelwood by now."

Sir Boris stepped forward again, followed by a line of beaming heralds. "As tradition demands, I must ask if there is any other knight who cares to challenge Sir Gareth in tourney today?"

Several knights found this an opportune moment to pick their teeth or kiss their favorite ladies.

"If any man cares to step forward," Sir Boris intoned, "let him do so now or forever—"

A horse appeared high on the hill.

"—hold his silence," he finished weakly.

Gareth pushed his visor back farther on his brow, squinting at the dark shape silhouetted against the afternoon sun. A balmy wind dried the sweat on his face. The list sank into silence.

The helmed figure lifted his lance. The crowd murmured at the obvious challenge, entranced by the mysterious figure. Gareth frowned. It was impossible to tell beneath armor and helm if the rider possessed Irwin's bulk. His challenger gave him no time to ponder.

Raising shield and lowering lance, the rider charged down the hill. Gareth slammed his visor down. The crowd caught its breath in a collective gasp as the white stallion's hooves left the ground, clearing the ropes strung at the end of the

list with a mighty leap. Sweaty palms grasped the rails a
the watchers wondered if the challenger was going to ru
Gareth down with the extra speed of his charge, castin
aside all rules of the tilt.

Gauntleted hands sawed on the reins. The stallion prance
to a rearing halt. Gareth blinked. An icy tendril of swea
trickled down the back of his neck. The stallion was no
Folio. Tufts of black starred its forelock and mane.

The stranger made a cutting gesture toward the marshal
and Sir Boris's words came tumbling out as if he cared very
little for the thought of standing between two such unpre
dictable opponents. "In-the-name-of-God-and-St.-Michael
do-your-battle!"

The heralds' response was gibberish. They shoved eac
other out of the way, heedless of the trumpeters they tram
pled.

As Gareth faced the rider an unfamiliar sensation tight
ened his gut. He was afraid. The fear infuriated him. If thi
was Irwin's idea of a prank, he would turn the lad over hi
knee after he bested him. He raised his lance with a grow
that sent the ladies in the gallery swooning into each other'
arms. The hair on the nape of Blaine's neck stood on end.

The stranger raised his shield. Two sets of booted fee
slammed into their mounts' flanks. One set wore spurs. The
other did not. The horses lunged forward, beating a cloud
of dust out of land still damp from the spring rain. The
stranger's shield was unmarked. Gareth could find no targe
to aim for. The ground rolled out from beneath his destrier'
hooves. Before he was ready, lance struck shield with a
jarring blow. Both riders swayed but kept their balance. The
crowd's cheer was muted as if they were still held in the
stranger's thrall.

There was barely time to wheel around before the ride
charged again. Gareth cursed under his breath, still reeling
from the last blow. He searched for any hint of humanity
beneath that unmarked helm. Sunlight glinted off the nar
row slits, mocking him with its deceptive brightness. The

visor held its secrets, sealed tight by shadows. He was only halfway toward the center of the field when his opponent's lance slammed into his own. His horse reared, hooves flailing at the air. Anger tightened his jaw.

He knew by now that he was not fighting Irwin. Irwin possessed neither the skill nor the grace to maneuver stallion, lance, and shield simultaneously. The rider came at him again, relentlessly driving his mount down the emerald swath of green between them.

In the flash of time before their lances clashed, Gareth straightened and held his lance high. The rider lunged forward, shield and body braced for the blow from Gareth's lance. When that blow did not come, the momentum of the stranger's lunge carried him into Gareth's shield, following the pass of his own lance through shield, then air. The force of the blow shuddered Gareth. He gripped the stiff saddle with his knees. His mount lurched in an awkward circle. The tip of his lance caught on the roof of the gallery, and the wooden stake ripped the peach veil in two. The coronal blunting the tip of his lance fell into Alise's lap.

Spurred by the rending of the veil and unaware of what had happened to his lance, Gareth swung the long pole around, hoping to catch his opponent off guard. Struggling to control his own stallion, the rider lifted his shield an instant too late. Sunlight reflected off steel. A woman screamed as the silver tip of Gareth's lance pierced the rider's armor.

The crowd came to its feet. All was silence.

Gareth stared in disbelief as blood poured over leather, staining silver to red. His lance thudded to the ground. The white stallion pranced sideways, away from Gareth. The rider slumped, clutching his pommel with rigid arms. One of the heralds began to mumble in Latin.

Time passed in a haze that knew no moments. No squire took the field to aid his wounded master. Gareth shoved his visor back, his blood freezing to ice in his veins as a horrible suspicion was spawned in his mind. The rider doubled over. With a determination that daunted Gareth, gauntleted fingers curled around the helm. He wanted to close his eyes, unable to watch the fall of long, dark hair he knew would follow.

The rider bent his head and wrenched the helm away. Wheaten curls spilled over ashen skin.

The list exploded into movement. Blaine screamed for a physician. The physician screamed for a priest. Alise fainted. A small, silver-haired figure detached itself from the farthest tent and came sprinting down the long stretch.

But it was Gareth who reached Rowena first. He plunged off his destrier, forfeiting his victory, and caught her in his arms as she fell. He eased her to the ground. The slickness of blood stained the stallion's pristine coat.

He cradled her across his lap. Golden curls poured over his surcoat. Her blue eyes were dimmed with a haze of pain. She ran a gauntleted finger along the curve of his jaw.

Her lips curled in a small smile. "I am free, milord. I have won myself."

Her sandy lashes fluttered against her cheeks as she lapsed into a merciful faint. An errant spurt of wind tore the veil from the gallery post and sent it soaring upward until it was only a splash of peach against a sea-blue sky.

CHAPTER 28

Big Freddie guided Rowena's head over the edge of the bed with swift, competent hands. His broad palm cradled her forehead as the meager contents of her stomach came forth. Her eyes did not even flicker. Her damp lashes lay against her cheeks like drowned spiders. Blaine reached out a hand as Gareth lurched past him and out the door. Big Freddie nodded as he gently lowered Rowena's still form back to the pillows. Blaine followed Gareth with Little Freddie trailing behind.

They found Gareth on the battlement, clutching the parapet and taking ragged gulps of air. He wiped his mouth with the back of his hand and turned to go back inside. Blaine stopped him.

"You need rest. You've had no sleep in three days. Give yourself some time."

Gareth shrugged his hand away. "She may not have any time. She needs me. I cannot abandon her."

"Big Freddie is tending her."

Gareth pushed Blaine's hand away a second time but stumbled as he started for the door. He turned abruptly back to the parapet, gripping the stone. He raised his face to the cool rain misting over the balcony and closed his eyes briefly. Tiny beads of moisture caught in the ragged edges of his beard. Shadows lay like bruises beneath his eyes.

They stood in silence, listening to the drowsy patter of rain tripping from a distant gutter.

"The sickness is good for her," Blaine finally said. "Th
physician says that the more of the wound's poison sh
purges from her body, the more chance she has to live."

"Are the fits good for her? I had to throw myself on he
with all my strength last night just to keep her from flyin
off the bed. Are the fevers good? Or the chills? Or th
nightmares?" Gareth's voice broke. His head dropped. Rai
drifted across the balcony in misty sheets until his hair hun
in limp strands around his face.

When Blaine could give him no answer, Gareth lurche
back into the castle. Blaine followed. Little Freddie stoo
staring over the gray bowls of fog that hung over the distar
hills. Blaine had stayed faithfully at Gareth's side sinc
Rowena had taken ill. No one knew what dark secrets th
two men had shared the first night they spent bolted i
Rowena's chamber. Voices raised in heated argument an
the echo of a hoarse sob were the only clues. Once ther
was even a loud crash like that of a body being slamme
against the door.

But when morning came, Rowena was still alive. Garet
had refused to allow the priest to administer the words tha
might grant her soul an unfettered passage into Purgatory
The Lord of Caerleon had willed that she would live. An
she had. Little Freddie felt his own lips form the words c
a prayer, stiff and half-forgotten from disuse. When th
words failed him, his eyes scanned the grim sky, pleadin
that God might recognize enough of His own arrogance an
passion in Gareth's love to have mercy on them all.

Little Freddie sat in the doorway, stroking the yello
hound that lay across his lap. Gareth dipped a cloth in wate
and dabbed at Rowena's parched lips. A waxy coolness ha
claimed her skin in the wake of the fever that had wracke
her body through the long night.

Her skin was stretched tight over the bones of her face
giving her once rosy cheeks a sunken pallor. He lifted he
to a sitting position and bent her slight weight over his arm

The bandage on her side was clean and dry. He plumped up the pillows and laid her back down.

Blue eyes stared up at him. Gareth's breath froze in his throat. Then one corner of her mouth lifted in a weak smile.

"Thank you, milord." Her voice cracked. Clearing her throat sent her into a shuddering cough that ravaged her body with its force.

She closed her eyes. Gareth leaned forward and peered into her face. Her eyes flew open again, huge and bright.

"Gareth?"

Her bright gaze was uncompromising. To escape it, Gareth picked up a comb and gently drew it through the limp strands of hair spread across the pillow.

"Aye, my love?"

"Are you terribly angry with me?"

His smile softened his answer. "Furious."

"Forgive me."

The brush froze in mid-motion as her head fell to the side. Her lips touched his wrist.

He twisted a strand of hair around his fingers, tightening it for a minute, letting the smooth skein cut into his hardened flesh. She yawned and nestled her cheek into the pillow, her breath coming evenly for the first time in days.

The curl he had made slipped out of his fingers. Gareth stood and strode out of the tower, stepping over boy and dog without breaking stride. He sat down on the narrow staircase, dropped his face in his arms, and quietly cried.

Blaine's head flew up as the door to the donjon crashed open. He dismissed the seneschal at his side with a careless flick of his hand. The man dropped the parchments he had been gathering with a grateful squeak and sidled past the hollow-eyed knight in the doorway. Gareth was garbed in mail and surcoat. A broadsword hung at his side. Blaine steepled his fingers under his chin, fearing the worst.

A pouch of gold sailed through the air, thumping to a halt on the oak table.

Blaine frowned at it. "I charge you no rent. You are my guest."

" 'Tis not for you. 'Tis for Rowena."

The taut lines of Blaine's body relaxed. He tossed the pouch back. "Give it to her yourself."

Gareth plunked the pouch down and leaned over Blaine, supporting his weight with both hands spread on the table. "I won't be here."

Blaine's brow puckered. He loosened the pouch's drawstrings and peered inside. His eyes widened. " 'Tis a substantial sum."

"Enough."

Blaine snorted. "Enough to purchase a small duchy."

"If she so desires."

Blaine leaned back in his chair and propped his heels on the table. "Is that what you wish?"

"She has won her freedom. That dower should give her the freedom to choose any man she wants." He added deliberately, "Or no man at all."

Blaine grinned sheepishly, picking a thread off his knee. "You trust me with her gold, but not with her."

"I'd be a fool if I did. I do, however, trust you with her brother. There is enough gold in there to ensure Little Freddie a proper education."

Blaine lifted a mocking brow. "You wish me to mold him in my image?"

"Heaven forbid. I wish you to mold him in your father's image."

Blaine's fingers tenderly smoothed a worn parchment beneath his hand.

Gareth studied it. "Flanking towers?"

Blaine shrugged. "Some old sketches of my father's. I was considering some additions to Ardendonne."

"Your halls were deserted."

"I sent the guests packing. With invitations for May Day, of course."

A smile touched Gareth's eyes. "Of course." He gave Blaine's shoulder a hard clasp and started for the door.

"Gareth?"

Gareth turned, reluctantly.

"What shall I tell her when she awakens calling your name?"

Gareth raised eyes as dark as midnight. "Tell her I am not worthy of her. I had no right to believe I was."

He was halfway through the door when Blaine's mutter reached his ears. "Damn your pride."

He whirled around. "Aye. Damn my pride. My pride almost killed her." His voice softened. "I'll not give it another chance."

With those words, Gareth left his friend staring blankly at the parchments in front of him. He strode past the alcove where Little Freddie crouched. The boy slipped out of the shadows as Gareth disappeared into the sunbeams streaming through the main door.

Little Freddie stood for a moment, fists clenched, then started for the stairs. His sure feet pounded up the curved staircase. He sped along a narrow hall, then up steeper stairs that seemed hewn from the rock of the castle itself. His breath came in quick gasps as he darted up a sloping corridor. His hands fumbled with a latch. He burst onto the battlements into a rush of sun and wind that whipped tears from his smarting eyes. His hands curled over the sun-warmed parapet.

Far below, a stallion detached itself from the stables, its reins gripped in a hamlike fist. The dark-garbed knight took the reins. Big Freddie slumped against the stable wall.

Gareth swung a long leg over the stallion's back. Little Freddie's nails dug into the stone. It was nearly impossible to tell where the black sheen of the stallion ended and the surcoat of the knight began. Gareth urged the horse into a gentle lope down the road that bypassed the lake, the long, twisting road that led away from Caerleon.

Little Freddie held his breath as he saw Gareth reach the

first curve of the road. The horse slowed, and Gareth guided it in a prancing circle. Even through the distance that separated them, Freddie felt Gareth's eyes find the sheen of his blond hair on the tower. The knight raised a gauntleted hand in a salute.

Little Freddie waved both arms wildly, leaning over the wall until the deepening green of the world below tilted. Gareth lowered his arm. He slapped the reins on the stallion's back. The faint tinkling of bells reached Freddie's ears. The stallion turned, breaking into a gallop, carrying its solitary rider around the bend of the curve and out of Freddie's sight. He came back into sight on the next curve—a lonely black speck on a never-ending ribbon of tan. Little Freddie was still waving when he felt the faint pressure of Sir Blaine's hands on his shoulders.

Tasting the salt of tears on his tongue, he swiped at his nose with his sleeve. "How will I tell her he isn't coming back?"

Blaine squeezed his shoulders. "He'll be back, lad. Don't worry. He'll be back."

Even as he said it, Blaine wasn't sure if he was trying to convince the boy or himself.

CHAPTER 29

A burst of wind and rain tore the leaves from the branches. They danced and whirled in a chaotic frenzy, taunting Gareth with their crackling refrain. The cold, damp breath of autumn blew down his neck. Beads of rain clung to his beard. He huddled deeper in his cloak, trying to conjure up the vision of his own warm hearth and Dunnla's face wreathed in a welcoming smile. The long, lonely months away from Caerleon, skirmishing with the Scots at Edward's side, had dimmed that vision, blurring it with other visions: a flash of white teeth beneath tangled, black hair; wheaten curls, heavy and damp from a bath, catching every scrap of light the fire tossed away; a bloodstained lance lying in the dirt. The horse jolted into a hole, and Gareth bit his lip, thankful for the cleansing pain. Visions were dangerous and best left alone.

A bundle of wet leaves slapped his neck. He peered upward. Between the black net of branches, the gray sky deepened to the charcoal of twilight. There was no sun to mourn the day's passing. Rain had fallen with leaden weight from dawn to dusk.

Ancient tree trunks lined the wide road, massive and knowing. Unblinking eyes watched him from sockets of bark and moss. Had they always been so menacing? He could feel their weight like the heaviness of his spirit, bearing down on his chest, constricting it until every breath was a burden. Tendrils of mist drifted between them, uncurling their gnarled fingers to beckon the weary traveler. Gareth shivered, cursing his own fancies. He clucked at the horse, hastening its walk to a gentle trot. A crackling fire and a flagon of ale would ease his imagination. One more bend and he would be home.

The tree above his head exploded in a flurry of leaves. A giant bat flung itself from the lowest limb with a bloodcurdling screech. There was only time to half raise an arm to protect his face before the creature was upon him. His yell of dismay blended with the beast's rabid squeal as they both went toppling from the stallion's back into the wet leaves. Gareth's head struck a dead branch. His ears rang and suddenly there were two beasts bouncing gleefully on his chest.

"Surrender," the creature growled, raising a menacing stick.

Gareth blinked. The two beasts blended into one. The bat wore a black helm with a dent where the nose should have been.

Gareth shook his head, silencing the irksome bells. His fingers slowly uncurled. He lifted his palms to each side of his head in a gesture of surrender.

"Ha!" came the triumphant cry.

The head bowed. Hands sheathed in leather gauntlets cracked with age reached for the battered helm.

A new set of bells took wing in Gareth's head—a mad carillon that would have put the bells of any cathedral to shame.

The helm tumbled to the leaves. Gareth was choked in a fall of long, blond hair. Rowena flung it behind her with a wicked grin.

Her eyes sparkled. "An easy victory, milord."

"I always was when it came to you." Gareth's hands reached for her. His thumbs encircled her wrists, probing and rubbing to insure she was bone and flesh, not just a tantalizing illusion spawned from his weary mind. "If you are a robber baron, I have no gold. A beautiful wench broke my heart and won my gold."

"Did she give you these?" Rowena neatly plucked a gray hair from the new sprinkling at his temple.

Gareth's hand slipped beneath her hair, cupping her beautiful sturdy neck. "Losing her gave me those."

" 'Tis just as well you are a pauper. I possess a mighty castle and all the gold I need." She leered at him. " 'Tis not gold I seek."

"Then why have you accosted me, wench?"

At her slight wiggle and coy sidelong glance, Gareth forgot his exhaustion. "I've been waiting many long days and nights for a knight to capture," she whispered.

"So you could carry him away to your enchanted castle and make merry on his body all the night long?"

She sniffed. "You malign me. My intentions are honorable. I have a priest waiting to hear our vows."

"And has he married you to every knight who traversed this road? Mayhaps you have a chest of headless knights awaiting me to take my place among them."

" 'Tis a chance you'll have to take."

She made his choice easier by leaning forward and gently pressing her lips to his. Gareth drew her down to a kiss that left them both breathless. He pulled her face to his shoulder with a reverent sigh.

Rowena gave a husky laugh against his throat. "Bested by a girl. Methinks you've grown soft in your travels."

"Carry me off to your priest and I shall spend my lifetime proving you wrong."

With a devilish slant of one eyebrow, he wrapped his arms tightly around her, molding their bodies together. His lips found hers again, drinking of the grail of sweetness he had found at the end of his lonely quest.

She pushed against his chest. "For shame, sir. You seek to do your proving without benefit of a priest." She drew a strand of her hair across the tip of his nose.

His nose twitched. He gave a solemn frown.

Rowena clutched his hauberk. "Why do you glower so? What ails you, milord?"

He gestured at the branch above their heads. "Before I make my oath, milady, tell me, is this what I have to look forward to every time I return to my bride?"

"Nay, milord. This is what you have to look forward to."

She threw both arms around his neck. They rolled over, oblivious to the sodden leaves clinging to them. Gareth stared down into eyes as blue as the skies of his childhood.

Rowena squealed as he stood and scooped her up in his arms.

He strode toward the castle, ignoring Rowena's half-hearted struggles. "Gridmore!" he bellowed. "Get out here and fetch some rope. I've captured a robber baroness."

He rubbed the tip of his nose to hers. Rowena froze, mesmerized by the desire in his eyes, the paralyzing tenderness of his smile. "And I believe I shall keep her."

She pressed her cheek to his beard, her voice muffled. "For the winter, milord?"

"Nay, milady. Forever."

Rowena lifted her head as they rounded the bend. Torchlight blazed from every window of Caerleon. The rain fell harder. Rowena's arm curled trustingly around Gareth's neck. Little Freddie pelted out the main door to welcome them. The sight of Irwin wrapped in a fur cloak and waving cheerfully from the battlement only deepened Gareth's smile. The Dark Lord of Caerleon had come home.